The Martyring
World Fantasy Award Finalist

"Thomas Sullivan is a master of description. Even readers who are not scared by things that go bump in the night may tremble as the most ghoulish creature since Hannibal Lecter stalks the pages of *The Martyring*. A tale of murder and unholy family relationships."   —William X. Kienzle

"A compelling read and the seed of nightmares. Classic Sullivan."   —Fred Bean

"Trying to pigeonhole Thomas Sullivan would be like calling Hemingway an outdoor writer or Fitzgerald the king of glamour and glitz. He's that good, moving effortlessly from one literary landscape to another, his cast of wonderful characters in tow."   —Lowell Cauffiel

The Phases of Harry Moon
Nominated for the Pulitzer Prize

"One is convinced that an outsize performer is trying his wings—a John Barth or a John Irving, with a touch of William Gaddis and maybe a touch of Kurt Vonnegut, Jr."
                              —*Chicago Tribune*

"Once in a blue moon, modern American literature captures lightning in a bottle, producing a work that is both important and entertaining. *The Phases of Harry Moon* is just such a work. In the hands of Thomas Sullivan, it is a serious character study as seen in a funhouse mirror. The reader will look, laugh, and come away changed."
                              —Loren D. Estleman

DUST OF
EDEN

Thomas Sullivan

AN ONYX BOOK

ONYX
Published by New American Library, a division of
Penguin Group (USA) Inc., 375 Hudson Street,
New York, New York 10014, U.S.A.
Penguin Books Ltd, 80 Strand,
London WC2R 0RL, England
Penguin Books Australia Ltd, 250 Camberwell Road,
Camberwell, Victoria 3124, Australia
Penguin Books Canada Ltd, 10 Alcorn Avenue,
Toronto, Ontario, Canada M4V 3B2
Penguin Books (N.Z.) Ltd, Cnr Rosedale and Airborne Roads,
Albany, Auckland 1310, New Zealand

Penguin Books Ltd, Registered Offices:
80 Strand, London WC2R 0RL, England

First published by Onyx, an imprint of New American Library,
a division of Penguin Group (USA) Inc.

First Printing, May 2004
10 9 8 7 6 5 4 3 2 1

PUBLISHER'S NOTE
This is a work of fiction. Names, characters, places, and incidents either are the product
of the author's imagination or are used fictitiously, and any resemblance to actual per-
sons, living or dead, business establishments, events, or locales is entirely coincidental.

BOOKS ARE AVAILABLE AT QUANTITY DISCOUNTS WHEN USED TO PROMOTE PRODUCTS OR
SERVICES. FOR INFORMATION PLEASE WRITE TO PREMIUM MARKETING DIVISION, PENGUIN
GROUP (USA) INC., 375 HUDSON STREET, NEW YORK, NEW YORK 10014.

For Fred Bean

Thanks to Karen Wydra, whose paintings are worth infinitely more than a thousand words and whose advice helped form mine, and to Molly Thiesse, Alyssa Stafne and Nathalie duRivage, who helped me construct Amber. Also, my gratitude to savvy Denny Solberg, Ginny Malikowski, my indispensable lad Sean Sullivan and the men of tomorrow: Chris Wilson, Richie Guillaume, Andrew Blair, Eric Barth and Spence Lewis.

*"For he who lives more lives than one
More deaths than one must die."*
—Oscar Wilde

The Site

1960

He saw them for the first time from the air, east of Baghdad, west of Basra. Like three dragonflies spread flat on the sand, they lay almost invisible in their dusky robes. Their symmetry was what caught his eye and made him aware of the faint ochre circle around which they were positioned like hours on a clock: four, eight, twelve. Facedown, they could have been worshipping. But worshipping what? The circle was about twenty meters across and utterly barren against the surrounding wasteland. No camel's thorn, no fists of vegetation. That was all he registered before the helicopter he was piloting beat off toward the marshes and Basra, where a tourist fare awaited him. But the three prone bodies went with him, connected to something he couldn't quite identify from his past. Or was it his future? A Ma'dan woman had told him he would soon recognize his destiny when he came upon it.

At age fifty-three, he thought he knew who he was: a slightly dissolute soldier of fortune freed to battle middle-age crisis by the death of his second wife. After World War II, Clayton Kenyon had hunkered down into a scavenger's existence selling military surplus in the Mideast, but now he co-owned a tour copter, if you could call the retrofitted Sikorsky S-55 a tour copter. Most of the time he or Bailey, his partner, ferried equipment and crews to the oil fields in Kirkuk or scrounged for odd jobs and parts to keep the helicopter in the air. But if he had managed to keep the chopper aloft, Kenyon knew he was going down within himself. It wasn't just the military coup of two years ago or the steady anti-Western diatribe over Radio Cairo that you heard in every village square; it was a feeling of failed personal destiny. Instead of freeing the warrior inside himself, each impulsive step here in Iraq had left him more desperate and lost. Like a gambler running out his dwindling stash, his bets got bigger and wilder.

The fare was staying at the Saint George Hotel overlooking the Shatt al Arab—a deepwater connector that drew the Euphrates and the Tigris into the Persian Gulf. Kenyon resented the rich tourists almost as much as the younger Arabs did. They came in gaggles, snapping pictures of "quaint" things, as if the struggling nation were a mere museum. By extension, he was becoming vestigial in their eyes too, a docent to something returning to dust. But this tourist was different. He came alone. Pug and plain, a geologist, he said he was. Demetrius Booth. He wanted to see Basra and the Tigris from the air and visit the traditional site of the Garden of Eden at Al Qurna.

So they overflew the canals crowded with dhows and the round reed boats called *gufas,* and then to the Shatt al Arab where freighters and a British destroyer rode at anchor. Sinbad the sailor had sailed from here. Kenyon turned the control stick in his right hand, and they glided off to the north over groves of date palms and up the Tigris a little ways to put down at Al Qurna and the Garden of Eden.

Here Demetrius Booth seemed duly reverent. Kenyon

didn't tell him that the Tree of Knowledge of Good and Evil that stood behind a palisade had fallen down a couple years ago, or that local enterprise had replanted it; he simply smoked and glanced at his watch as the little Greek took rapid notes on a yellow pad. When they were back in the air, he had a sudden impulse.

"Want to see another site?" he shouted above the roar and vibration.

"Eh? What is it?"

"Don't know. Funny-looking terrain just the other side of the marshes."

The red circle, he was thinking. Prostrated worshippers. Maybe it was valuable. Some mineral fluke with strange properties there in the desert. A geologist might know. Whatever Demetrius Booth replied beneath the din, Clay Kenyon was already banking off toward the west.

Below them passed the marshes of the Ma'dan, gerrymandered with waterways and floating villages of reed huts all facing southwest toward Mecca and long canoes and water buffalo and—once—a wild boar. Each village had a *mudhif*, or tunnel-like guest hall, built entirely of twenty-foot-long reeds bundled into vaulted ribs as thick as elephant legs.

Beyond that was the barren emptiness of haze and dust where nothing moved and no more dogs pantomimed barking below. They flew northwest until Kenyon knew he had missed the odd red circle with its trio of votaries. He turned back, banking, zigzagging. Three times he traversed the zone. He glanced at his watch again. He had been doing that a lot lately, as if time were running out. Where was it? Usually he flew to the south, carrying tourists to Babylon or Ur near the Euphrates. "*You will come upon your destiny like a falcon diving on its prey*," the Ma'dan woman had told him when he was sharing sweet black tea with Dakhil, who occasionally worked for him.

And so he did.

Again.

It was there soon into the fourth pass, a nearly perfect crater of red against gray sand. And there were the three prone figures, nearly invisible in their gray robes. They couldn't have been lying there all this time, he thought. Not unless they were dead, and if they had somehow all died together with such symmetry, then where were the carrion eaters who would have torn their garments and picked their bones? No, the men had fallen on their faces at the chopper's approach. Like desert chameleons', this was their camouflage. Pushing the stick in his left hand, Kenyon dove down and hovered, the rotor changing pitch as it drooped like a shallow parasol. Against the teeth-rattling percussion he merely nodded toward the site for the benefit of Demetrius Booth.

The geologist leaned forward, causing the cabin to dip slightly. Fluidly, Kenyon nosed the craft forward to dissipate the nod; there were days when he steered just by shifting his body weight. When their wash lapped at the crater, Kenyon brought them up slightly. He didn't want to disturb the site, even though he disliked flying at an in-between altitude. If you lost power under thirty feet, "ground cushion" would mitigate a crash. And if you lost it above three hundred feet, the windmill effect on the rotor from that height could build and act like a parachute. "Autorotation," they called it. Helicopters went down more than planes, but they had fewer fatalities because of these soft crashes and because wreckage tended to spin away from the occupants. But not in between thirty and three hundred feet. That was the death zone.

Suddenly the dragonfly on the near side of the crater lifted smoothly from the sand and in one clean motion brought a rifle—a Kalashnikov—into line with them. The sound was lost in the hammering beat of the Sikorsky, but the muzzle flashes were vivid and succinct. And by the time the other two figures on the ground had sprung up, each with his own Kalashnikov, they heard the pings off the rotor and felt the lurch. The chopper yawed violently and began to spin.

Instinctively Kenyon's palms and fingers melded with the two controls. His left hand twisted the grip, feeding fuel while he moved that stick to change the pitch of the blades. Simultaneously he used the right control so that the rotor swept them forward. The copter righted itself. But the ground fire was murderously close. If he banked away, he would make a broader target. Without hesitation, Kenyon turned head-on and dove for the figures on the ground.

It was a game of chicken. For the figures on the ground, the terms were stand and fire versus fall and be saved. But all three stood, apparently willing to die if only they could bring down the chopper. Their gray robes billowed in the wash and the blinding swirls of sand, and still they fired. In the sudden maelstrom it would certainly have taken luck to hit anything. Add to that disorientation the deafening resonance and tattooing of mechanical things. But as low as the Sikorsky swept and as near to the target as the blinded shooters were, no heads rolled and nothing penetrated the skin of the craft. The assailants turned to follow the sound, still firing wildly and perhaps in danger of hitting each other.

Kenyon glanced at his watch.

When he looked across at his passenger he was struck by the grim stoicism on the geologist's pug features. Tough little man. Where had he fought before? They flew straight north, looking back at the curious spot of red already fading to orange and at the figures blending with the sand. The smell of gas was in the cabin, but the gauge was holding steady. Banking in a wide circle, Kenyon headed back toward Basra.

Despite his relief it nagged at him that they had missed. The only hits were those "pings" that had come at maximum distance after the firing began. Why hadn't their accuracy improved just before the ground wash enveloped them? He had flown at them to make them duck, but failing that, they couldn't have missed. Unless they wanted to. Was it because they didn't want him to crash in the red crater? He had a feeling that bringing a helicopter down in the desert would not have been a problem for them—that more of them would have come to remove anything that compromised the site. These were not worshippers—at least not *just* worshippers—they must have been guards. They would have hauled off the wreckage like ants carrying away leaves, like carrion eaters picking bones. And yet they wouldn't risk having him crash in the red crater. What could be so valuable there? And who the hell were they?

Servants of the Circle, Red Sentries, Keepers of Silence, Defenders of the Cradle of Dust—the names trailed back fifty centuries into the dawn of social order. Jealously guarded from the beginning, the site had rarely become known outside the region. And when it had, the knowledge eventually faded into the mists of time and legend. Dozens of sects back through Mesopotamia and Babylon had sustained the watch. Some had done so out of fear, some out of love, others merely because of tradition, some simply because of the magnitude of a sacred trust. All had felt awe.

In the time of the Ottoman Empire there had been outposts in a ring around the crater, and so far removed from it that only a camel could cross from an outpost to the site in a day. But the ring itself had drawn attention, and eventually a traitor and a massacre had caused the strategy to be changed. Now only a trio of servitors stood guard. Three members at a time out of the fifteen permanent initiates. They came on foot at night across the moon-haunted desert, so that no horse droppings marked the way. The first seven of the nineteen kilometers were trekked through a brook; the last twelve along various routes in the shadows of sarsens or where the wind would sweep away traces. They stayed at the red crater for twenty-fours hours, until the next sentries arrived. No outsider knew of the site. No outsider could know. These faithful were celibate, and they would turn ruthlessly on each other if any weakening was suspected.

They were supported by the elders at the ruins known as Tel el Muhunnad, but only two patriarchs of that small, impenetrable sect actually understood exactly what it was they were guarding. The power in the crater was enormous, staggering, and yet it was a mere residue, beyond the province of man to harness and blasphemous to try. Not gold, not silver, nor precious stones. There was nothing of value here in the commerce of civilization. Nothing at all . . . except red dust.

"You will come upon your destiny like a falcon diving on its prey."

So Kenyon had. A robust, manly destiny befitting the hunter in him. The tangible goal of riches; the intangible one of revenge. But it wasn't just anger or even greed that drew him back. It was purpose. Something to pull his life together and stop the slide. He didn't care what the danger was. He was more afraid of living than of dying. It came out less philosophically when he made his pitch.

"There's something extremely valuable at that site,"

he told each of the men he recruited. "Something they don't want to move."

This played well in the impoverished harshness of the marshlands for the man named Dakhil. And there was another reason it was effective—something that bordered on religious destiny for the superstitious Ma'di. The stalwart Dakhil had always believed in the *Hujaidk,* a magical island guarded by spirits who could make it invisible and drive visitors mad, and thus the island of red sand and its nearly invisible guardians struck a chord of recognition.

And Saladin, the Kurd who ran routes with Kenyon from Mosul to Kirkuk, also found it attractive. His Yazidi sect believed in the ultimate power of God but deferred in the short term to Shaitan—the fallen angel Satan—who after all was in control of the present earth. You could take God's goodness for granted, Saladin had once explained, but *Malak Ta'us* (the Peacock Angel, symbol of Satan) was unpredictable and required appeasement. If the guardians of this red crater were holding the earth hostage, then maybe there was justice in destroying them. Saladin reasoned this with mounting fervor, but it was Kenyon's speculation about something valuable that made his eyes glint.

Sadam Salah, from Baghdad's famed River Street row of silversmiths, needed no spiritual justification. Apprenticed to his uncle and feeling trapped in a family craft that smothered his young ambitions, he had always responded favorably to Kenyon's propositions. Either money or adventure alone would have persuaded him. The prospect of both was extravagant.

A Ma'di from the south, a Kurd from the north, a Shiite Muslim from Baghdad. Truly strange bedfellows. Kenyon had never worked with all of them together before, nor had his partner, Bailey Burke, a veteran pilot who had flown Shawnees and Chickasaws for the Air Force.

Bailey had reservations. "These guys know who the enemy is?" he grumbled. That was unusual for Bailey, who never seemed to worry about anything. If Kenyon was forever glancing at his watch, Bailey didn't wear one.

And then there was Demetrius Booth—always a surprise. The Greek geologist kept everyone at arm's length with his bad breath and Coke-bottle lenses, but he had responded to Kenyon's request that he help them assay what might be there in the red crater by insisting that he wanted to go along for the kill. It provoked an argument between the two partners that was settled only when Demetrius offered to pay for the Kalashnikovs that Saladin was to obtain.

"Do you know how to use an automatic rifle?" Bailey demanded of Booth.

"With my eyesight, anything that keeps pumping out bullets is the weapon of choice," the Greek said, and if that wasn't a satisfying answer, the wad of dinars he pulled out of his pocket was.

It took six days to put it together—the repairs to the rotor, the travel, the bringing of arms through border passes in extreme southeast Turkey near Semdini. Six days. Long enough to create a universe. And though God may have rested the next day, on their seventh morning the little sortie group went in under an ancient sky without a clue as to what they were disturbing.

As an attack, there was no real element of surprise. The strategy was six against three. Kenyon made a low circle, keeping almost half a mile from ground zero, dropping off Dakhil, Booth, Salah and Burke ninety degrees apart from each other. Then, with the four on the ground closing in and drawing fire, he attacked from the air, roaring nose-on toward the red crater while Saladin hung out of the retrofitted port on the Sikorsky, firing his Kalashnikov.

It was Salah who went down first, catching a burst in the throat and chest less than fifty yards from the object of their assault. The defenders were skilled, and they had built up around the crater a concentric ring of redoubts whose slight elevation was undetectable from the air, but from the positions they took to fire outward, Kenyon could see this now. And he understood too that the redoubts had been built because the defenders would not step down into the crater and use the rim for protection. Had he been a man of faith, he might have imputed this to some religious cause. It was easier to believe that something of secular value lay in the crater. Or even that the red dust was dangerous. At any rate, it was too late to second-guess. Now it was a fight for the sake of a fight. Reason enough to live for a soldier of fortune; reason enough to die for a man who had been dying for a decade.

Boldly he swept over the crater, gambling that they wouldn't shoot down his chopper as long as it hovered over the red dust. With Saladin firing on the pinned defenders, Kenyon moved the stick in his left hand, dropping, dropping. They were perhaps sixty feet in the air—that in-between altitude he hated. If he could get it under thirty feet, he would feel safer. And his gamble was working. The robed figures writhed below him, torn between getting off bursts at the ground attackers and shooting up at the vulnerable target that was descending on them like a falcon diving on its prey. Fifty-five feet . . . fifty. It happened faster than the telling. But now the wash began to kick things up. Swirls of dust, swirls of time, men coming apart as they came together, passion and will apart from God, blind, forever blind . . .

The Servants of the Circle squinted within the pillar of red, trying to determine whether the blasphemous machine was yawing and pitching itself clear of the holy site. Did it even matter, when they would momentarily be dead anyway? Who would protect the Circle then? Better to bring it down if there was a chance that they might keep control of the site. One of them sat up, his left arm raised against the dust, his right cradling the Kalashnikov. In an instant he was raked by Dakhil's deadly fire. Immediately a second defender rose to his feet, firing blindly into the demonic roar.

The Sikorsky was above forty feet when the engine cut out. Too low for autorotation to save it; too high for ground cushion to have an effect. It fell like a stone in the middle of the crater and exploded into flame. The blast threw clear bodies and riving shards of metal. The heat kept everyone at bay. One of the defenders was still alive, his robes afire, his kaffiyeh missing, clawing for a great curved knife in his sash. It frightened Dakhil, who nevertheless edged forward the final few steps. ". . . *Hujaidk*," he murmured and fired conclusively.

Burke, Booth, Dakhil. Everyone else was dead. In astonishment the survivors watched the remnants of the Sikorsky burn. The fire was intensely red, almost phosphorescent, the heat ferocious. And it didn't just eat away consumables, leaving blackened scoria and ashes. It hissed and vaporized like a fuse. Strangest of all, there was no smoke. There should have been billowing black clouds going up, but there was absolutely nothing, as if matter were not just transmuting but being annihilated. In a few minutes the red crater lay as before, with only a glassy patch marking the spot where the chopper had exploded on impact and burned.

It was Demetrius Booth, the geologist, who stepped down into the crater and walked carefully to the spot.

His Coke-bottle lenses were riveted on the glazed sand.
Slowly he squatted, extending an index finger until it
punctured the translucent crust. "Natron . . ." he murmured.

"What is it?" Bailey hollered at length from the rim.

Booth stood up. "Sand," he said, ". . . just sand."

They probed, they dug, they searched. *Sand*. An extremely fine red sand. An anomaly, to be sure. The Sa-
hara was sand, and the Gobi was like the valley of the
moon, but the Iraqi desert was inclined to barren wasteland with shale and tufted vegetation. They found the
guards' meager rations nearby. Water, some nuts. Empty-
ing one of the jugs, they filled it with red sand and began
the long trek toward the marshes.

It was two days before they were back in Basra, two
days of walking and Ma'dan hospitality and clouds of
mosquitoes in the marshlands. Booth confirmed his
analysis soon after: a fine red sand you could call dust,
not typical of any formations in the area.

"So why is it valuable?" Bailey wanted to know.

"I haven't the faintest idea. These people will attach
legends to any anomaly. Maybe a meteor crashed there.
That circular crater . . ."

Demetrius Booth had lost whatever interest he had in
this madcap diversion. His second night back in Basra,
he checked out of the Saint George and disappeared into
the global mists from which he had come. Dakhil also
left, shrugging and quietly returning to his archipelago
village built of reeds. Life was a struggle; he did not
have the luxury of guilt, grief or regret.

Bailey did. He was angry at first, his blood still
singing with the violence of the raid. He was angry at
the strangers he had assaulted. Angry at Kenyon for getting killed. Angry because he could not understand what
had happened. But then the futility and stupidity of what

they had done sank in, and he began to feel humility and remorse. Clay Kenyon had a married daughter by his first wife in the States. He had one of her letters in his pocket, which he had neglected to give his partner before the raid. At least he would write her to say that her father had died in a helicopter crash. Then he would get out of Iraq. Go to Europe. Look up an old girlfriend who would drink with him and hear his confessions for a while.

Booth had transferred the red dust to a plastic bag, and Bailey would have thrown it into the Shatt al Arab, except that on the third night in Basra, while he was staying in the Greek's paid-up room, someone broke in and tried to steal it.

In through the balcony came the thief, a slight man dressed oddly for his mission in a double-breasted British suit coat, white native trousers and a kaffiyeh on his head. Bailey, stocky and with a grip like spring steel, got him by the throat as he was escaping.

"I get real testy when someone wakes me," he growled, bending him over the rail four stories up. "So tell me a bedtime story so I can get back to sleep."

He got a thin wheeze of Arabic.

"No English? Too bad." He tipped the body a little more.

"Wait!" The agile man clung as Bailey rocked him back to the pivot point.

"Ah, I thought you might be a linguist."

"*You* stole it," the thief piped recklessly.

"Yeah, that's true."

"I am not stealing it. I am getting it back."

"We won't dispute that. Now, tell me exactly what it is I've stolen."

There was a moment of calculation while the intruder registered Bailey's ignorance.

"You were guarding it, Bucko. It must be valuable," Bailey prompted.

"It is not valuable."

"Don't tell me . . . a holy site?"

"No, no, not holy." Lameness in the voice.

"A holy site," Bailey repeated with disgust. This was what Kenyon had died for.

"I swear, it is not."

Bailey teetered him over the rail.

"I will tell you! I will tell you!" He was breathless now, fumbling for a train of thought that Bailey kept shaking him to derail. "It . . . it is the dust of . . ."

"Spit it out."

"—of Creation." This came out a half sob—agony and fear—and as the intruder was swung back onto his own center of gravity, he trembled like an abject puppy let back in from the storm but facing the shame for which it had been banished.

"Creation," Bailey sighed, his arms relaxing like depressurized pistons. "Adam and Eve. If you people found a snowman, you'd think it was the Holy Ghost."

But if for Bailey the drama had all gone out of the mystery of the red dust, his reprieved visitor was now intent on denying what he had just blurted out for the sake of his own skin.

"I did not say it was holy. There is a legend . . . a legend of a master race . . . coming from the stars. They made us. They made men and left the red residue."

"Religion."

"I'm telling you, it has nothing to do with religion. Scoff at what I've told you, if you like, but do not spread rumors that could cause a sensation."

Bailey was laughing. The fellow was frantic with smoke screens. "What are you—a priest? You're not like those fighters out there in the desert." Bailey pulled him all the way up. "Here." He retrieved the plastic bag of red dust that had been dropped on the balcony. "Take it. Save me the trouble of throwing it away. Take a 'powder.' Am-scray. But use the door this time."

Thunderstruck, the little man in the double-breasted suit and loose native trousers moved a couple of cautious steps. Then, gathering the bag to his breast with both hands, he fled as comically as a broken-field runner through the apartment.

And that would have been the end of it, but in the morning Bailey saw the rest of the red dust, which Demetrius Booth had poured into a glass flask for analysis, and decided that it would serve as ashes in a funerary urn. So he wrote Kenyon's daughter that her father's ashes were enclosed—a little white lie to give her some closure for her father, and himself some closure for his partner—and by noon he had packed the thing in a wooden box filled with excelsior and shipped it to America. Now he could get on with his life. By nightfall he was floating in the Shatt al Arab with his throat slashed from ear to ear.

Creation

2000

Ariel

Lightning blanched the side of the farmhouse, freezing a flash photograph. Thunder shook the thin windows in anger, as if they were so many wall frames whose portraits had been stolen. There were faces enough in the history of the house to fill each one, three to a casement. A century and a half of faces had sheltered behind the glass, contemplating spring floods, summer droughts, winter freezes. The thousand storms that had laid siege to the roof and the foundation had never penetrated. All those generations kept safe and sound until now, and the house was still a virtual fortification. But the need tonight was not for refuge. The need tonight was for escape.

She stood there in the weather-ravaged window frame high up on the third story, a white-faced hag, her stare bulging with just a hint of Graves' disease out at the storm. This was Ariel Leppa, whose once clear eyes were now becoming opaque. They saw nothing in the present, nothing in the future. And the past, which remained so vivid in her thoughts, was like a single day. The compression of life into one day was not so strange considering that time had shunned her.

It had taken seventy-four years to live that past, but

now it was like a single day into which she had arisen, stupid with hope and trust, in the morning. And even when the afternoon of that solitary day was upon her and the details of her personal reality had begun to crush her, she had still believed. Stupid. Because by that time she had shallow friendships of convenience, and a husband who "kept" her like something in a drawer, and a headstrong daughter she had raised but never controlled.

Beyond the tyranny of marriage and parenting, the unending day had been about omissions—things that had never truly happened. Like friendship and respect. Ariel had gone to school, church, dances; she had worked for a time in the world. Why had all her relationships been variations on the single theme of rejection? Ariel Leppa. Ariel the Leper. Her successes had been defaults, her minor ascendancies consolations. She had never been anyone's first choice for anything. They had merely taken her in. Tolerated her. And when better options came along or they felt acquitted of charitable obligations, they shoved her back into the shadows. That's who she was and who she wasn't.

But now it was over, if only because the major players in her melodrama were dead. They had gone down one by one like autumnal fireflies winking out in the cold. Except for her daughter. Amber might as well be dead, partially paralyzed and on dialysis at age forty-four because of a fall in a rock climb eleven years ago, living—if you could call it that—with a husband and a grown son. How dare Amber be happy in such a state when her mother, whole in mind and body if not spirit, was so miserable!

Ariel stood in the skittering flashes and bombast of the storm, waiting to feel vindicated. *(See who is left standing!)* But all she felt was cheated.

When the lightning flashed again, the high window

frame was empty. Ariel Leppa was flying through the house like a Valkyrie. *Wait for me!* Tonight she would rejoin the context of her life. No tepid suicide hers, no whiny note or play for attention. Her death would be a temper tantrum equal to the storm outside. Hurling her own thunderbolts, she swept the nightstand and dresser clean. She had a cane she used but did not much need, and this she raked along the upper corridor between the doors, tearing down pictures—faces and places that kept the wounds of condescension fresh. What malevolence deemed that she, the most unwanted of her life's circle, be the survivor? All those funerals she had attended, most recently her husband's—that tyrant. Even he, the invincible Thomas Leppa, was in his grave. What a shock to discover that she needed them, wanted them back. Why wasn't she triumphant to have outlived them all?

It was because she *hadn't* lived. She was still waiting to live. And they had been her audience who might yet applaud, might accept her before the curtain rang down, might give some meaning to the play and her performance. And now the best she could do was exit stage left to an empty . . . house.

Down the staircase she hammered, stiffness be damned. The resistance in her dried-up old joints made her a frightening spectacle, stumbling against the banister, scrawny limbs advancing with jerky animation. A good headlong pitch to the bottom might do it, flashed through her mind. But what if she wasn't lucky enough to break her neck? What if she survived only to go on existing in a wheelchair, like Amber? Better to start a fire on the first floor. Better to go up to the roof where she could fall three stories, glaring at the world all the way down. No one ever got an Oscar for a quick death. She hadn't been up there since she was a little girl, she thought, and suddenly the image of her childhood attempts to touch the sky tore through her with softness and light. She faltered against the wall and slid down hard on the bottom step of the staircase. A blue flash filled the side glass by the front door, followed by a sharp bark, like heavy furniture being nudged on a wooden floor, and then the lights failed exactly like house lights going down for the start of a play.

The rain beat steadily now, drumming up a deluge of memories and memories told to her. She had been born in this house, breathing the dust left over from another century. The foundation had been laid in 1856. So sayeth *The History of Minnesota: A County Survey* up in the sewing room. It was a proper house, the first real one in the area. The cellars—plural because there was a subcellar that sloped down from the main one—had gone in first. In those days, five years after the Dakota Indians sold their lands to the government and two years before statehood, you couldn't know that disgruntled bands wouldn't come back to burn you out. The charred bones of many settlers mingled with ruins still traceable in local lore. A civil war came and went, and a whole Victorian age. The new century had brought, among other things, a chic decadence, and there was a dark chapter where her grandfather had permitted mobsters from far-off Chicago to run Canadian whiskey that had been stored at the farm into Saint Paul. That too she missed, but just barely. She had heard that tale fresh: how men named Torrio and O'Bannion had stacked cases of smuggled bourbon in tunnels that had been extended from the cellars; and how five of their gang had been gunned down with Thompson submachine guns right there; and how her grandfather had then sealed off the tunnel. Were dead men still in the cellars? No one could or would answer that, and she had loved exploring the tunnels as a little girl, discovering quaint tools, puzzling over Chautauqua souvenirs and patent medicine relics. The cellars became her first studio. She learned to draw down there and later to paint. Painting was all she had ever accomplished. It had saved her from loneliness at the same time that it condemned her to be alone, because two-dimensional people done in oils became her three-dimensional society, her friends, her lovers. . . .

But she couldn't paint herself a husband, and her father had volunteered to fight Hirohito and neglected to return, leaving her mother to claim abandonment and file for divorce, so the farm had no man. And then Thomas Leppa stepped in. He was no more attractive than she, a fact they both understood. But Ariel was almost thirty, and no one else was looking at her, least of all the undeclared inamorata of her life, Kraft Olson, who only had eyes for a woman named Danielle, so she married Thomas Leppa, and he gave her Amber and a lifetime of abuse.

When the farm began to fail in 1960 they leased the lower floor of the house to a Lutheran country day school, and a wing was built that extended the house closer to the barn. After that they lived in the upstairs while nearly four decades limped by. They were still farming at a subsistence level when the Lutheran day school closed its doors. But the loans had all been paid off by then, and there were just the two of them. And then there was one. And by dawn there would be none.

Except . . . that she couldn't just end herself without a final statement. Wasn't that funny? So much never accomplished, and now she needed something for closure before she could give it up.

She rose stiffly from the step and stumped through the rooms on her cane, pausing for lightning flashes to show the way. With her eyes she took diluted pictures at each illumination: the floor lamp, the morris chair, the ottoman drained of color—ghosts standing, sitting, lying. And suddenly it occurred to her that she couldn't remember what her father looked like. He was the first to abandon her. Was that when the pattern of rejection was set? He had said he loved her—he wrote that he loved her. He wrote when she was thirty-three. *A little late, Daddy . . .* He must have known that, because what he actually wrote was that he had "always" loved her, as if he had finally figured out what a little girl needed to hear, to feel. She had never before been able to laugh at this absurd tardiness, so typically male, and for the first time in the forty years since she had learned of his death she wanted to forgive him, embrace him. But he had died in Iraq, in a helicopter crash, and his ashes . . .

Where were his ashes?

Those oddly red ashes his partner had sent. She hadn't seen the glass flask since before Amber's accident. It had gone from the mantel to the study after the Lutheran day school leased the lower floor, but it wasn't there now. She was sure of that. Had it been thrown away? On the brink of self-destruction, the thought that her father's ashes had disappeared from her life seemed apocalyptic.

Another spasm of lightning, and she twisted to scrutinize the shelves, too late to catch anything but afterdrift. She groped through to the next room and the next, and then, in the dining room, where a curved glass highboy sat, she saw something that afterward seemed like a silver finger pointing from her father's grave. Breathing heavily in the dark, she waited until a sustained flash brought back the silver glint precisely where she was peering. Dust within glass within glass, she saw. The flask sat on the middle shelf of the cabinet, crowded against mugs and knickknacks that were leather or pewter or clay.

The bramble of lightning died as she shuffled toward the highboy—the darkness where she had last seen the highboy—and her cane thumped on the hardwood floor and her other hand paddled the air as if it were webbed. Her nails scrabbled against the glass, and the door opened with a yelp. Aromas of leather and lacquered wood puffed out. She fumbled past objects, trembling as though she were really reaching to touch the hand of the man who had authored her being. A millisecond flash from the window guided her, and she clamped on to the flask as if it were the last rock before the dizzying drop of a cataract. Conception and death, the bookends of life . . . her father the witness to both . . . alpha and omega.

Something fell, something broke, and she caught her breath for an instant, even though she knew it was not glass but the muted grate of ceramic. Slowly she withdrew the flask. By weight alone she was sure it was intact. Hugging that Holy Grail to her breast, she beetled back through the house to the staircase just as the electricity came back on. Up the steps she climbed to the third floor, past the framed photos she had raked from the walls, past her bedroom into her inner sanctum: the studio.

She could tell by the smell of a painting how much it had dried, and the last one wasn't ready for varnishing yet, but she tumbled it from the easel. Still clutching the flask, she toted a fresh canvas out of the pile she had ready and bumped it awkwardly into place. Then she went to her bench and squeezed out her paints. By habit she always did this in the same order: cool colors on the short side of the rectangular palette, warm colors to the right, separated by white. When she pulled the glass stopper from the flask, she hesitated. Her eyes scanned the shelves, and now she culled containers and pigments, a mortar and pestle, linseed oil, a rack of glass jars, a ring of plastic measuring spoons, rags and clean stir sticks broken down from larger sticks. Again she hesitated, weighing alternatives. Then she picked up the palette and scraped the oils into the glass jars. Like a master chef working from scratch, she prepared her stock according to instinct and imagination, cutting—always cutting with the turps—until the paste was thinned into a liquid in the jars. The colors blended swiftly now: first a basic array, then the flesh tones, then a very subtle viridescence for the eyes, and finally a variety of flaxen tints—she would have to experiment as she painted—for the hair.

This was the cognoscente Ariel Leppa. This was what her innermost passions, left to their own designs for a lifetime, had become. She was unschooled but sure in her craft. She had sought no help, been offered none. She knew painting, knew herself, knew what she saw and how to put its essence on canvas. But tonight there would be one difference, one new element in her alchemy.

Crying dry-eyed, not daring to inhale or exhale, she unstoppered the flask. Cautiously she lowered a kind of pointel made of glass with a tiny ladle on the end into the mouth. She expected the fine red dust to be compacted, or at least to have formed a crust, but there was no tension there at all. The glass ladle slid in as if it were air. Slowly she withdrew the measure and bore it to the first container, and there she sprinkled it.

It lay on the surface like nutmeg on a soup, not sinking, not changing color at all. She picked up a flat stick and stirred it into suspension. Then she scrutinized the color and texture with satisfaction. No detectable change. She could cut it again and the fine red dust would not make its presence known. The difference in handling would simply be the thinness she chose. And thinned paints were her forte.

Because she didn't have time to let things dry. No time at all. Thick oils could take months to set completely, even years. Two weeks minimum just to dry to the touch. She had gone to galleries and talked with painters and knew she was right about this. But she had also learned to control the use of washes of turpentine, and even a drying and thinning medium like Liquin, so that she could finish quickly without sacrificing detail. The secret was a technique called *alla prima*. And no one, she thought, did that better than she.

Wet on wet. She would work that way, using all the tricks she had accumulated in a lifetime. The painting would glow a little, look a little pale, but that was all right. It would be complete and detailed despite the wet layering. Details were another strength of her art. Not the kind of bigger-than-life detail of the masters, but a pure skill in creating likeness. At an age when other painters began to depend on memory and habit, Ariel Leppa still saw with an evolving interpretation and possessed a flawless transfer from mind to wrist and fingers. And now she was ready for her last painting.

A painting with her father's ashes, but not his face. Because her mother had destroyed the photographs, and the recall of the child who had wiped his image irretrievably from her memory was only of Old Spice shaving lotion, and a raspy cheek when he hugged, and the faintly mellow molasses smell of tobacco in his pocket in that same hug. Try as she might, she could never pull his face into focus, as if admitting it had existed was to admit it had departed. But now she needed his presence, because the final distillation must testify to some meaning or coherence that might have been. So she merged the three critical elements of her life: her skill, her father, and the hallowed subject of her final portrait . . .

Amber.

No shortage of Amber photos. From studio poses to blurry snapshots, monochrome to noir, seraphic smiles to glowering outrage; and a progression from bassinet to wheelchair (the last one taken at Amber's insistence because Ariel didn't want a photo of her daughter in that contraption). But Ariel Leppa, nee Kenyon, didn't need a photograph for this painting. It would be Amber at age nine. Amber when her hair was golden and her eyes were a cat's green, and when there was something indefinable on the verge of rebellion in her soul and body that was still contained by childhood and a mother's call. That was just before Ariel lost her. Lost communication and insight.

She would have preferred to paint in the daylight that entered the upper-story studio, but she didn't want to see another sunrise. With the easel moved to catch the bench lamp full and her thinned oils and solvents within reach, she made the first broad strokes and instantly the lines of force were unmistakably Amber. Amber from head to toe, a ghost, a spirit of turpentine barely visible in the first layer.

From the slashing pyrotechnics outside the house she had Sturm und Drang, and that seemed to be the right anthem. The rain drove straight at the windows as if trying to get in, trying to dialyze the oils and wash out the dark miracle that was taking place on canvas. But Ariel painted calmly, implacably. If she had ever permitted anyone to watch, they would have imagined that painting was her therapy. The physical tension that gripped her when she worked never showed. She moved like a dancer, holding poses through sheer tensile strength while appearing effortless and graceful. It exhausted her.

But the old energy was there this night, flowing to and from the image as never before.

She painted Amber standing in a white pinafore, and it was like caressing her features to life: the frail, downy forearms and agile fingers . . . the crown of her head, so full in contrast to her pixie chin . . . the tiny fissures of her rosebud lips *("Stop pouting, young lady!")* . . . and the eyes—which expression to choose for the endlessly changing eyes? She summoned Amber's Queen of the Nile look—a touch of impudence and boredom within a sleepy knowledge beyond her years. And outside, Zeus hurling fire. On she painted, layer by layer floating independently, like pastry, a diaphanous miracle of *alla prima*.

It was still dark when she realized she was finished. She had been staring for several minutes, the brush idle between her fingers, as if waiting for her child to speak. But it was the final uneasy whisper of the thunder that she heard. No more fulminations through the window. Just blackness. The downspouts murmured, as if things were fleeing. Something had left the house, something had arrived, and all was quite still.

She knew it was her best work ever. An utterly ephemeral creature sat on the canvas, like a butterfly that would presently palpitate to life and resume flight. Speed had forced her to capture just what was essential, and yet the portrait was complete. Not one painter in a hundred could have done it with that technique. Maybe not one in a thousand. They would have ended up with a surreal wash, a wax figure on a hot day.

The flush of exultation ebbed, and Ariel felt the stiffness in her elbow, the shakiness in her legs. Where were her aspirins?

Oh.

She wouldn't need them. Except perhaps as an overdose. Because she still had to commit suicide, didn't she? But she was too tired to kill herself now. Wasn't that funny? Too tired to sleep forever. When she woke up, then she would do it. She turned the easel and crossed the room to slump on the ratty Chesterfield sofa. Perhaps she would die effortlessly if she just closed her eyes. They would find her a week from now, or a month, whenever the first stray dog began howling outside. Her corpse would be awful by then. Serve them right. And they would see the painting, and maybe they would even understand when they wrote her obituary: *Ariel Leppa died in childbirth at age seventy-four . . .*

Amber

"Mother?"

Ariel's eyelids lifted like mechanical shutters. Something urgent and external was trying to reverse the entropy of her soul. And then she saw Amber and she knew she had died after all, right there on the Chesterfield. Everything else—the studio, the hum of the sump pump, the wind flapping a shingle on the roof—was like the hell on earth of her past, but here was her angel, whitely radiant with only her cat's green eyes for contrast, that and the faint gloss of her pink lips.

"Mother-rr, get up!"

And that unheavenly impatience brought Ariel fully awake. A great fear swept over her as she struggled to a sitting position. Her old heart was beating like a fist on a mossy door. How could this be happening? She twisted around to stare at the painting. The image was unchanged. Amber had not stepped out of the frame, life size, leaving an empty canvas. And yet she *had* stepped out of it. How could flesh arise from paint? As if the oils were embrocations that had moistened some desiccated phantom of memory to life. But it couldn't be the pigments and oils—those same elements Ariel had mixed time and again—could it? It had to be the ashes. Her father's ashes.

Dysfunctional, desolate, disenfranchised Ariel Leppa had no trouble believing in magical interventions. Earth had failed her. She had lived in the shadows of life with only the hope of a retributive change—why shouldn't she be compensated? She had grown old waiting for her due, and the people who were required to pay it were now dead—the possibility of justice on earth was dead—so why shouldn't Amber be restored to her? Why shouldn't her guilty father make reparations from the grave? You didn't question magic. It just was. In a world of stumbling science and evolving impossibilities, call it a mutation of reality. If it worked, it would hang around. If it didn't, it would disappear. In the last summer of the millennium, in south central Minnesota, magic had appeared.

"Oh, my dear . . ." She sighed brokenly with awe and delight.

Trouble in the cat's green. A dart of annoyance. And the ten fingertips that had been bunched together in childlike indecision flew apart with a sweeping gesture at the room. "What's going on? Where's the wallpaper, and the picture of Sir Aarfie?"

Ariel struggled to her feet, doubting again. The stiffness in her body was all too earthly. And Amber was forty-four years old and in a wheelchair. How could she be standing here disoriented, talking about wallpaper and Sir Aarfie—that absurd name given to a dog killed by a pickup truck decades ago? But there *had* been a picture—a painting Ariel had done of the toy collie—that hung in the studio, and the walls still would have been papered when Amber was nine. And then the clincher, spoken by Amber with horror, as Ariel moved fully into the light, her sweater collar falling away from her face:

"You're not my mother . . ."

And that disavowal more than anything else convinced Ariel that somehow her nine-year-old daughter really had returned. Because of course she *was* Amber's mother. And who else could have been at odds with her after only a few seconds?

"What a shocking thing to say," Ariel spat out.

Amber shrank back, her fingertips coming together again like ten tiny magnets. "You're ugly. You're old."

Ariel made a breathy sound of indignation, even as she teared up and reached, trembling, for her daughter. "Well. *You* haven't changed."

Amber peered hard at the woman who said she was her mother, and by then Ariel had her by the wrist, pulling her into her arms. A cold, bony hug. When had it ever been different? But then the little girl jumped away, and they stared at one another for long seconds.

"You don't remember growing up, do you?" Ariel said. "Then nothing has changed for you. Amber, Amber, it's really you."

"Why are you talking like that?"

"Never mind," she laughed, her inexplicable joy deepening the scowl on her daughter's face. "Listen, listen, Amber, if everything is strange, don't be upset. I'll explain it. But let's not rush. We've got all the time in the world for explanations. Do you understand?"

"No."

Of course she didn't. She was asking about her dog. Soon she would want to know where her father was, and why yesterday wasn't yesterday. She would just have to know the truth, except . . . What was the truth?

"Then don't think about it, dear. We won't think about it. We'll just—"

"Where's Sir Aarfie?" the nine-year-old demanded again.

"Gone."

"Gone where?"

"Amber . . ." Amber was backing toward the door. "Amber, don't go out yet."

"Why not?"

"We're not done talking."

"I want to look for Sir Aarfie." And she called the animal's name in her child's clarion voice that rang painfully in the boxlike studio. Then she was out the door, her pure cries for the dog stabbing through the house.

Ariel struggled to the window, afraid she had lost the apparition that only a few minutes ago she had been afraid to discover. But no, there she was, circling the basswood tree.

"Father . . . Father, is this from you?" she asked, the first prayer she had ever addressed to him.

She hobbled to her workbench and snatched up one of the bottles of paint. It looked the same, smelled the same. It lapped viscously when she twirled the bottle, just like any other mix. But the red dust was in there, as invisible as the hand of God. And then it occurred to her that she could have painted anyone with the red dust. Any mortal flesh—

Don't even think about bringing them back!

They were dead. Dead, buried, corrupted. It couldn't happen again. What had taken place was something unique and specific. Amber. Flesh of her flesh. A gift back from God . . . or her father. But why? To make up for abandoning Ariel? Was it something to do with her own intensity? No question she came from a long line of impulsive, willful, even—shall we say—ruthless people. And then another little shock set in. If Amber was here, and nine years old, where was the daughter who existed in a wheelchair?

Cue the ringing phone. For an instant she sensed the swelling of air that anticipates a clamoring phone with dire news. But the instrument remained dead in its cradle. Instead what she heard was a joyful noise, a wonderful, significant lament from her nine-year-old daughter, searching below: "Aaaaar-fie!"

Dear God, what a staggering resurrection had taken place. What a staggering potential for more. Red dust, red dust.

She couldn't get away from the thought. Stumping downstairs, seeing the photos of the people who had stunted her life and then died out of it, looking at the dull stain on the antimacassar where her husband's head had rested for most of half a century as he hawked his throat and browbeat her—*red dust*. What if they *could* come back? Where would they go? How would they fit back into society?

All afternoon she watched her daughter. Amber in the yard drawing with sticks. Amber in the kitchen searching for cookies. It wasn't so different having her back again. And it wasn't too late. The child seemed more enthused with discovery than traumatized by change. Even when Ariel told her the truth, as she understood it—which was, at best, lame—even then, it didn't seem to register on Amber. She was more interested in the VCR and television. Nineteen sixty-five, that was the year she was nine—1965. Twenty-first-century ads and movies must look like science fiction to her. And then again, growing up was like that, wasn't it? Mundane miracles that you accepted without question. There were some troubling details, but this was going to work. At least some of Ariel's life was going to get relived.

Red dust.

One of those troubling details was taken care of that evening. The inevitable phone call she had feared and feared hoping for came just after seven o'clock. Amber was dead. That Amber. The one in the wheelchair. Ap-

parently she had died just about the hour when nine-
year-old Amber returned. Ariel didn't know what to feel.
How could she mourn? Even though she knew, for a cer-
tainty, that she had killed her adult daughter. Caused her
death anyway. Perhaps not even inadvertently. Perhaps
she had wished for it and it was implicit in her last painting. Last painting? Hardly her last.

Red dust, red dust, red dust . . .

She told herself it was for Amber that she did the next
one. Amber needed her father, and Ariel had his photo.
Though she never even glanced at it as she painted.
Cheerfully, breathlessly, she did it. She brought Thomas
Leppa back from the dead.

Unlike Amber, he came back knowing how his story
had ended, because there was no killing off to do this
time, inadvertent or otherwise. He had died naturally.
Finis. Therefore, he remembered everything from his
life, and perhaps everything thereafter. This last was a
matter of great interest to Ariel: where had he been since
the funeral? He wouldn't tell her what it was like. Of
course, he was angry, and that might have had something
to do with his obstinacy. Angry and afraid. Because Ariel
made one slight alteration in the circumstances to which
he returned, one little addition (subtraction, technically)
to ensure that life—Ariel's life—would be better this
time around. Some might have seen some irony in it, almost a cruel joke. Because Amber had come back standing tall and freed from a wheelchair. But Thomas Leppa
returned sitting down in one.

Denny & Martin

"Happy Y2K," Denny Bryce told his father on New Year's Day, 2000.

"Happy Y2K," Denny Bryce told his father on New Year's Day, 2001.

He used the very same words, because you couldn't be sure exactly when the new millennium started—what with everyone arguing about the year zero and all that—and because it didn't matter to his father anyway. Even if his father were capable of remembering that Denny had said the same thing, it wouldn't have mattered. Martin Bryce didn't know what millennium it was, or even what century. He didn't know the year or the month or the day, or what Y2K meant. His father had heard all of these things on the periphery of the chair he sat in, but he didn't remember them, didn't care—though he kept asking the time, like a man waiting for a train. He had given up trying to hang on to the thread of a television show through the commercials, and doing his quarterly taxes, and driving (thank God he had stopped asking where the car keys were!).

There was only one thing Martin Bryce did care about, his son knew. Something as fundamental as his own identity. Beth. His once and forever wife. For sixty inviolate years they had been married.

To the best of Denny's knowledge, his father fell in love with his mother after he retired. He wasn't sure what had preceded that. Lust, loyalty, friendship. Something practical and durable, passionate perhaps, but not the absolute and total love that had followed. Not the kind of altruistic love that almost no one ever gets. No. Not gets. *Gives.* Because you don't get it without being worthy of it, and you aren't worthy of it until you stop trying to get it and just give. It isn't "give until it hurts"; it's give until it stops hurting. Funny that Denny knew that, because at age fifty-one he had never experienced it live and in person. But he still thought he would. If he could just meet the right woman.

"Beth?" his father would call at all hours with expectation in his voice, as if she would come smiling from the next room. And Denny would remind him, often with aggravation: "Mom's dead, Dad. She died in the car accident two years ago, remember?"

Then the stoic old man would hang his head and swallow dryly and the mask would tighten over his eyes— waterproofing. "I forgot," he sometimes apologized in an airy whisper that didn't risk a tremble in his voice. Then, in that brief instant of shock and recovery, Denny would see all of his father, all of the emotional accumulation of the past he kept hidden. Because his father was a walking X-file: trust no one. Denny knew that his grandmother had been murdered when his father was six, and that his mother had tried to fill that void belatedly. There was more to it than he could fathom, but he didn't know how to compensate for his mother's role, and that was why it just killed him when the old man forgot—*Beth? . . . Mom's dead, Dad.* And the more he hated his father resurrecting his mother in this way, the more the old man did it, remembering what she had done that morning, it seemed, and how he was going to take her to Olive Garden that Sunday, and announcing that she was the best thing that had ever happened to him. And when the illusions collapsed in stark moments of lucidity, together they would have to bury her all over again.

So Denny Bryce knew the drill. And he knew his father was transferring trust to him. And he knew that he was about to betray that trust.

He had hung on as long as he could. The toileting, and the logistics of survival, and the endless business envelopes containing bills and statements that were beginning to rain down on him like tombstones. But now his father was wandering, turning up lost at a bank or a supermarket, or coming home in the back of a police car. When Martin Bryce answered the phone and set down the receiver, he never came back; and he left the stove on and water running and doors unlocked. Last week he had melted bacon fat in a Teflon pan, as if it were an old iron skillet, and then forgotten that he was going to fry eggs. The scorch marks from the resulting fire were still on the ceiling. But the most painful part of it was that the old man knew he was slipping and was ashamed and diminished by it. Denny didn't know how to deal with that.

And it was bad enough to hear meek apologies and hateful self-denigrations from his normally taciturn parent, but it was the thing with the mail that really brought his father's humiliation home to Denny.

"I've won a million dollars," Martin insisted after studying the contest advisory notice he had received.

Denny had to read it twice to see all the loopholes and deceptions. Then he made the mistake of laughing. He was laughing at the rhetorical frauds, but his father grew defensive and obstinate about having won, and they argued until the son took the letter apart line by line, resulting in the old man at last waving it off with a declaration of his own worthlessness. If Martin's memory hadn't been hemorrhaging, the tiff might have lingered. As it was, he lapsed into a kind of obedience that seemed to reflect his decreased self-esteem.

Denny didn't like his father becoming subservient. He wished he had congratulated the old man for winning the million dollars and just played it out until it was forgotten or they had blown money for the commercial toll call that was part of the scam. The next delusion was even more groundless, and Denny handled it better.

"The doctors say I need an operation," Martin told him solemnly one morning, and he waved in a general way toward his torso.

They talked it out, and Denny gently relieved him of the notion, but he could tell by the way his father closed his eyes and sat tight-lipped pretending to sleep that it was another blow.

And then there was the garage. That was the galvanizing event, the thing that doomed the status quo.

When Denny came home that afternoon from the school where he worked as a counselor, Martin was gone. He saw that the side door was open, and after a quick check inside, he drove all over the neighborhood before it occurred to him that his father had never used the side door except when he was going to the garage. Fearful that he had taken the old Buick Century out, Denny raced back. But when he hit the door opener, the cantilevered panel swung up, revealing first his father's ratty slippers and mismatched socks, and then the rest of him sitting in a dusty lawn chair next to the car. The old man pretended he was just resting there in the hermetic gloom of the cluttered garage, but it was clear what had happened. He had raised the door from the button in the house, had gone in and somehow closed it, and then couldn't remember how to open it again.

Denny disarmed the thing, but he couldn't disarm the world that threatened his father.

How could he protect him without abetting the irony of being alive but not really living? He had to do something for this man who had fathered him, who had gone to work each day to provide for him and sacrificed without limit for his family's well-being. He had to care for him. No question about that. Only how could he do it when he himself had to go to work each day? How could he stand guard through the nights when his father, having slept most of the day, suddenly got up? So he did something a Bryce male never did. He reached out to others. He reached out to everyone. The parade included a volunteer elder aide, Meals on Wheels, then Medicare, an agency and a visiting nurse, who assigned a visiting caregiver. But it was all stopgap, and then one day after school had ended for the semester and the counselors had finished their year-end record keeping, Denny Bryce found himself driving around to the assisted-living complexes and nursing homes whose mailings he had steadfastly thrown away over the past decade. Enlightenment was ghastly.

Most of the homes maintained common areas suitable to the mobile and the sentient, but go beyond that and you were in the corridors of the damned. Here were urine smells and feeble calls for help and waxy flesh straining to coat skeletons and an infantry of nurses maneuvering two-wheeled personnel carriers. You talked above hoary heads and studied antiseptically clean linoleum or looked at light caught in the sheers of windows that never seemed to brighten the interior. You pretended these were not warehouses for the dying. *Welcome aboard the* Titanic! In the end, Denny could not consign his father to such a place. He just couldn't do it.

And then he came upon New Eden.

KNEAL the small hand-painted placard below the rural mailbox read. If he hadn't stopped at the turnoff while trying to find his way back from Mankato, he wouldn't have noticed. He had gone to Mankato hoping that Golden Years Senior Living was the answer, and he had left in despair, grasping at straws, praying for deliverance, ready to trade in the Yellow Pages list of facilities he had been using for cues and omens. And suddenly here was this unimposing sign with that phrase again, that shibboleth that promised there wasn't a contradiction between freedom and confinement: "Assisted Living." Kenyon New Eden Assisted Living. KNEAL. Out here in the middle of nowhere.

It looked like a wood-frame farmhouse, but there was a long wing built of bricks, and it was pastoral and refreshingly distinct from the urban compounds and contrived facades of green over gray that clamored for the abandoned and the dying. Still you couldn't take the place seriously with that tiny sign, an afterthought, as if it needed to fulfill some regulatory declaration but didn't really want to be discovered. Maybe they were hiding a good thing. Maybe God had finally stepped in with a few misleading road signs to facilitate an answer for him. KNEAL. He was too frustrated and desperate not to pay attention.

The driveway was an archipelago of surviving chunks of asphalt that eventually led to a barn, but there was no parking area—no cars, in fact. And then he saw the last vestiges of a curb that ran parallel to the red brick addition. Goosegrass and dandelions were growing on the compacted area, and there were no tire tracks. What was going on here? A permanent bed and breakfast for enfeebled octogenarians? It just couldn't be legit. Some informal home-care facility qualifying for funds by listing

itself as assisted living? Probably be out of business next
week. But all he really knew was that it wasn't what he
had already seen at a dozen geriatric prisons across the
state.

He parked his Tercel under the umbrella of a willow
and strolled up to the porch. Nothing stirred in the windows and the house was strangely mute, as if caught in
its afternoon nap. Maybe everyone inside had died a
decade ago, he thought; maybe he was walking into a
mausoleum. He almost felt he should knock, but you
didn't knock when you went into a business, so he
turned the flecked metal handle and stepped across the
threshold . . .

And it was like coming home.

In fact, he still wasn't certain he wasn't trespassing on
someone's living room. But that wasn't all bad. Because
the white-glove cleaning patrol, and the smell of disin-
fectant, and the receptionist with the lily who probably
did double duty as an instant mourner, and the rattle of
trays on gurneys, and the snail line of wheelchairs at the
elevators, and the donated *National Geographic*s and
Reader's Digest books, and the WanderGuard detectors
behind plastic plants, and the flashing call lights screaming silently on a switchboard or unanswered above a
grim portal where the grim reaper leaned on the door-
frame—*all those were missing!* True, you could just call
this place ill equipped, but he liked the homey informality. Did it actually run? It came down to the people,
didn't it? And that was when he realized that he was
looking at two of them.

They sat, as still as lamps, on an ottoman. Two white
faces—a man's, a woman's—trained on his, but with ra-
diance awakening in their eyes. The woman especially
seemed to glow at his presence, her eyes huge behind
Hollywood glasses with glitter on the frames. She was a

tiny woman in shrieking colors, and her red lipstick had rubbed onto a prominent eyetooth.

"Got a cigarette?" she asked hopefully.

The man—burly, leathery, in a shirt buttoned to the neck—leaned forward also intent on Denny's answer.

"Sorry," Denny said.

"She won't let us smoke in here anyway," the woman murmured dryly.

She.

And suddenly there was another woman in the archway, a good deal younger than the other two, fiftyish, though nothing else about her suggested the formality of staff, except that her calves and forearms were plump and muscular, as if she were a twist balloon put together in segments. She had a shoe button nose, liquid brown eyes, jet-black hair with two white streaks like meteors in the night, and her voice held a hint of challenge: "May I help you?"

"I saw your sign," Denny said. "I'm inquiring."

"About . . . ?"

"Residency for my father."

"Does he smoke?" piped the woman on the ottoman, and the man next to her grinned.

"Now, you know we don't have any openings, Beverly," said the plump woman by way of informing Denny.

"How about a waiting list?"

The pair on the ottoman laughed.

"We don't keep a waiting list either."

"Plenty of room, Molly," the burly man put in. "You ought to ask Ariel."

Denny gestured loosely. "I didn't see you listed in the phone book, but you've got that sign outside—"

"We're a private home."

"Just what I'm looking for. How do people apply? You must be regulated or you wouldn't have that sign."

The word "regulated" entered the room like a hornet looking for a place to land.

"Wait here," Molly said warily and squeaked back through the arch in her ripple-soled sneakers.

Beverly, the tiny woman with the Hollywood glasses, stroked her chin with an age-spotted hand. "She's gone to get Ariel," she said. "Haven't seen that before, eh, Paavo?"

Paavo danced his feet on the floor—one step each— and nodded, his hands folded between his knees, his mirthful expression directed straight before him.

"Is Ariel the manager?"

"Oh yes. She manages us." Beverly nudged her glasses back up her petite nose. "You're almost a red-head," she assessed with the tactlessness of the very bored.

"Almost."

"I had red hair once. *Naturally* red hair. You wouldn't know it now, of course, but it was my best feature." She turned to her companion. "Apparently Ariel didn't like it."

The burly man restrained his amusement. He had square, pink fingernails and a strong face that was just starting to collapse with gravity. "Your hair's not all she may not like," he said to the woman.

"Aaah, to hell with it. I'll say what I like."

"Do I detect a Norwegian accent?" Denny addressed the man.

"Paavo's a Finn," said Beverly. "Paavo Seppanen. His wife is Ruta. She was a Lanoki before she married this old galoot."

Denny nodded too many times. "How long have you lived here?"

"About a year."

"You came at the same time?"

Paavo's smile seemed to freeze.

"Just about," Beverly said.

"So, do you like it here?"

"Hell, no. I'd like to be twenty-four years old and on the French Riviera, that's where I'd like to be. But it's better here than where I was."

"How's the food?"

"Food's good," Paavo said.

"And the medical staff?"

Again the tandem exchange of faint smiles. "Infallible," said the woman. "No one gets sick here. Not for long anyhow."

And that was when they heard the cane thudding on the wooden floor, and Denny saw their eyes go down. Molly reappeared in the arch, followed by a somewhat regal figure—a woman, tall, thin, gray hair cut short, and wearing a dress that a dowager empress might have worn in another time. She had very white skin and her hawkish nose seemed aimed at Denny like the bowsprit of a ship.

"Bring him back," she crackled at Molly.

They took each other's measure for the first time not in an office but in a kitchen, Ariel on one side of an immense worn butcher's block, Denny on the other. The looks between them were guileless.

"We're not taking residents at this time," Ariel declared softly, and when he replied that he had been told they had plenty of room, she looked to the doorway as if Molly were still there. "It's a matter of choice," she said.

"But you haven't even met my father."

"—which should tell you there's nothing personal in it."

"But . . . you can't be running a business that way."

"Do we look like a corporation?"

"No. But you have the sign out front. You must be

regulated. Are you getting funds or tax breaks or something?"

"It's not a big sign. We don't advertise."

Funds, taxes. She was getting some kind of financial advantage.

The sun was on the other side of the house, and the light entering the kitchen was mugged of its color by the muzzy sheers. Ariel and Denny went back and forth in a black-and-white chess game where neither knew the rules and the moves were mostly pawns falling one by one.

"I'm willing to pay the going rate," he said, "even a little more, and you don't seem to have the overhead that others do. More than the going rate for places with full programs, I mean."

"We meet all requirements, you can rest assured of that," she snapped.

"So if I went to check out your credentials, you're a viable business? And you have a qualified medical staff."

"No one complains. You might say our doctor is a miracle worker."

"What kind of staff *do* you have?"

"For the record, there are only a dozen people in this house, Mr. Bryce. We all pitch in. That's why they call it assisted living. Things get done and we manage well. No one has ever had a serious illness or died."

He was not an intuitive person, but something of the informality of the house connected with his protective feelings toward his father. "My father isn't the ordinary beast," he said. "All those frantic social programs and interventions at the other places—he doesn't need that. He doesn't need stimulation—he needs a sanctuary. He's kind of a paradox. The less fussing, the better he likes it. Memory going bad—he's on Aricept—but other than that he just likes to be left alone. When I'm home, he's fine. If there are people around, he just hunkers down. But I have to work and when I'm not there he goes looking."

For a moment she seemed to consider the possibility, but then she said, "We don't handle dementia patients."

"Is that what your certification says? I've heard that term thrown around, and I don't know what it means anymore. My father hasn't had a firm diagnosis, and anyway, no one has used that as an excuse to rule him out of a facility. Like I said, we'd pay you well."

"Are you . . . like your father, Mr. Bryce?"

He tried to stare her down, but she was not easily flustered. "Does that matter?"

"Do you live alone with your father?"

"Yes."

"I was just wondering why your family couldn't answer your father's needs."

He had a sense that she was fishing as much as resisting. She wanted to know how far she would be reaching out into the world if she took in his father. "We have no family left," Denny said. "We aren't fussy, and we aren't demanding, and we're very solitary. I've tried all the home-based programs, and now I need help."

"Be that as it may, the residents here have no connections to the outside world. None. They are here for life. They never leave. No shopping mall trips, no churches, no outside medical management. I'm the only one who goes into town."

He thought. "I don't see a problem with that."

"And they have no visitors."

"I'd be the only visitor my father had."

"That would be a problem."

"Why?"

"It might interfere. It might make the other residents resentful."

"But you said they had no families. Are you saying no one is *allowed* to come here?"

"You came here," she pointed out. "I'm just saying we do better without disturbances."

"I would want to see my father as often as possible—maybe every day—but I wouldn't disturb anyone. I don't see what the problem is. If you're a licensed home, you know you can't prevent access."

"It's not a rule, it's a policy. We might make an exception for your visits, but you did understand when I said the residents are here for life? I won't accept anyone who doesn't agree to that."

If there was a problem he would get his father out one way or another, he was thinking. And he wouldn't sign anything that said otherwise.

To his amazement, he didn't have to sign anything. God help this woman if anyone ever took her to court. He wondered what her books looked like. In the end, Ariel Leppa and the house manager, Molly Armitage, took him on a brief tour that didn't change anyone's mind. And then—looking somewhat astounded, he thought—they accepted his thirty-five-hundred-dollar check for a month in advance. In less than an hour from when he had first seen their sign he was back in his car, heading home as if the surreal visit to New Eden had never happened. On the radio, the Eagles' "Hotel California" was playing, recounting a residency where checking out but never leaving was not a contradiction.

New Eden

2001

1

"Why don't you ever call me by my name anymore, Molly?"

"I didn't realize—"

"I don't want you to be afraid of me. Say it, please, my name."

"Ariel."

"That's better. We were friends. That's why I brought you back."

"I could have been a better friend. I know that, Ariel. Believe me, I know that."

"That's true. I'm glad you realize it. But we're friends now, aren't we? Why are you all afraid of me?"

"I don't think anyone is afraid, exactly. But everyone knows you were treated badly. It's awkward, that's all."

"Awkward. Not sorry, not guilty—awkward."

"Of course we're sorry. And . . . and a little guilty about it, if you want to use that word."

"I just want to know what word you all use, Molly. I want to know what you feel. Does anyone ever say anything? Do you talk about what happened in the past?"

"Maybe not in so many words, but there have been changes. We know what we were before. The petty jealousies, the pecking order—"

"And there's no pecking order now?"

"No, of course not."

"No . . . jealousies?"

"No, Ariel."

"But Dana is younger than you. And you're younger than everyone else."

"I haven't noticed any resentment to speak of. Maybe from Ruta, but that's . . . Ruta."

"Yes. She was always vain and competitive. That's why I kept her more or less the way she was just before she died. Not as a cross to bear but to make her a better person."

"Exactly. I know that. We all know that. Ruta probably knows it too—deep down."

"So why are all of you afraid of me?"

"No one's afraid. They're all . . . grateful."

"Ah, not guilty. Grateful."

"Ariel, you're mixing me up! What if we are a little afraid? After all, you've given us so much back. It's natural to be afraid of losing it. You can understand that."

"Then"—Ariel cupped her chin in her white fist, pretending to ponder, and shot a finger in the air—"they think I might take that away?"

"I don't know."

"Do you think I might?"

"Don't do this to me, Ariel. I think you're a miracle worker, you know that. Haven't I been loyal? I'll do anything you ask."

"Stop begging, Molly. I didn't like playing God, but I had to decide. I had to re-create you. It was an awesome responsibility, and I did what I thought was best. Do you think I want to make a mess of my life a second time? Whatever your sins—and their sins—we've all got a second chance. That's why I need you to be honest with me, and to tell me what they need, and what they want, and what . . . they're thinking."

"I have."

"But you say Ruta is jealous. I didn't know that. What is she saying?"

"Nothing against you. She just complains about her looks, and I think she wants her megavitamins and herbs."

"She doesn't need pills. I can do better than pills with my paintbrush, if she earns it. What else?"

"Nothing else."

"They don't want things?"

"Another television, maybe. The men don't like the soaps."

"I'll think about it."

". . . And . . . and some are thinking about telephone calls."

"That's idiotic. You know we can't contact anyone—people who would know, people who were at their funerals!"

"You asked. I'm just being honest."

"Be honest."

"They want to know how their families are—you can understand that. The Seppanens both passed over ten years ago, and they want to know who might have gotten sick since then or what their situations are."

"No one can go back to their families."

"They know that."

"It would jeopardize everything, create a sensation. We'd be dragged onstage, and I don't know what would happen then, but it would all be over."

"Over?"

"Over. Finis. Kaput. What did you think I meant?"

"No one would blame you, if you . . . undid things."

"What difference does it make how it would end? It

would end. We couldn't hold up to scrutiny. Quickly or slowly it would end."

"They don't want it to end, Ariel."

"Then keep me informed, Molly. I need to know if anyone is becoming foolish."

"None of them want to go back to where they were before you brought them here."

Ariel sat forward then, her stark stare catching Molly's every nuance. "And where was that?"

A look of weary dread sprang into the plump woman's eyes. "It's impossible to describe."

"How can it be impossible? Evidently everyone was aware of their surroundings. Was it good, was it bad? Heaven or hell, Molly?"

"I don't know."

Ariel turned her right palm up. "Could it have been heaven? But then you wouldn't fear going back. And if it was hell"—she turned up her left palm—"apparently it wasn't Dante's Inferno, or Michelangelo's ceiling, or anything biblical, because you could have described those. But you were aware. How interesting. Reassuring, in a way. Were you in between, Molly? All that time, were you in limbo?"

The woman tried to answer, her fleshy cheeks fluctuating like a small bellows but with nothing coming out. She had a cartoon simplicity to her face that couldn't survive complexity. That was why she was Ariel's factotum. Fear and reward not only mirrored in her expression; they were rooted in her every task. Ariel liked this transparency. But Molly had her limits. Ask her simple questions and you got simple answers. Ask her the profound and you got a wall of emotions.

"What about you, Molly—what do you want? Do you miss your family?"

Molly took a cavernous breath. "I'm not going to lie

about that. Anybody would want to return to their family. Even though her family wouldn't be able to understand or to accept her coming back this way. I just wonder about my granddaughter, that's all. You remember Lindsay—you saw her at my birthday party five years ago. She's got cystic fibrosis. I don't know how she is, or even if she's still alive. She should be, though. Five years. She should be alive. And . . . and I just wonder sometimes, you know, what if she had been painted back instead of me. Maybe that would have been better. . . ."

"Molly, you know I can't."

"I suppose not."

"I don't even remember what Lindsay looks like. I'd have to get a photo. And then what would the others want me to do for them? I'd have to deal with that. There would be no limit to the things we'd all want for the people in our past. It would get out of hand, jeopardize everything. You can see that."

"She was so young, is all. Barely three. She'd be eight now."

"You don't know what you're asking. The sick child they have now would die, just like Amber did."

"—Paavo or Dana could go and make some excuse to take a photograph. I don't think they would recognize Dana. Or Kraft."

"Kraft doesn't remember things. He could get lost. If he was picked up and his picture was in the paper, someone might recognize him."

"Sometimes he remembers."

"Really? I'll have to look into that. But it doesn't make any difference to your granddaughter, Molly. Even if I did paint her, she would be here with us. How would we get her back to her parents? And what would they think when they saw her healed and alive after they had just buried her? Alien abduction?"

"It wouldn't necessarily connect to us, whatever they thought."

"No, Molly . . . no."

Kraft remembering? Molly had said Kraft was remembering. Ariel looked in the mirror, patted the bags under her eyes, stroked the sagging flesh beneath her jaw, drew her shoulders back. *Why don't I paint myself younger?* A fold of gravity here, a tuck of time there. A half-dozen brush strokes could correct what she saw in the mirror. Health insurance. Life insurance. A different vanity from Ruta's. Ruta needed to fool herself. Ariel would use vanity like a utilitarian thing, fooling just the world.

She descended into the house without turning on lights, waggling her walking stick to touch familiar objects, groping through the rooms to the school corridor. When she reached Kraft Olson's room, she made three faint raps with the neck of her cane. No response. A push, a peek. He was sitting at the window, his features hidden in silhouette.

Why don't I paint myself younger?

She wanted to see his eyes. In she came, setting the cane aside and crossing the moonlit room with as easy a gait as she could manage.

"Hello, Kraft."

"Hello."

His eyes now, empty, hollow, vacant.

He might not recognize her, but, oh, she recognized him down to the last brush stroke, the last atom. She had done a wonderful job, especially the hair and the eyes. Perfect hair that he had always seemed to take for granted. No preener this man, grooming himself with surreptitious sweeps of a comb. She had spent more time brushing his hair to life on canvas than he ever had in real life, she felt sure. And the spectator eyes—she had captured those too. So where had the old cavalier glint gone since? Now his eyes looked dull, their fire banked. She had painted him younger, she thought, than when his Alzheimer's had become pronounced. In his midsixties, she had made him, because he hadn't begun to lose it until he was at least seventy. But how could you tell with dementia, especially with someone as smart and articulate as Kraft had been? It was odd, because the others remembered what had happened up until their deaths, unlike Amber, who remembered nothing. Maybe with Amber it had been too great a span—age forty-four back down to nine—or maybe it was because she had been alive at the time of the re-creation. But even with dementia Kraft had recognized her and the others at times up until he died, so she had thought that giving him back a few years would ensure he knew her. But Kraft Olson did not remember her at all.

Maybe that was good. Maybe she would have a chance with him now and he would forget Danielle Kramer. *Why don't I paint myself younger?* Or was this just an ancient hurt to her pride too absurd to rectify?

She wanted to be humble, and that was the paradox. Pride demanded that she be humble. Because the potential to look like a mad egoist out for tyranny and revenge was obvious. Ariel the leper in charge of things. Pay her lip service, pay her tribute, an altar here, a statue there. But that wasn't what she wanted. What she wanted was to be worth something. They didn't have to suck up to her, but why weren't they grateful? Molly said they were, but they weren't. They were afraid. *Fear thy God*—and if she wasn't their God, she *was* the instrument of their creation, so it amounted to the same thing. She didn't want their fear. Only fundamentalists and fa-

natics used fear and took it on themselves to act as prox-
ies for God. Every horror in the history of the world was
at heart intolerance. You could create the illusion of
love, obedience, worship, but you would never really
have any of those things if you forced them out of fear.
Gratitude, on the other hand, should have been a given.
And gratitude was a kind of love, wasn't it? The beginnings of love anyway. So why weren't the re-created at
least grateful to instead of afraid of her?

"Do you remember me, Kraft?"

He looked at her blankly.

"I'm Ariel. Your friend."

"I don't remember you."

"No? Who *do* you remember?" She looked hard into
his eyes. Was he sentient enough to remember Danielle
Kramer? "If you could have anyone you ever knew here
right now, Kraft, who would it be? Tell me. Don't be
afraid. I can bring people back, you know."

His eyes remained rigid. He could be thinking she was
insane, or he could be hating her with those eyes.

"Think about it, Kraft. Who? Your mother? Your
brother? . . . A lover? Give me a name, and if it's someone I've got a photo of, I'll paint them back." She had
lots of photos of Danielle buried with the others in a
wicker basket upstairs. "Remember how I used to take
pictures, Kraft? All of . . . our gang. I always took the
pictures. That's why I'm not in very many of them. You
always asked me to take the pictures."

She plucked a thread from the sleeve of his shirt,
brushed his shoulder. He had always been a sharp
dresser.

"Maybe it was a good thing," she said. "Because now
I can paint back almost anyone you knew. *Anyone.* So if
you have a name, let's hear it." He was looking around.
". . . Now or never." Wetting his lips. "Just say the name

of anyone you want, and I'll deliver him—or her—to you, Kraft."

"I don't remember anyone."

Well. She really should paint herself younger.

But if she did, what would happen to her body? Would she still be there, dead, like Amber slumped in her wheelchair the moment her reanimation at age nine had appeared? Now, that would get everyone's attention. Dropping like a fly, a little terror in the parlor. *Fear thy God.* . . .

She wished she had gone to Amber's funeral, seen the body. But how could she when she had to take care of the nine-year-old reincarnation of the corpse? "I'm too upset," she had told her son-in-law and grandson. There was no love lost between them anyway, and they hadn't tried to persuade her to attend, and except for Christmas cards there had been no further communication. She had considered taking nine-year-old Amber to her own funeral— who would recognize her?—but she had feared that Amber might get hysterical. Later, when she took Amber to help her find the grave site, she found out how she would react.

"Is that me?" the child had asked, staring down at the cold stone.

"No."

"Yes, it is."

"That was who you will become, if you're foolish again."

The rosebud mouth tightened and the stare locked. "What was I like?"

"You were partially paralyzed and in a wheelchair."

"But what was I like? Didn't I have a life?"

"You sat. You waited to die. You couldn't climb things anymore and you were unhappy."

It just could be that if she repainted her creations there

wouldn't be any bodies, Ariel thought. After all, the paralyzed Amber had been a natural, living being, born of
parents and still alive, while the others had all gone to
their graves before being brought back. So in the case of
those who had died before reincarnation, if their bodies
remained at all, they were already buried. But because
she too was a naturally living person, she could expect
the same thing that had happened to Amber to happen to
her. She would have to dispose of her own body. Drag it
out of the house and dig a grave and bury it somewhere.
The thought terrified and disgusted her.

"Paint me again," her husband, Thomas, pleaded that
very night. "Paint me with legs."

"I'd have to get rid of the body you have now."

"I'll bury myself."

"What was it like to be dead?" she asked urgently.
"Are the bodies still in the graves?"

"Paint me whole and I'll tell you."

"No, thank you. I've already lived that life."

"You're insane."

"Careful, careful."

2

Denny Bryce rehearsed it all evening and in the dawn. The delivery. The four words. And each repetition sounded more like a lie. Finally he said it to his father: "Let's go see Mom."

The old man sat in his chair—the recliner throne about to be abdicated—and his eyelids pulsed without opening. "She's in the kitchen."

"No, Dad. She died, remember? You were at her funeral."

The eyes opened, the head came up. Martin Bryce gasped as if the wind had been knocked out of him. Beth dead. The terrible reprising of shock, tension knotting at the bridge of his nose, his lips spreading in a grimace to contain the pain. "I forgot," he said apologetically, and Denny stroked his silver hair.

"It's okay, Dad. It's okay. I meant her grave. Let's go visit her grave."

He felt lower than a scavenger, as despicable as a bully. His faithful, hardworking, dependable, trusting father. *Throw him out, Denny. Take away his house, the only thing he has left, the citadel of his memories. Let me see you do that.*

"While we're out, I'll show you some things. . . . Okay? Okay, Dad?"

Nod.

He isn't listening. Tell him, but don't tell him. Soothe your guilty conscience. He doesn't understand. But you can pretend he did.

He had never lied to his father in these latter years. Never manipulated him. Not since high school. He had told him straight up what the medical prognoses were for his mother, for the old man himself. He had told him the truth about his sister, Tiffany, when she had committed suicide seven years earlier. Wretched Tiffany, who at age forty-seven had finally tired of fighting drugs and depression. He could have said it was an accident or a medical thing—God knows she had enough wrong with her—but he hadn't. Why let his parents doubt? He had told them. Told them everything on his almost daily visits. Investments, mortgage, insurance, repairs, scams, health—everything. More than they understood or needed to know, but they listened to hear him taking care of them, like he always did, mowing the lawn, shoveling the drive, plunging the toilet, changing the screens, raking the leaves. Acts of love to which his parents were happy spectators as well as recipients. How grateful they were, and it was sometimes hurtful to see that—as if they were surprised that he should give back to them. So, above all, they trusted him.

"What do other old people do who don't have a son like you?" his mother would say.

Nothing she had ever given him—and she had given him everything—could be as important as that.

And now the great betrayal. Why couldn't he just sit down on the couch and tell the old man that the Twins were still leading their division? "They'll blow it," his father would say, and he would take his mother's role of optimism and remind him of the World Series victory in '91. Then they could just go on like that. Small talk forever.

"Guess we'd better get going, Dad. Do you have to go to the bathroom?"

Martin stood in the living room, breathless from having donned his sweater. It was summer, but he was always chilled. He shook his head, moved his lips as though he wanted to say something else.

"Do you want your hat?"

"No."

"Okay, then."

What he really meant was Say farewell to your life. Say good-by to the house you're never going to see again. Walk away from every semblance of your life, the old familiar things, the artifacts, the sacred surfaces that Beth and Tiffany touched a million times and that will be profaned by the next garage-sale shopper, or the next owner of the house, or the sanitation engineer when he leaps out of his truck to make the heave. That was what he meant to say.

And through the opacity of his father's expression, there came just a glint for a moment. Not a doubt, really, but a question. Denny turned away and pulled the door open against the swollen jamb, trying in vain not to stir the clapper in the little bell his mother had hung there.

Then came the slow, unsteady journey onto the steps, his father groping for the grab post Denny had installed on the porch (four lag bolts—see how much I love you?), shuffling down the sidewalk, stopping for breath, opening the car doors, moving the seat back—a crude ballet of clutching hands, lowering, pivoting, ducking. The terminal sound of slamming doors. Then the key turning in the ignition. *Look, Dad! Look at the house.*

*You won't see it again. Don't you want to see the house
for the last time?*

But he didn't know it was the last time. Did he?

Denny's emotions were singing so loudly that even
the old man must have heard. He was swallowing sand
by the mouthful. His father, though a great pragmatist,
nevertheless had his intuitive moments, and this could be
one. The silence between them became expectancy, as if
Denny should explain, but the merciless car made all the
irreverent noises that cars do. You couldn't say delicate
things with the bumpkin thud of gears in the background, or the hiss and oscillating whine as you rolled
down the drive pumping the brakes. So they got under
way, the center of his father's life receding behind them,
and each ticking second was like another foot of safety
rope.

He started out for the cemetery where his mother was
interred, but it wasn't five minutes before his father
asked aloud where were they going. And what was the
point of following through with the awful misdirection if
his father had forgotten? Just get to the place. Don't go
to the graveyard in Little Canada. Get out of the suburbs,
away from the Twin Cities. Take him to KNEAL. New
Eden. Home . . .

"I can't leave you alone anymore, Dad. You wander,
you start fires. What's going to happen when I'm back at
school full-time this fall?"

"You don't have to worry about me."

"Yes, I do."

"I can take care of myself."

"Dad . . . you can't. That's a fact—you can't. I don't
want to hurt your self-esteem or mess with your inde-
pendence, but you could get hurt or killed."

"What difference does it make?" Martin asked wearily.

"Your mother was the only reason I was alive. She was the best thing that ever happened to me."

"I know. But you can't expect me to let go of you like that, Dad. When God calls you in . . . okay. I'll accept that. But you can't ask me to just ignore you. What kind of a son would I be if I did that? You care about me, don't you? You wouldn't want to leave me with a legacy of guilt."

It was the only thing that worked anymore. This suggestion that his father still had an obligation to him. They lapsed into silence until they were jouncing up the eroding asphalt drive to the old farmhouse, and then Martin asked: "What's this?"

"New Eden, Dad. It's a great place. We're gonna try it, okay?"

After that it was all like a bunco game in which Denny was a shill, infusing his old man with words, will, illusions as they migrated somehow through the greetings and the rooms to the chamber that had been cleared for his father. It was large—once a small classroom, according to the woman named Molly—and now there was a miscellany of old furniture on the tile floor and an immense open spot for the bed Denny was to bring on another trip (the bed was central) and there were paintings that looked like originals on the walls.

"This is pretty nice, Dad, and you can go anywhere you want in the house. It's all yours. Along with the other residents, of course. It's what they call assisted living. You're on your own, except they take care of your food and medical and other necessities. And I can come see you every day."

His father shuffled, breathless, to the captain's chair by the windows and collapsed onto the pads tied to its spindles. He seemed to be listening from a long way off.

"I'll be bringing your other stuff, Dad. Your bed, your

dresser, your nightstand. Photos and everything too. Anything you want moved, you just say so. I'm going to pick up the rental truck now. I've got a student to help me. Okay? I'll see you in a little while."

From the window ledge his father picked up a framed photo of a woman in batwing sleeves, as if he knew her.

"We'll take good care of him," Molly vowed with empathy, and Denny allowed himself to be drawn into the corridor.

The little woman with the glitter glasses and the perpetual smudge of lipstick on one of her eyeteeth began to shuffle past as they came out.

Denny made two trips in the rental truck, and on the final delivery he faced Ariel in the parlor. Paavo was there, as well as two women introduced as Helen Hoverstein and Marjorie Korpela. For the first time it struck Denny as odd that an old matron—older, it seemed, than the residents—should be in charge.

"Your father will be fine," Ariel assured him. "In fact, I'd advise you to leave him alone as much as possible. If you come, it will just make it harder for him to adjust."

"I'll think about it," Denny said.

"Well, if you do come again, I'll take your photograph— a nice photo of you and your father in his room."

For just a second, Denny Bryce thought the room inhaled. The woman named Marjorie stiffened and sat a little straighter, and the enormous eyes of the one named Helen froze on him with something like urgency. And did ramrod Paavo, his shirt still buttoned to the neck, lean back slightly as though buffeted by an invisible current? But as he stood up to leave, Denny noticed something he found reassuring. It was a painting of the Garden of Eden. Not the ubiquitous print that hung on Sunday school walls and in rectories; this one was an original. Whatever the quirks and foibles of this buttoned-up grandame who ran the place, she was steeped in traditional morality, he thought. A little hard to live with but scarcely neglectful. No, he decided, there wasn't any trouble in this paradise.

Out on the porch he found himself confronted by the woman with the lipstick-smudged eyetooth. "Forget about having your photograph taken," she said. "It's a bad idea."

"Why?"

She tried to peer past him through the screen door. "It just is." Then she moved aside and, in a stage whisper meant to carry into the house, added, ". . . So, bring some cigarettes when you come again."

3

Martin Bryce awoke nowhere. It was as if he had been trolleying along over the axons and dendrites of his brain and gotten derailed. He left the tracks almost every time he awoke. If he wasn't in a black gulf, he was at a way station that had no rail lines coming or going. The sense of utter loneliness that came with this never lessened, because it was always the first time. He didn't remember it happening the night before, or the night before that. Those tracks too no longer existed.

It was the green glow of a clock radio that usually reeled him back to real time. That thirteen-year-old radio *she* had given him on their fiftieth anniversary. He saw it and knew it was part of his marriage and that Beth was lying on the other side of him. But there was no green glow tonight, and she was not beside him.

"Where is this place?" he whispered.

The walls seemed too far away, and the air was sticky and heavy in his lungs. He closed his eyes, half dreaming, half remembering, and when he opened them again he had a context. The motes he saw swimming in the air were no longer a common symptom of his dementia but a semitropical plague of insects. And the chirrs he heard came from a swamp. A dog barked a long way off on the perimeter of the encampment. *He was inside the bullpen.* All the prisoners were standing up because they couldn't fall down. Bodies pressed against bodies, penned up for the night, some with diarrhea, some with dysentery, some dead, all dying. The thirst, the heat, the reeking suffocation were all part of hell on earth. And in the morning when the sun had boiled them enough, the dusty march would continue. So Martin let himself die for a few minutes until the toxic tide ebbed away, and when consciousness washed in again he sat up, stood up.

He was in a room, barefoot but with his clothes still on, having gone to bed fully dressed, and the phantoms of war—that default realm he always returned to in his worst night sweats—were still with him. He was Lieutenant Commander M. B. Bryce, USN. And he was in a barracks somewhere, and he didn't want to wake up Beth, because she shouldn't have to march with the rest of them. What had she ever done to the Japs? So he left her sleeping in the green glow of a clock radio that would keep track of time and space while he went back to the road in the province whose name he couldn't remember, but which history records as Pampagna on the peninsula of Bataan.

He remembered two things: a truck slowly flattening the bodies of those who had fallen at the side of the column, and the Japanese soldier who had taken Martin's canteen to give a horse water, then thrown it away. Water. He needed water. Not the dirty stuff in some carabao wallow, but a tall tumbler full of crystal cubes and pure, transparent water. Pawing through the air to avoid barbed wire, he shuffled toward the seam of light that lay on the tile floor of New Eden.

Heat lightning flickered on the horizon, and the north half of everything was suddenly vivid. Half the fields sprang to life, half the trees, half the farmhouse and four sides of the odd structure sitting on the roof. It was an octagonal cupola, the odd structure. Big enough to hold a person, Amber thought. Or maybe just half a person. But she was half a person. She waited for another wink from the horizon.

"God has a loose bulb in his lamp," her father used to say about heat lightning. Used to say. Now he hardly ever talked. He was suddenly old, like her mother, though that wasn't why he didn't talk the same. The reason he didn't talk was because he was mad, Amber thought. And sad. And—she wasn't sure about this—but maybe because he was afraid. She understood a little why her mother had painted him in the wheelchair. Before he lost his legs, he could be a grouch, even mean. And Amber had seen a lot of TV in the last year—*Rosie* and *Jenny Jones* and *Ricki Lake*—and she knew a lot of women were victims of men now. Actually they had always been. But now everyone knew it. So in a way this was new. She herself hadn't had any idea before that men could be so bad. Not all men, of course, but almost all women were victims. So maybe her dad deserved to be in a wheelchair a little, only she didn't think it should be forever. Maybe a week or a month, that was all. And it had been a year now.

More winks from the horizon, and this time she was sure she could get to the cupola. Not from the ground where she was standing now, looking up at the house where everyone was asleep, but from the window. She could climb out the window upstairs and push off the lightning rod with her foot while she pulled herself over the gutter, and then it was just a couple of steps along the edge before she could grab that funny-looking pipe sticking up through the roof, and then a couple more to reach the chimney, and then, with the chimney to block her slide if she fell, she could go up. The roof was steep, but she could keep trying until she made it. Shingles were like sandpaper. Your tennis shoes could grip. So she could make it to the ridge, and then it was a piece of cake to reach the cupola.

She liked the night. The world seemed bigger at night. Not just an old folks' home and a farm with no kids—and no animals anymore either—but a half-painted world where the shadows could become anything you wanted. She wasn't allowed to go to school, or to shows, or shopping when her mother made her weekly runs to a strip mall, so there were lots of things she wanted. At first she had liked the idea of staying home from school ("No more pencils, no more books, no more teachers' dirty looks"), but she had zilch friends ("zilch"—kids didn't say that anymore). Her mother said her friends were all grown up, that they were in their forties. She supposed that was true, but it was hard to believe, and if they were truly grown up then she really didn't care about them anymore anyway. She wanted to meet new people. So she liked the night, because she could explore and pretend there were lots of people around.

They really might be around too. Hadn't her father told her about the ghosts? That was before he was in the wheelchair, and he would show her the cellars or wave at the fields and say that the red corn they grew down by the woods was red from blood and corpses. Her mother called it Indian corn, or sometimes Winnebago, but her father said it was because gangsters had been murdered in the cellars and that they sometimes walked, gushing blood, the fields at night. They were still in the house too. In the tunnels or maybe the walls. Amber had looked for them many times, even though her old friends used to tell her she was freaked out. Now she wandered all over the house after everyone was asleep, and some-

times—like tonight—she climbed out a window and
went through the fields to the woods or hung around the
yard in the moonlight. There was a rope swing still on
the basswood, except that the rope was yellow plastic
now, because the Lutheran school that had built the new
wing had changed it, and she sat on the tire and swung
and pretended there were hands reaching for her as she
gyrated to avoid them. She liked to scare herself. Liked
to take risks. That hadn't changed. Because even if she
was scared, she was lonely too, and she didn't think
she'd mind meeting a ghost or two.

Now she looked up at the cupola and thought, *Maybe
that's where they are?*

She had never looked there before, so it might be. Another series of flashes winked on the horizon, almost as
if someone who couldn't speak was signaling to her. *Yes,
yes, yes! . . . The cupola. That's where they are. Climb up
and see.* So she jumped off the tire swing, and snuck
back into the house, and tiptoed up the stairs, being careful not to step in the center of the squeaky treads—
which didn't matter, because you could beat pots and
pans and not wake the living dead in the house, who
were mostly about a hundred years old—and Amber
went to the sewing room where the window was that she
had chosen from the ground.

She checked to make sure her new Skechers were on
tight, and then she tugged open the window and stared
down three stories to the ground. Scary, for sure. But she
had things to hang on to, and except for that couple of
steps near the edge above her, there wasn't any risk. The
trick was to pretend you were on the ground. That's what
her father used to tell her. You could jump and dance on
a two-by-four lying on the ground and never fall, so why
couldn't you do it if the two-by-four was in the air? You

could. You just had to think about what you were doing instead of thinking about falling. Amber never fell.

She sat on the window ledge and thumped her feet on the side of the house, just like sitting at the dining room table. You couldn't fall off a chair, and this was a chair. Then she crouched. No problem. Easy as pie. Standing up, though, that was a little harder on account of the window being in the way. But she had one hand outside the window and the other on the wall inside the house, and she rose up about a foot before the sash checked her shoulder. Letting the hand on the wall slide back a little, her fingers dug into the old window frame and she wiggled her shoulder free of the sash so that only the crook of her elbow touched it, and then she stood up another foot.

Hello, stars . . .

Five fingers were all that separated her from soaring, and it was tempting to just let go. She liked to think about that, because she wouldn't actually do it, of course, but she was that close to being free. No one could follow her here. She was the boss now. And there was the lightning rod, against which she wedged her left foot. Solid. She wouldn't push off it very hard, though. Just enough to hold her while she pulled herself over the gutter with her left hand as she let go of the window frame with her right. It would only take maybe half a second to make the transfer. Then she would have both hands on the gutter, and her foot pushing off the metal rod. Already she was feeling the shingles above the frame with her left hand, and they were like thick book covers that she could tug on, she thought. If she slipped, she would just grab the lightning rod. Hadn't she heard stories about how the kids used to shinny up and down the thing in the old days? It went into the ground, so it

wasn't just attached to the house. She bet no one ever
went up to the roof this way before, though.

Bracing herself with all the lightness of being in the
mind of a steeplejack, she pushed and pulled, calculating
the energy required on the fly, her weight more or less
ricocheting from the ledge to the rod to the gutter. It was
the gutter that threatened to undo her. A big galvanized
gutter that had probably supported more than one two-
hundred-pound man in its day but that now had begun to
loosen in the rotting fascia board. Still, a seventy-pound
will-o'-the-wisp, shifting quickly as she redistributed her
weight, weighed less than some of the ice dams it still
held up for months all winter. Faster than you can say
"Fools rush in where angels fear to tread," Amber Leppa
found herself scrabbling onto the shingles above the
world.

She stretched out almost at the same steep angle as the
roof, daring only one glance at the murky yard an infinity away. Her heart fluttered, because already she sensed
the need to keep moving, to use her momentum before
gravity could test the stingy friction and fling her down.
There was the black pipe sticking up out of the roof. But
she saw now that it had a kind of base to it, like the brim
on a stovepipe hat. Did that mean it didn't go down into
the house? Maybe it was just shoved under the shingles
and wouldn't hold her.

Too late. The edges of her Skechers pressed harder
into the roof. Either she went for it now or she would
slide back toward the lightning rod. Pushing sideways on
the shingles with her hands, she flung herself with
enough momentum to achieve two steps, and that put her
within reach of the pipe.

Her right hand caught it first, and she felt the give, felt
the shingles lifting. It was not going to hold. As soon as
her weight was centered over it, it would tear out of the

roof and she would sled with it right over the edge. But in that parsed second of time before her left foot came down, she saw the nimble possibilities. There was the gutter, of course. She could grab that as she went over; but from her brief testing of its strength at the window, she knew it wouldn't hold. So that left the chimney. Instead of stopping at the pipe, she could just push off it as she had the lightning rod, and hope she got enough shove to reach the chimney. But that too failed her preview, because the pipe was going to slide right out from under the shingles.

And then her left foot planted just short of the pipe, and she felt the shingle reseat itself flat to the roof, and she knew instantaneously that the base of the pipe extended out under the shingles and that her left foot was pinning it down. So now she dropped her right foot on the other side, pinning that half too, and grabbed the pipe and squatted back on her fanny with her weight still pressing down on the hidden extension of the base. Nothing moved.

Equilibrium.

It wasn't the kind of thing you'd want to try after a heavy meal—she could feel the delicate friction beneath the soles of her shoes as she rocked slightly—but she could land like a butterfly, and all she had to do now was push off evenly. Which she did. Changing from butterfly to grasshopper, she leaped with both feet at once, and in another moment she had the chimney to brace on as she gazed up at the eight-sided thing on the roof.

Even if it took her a couple of tries, she would definitely be able to scramble all the way up because she could push off as hard as she wanted from the chimney, whereas the lightning rod would not have given her enough momentum. Some of the slats were broken out of the cupola, and she thought she could wriggle in once she reached the ridge. There was one thing, though. What was *in* the cupola? Meeting ghosts didn't seem all that good of an idea, suddenly. Because the way the slats were broken—all jagged and pointing in one direction— it looked like something had smashed its way in with one swipe. And even though she couldn't be sure it came from the cupola, she smelled a new kind of dampness and rot. Like the black mud down by the marsh. Decayed like that. You inhaled it and you felt like you were underwater, gulping down mouthfuls of green slime and gritty stuff that swam and multiplied inside you. She didn't mind heights, but she didn't like to be touched when she couldn't control the contact. And when slimy things touched you *inside,* you had no control at all.

So the more she thought about it, the less she liked it. Something up there might be watching her, and she was about to rush into its claws. *Well, well, my dear, you've come just in time for dinner—and you're it!* But what if there wasn't anything up there? It really was a neat hideout, a cool place to crash whenever she wanted, high above the world, like the eagle's aerie back in the woods her father had talked about, a place where she could be sure no one would reach her. At least she could climb to the ridge a few feet away from the broken slats and check it out, she decided.

Bracing one foot against the chimney, the other under her body, she rocked back and charged the steep pitch. Up, up she went, half standing, half lunging, until just when she had lost all momentum her fingers caught the crest of the roof. For a critical second while she straddled the ridge she lost track of the octagon. Time enough for something taloned or fanged to fly shrieking into her face, tearing at her eyes or the softness of her throat. But then she faced around and heard only the rattle of grit or maybe a rat in the leaves banked where the valleys met the eaves. Silence followed. Nothing moved in the cupola. Nothing scurried or fluttered or rushed out at her.

She inched forward, using her knees and her hands, hoping she remained in line with the chimney in case she had to bail out but afraid to look away from the inky darkness beyond the slats. The stench—that bottom-of-the-world odor—was overpowering now. Things had probably died in the cupola, she thought. Pigeons and things. So the smell of decay wasn't really surprising. She crept closer, right next to the broken facing now, and that was when she thought she heard a rustling. It wasn't a big rustling. More like a mouse. Would a mouse stay there if something bad was inside? Drawing her legs up one at a time until she was balanced on the ridge, she poked in.

Something breathed past her face. The spirit of the cupola leaving. Gone before she could become alarmed. Carefully she pawed the darkness, then waddled through until she found herself crouching on a platform. The funny thing was that the odor inside wasn't so bad, even though it had been outside. The second thing she noticed was that she could see the blue velvet sky through all the slats. In a few seconds she could make out the geometric contrasts of board ends and wood frames. Then she distinguished shades of gray. Then she could separate the eight sides. Cool, she decided (kids still said "cool"). Except for a couple of slippery spots where rain had dripped on the platform, it was dry. She felt safe here, like she was wearing armor. Girl in a cage.

But no ghosts. A little disappointment; a little relief. She really would like to meet a ghost. Not one gushing blood as it staggered across the fields maybe, but a nice sad one floating around lost. Like Topper. You couldn't get *Topper* on TV anymore. Not even reruns like she used to watch in the '60s. She sat in the cupola a few

minutes longer, listening to the wind and thinking about
the things she could move up here to make it a kind of a
clubhouse, and then she crawled back out to start the descent.

Sliding down to the chimney was a piece of cake, and
now that she knew how to keep her weight straddled
around the base of the pipe and push off again, that was
no problem either. The lightning rod was a little trickier,
because she had to stop her momentum by going a couple of steps against the pitch of the roof, then dragging
and scuffing as she slid so that she didn't hit the gutter or
the lightning rod too hard. But she did that okay too, she
thought. One scrape from bracing with her elbow coming off the shingles, but heck, she got those just leaning
her elbows on the dinner table.

She lowered the window sash in the sewing room and
passed downstairs, listening for sounds from her
mother's room. If anyone heard her on the roof, it would
be her mother, though probably she would think it was a
raccoon. So Amber wasn't expecting anybody when she
got to the first floor. And that was when she saw the
ghost.

It was floating slowly through the dining room beyond the arch. Tall, thin, its silver hair kind of glowing.
She froze at the foot of the stairs, waiting to see if it
would know she was there and turn and grin with rotten
teeth and maybe lift its hands like a strangler. But if it
knew she was there, it didn't care. And it kind of groped
through the gloom, touching things, melting into them
and reappearing again. A ghost for sure. She took a step
to follow, and then another—long and darting—like a
game of Mother, May I or Red Light, Green Light,
where you snuck up as close as possible while the person had his back turned. And now she could see that the
ghost wasn't walking right through objects, but just

passing through shadows. And then she heard it breathing.

Breathing?

Ghosts didn't breathe. The hair on this one wasn't really glowing either. Up close it was thin and white and stuck up where it kind of gathered the moonlight. She waited until he reached the faint illumination that crossed a threshold from the sunporch with its large windows, and then she hopped alongside.

"Who are you?" she challenged.

He stopped as if not sure where the voice had come from, then turned his straining eyes on her. "Where are we?" he asked at last.

"In the house, of course."

More peering, as if to reconcile contradictions.

"You're the new resident," Amber said.

"I am?"

"I'm Amber."

"You shouldn't be here."

"Why not?"

"It's dangerous."

"You're here."

"That doesn't matter. I've lived too long anyway."

She studied him. "Why is it dangerous?"

He looked back at her, looked away, looked back again. "They might find you."

"Who?"

"Better get rid of your Japanese money, if you have any. They'll cut off your head, if you have anything you've taken off a body."

"I don't have any Japanese money," she said.

"Good."

"Are you trying to find your room?"

". . . No. We've got to steal some food and take it back."

He craned in the direction of the light.

"I can get you food," Amber said. He looked like he might be starving, she thought, but that was because he was old—older than anyone in the house probably.

She led him a few steps at a time, pausing for him to catch up, until they were in the kitchen, and there she opened the refrigerator and stood aside.

"You want some yogurt? The lemon is the best. But the cherry is good too. You can have both, if you want." The light from the refrigerator fell on her, and his eyes were suddenly intent. "Why are you looking at me like that?"

"I didn't know it was you."

"Yup. It's me, Amber."

"You're Tiffany."

"I'm Amber."

He lost half a beat, huffed a curt laugh of disbelief.

She considered. "You can call me Tiffany, if you want."

"Mm-h," he said with a nod. "Where are we?"

"We're in the house. You said you wanted food."

"I'm not hungry."

"You said you were."

He shook his head. "I don't know what you're talking about."

She puckered her rosebud mouth, tilted her head. "You got that Weisenheimer disease or something, mister? I seen it on *Oprah* last week."

"Mm-h. Where are we?"

"I'm gonna take you to your room, okay? I saw them cleaning it out for you a couple days ago."

He let her pluck his sleeve and lead him to the corridor, and twice he hesitated before a door, thinking it was his own. When she took him to the right place and helped him lie back on his mattress, the energy that had gone to his body seemed to flood back into his face. "I've got to get food for the others," he said, trying to sit up.

"It's okay. You stay here, and I'll bring you food every night, if you want. Just don't leave any crumbs, okay? Molly gets mad if you leave crumbs."

He lay back again.

"I'm going now, mister."

He called to her again when she was at the door. "You don't have any Japanese money on you, do you?"

"No. I got rid of it."

"Good. They're beheading anyone with souvenirs."

It was sad to be that old. Sad to say you didn't care if you died. Amber climbed back to her sanctuary on the roof and thought about her father in a wheelchair, aging like that. It didn't seem fair. Why had her mother brought him back? Even though he was an abuser, you shouldn't punish someone forever. If he was bad, he would've been in hell and probably come back all burned. But he wasn't burned, so maybe he wasn't so bad after all. The heat lightning flashed from the horizon, stabbing between the weathered slats of the cupola, catching the whites of her eyes. Too bad she wasn't the magic painter instead of her mother. Too bad she didn't have the magic paints. And that made her think: why not? She could steal the paints. And then she could practice. And when she was good enough . . .

4

"What is this place?"

Martin squinted up from the bed like he'd been lying there since yesterday just waiting to ask the question. Denny felt guilty already.

"It's called New Eden."

"Never heard of it. I want to go home."

The Nightmare Assertion. Denny had known "I want to go home" was coming, known he would have to deal with it, knew there was no answer for it. He kissed his father's forehead, and the old man's muzzy blue eyes followed him to the captain's chair by the windows.

"I know you do, Dad, but you weren't safe at home."

Martin Bryce looked away, and his chest seemed to collapse a little. "Who cares?"

"I care."

"I don't know why I have to live so long. You should just . . . just leave me alone."

"You know I can't do that, Dad."

"Why not?"

Let me die. Call Doctor Kevorkian. Time for Jack the Dripper. Bring in the elixir of death, set up the tubes and the bottle. . . . Denny had heard it a thousand times. Was defeated each time his father wished for death. It was bad enough when his mother had been alive—so hard on her—but his father hadn't meant it then. Now he did.

They argued in that slow, loving way that had evolved somehow. Pathos, humor. Negotiating death. The father reviving slightly with the son's attention; the son dying a little:

If you don't care for any other reason, then care for me, Dad. You can't ask me to let you go like that.

Why can't I?

I'm not trying to keep you alive beyond your time. But you're healthy. You're not in any pain.

I am in pain.

Hey, old man, when God puts the death certificate in your hand, I'll sign off, but not a moment sooner. Maybe I'll even leave your head sticking out of the ground for a tombstone. Okay? Okay?

Polemics. The flow was circular. Stalemate.

"Ariel is complaining about you, Dad. You've got to cooperate, you know."

"Who's Ariel?"

"Woman who runs this place."

"They're all women here."

"Mostly. I guess that's the problem. She says you keep going in other people's rooms. She says one of the women found you asleep on her bed and that you tried to hug her. Nice goin', guy."

Frail smile. "Some people are all about wish fulfillment."

His father still had a sense of humor sometimes. "Yeah. Anyway, try to remember which is your room, okay? And wait for formal introductions before you hug a woman."

"There's no woman for me except Beth," he said. "Best thing that ever happened to me."

They were silent for a while, and Denny wished he

could think of something to say, because he could feel the lucidity draining away like heat from a car left in the cold. Just to make a noise, he pulled open the nightstand drawer. Oh, shit. Three pair of glasses, only one his father's. One of the other two had Hollywood glitter frames. He lifted them out, shoved them in his pocket. Best to leave them inconspicuously around the house when he was on the way out than draw attention to senile larceny.

"What is this place?" his father said.

"New Eden."

"Tell Tiffany to come in here."

"Tiffany's not here, Dad."

"Where'd she go?"

"I don't know."

"Then get your mother for me."

"Mom's not here either, Dad."

"Tell Tiffany to come in here."

Denny hesitated. "Tiffany has never been here, Dad."

"I saw her last night."

"Tiffany died seven years ago."

"I saw her . . . she's getting tall for her age."

"Dad. Tiffany was forty-seven. She died of a drug overdose. She was in bad shape."

His father listened attentively, as if the news were freshly arrived and pummeling him, and Denny couldn't stop telling him the truth. There was no reason to dredge up his sister's miserable life and fate, but he did, because it was the truth and he couldn't spare his father the truth, couldn't let him slide into whatever merciful dementia was scattering his memories. If the memories went, what was left?

"I saw her last night," Martin said. "My little girl. She's got her momma's green eyes."

". . . Yeah."

"I don't know where she got that blond hair and those pouty lips, though."

"Yeah." His sister's hair was steel gray when she died. She had looked sixty on her best day. The blond hair, the rosebud mouth, the green eyes—that was the nine-year-old before the fire in 1956. After the fire she was scars. Grafts and operations had traumatized her adolescence, leading to drugs and worse. By the time she took her last overdose in 1994, addiction and prostitution had taken their toll.

"When is her birthday, son?"

"November."

"Is it November now?"

"It's summer."

"Oh. Remind me when it's your sister's birthday."

"Okay."

"And tell your mom I want to see her."

"She's not here, Dad. She's never been here. And Tiffany's not here. She's never been here either."

Befuddled look. "Well, then who did I see last night?"

"I don't know."

"She had blond hair. She had your sister's green eyes and pouty lips. Who was she, then?"

"No one."

The denials were like plunging a knife into his old man. Stabbing him again and again in the brain, the mind, the soul. Fragmented memories kept rescuing his father from reality, and Denny kept dragging him back to the present. He wouldn't let go. Couldn't. Because then the figure on the bed wouldn't be his father anymore.

"—Dad. Listen to me. I know it's hard to remember, so that's why I keep repeating things and writing them down for you. And you've got your tape recorder here, remember? I made you a tape. I told you to listen to it any time you couldn't remember. It's the same tape we've had for years, but you never play it. Momma used to play it for you so that you wouldn't keep thinking you had to do your taxes."

He didn't like the faint echo that dogged his words in the oversize tile bedroom, and he moved to the black vinyl chair by the bed.

"You've got a common medical condition that sometimes keeps you from remembering. You're the same grouchy old guy you've always been—you're wise and you're funny—but you lose track of things because of the condition. I'm not gonna treat you like a kid, dad. I'm gonna take care of you and make you sure you don't have any pain or indignities, but I'm not gonna treat you like you're less than what you are. You're my *dad*. So try not to be frustrated if I keep at you, okay? Okay, Dad?"

"Okay."

"I'm not telling you you've got to live forever, but I don't want to lose you before you tell me the secret of why you've got more hair than I do."

Faint nod. "You must take after your mother's side."

"Yeah. Well, that's not all bad."

"Send her in again, will you?"

". . . I can't, Dad."

"Why not?" The look. Then slow tears welling up. Nothing else. No movement of the sagging, worn cheeks, the reddened throat. "I forgot. She's dead, isn't she?"

"Yeah, she's dead."

"And Tiffany . . . ?"

"Tiffany too."

"She was burned in the fire—I didn't save her."

"Dad—"

"I tried, but I couldn't."

"You did save her, Dad."

"She was already burned."

"Dad."

Sniffling now, both of them. Fighting it. Big, stupid men unable to turn the valve and let it out. Tears aching in their skulls, teeth clenched, blinking blurry-eyed at each other. Silence and irregular breathing. A rough, dry hand on top of a rougher, dryer one. "Hey." Denny pushing himself to his feet. "I came in here to tell you to stop groping the women."

Martin nodded but wasn't sure the words they had spoken matched his memories. "So everyone's dead."

"I'm not . . . you're not."

And that's how Denny left—fleeing out of the house, avoiding everyone. Ariel Leppa with her magic camera, trying to capture his soul. The glasses still in his pocket—*Stop, thief, you're robbing us blind* (ha-ha)! But as he turned his Toyota Tercel in front of the house, he caught a face in an upper window, and for just a second he thought he was looking at his long-ago sister. Tiffany, before the fire. Blond hair, green eyes, rosebud mouth. Momentary, because it backed away. Probably just the imperfections of a windowpane in a vintage farmhouse. Wavy, distorted. Fade to black.

5

Why don't I paint myself younger?

Such a temptation, and therein lay the evil. Like a cough that would inevitably become a cold, Ariel fought it. Humility—she must keep her humility. And, of course, there was the problem of the corpse. Some revitalized version of herself dragging the dead one into the woods and digging a grave. Not an appealing prospect. She couldn't paint herself out of existence, like she was sure she could do with the others, who had already gone through natural death and now existed tethered to those paintings, as if those seminal portraits were their spirit guardians. She would have to die like Amber had when her younger self came into being.

But already Ariel had an idea of how to take care of the burial, if she could only trust that it would work. She knew the painting had to dry before the creation was finished. And that would give her time to . . . arrange things. She could paint herself, and then she would have an interval before there were two of her—one dead, one alive. And in that interval she could go out into the woods and dig her grave and lie down in it, and wait for the second Ariel to come finish the job. She wouldn't have to drag the body, dig the grave or trundle the cadaver in. She would just have to fill the damn thing. Shovel dirt in a hole. Not so bad. She wouldn't even look down in the hole at herself—black clods raining over her face. She wouldn't have to see that. You could sling dirt without looking. Hard to miss a hole.

But what if she didn't remember what had happened from her previous life? Amber didn't. She wouldn't know that her former self was lying in an open grave out in the woods. What then? But she *would* remember. The two Ambers had been separated by thirty-five years, that was all. The child and the adult. Vastly different beings. In that respect, she would be like the ones who had died naturally. They remembered their previous deaths— remembered past them, in fact—even though they wouldn't tell her what it was like in their graves. And she could write a journal for herself about all that had happened in the last year, just to make sure the reborn Ariel would know.

The power she had was still dawning on her a year after that first painting. She had resurrected the major players from her past, because they had died, but there were others who had died that she could bring back and wouldn't. Like her parents. She didn't remember her father—didn't have his picture—but her mother, well, Ariel was still thinking about that. Did she want to compete with her and deal with issues of control that she could take for granted with the others? Did she want to have absolute power over her own mother? If she brought her back younger than herself, what then? No, she didn't think she would be resurrecting her mother. Rest in peace.

There was so much more to learn, and she had barely begun to experiment. The subjects wore the clothes she painted on them, and came to life in the settings she chose. She had always re-created them in the studio—

that was the birth chamber—but she could have re-created them anywhere, she thought. She had been extremely careful to let it happen just the way it had the first time when Amber's voice woke her up. In fact, she never watched. She left the studio and listened for the sudden steps or the tremulous cry, and then she presented herself, and the person knew instantly who it was that had brought them back. Ariel saw it in their eyes—a complex look she was still deciphering for the glints of cunning and fear and pleading. She had brought them back from the grave, and they knew she had power over them.

She had made things happen in the fields and repaired the barn too. She could paint chickens and cows and sell them. She could paint vegetable gardens already grown, flowers in bloom. Anything organic.

. . . Or inorganic, she thought.

For some reason this spooked her almost as much as the thought of bringing people back outside the studio. Except for rudimentary needs, supplies and repairs, she had been very cautious about creating inorganic things. As if this might be tampering with unknown consequences—*deus ex machina.* And she still drove to the local strip mall once a week.

People were the substance of her life, not things. She knew people. This was her sphere of injustice to set right. She wouldn't, for instance, paint back JFK. But she could, if she wanted. She could change history; she could solve a lot of problems or, perhaps, create unforeseen cataclysms. But . . .

Why don't I paint myself younger?

That night she went so far as to make a sketch on canvas of how she might look. Melting the flesh that sagged at her throat, tightening the corners of her eyes, softening the discoloration where her skull was starting to thrust through her cheeks and the bridge of her nose. She had a foolish urge to carry the sketch downstairs and stick it under a certain someone's nose—"Is this better, Kraft? Do I make the cut if I look like that?" But she had to recognize that the inertness of his feelings for her had been conditioned over a lifetime. That was what she had to overcome. She had tried humility and free will; now she should try the direct approach. Why not? He was a docile old man, confused and lost. He would never be more susceptible. She could talk to him plainly, condition him, reprogram him, and when his mind was purged of all the old reflexes and negative associations, then maybe . . . maybe she would see about painting them both younger. Leaning the sketch of herself against the studio wall, like a number painting waiting to be filled in, and resisting the impulse to check her appearance in the mirror, she negotiated the house to his room.

The suave Kraft Olson of yesteryear would have been implacable, but this one lowered his chin slightly when she entered his room, like a cornered animal protecting its throat. She wondered if Danielle Kramer had come in instead of Ariel Leppa, would he have made that little cranial nod?

"Hello, Kraft."

"Hello."

"Do you remember my name?"

"No."

"I don't believe you. Molly says you remember lots of things." He was sitting in the chair with the lamp on, and it annoyed her to see those wonderful eyes of his go dull and flat in the light. "I'm going to make a fool of myself, Kraft. If you really don't remember anything, then I suppose it doesn't matter, because you won't remember me doing this."

She dragged a bentwood chair across the linoleum and

sat knee-to-knee with him, and when she had his slightly askance gaze locked in, she took a long shaky breath and plunged ahead.

"We've known each other for over half a century, Kraft, and I've been in love with you all that time. There is no one in your whole life who has felt this way about you for that long. Even when you started to lose your memory, I felt the same. I guess you know all this."

He could have been watching paint dry, for all the effect her confession had on him. Ironically, she suddenly felt more comfortable. Rejection suited her, she realized; she knew how to handle rejection. She didn't know how she would handle love. Probably stupidly, giddily, gullibly, vulnerably. But, oh, how she would like to give it a try.

"You know, I've still got the Valentine card Mrs. Dulmeir made you give me in fifth grade," she said. "Do you remember that? Everyone had to give everyone else one of those little heart-shaped Valentines she brought in, and you tore mine up in front of the boys after school. You were very good at throwing cold water on me, Kraft. You tore my heart up, but I kept yours. . . . "

Another pause. Another cue for him to ignore. She smiled a melancholy smile. Here she was, lecturing him like it was a time-out from life, but he had the barely tolerant look of a dog about to be immersed in a tub of water.

". . . So you see where we are, my dear. I'm the survivor in your life. No one else is. And, in fact, you owe your very existence to me. I think you know that. I think you remember just like the others that you were once dead. And if you don't, then I'm telling you: I brought you back. Not that I had any illusions. I think I brought you back just to see if you still . . . find me unacceptable. Do you?"

He just kept staring at her.

"Well, it can't be because of anything I did to you, Kraft. And I could still give you a lot. Can't you see what's in your own best interests? You could decide to love me, Kraft. You could work at it. I brought you back. I can make us both younger. Was I so bad before? I was devoted to you. I gave you my loyalty. Give me yours. Well? Talk to me. How am I doing?"

Horribly. She had emasculated him, then demanded that he want her. He sat there, tense, breathing deeply but in the surreptitious way of someone gathering resources to bolt. Would he be so wary if he weren't pretending? She took her own deep breath. The stone lioness of ultimate justice crouching inside her had made yet another thinly veiled ultimatum.

"Think about it, Kraft," she said.

Well, that took care of that, she thought, climbing the stairs with frequent pauses to slide her hand up the banister. She was artless and direct, and however much they bitched about Delilahs and Mata Haris, men always found that distressing in a woman. So what now? A complete personal makeover with miracle paint? It was too late for humility, but it was absurd to go through with the portrait. They would laugh behind her back. Ariel Leppa's desperate attempt to turn herself into a slightly overripe centerfold. What was her purpose anyway—to change them or to be changed by them?

And then she switched on the studio light, and it looked almost the same. Almost. But the paintings stacked one behind another were not lined up as before, and the sketch she had just done of herself leaned at a different angle against the wall. She hadn't locked the door because she had thought everyone was asleep. Clearly someone had been waiting their chance. She slowly circled the studio. The dampness that had sprung

to her eyes as she left Kraft's room glazed to ice, and her
gaze came to rest on the glass jars. Something she saw
there made her insides begin to shear off. The containers
that held her paints had been disturbed—she would
never have left them staggered like that. And a thin cuti-
cle of red rose to the lip of one glass jar, as if some of it
had been poured out. She looked inside, and it was almost empty. Just the coated sides gave the illusion of a
full jar. Not seeing red was making her see red.

Who?

The red itself was a clue. Like makeup. Like the blush
of youth. *Ruta*, she thought.

She stooped over the stacked paintings, her long fingers flipping them like file folders until she found Ruta's
portrait and yanked it up. Back to the bench she took it,
scrutinizing every brush stroke, tilting the canvas to let
the light glaze over any moisture. It was unchanged.
Who, then? Molly? For the child with cystic fibrosis?
Molly had no artistic ability whatsoever. Maybe the
game was to steal a little at a time, hoping it wouldn't be
missed, and when a full palette was possessed by the
thief, take it to another artist. Something flared hotly inside Ariel, something she hadn't known was smoldering
there.

The first sin had been committed in New Eden, the
first blasphemy, because it challenged the source of her
power. (*Thou shalt have no other artists before me!*) Her
chosen family was flawed now, and she would have to
make a change. Root it out, Ruta out. Or Molly, if it was
she. Sad to have to make a display of punishment and
fear, but someone had defied her will. . . .

"Our father, who art in heaven, thy will be done, thy will
be done."

Kraft prayed not to God but as a protective mantra to

drown out the croaking voice inside him. Yes, yes, he remembered. He remembered everything. The green hellscape. The obscene carapaces of gangliate things that lashed across the void. The bloated, feral entities that smote the walls of limbo, like rapacious predators waiting at a food gate in a cosmic zoo. Had he really been dead, or to put it another way, had he ever really lived? Mad thoughts floating in a mad universe, simply because all possibilities must exist . . . navigating the zero coordinates of Chaos and Night . . . seeking to connect, to adhere to something . . . two being infinitely better than one, because two is mutually corroborative . . . giving rise, therefore, to the demiurge of the universe so as to make more evidence of being, because otherwise YOU DID NOT EXIST!

So he had heard the croaking voice that had followed him from the grave, a groaning ship's-timbers voice that for all its terribleness implied that there was a way, a light, a form of real existence. And the voice had told him what he must do, the gateway he must open and how to serve if he wanted to leave the darkness that otherwise awaited him. Only, for a year now he had been surrounded by vivid color and light, and he had let himself doubt that there ever had been a voice. Voices were sounds you heard through ears, and he had ears now and they no longer heard the deep, resonant croaking. Voices were articulated chains of thoughts and feelings. Voices were not groaning ship's timbers that erupted into consciousness, gone before they registered, heard almost as echoes. But the memory of soul terror is soul deep, and he listened to Ariel and dared not speak. As if he could fool not just her but the giver of mandates.

". . . But deliver us from evil, from evil, from—"

His chin was down, covering his throat, and his eyes were fixed on his hands when he saw the smoke begin to curl out from under his fingernails. It was just a wisp at first, fed from bubbles moving up from the quicks. But suddenly it foamed into the air, thick and yellow, and the flesh of his fingers turned white-hot. He opened his mouth to scream and something thudded softly onto the carpet. He did not want to see it, because he could taste gouts of blood now, warm and salty, and his voice was a wheezy ululation, all vowels and no consonants. No, it was not his tongue lying there on the carpet, torn out by the roots. His insides were not crawling with vermin, cankers were not eating through his lips, sucking things were not draining away his *vis vitae*. These were his nightmares—imagination turning in on itself. Tomorrow he would be whole again. And the tomorrow after that. Only, he was on borrowed time and the tomorrows could not go on forever, and when they stopped, as they inevitably must, it was right back where he had been, where he was doomed to be, forever and ever and ever and ever and ever and ever—UNLESS . . . he accepted the mandate.

"Our father, who art in hell . . . thy will be done, thy will be done, thy will be done."

6

Amber saw him. He was just sitting there outside her bedroom when she decided to make her move. By that time she could hear her mother on the warpath, and everyone was circling around the house like leaves in the wind, so here was Mr. Olson outside her bedroom door. He hardly ever talked and he couldn't remember things, so she thought he probably didn't know what was going on. And anyway, she had to move her stuff super quick, because sooner or later her mother would figure out who really had stolen her paint, and then she would come through her bedroom like Speedy Gonzalez.

Amber couldn't move everything to the cupola at once because she needed her hands free to get across the roof, and she didn't want to crumple the paper or drop the brush or spill the paint. But she should have moved the paint first. Leaving it behind was stupid. Because that was when someone else got into it. She still didn't think it could've been Mr. Olson, but you never knew with adults. Especially old ones like that. He could've got right up and gone into her room and taken some, and then she would never know, because he wasn't there when she came back for the second trip. The reason she hadn't taken the paint with her on the first trip was because she wanted to make sure she could do it with one hand—like a practice run. And she could, she found out. And she did, on the second trip. The screw-cap jar from the kitchen was just like her mother's jars, and that kept the paint from sloshing out when she jumped for the pipe and then the chimney. It coated the whole side of the glass by the time she got to the cupola, but nothing leaked out. That was what was funny, though—and why she knew someone had been in her room. Because the glass above the paint line was already smeared when she came back for it. So someone had poured some out.

If Mr. Olson took it, he probably didn't know what he was doing. He probably thought it was ketchup or something. And now he was gone, and it occurred to her that maybe it was good that he had the paint, because if her mother found him with it, she would blame him.

So Amber Leppa went up to the cupola again and began to paint sitting high above her kingdom, and for the next quarter hour the evolution of life on Earth made startling quantum leaps. There were spiders with huge eyes and fangs and ten legs—call the class decarachnids—because her mother hated things that crawled. And almost everything else had batlike wings, because it had occurred to her that they couldn't get off the roof if they couldn't fly. But by then she had done the first thing, and it didn't have wings. That was a scarecrow, and she hoped it could climb down the lightning rod. She had also discarded a few attempts at painting Aarfie the Wonder Dog, which, because they were painted from a specific memory, weren't shaping up just right. In fact, they were very wrong. Mutant beasties. Natural selection. And all of these things shared one link in their ascendancy from the disparate elements of the cosmos: they were bright, bright red.

Sunshine blazed between the slats, dismembering the

face of the child into composite strips of light and shadow. Radiant blond hair . . . murky alabaster brow . . . scintillating emerald eyes . . . smoke-gray button nose . . . pink lips the hue of sugared rhubarb . . . chin sharp and dark. She gazed out in regal reflection at the world, trying to decide what else it needed in order to become exciting and fun. And all around her on the rotting platform, the papers she had painted were drying, starting to thicken . . . rustling.

The first spiders she had painted were drying the fastest, because she had gotten them down to quick circles (for the bodies and the eyes) and daggers (for the fangs) and crooked lines (for the legs). But where had they gone? The breeze really zipped through when the branches of the basswood tree swayed, and her paintings were moving around a little. So she knew with a glance to the pictures left and right that the spiders must be behind her. She twisted as far as she could but still couldn't see, and if she moved her legs she would brush some of the others paintings, so she didn't turn around completely. Just enough to see that the paper was still there. And she thought she caught the red too, only there was more of it at first. Your eyes could do that, she had noticed, when you strained to see out the corners like that. You got all teary, and then whatever you were trying to see would blur into other shapes. But then she made a super effort to twist, and that made the extra red go away. She even thought she saw it disappearing into the dark, damp corners of the cupola where it joined with the rafters in the attic.

Enough, she decided about populating the world. She had better get back into the house so she could look innocent when her mother came looking for her. And she wondered if Mr. Olson had been caught with the paint he had taken. He couldn't have taken much, because there was still plenty left in the jar. Just that smear, like a finger had been dipped into it.

Kraft Olson. Standing in the parlor in front of the painting of the Garden of Eden. Trembling. Especially his right index finger—TREMBLING. Because it looked like it had been severed. Crimson from knuckle to nail. And because it was stabbing out at the painting, slowly, slowly, trying to muster the dexterity to touch it right where it must.

Ancient things—incredibly ancient things—had persuaded him. They had shown him the bedrock of the universe. Traveling down beams from the moon in hideous, giggling packs, erupting out of the stench of buried death, bubbling through swamps and sewers and fecal decay, they came at night. He had seen the horrors of the grave, been on the wrong side of the river, breathed the ethers of miasma and effluvium floating out from the black islands in the green mist, and if he wanted to escape the howling abyss, they offered the only way open to him. Because it was too late for him to follow the light.

So he reached out to the painting of the Garden of Eden with his wet crimson finger and touched it just there, like God and Adam reaching across the ceiling of the Sistine Chapel. Touched it and followed the helical coil of the thing, tracing wet paint over the form that wound around the Tree of Knowledge.

Done!

The slithering viper was unbound from its pit now. As good as if Ariel had eaten the apple. Because what was an Eden without a serpent?

7

Denny Bryce's thoughts were drifting with the ball scores, and the whole thing happened so fast that he could have been mistaken. One minute he was tooling serenely along the empty road in his Tercel, and the next his heart was flopping around his chest as he fought for control of the wheel. The car fishtailed just before he hit the creature, just before he thought he hit the creature, and so he wasn't sure whether the jarring was an actual collision or maybe—*sweet Jesus, let it have gotten away, whatever it was*—the suspension system tying up in some way.

. He hit the shoulder with the wheels locked and made a washboard stop just shy of the ditch. A glance in the mirror showed empty road. Out of the car, around to the front, onto his knees he went, inspecting for damage. The left side of the bumper was smeared with viscera and a swatch of fur—red fur. Very red. What the hell was it? He peered back up the road. Smoothly capped. He hadn't seen the animal flying off to the side after the jar, so it still must have been moving on its own. But, Lord, it appeared to be already injured *before* it ran across the road: bloodied and misshapen and . . . and— he thought—it only had three legs.

Long, skinny stick legs.

But then you couldn't tell that much, since it was running. It had to have been wounded before it loped out into the road like that, though. Maybe it had been in a fight with another animal. Only, it was big enough where you wouldn't think it would fare so badly. It must have been a dog. Chewed up by another dog or hit by a truck. And the red fur, that was blood.

He pulled the few hairs off the bumper and saw that they were dry and smooth. Not bloodstained, just red. Redder than a red fox. Of course, you couldn't be sure with such a small sample. But that was one horribly mutilated pooch. And yet "mutilation" wasn't the word. Because it was smooth, almost featureless. He had seen the eye, the sharply pointed ears, and one more thing he was obviously mistaken about.

He could have sworn it didn't have a mouth.

There in the sunshine of a pastoral midday, Denny Bryce sensed an unseen actor just offstage and twisted around suddenly. He scrutinized the underbrush beside the shoulder of the road. Then the trees. Very still. No squirrels, no tattletale jays, no grasshoppers or butterflies. He wanted to go back and look for whatever it was he had hit, but something warned him: *Get back in the car.*

No way for a rationalist to act.

He stared hard at the embankment, but the feeling persisted that the stillness meant just the opposite—an invisible turmoil. It was like one of those puzzle pictures where you searched for hidden animals. Was he picking up bits of some nearly discernible form in the underbrush, hearing a faint patter? *Nyet. Nein.* Nonsense. Turning in a complete circle, he crossed the road and stood on the edge of the ditch.

Some kind of vine had taken over the embankment.

Up close he could detect that its green, heart-shaped leaves were faintly trembling like the skeins of a vast spider web. He looked toward where the creature had crossed in front of his car. Dead still. The leaves stretched like ivy, unbroken as far as he could see. And then he saw a ridge appear in the glossy green bank and begin to ripple toward him. Exactly like an ocean swell it came, lifting and accelerating with a rush. It was the acceleration that finally got to him. He jumped, turned and skipped to the car.

When he dove into the front seat, he slammed and locked the door. Then he felt silly. The wave or the shadow, whatever it was, did not pass him. He craned around to look and saw the same even green ground cover as before. A breeze, that was all. He had let himself be mocked by a breeze.

It was only another half mile to KNEAL, and when he arrived he was surprised that the stagnancy he had sensed on the road seemed to reach this far. He got out of the car and stood beneath the willow, rubbernecking the branches of all the trees he could see and the roof of the farmhouse and the window where yesterday he thought he had seen the face like his dead sister's before the fire had scarred her for life. It felt like aftermath. Whatever had happened up the road seemed to have happened here as well. It was like hunting season, where the first shot recoils through the woods and everything freezes. And you know that the next shot will bring pandemonium.

"So, did you bring my cigarettes?"

He looked up just as the screen door banged the jamb. It was the brightly dressed erg of a woman who had warned him not to have his picture taken—Beverly Swanson, her name was. She smiled effortfully and for once neither of her eyeteeth was smudged with lipstick.

"Sorry," he said, reaching into his shirt pocked as he strolled to the porch. "But I think I've got your glasses."

She slid off the blue pearled pair of spectacles she wore and, with a jeweled finger, pressed the bridge of the glitter frames he handed her to seat the stems over her ears. "So it was you. I'd pegged your old man."

"I found them lying around."

"You don't look like a kleptomaniac."

"What does a kleptomaniac look like?"

"Like your old man. Martin collects things as if civilization is on the verge of collapse."

This time he didn't deny it.

"Quite a ladies' man," she added.

"Dad?"

"Lets you know how he feels, that's for sure."

"Oh-oh. What's he done now?"

"Nothing James Cagney wouldn't have done."

"I don't get you."

"Well, they'll tell you, if it's worth telling. I'm not a gossip. I came out here for cigarettes, and you don't have any."

She *was* a gossip, but she had learned how to control the flow of information to disguise that fact. "What kind do you smoke?" he asked about the cigarettes.

"Do I look fussy? Anything but chocolate or peppermint."

"You look elegant. Like you might use a cigarette holder."

"Aren't you the sweetheart, telling a wart of a woman things like that. If you want to humor me, get something without filters and enough nicotine so that I don't bust an artery sucking the damn things."

"I'll do that."

"And don't worry about your old man. Everyone's

upset about last night, and I guess your dad sensed that.
He's lost, poor guy."

"What happened last night?"

"Cat burglars. Or maybe just cats. Something yowled
on the roof and fell off. Ruta swears it was a red scarecrow trying to climb down the lightning rod. But that
woman thinks she's gang-raped once a week by horny
aliens, so who knows what she saw?"

Denny exhaled a laugh. You had to like this woman.
Never mind that he couldn't make sense of half of what
she said.

"Mr. Bryce?" Someone calling from the shadow of the
screen door.

"Excuse me," he said and passed into the house.

Molly faced him with the assurance of an accuser.
"Did Beverly tell you?"

"Tell me what?"

"Your father hit one of the women."

"What?"

"With his fist."

"You mean an actual punch, or just a push?"

"It wasn't ambiguous; he looked like a boxer. Your father doesn't like to sit for photographs, does he?"

"No, but—"

"The photograph was when he started to get testy.
Then when Dana tried to get him to take a shower, he hit
her."

"Is she all right?"

"He left a mark."

The big woman looked at him with her cartoon-perfect
button nose and large brown eyes, and Denny got the
mandate. "All right," he said. "What was her name—
Dana? Let me apologize to her before I talk to my dad."

"Fine. She's doing laundry."

The narrow steps were cupped and worn to velvet,

and the side walls leading down were damp stone mot-
tled with runes of mildew and mold. No handrail. Haul-
ing baskets of laundry up and down would be a feat for a
British charwoman, and Denny pictured Dana as stalwart with a yellow brick for a face and a right cross that
could have dislocated his father's jaw. The light in the
cellars banked from the left at the bottom, and he found
himself on a hard dirt floor in the splintered glare of a
single naked bulb. It was dusty and oily and dank, and
the temperature was at least twenty degrees cooler than
that of the level above. The opposite end of the storage
room funneled into darkness that emitted a steady churn-
ing. This must be the washer, of course, though in the
context of the bowels of the house it sounded gastric and
digestive.

He found a vague illumination in the passageway after
all that guided him through the kink into the moist
chamber that held the washing machine and three slate
set tubs. The ogress of ablutions had her back to him as
she worked in the middle tub with a stick, but she had
ankles and calves more like a Swedish Cinderella than
the Brit charwoman of his expectations. And the way she
jumped when he spoke suggested a certain frailty.

"Sorry." He stuck out his hand. "Denny Bryce."

The fingers that had flown to her breast came forward
in a limp grasp. "Dana Novicki."

They had to shout above the noise of the washer, and
so they moved to the near end of the laundry room. He
took note of her slate blue eyes, sandy blond hair, tiny
ears, slender fingers, thin pert nose and dull rose ample
lips. Her cheeks had that ephemeral ruddiness of women
who blush easily and always look a little surprised. She
could have been either side of fifty, but age seemed irrelevant to her quick and graceful movements. And the last
thing, more damning somehow now that he saw how

diminutive she was: she had a faint mouse developing above her right eye.

"I can't tell you how upset I am about that." He nodded at her brow.

She waggled fingers, shooing away the reference.

"He's never mistreated a woman before."

"He was just confused."

"That's no excuse."

They looked at each other somewhat helplessly, because they were still shouting and the relentless chug of the washer was going to defeat any delicate conversation.

"Let me make it up to you."

She shook her head. "Not a problem."

"Let me take you to lunch."

"Really, I can't."

He pointed upstairs. "We'll talk."

She nodded and he A-framed his hands in a gesture of indebtedness before starting toward the wrong end of the room to make his exit. But there were two tunnels in that direction, he saw. You could lose a minotaur down here. At least she was laughing at his wrong turn, he noted, though he could only hear the crescendo of the spin cycle.

His father didn't remember the incident. Didn't know who Dana Novicki was. Sometimes he faked forgetting, but Denny didn't think he was faking this morning. "So, you got your mug shot taken, old man?" he asked, and the vague way Martin Bryce went along with the statement made Denny sure he didn't remember that either. He stayed with him for an hour, then spent another ten or fifteen minutes trying to relocate Dana. No one had seen her. No one had any idea where she might be.

He sat down on a chair in the parlor, aware of the curious looks he was getting and pretending to study the

painting of the Garden of Eden that hung on the opposite
wall. Something odd caught his eye. He got to his feet
for a closer examination. The serpent was missing. The
artist had failed to paint it in. How had he failed to notice that before? But then again there was a ridge of
paint all along the outline that wound round the Tree of
Knowledge, as if someone had scraped the coil right off.
Strange. Snooky snake gone missing.

Suddenly something else that was undersized caught
his attention. A flash of blond, a glint of green, and a
girl, no more than ten years of age, darted through the
archway and up the staircase. *Tiffany! My sister.* Only, it
had to be the child he had seen at the window. What a
striking similarity to the memory of his sib. Obviously a
grandchild, but whose among these aging women?

Like a missing piece returned to a jigsaw puzzle, that
faint restoration of credibility to his father's insistence
that he had talked to Tiffany seemed to make his old
man whole for a moment. *Always take him seriously,* he
reminded himself. Nothing infuriated him more than to
have people talk over his father's head as if he weren't
there, weren't in command of his daily destiny.

Jigsaw. The painting had suggested that. A missing
piece. And Dana Novicki was missing and he couldn't
wait any longer, so he decided to check the cellars, even
though she must have returned from there over an hour
ago.

He flicked the light switch at the top of the stairs and
the naked bulb in the storage room came on. Down the
worn narrow steps he went, through the first cellar and
the passageway where grayness squeezed to nothingness. The masticating washing machine was silent now.
He groped forward with the light at his back, and suddenly on his left there was a pitch-black rectangle. This
was where the passage took a peculiar U-turn and then, a

few feet farther, another one. Why? What could be in the earth that had to be negotiated around? It almost seemed like a diabolical contrivance for an ambush.

He had been guided by light from the laundry on his first trip through, but now it was midnight in front of him. There was no point in going on. "Dana?" he called, to make sure.

And yet she wasn't upstairs.

How had she turned on the light in the laundry room? He ran his hand around the corner of the black rectangle. The cold stone was damp, but not from sweating. It was saturated. The earth on the exterior side of the wall must be a quagmire. It made him wonder if the passageway led beyond the foundation of the house.

No light switch. It must be in the laundry room.

Well, hell, only a few feet and a couple of turns. Dana had done it. What if something had happened to her? She could be lying on the floor in there, though that would still leave the light burning, so maybe she had turned it off first, or . . . shit.

He groped ahead. One step, two—hands scraping for reference points, reaching for an end. Something like fur passed under his fingertips, only it was brittle and it slurried under his touch. The white crystalline mold, he thought with disgust. Enough spores down here to kill Mr. Clean. And now he imagined great puffballs and fruited fungi spewing around him. And could that be the faint phosphorescence of a minute fairy ring on the wall directly in front of him? Something was glowing. End of passage. He took the second U-turn, and a few steps later the clammy air of the laundry room expanded around him.

"Dana?"

He had the same feeling that had come to him out on the road after the thing with no mouth loped across.

Alien senses apprehending him—watching, smelling, feeling his heat, picking up subtle signatures. You couldn't have a place like this that was perpetually in the dark, in the damp, in the earth, and not expect unfamiliar things to take up residence. Small, probably. Most of them. Very small. Bats, rats. Things like that. Even smaller. Noctivagant forms, feeling out territory, contriving their means of sustenance. They lived pretty much off juices of things that were even smaller or the organic cells that dropped off laundry, but not human blood or big chunks out of your neck or something. So he, Denny Bryce, was the big kahuna down here. No sweat.

At last he found the wall plate and threw the switch and the Cartesian world flooded back into being. Washer, dryer, three slate set tubs. No Dana Novicki lying there, sucked dry by vampire gnats who afterward turned off the light. But . . .

What the hell was that?

He could have sworn he saw something red shrinking back into one of the far passageways. Small—or at least low to the ground—receding from the light. He probably would not have seen it, in fact, except that it was so red. Crimson.

Red sweat sock escapes laundry room! Last seen limping into tunnel.

Yeah, well, enough of this shit. She wasn't here. And he had done the brave thing, half out of curiosity, and now he wasn't curious anymore, and so he backtracked through the labyrinth and left the house and drove home, or at least to the spot where that other red thing had crossed the road. There he pulled onto the shoulder and studied the panoply of green heart-shaped ivy. Because there was something there now, he could see. Definitely a gap in the ground cover. And it was bright sunshine everywhere, so he got out of the car and leaped the ditch and waded through the ankle-grabbing network of vines until the flies all lifted in a blue cloud.

"My God . . ." he murmured.

Whatever it was—whatever it had been—there was nothing now left but viscera and an incomplete skeleton. Purplish masses of tissue wrapped in bloody sinews, gnawed bones that didn't assemble right in his imagination, shreds of glistening gore, swatches of red fur that he knew weren't blood soaked and a savaged skull with a very pronounced anomaly. The skull was licked clean by something that had worked rather diligently at getting the brain out through the eye sockets, sinusoidal cavity and spinal opening. And that must have been a task, because the latter orifice was quite small. Which is what you get when there are no teeth, no jaw, no mouth . . .

8

"Ammmber?"

She said it in that slow, measured way adults have of leading you out of a lie, hinting at their power over you. And Amber was afraid of her mother's power. But she was still going to lie to her face about stealing the paint. Because if she gave up what she had—or what her mother thought she had—then she would be helpless again. "You always blame me!" she shrilled.

"That's because you're always to blame," Ariel said. "Do you expect me to accuse Ruta Seppanen of riding a bike through the flower bed or Marjorie Korpela for thundering around on the roof?"

"That wasn't me!" A twitch of a smile broke her anxiety at the thought of Mrs. Korpela prancing around on the roof. Everyone knew she had a limp.

"Do you think this is funny?"

"No."

"Then what were you doing up there?"

"It wasn't me."

"My dear, you are the only one who could have made that much noise. It sounded like a herd of wild animals. All that flapping and scratching—oh. Dear God. It wasn't you. Amber, what did you paint?"

"I didn't."

Raspy and desperate now. "WHAT did you paint?" Hands encasing the child's shoulders, squeezing, strong as a butcher's. "What did you paint, I said! May God damn whatever it was—tell me! What did you *paint?*"

"I didn't, I didn't." Little girl's dissembling tears. It was transparent now, and either she would gut it out or cave in. But as soon as her mother had the paint she would punish Amber, and punishments weren't the same anymore. Amber didn't know what her mother might do. So keeping the paint was protection against something really bad happening to her.

"Amber," said Ariel with sudden pathological calm. "You're going to give it back."

Silence.

". . . And you're going to tell me: what did you paint? Was it one thing?" Pause. "More than one?" Voice rising, eyes blazing. Then a gasp of revelation and dismay. "Where are they?"

"Where are what?"

"The paintings. Where are they?"

"I don't have any."

This was almost true. Most of them had blown out into the fields. She hadn't been able to find them— except for a couple, one of which was completely soaked because it had been lying in a furrow of the vegetable garden after the rain.

As soon as she had heard the screams and the clawing she had known what was happening. It was lightning and thundering outside, but inside the cupola her paintings were drying. One by one they were coming alive— and some of them *not* one by one. Some of them were coming alive together: animals with fangs and tusks, and ten-legged spiders, and the scarecrow. Mrs. Seppanen kept babbling and crying because she must have seen the scarecrow falling, and there were wings flapping and wood splintering. The next day when Amber had gone up there, she had seen that they had shoved right through the side of the cupola. There were big white gashes on the basswood tree too, as if something had leaped from the roof to the trunk. She had thought there might be dead things left inside the cupola, but when she dared poke her head in it was empty, except for splatters of blood with bits of fur stuck in them. The pictures, of course, were gone, and that was when she had searched for them in the fields and found only the two. She had also found the actual remains of one of the things that had left the cupola alive. It was more like a stain than an animal. All puddly and with the eyes floating around and one red claw. That one had come from the painting that was partly ruined in the rain, and so it was partly ruined too. And the other painting she found—that was the scarecrow. It was probably messed up now, or maybe even gone, because the colors had all run on the paper and it sort of made it glow. But it was just a scarecrow, and scarecrows didn't hurt people.

"What do you mean you don't have any?" Ariel demanded about the paintings. "I want them, Amber. I *have* to have them. You understand why, don't you? You know what you've unleashed? I need the paintings to undo what you've done."

Amber was shaken and uncertain because her mother looked so intent, with her short gray hair all choppy like that and dark circles around her eyes. "I don't have them, Momma," she delivered with shudders.

Stalemate.

Amber spent the rest of the day trying to look innocent and avoiding her usual haunts. She didn't dare climb to the cupola. Downstairs everyone seemed to know she had something to do with the noises on the

roof and the thing Mrs. Seppanen had seen falling off the
lightning rod. Mrs. Armitage was spying on her, and
Mrs. Swanson was giving her hard looks, and even Miss
Hoverstein—who had never been married and always
treated her like she wished Amber were her daughter—
was avoiding her. She didn't care about Mrs. Armitage.
Mrs. Armitage was a big beluga butt her mother sent
after her every time she did something wrong. But Miss
Hoverstein was nice and read a lot of travel books and
told her stories. Like the one about the Taron pygmies,
who lived in a place called Myanmar that used to be
called Burma, and how they were all going to let themselves die out. Amber liked stories about faraway places
and people who were sad and struggling to survive. And
Mrs. Swanson could be nice too. Like when she watched
the soaps on TV and told Amber everything that was
going to happen or did her torch singer imitation while
Mr. Seppanen played the piano.

The worst time was dinner. There were mashed potatoes, but Amber just played with her food and put one
elbow on the table because no one was talking to her.
Ordinarily she liked old people. They gave you stuff,
and even if they were hard of hearing, they listened or
pretended to. But no one asked her what she had been
doing or said she had "grown a foot since yesterday."
She put both elbows on the table. Still they just munched
away, everyone minding their own business and leaving
one by one when they were done eating, like they had
suddenly remembered something they had to do instead
of sitting around talking about the olden days or what
was happening on the news.

"I'm going to go to school this fall," Amber said when
it was just Mr. Seppanen, Mrs. Swanson, Mrs. Korpela
and Miss Hoverstein left.

That got their attention. They knew she couldn't go to

school. And then Mr. Seppanen got up and stood there in his khakis with the high-water cuffs, holding on to the back of his chair, and said, "Maybe they'll put some sense into your head."

Pretending not to notice, Amber turned to Miss Hoverstein. "Tell me about the pygmies."

"I don't remember," Miss Hoverstein said.

"Yes, you do. You said they're all just one family that lives in the mountains and all their babies are misshapen or retards."

"I didn't say 'retards.'"

"Tell me, then."

"You've just said it."

"No, tell me the sad part. How they decided not to make babies anymore, because the world shouldn't have them."

The others were looking at Miss Hoverstein now, a funny glint of curiosity and something like fear in their eyes, or maybe it was worry. And Miss Hoverstein seemed almost to speak to them instead of to Amber. "The Taron pygmies of southeast Asia say that they don't belong in the world, so they've chosen to make themselves extinct. There are only twelve of them left."

"Cheery," Mrs. Swanson said then, pushing back from the table. "I think I'll go pretend to smoke a cigarette."

Wordlessly Miss Hoverstein followed.

So then it was just the two of them, Amber and Mrs. Korpela, and that was how the game began. Because no one could make Amber get out of their sight. She would be in their face until they paid attention to her. She would be like poison. If they wouldn't talk while she was there, she would hang around until they left.

Mrs. Korpela had once been Amber's mother's boss at Kresge's or some place a long time ago, and Amber thought that was strange. She wore suits and dabbed her

lips when she ate and never bad-mouthed anyone.
Amber leaned on one elbow again and chewed mashed
potatoes with her mouth open and twiddled the handle of
her fork, but Mrs. Korpela paid no attention. Then
Amber remembered. The limp. Mrs. Korpela was always
sitting there when you showed up for dinner, and she
would wait until everyone else left before she got up, because she didn't want anyone to notice her limp.

Well, she would just have to talk to Amber if she did-
n't want her to see. She would have to say something,
like ask her why she wasn't eating, or why didn't she go
outside and play while it was still light. It wasn't really
being cruel, because Mrs. Korpela was being cruel by
giving her the silent treatment.

And suddenly the straight-backed Marjorie Korpela,
for whom quiet, unobtrusive dignity had gotten everything she had in life, edged her seat back in a series of
feeble thrusts, stood and sidled out from her prescribed
position like a bowling pin rocking off its mark. For a
moment she leaned there, looking straight ahead. Then
she said in a very high-pitched voice, "You're just like
your mother."

Amber looked down at her plate but couldn't blot out
the halting progress to the arch and thereafter the lisp of
an uneven gait retreating on hardwood floors. *I'm not
like my mother!* she screamed inside. *I hate Mrs. Korpela. I hate everyone. I hate Mrs. Armitage and Momma
and . . . and—*

But not Daddy.

It might have been because of the lameness that she
thought of him just then. Mrs. Korpela limped and her
father was in a wheelchair. Her father was even worse
off than Mrs. Korpela, but he had never stopped talking
to her or been cruel. Late in the day she went up to see
him. She snuck up to the room her mother kept him in

and knocked really softly and then opened the door, because you didn't expect him to answer. And then she walked around the room, touching things and stopping at the window until she was sure his eyes were following her.

You had to do that because it was hard to get his attention. She didn't think he saw too well, but except for her and Mrs. Novicki, no one ever tried to find his glasses for him. Other times, though, his eyes were all gluey and wide and she thought he was looking right through her. He was still big. Even in his wheelchair he was big, but he had lost his shape, sort of like a pyramid of corn sitting out in the rain that gets rounder and rounder by the day. His lips were all dry too. And when he whispered you could hear his tongue like it was sticking to the roof of his mouth. Sometimes he just nodded and grunted and only said hello and good-by. But still he listened.

Except for today.

Today she didn't think he was listening at all, even though he looked right at her. She told him lots of stuff, all about the cupola and taking the paint and, finally, about the things she had painted. But he didn't seem to hear. Then she put her hand on the back of his chair and leaned against the wheel. "Tell me about the red corn," she said. "You know, about the gangsters in the tunnels and how their blood turns the corn red."

But he just stared through her, and she felt a little scared and maybe hurt, because she didn't have any friends and friends were the most important thing. That's why she had painted the animals. So she would have friends. She wanted Sir Aarfie back. But trying to paint him back had been a mistake—a horrible mistake. She could see that now. It had gotten out of hand, because she lost most of the paintings and now there was no way to undo them, like her mother said.

She left her father to his depression and moped around all evening, and when Molly told her that her mother wanted her to take a bath, she didn't protest. She went into the bathroom and took off her clothes. Then she climbed into the old tub and turned on the faucets, stamping a little in the splash until the temperature was just right. She looked in the soap caddy and behind her on the curved rail for the rubber plug, but it wasn't there. Sometimes it dropped onto the floor and rolled under the tub, so she got on her hands and knees in the cascading water and leaned out to see. It was there, all right. Behind one of the feet. She snatched it up and turned back to jam it into the drain, and that was when her heart took one gigantic beat and stopped.

Because she wasn't alone in the tub anymore.

It came out of the drain. Even though it looked too big to fit down there. Crimson, with huge eyes and dagger fangs and too many legs—more than eight, just like she had painted them. Her mother hated spiders and crawly things, so she had wanted them to have lots of legs. Only now this one was zigzagging around her like a bullet, trying to stay out of the water and looking at her and crouching to spring like she might be an island. She tried to scramble up, but as soon as she planted her foot the scuttling thing stopped and faced her, and by the way it raised its fangs and front legs she knew she had better not move again.

Because it could leap. She was sure of that. It looked like a hideous cartoon with its funny bent legs, but she bet it could jump up on her bare flesh and bury those oversize fangs in her throat or her heart or—and this frightened her more than the other possible landing sites—her eyes. She thought somehow that its great goggle eyes were focused on hers.

Maybe it had venom, and maybe it could shoot the

venom and blind her. She had seen that in a documentary
somewhere—a great fanged spider in India, or some
place like that, that blinded its prey with a stream of poison. Just like that. This one was bigger than the spider in
India. As big as her hand maybe. She drew back her
face, and it seemed to rise up like it was tracking her.

The impulse to scream (were spiders deaf?) rose in
her throat, but she fought it down. They must be able to
pick up vibrations, because that was what they did with
their webs, and she was in a tub that sounded almost like
a bell when you hit it, so if she screamed the spider was
going to know it, even if it was deaf, and it would probably strike just like they did when a web vibrated. She
couldn't jump out, because she only had one foot under
her and by the time she thumped around and got her
other leg unbent it would be too late.

The red spider was sitting right where the tub sloped
up at the back. It was crouched to spring because the
water was coming in faster than it could go out. And it
was coming in hotter and hotter. In a few seconds they
were both going to be scalded. So it came down to who
was going to move first. The spider wasn't wet yet, but
Amber's toes and ankles were starting to sting.

And then the spider nudged up the slope a little. Tried
to nudge up the slope. Because it immediately slid back
some, and then its fangs came down and it rotated like
the faucet handle and began to drum its legs. There was
no way it could get out. Maybe if it had leaped before
the level got too high, but it slid all the way down now,
half in the water, and that was her chance. She cleared
the tub with barely a ripple.

The spider's legs were turning over like a combine
harvester and going nowhere, but as the water rose, it
rose too. She was going to have to kill it, she knew. Kill
it and not tell anyone. They would all blame her for

whatever didn't die outside the house—and inside now too, she guessed. She had a chance to take one off the list. Probably some of the creatures she had created would kill each other, she thought. But then again, maybe they would mate. No, they were too different, weren't they? They couldn't get together and make babies.

But they might.

And spiders had lots of babies. Thousands and thousands, some of them. So now she groped down into the tub and found the rubber drain plug and jammed it home. But then she thought what if the water got so close to the rim that the red spider could make it out? So she spun the faucets shut, and now the thing began bobbing around the edge, its front legs still going in a furious blur, and its awful eyes bulging out so that no matter where she stood, it seemed to be looking at her.

Standing there naked, she felt like it could touch her too easily, so she wrapped a towel around herself. Then from the other side of the tub, she began splashing water at it. But each time she drove it under, air bubbles seemed to protect it. Again and again it swirled to the surface. So of course she made bigger and bigger waves. Which was a mistake. Because the third one actually lifted it out of the water onto the slope just inches from the rim of the tub. And if she thought the legs were going fast before, now they were like egg beaters. She jabbed at it, gauging whether she could knock it back. But the eyes seemed to spark with something she didn't like. So then she blew on it. Blew and blew and blew, trying not to lean too close. And whether that made any difference or not, the red spider suddenly lost momentum and slid back into the water.

She wondered if it was getting scalded. It hated the water for sure, but it didn't seem affected by it. How could she kill it? She thought about throwing her shoe or hitting it with the toilet plunger, but she would have to drain the water to do that, and if it got onto the flat of the tub again, it might try to leap.

The toilet plunger, though—what if she got the rubber cup around it? Then she could push down and squash it. It wouldn't know about toilet plungers, so it would probably want to crawl into the cup on the end.

She dashed to the sink where the green wooden handle with the black rubber cup sat underneath. Returning to the tub, she took dead aim. But right away it knew. She could tell by its eyes. She had made it intelligent by painting those eyes, she thought, and now she would just have to stab it. One quick stab and she would have it pinned to the side of the tub.

Bracing her feet and taking the green handle in both hands, she thrust. But quicker than she could follow, the thing was over the black rubber rim and flying up the wooden shaft. She had just enough time to fling the plunger away as she uttered a short cry.

It fell into the water and the spider more or less clung to it, a rolling island of wood. But Amber didn't like the possibilities. The plunger would soon touch the side of the tub or drift near the overflow drain near the rim, and that would turn it into a bridge.

She had another idea. There was a gray plastic pail under the sink, and if she could somehow scoop the spider into the toilet, she could flush it away. It had fit through the tub drain, so it would go down the toilet. She didn't know where toilets led, but it had to be away from the house. So she raised the seat and grabbed the pail and tried to act like she wasn't going to do what she was going to do, because the spider seemed to know everything.

Her heart was beating wildly when she confronted it.

It knew, but what could it do? She scooped the pail over the surface. There was no way it could not be caught in her trap this time. She never gave it a chance to get its bearings. Without even straightening the bucket, she let the momentum carry the red spider and the water out of the tub and into the toilet. One big wave with a flash of crimson, almost like a goldfish, going down into that little hole. And the water was enough to make the toilet flush, which it did. A frothy swirl and a single gulp that took the level down to the bottom of the bowl.

And that was it.

Except that the spider must have wedged itself into the bends in the toilet, because no sooner had the water begun to ebb back to its normal level than she saw red legs scrabbling frantically around the curve of the hole.

Trembling at the invincible will of the thing, she plunked down on the tank handle. Ridges of water spiraled around the sides, agitating the surface and carving a hole right through to where it clung. She could see the legs flex and grip, completely exposed now, except that the flow was sucking at its body. It wasn't going to be enough, she thought. The horrible creature was going to hang on. But just before the final swirl, it suddenly let loose and was gone.

She didn't wait to see if it came back this time. She didn't want to know. She just slammed the seat and the lid down. Then she drained the tub without taking her bath and grabbed her clothes and fled to her bedroom.

Let it be dead, let it be dead, she prayed.

For a long time afterward she listened. Because if it was still alive in the house plumbing, sooner or later someone was going to scream very, very loudly.

9

Martin opened his eyes just before midnight and saw the green glow. It was the clock radio he had given his wife for an anniversary present thirteen years ago, but without his glasses on and with his eyes crusted with sleep, the 11 throbbed phosphorescently.

"Beth . . ." he said and closed his eyes again.

The green glow went with him as he fell and fell back to an outpost of memory where deeply etched events fired cerebral salvos like pom-pom guns on the beach of a Pacific hell. Distant flares on the deck of a flattop homed him in. When you were flying in at night like this, the first thing you saw was that glowing green number 11—two flares—throbbing phosphorescently. *Split it, Marty. . . . Split the uprights!* But he didn't split them. He ditched. And here the geography became muddled. Night was now day. The F4F Wildcat was scattered over a quarter mile of ocean. And he was being lifted—crawling, lifted, crawling—by waves over a sandbar. The murmur of surf blended with chatter in Japanese. Then he was being dragged, interrogated, beaten with a two-by-four, and when he was on his feet again, he was trudging through the dust from bullpen to bullpen, camp to camp—Capiz Tarlac, O'Donnell, Cabanatuan. The guns of Corregidor faded as he marched. Men died, hundreds a day from starvation, from beatings, from the "sun treatment," from beheadings. *Get rid of your Japanese tokens. . . . Throw away your money.* And then his eyes were open again, and he was sitting on the edge of the bed in New Eden, trying to decide what to do . . . what to do for the men.

"Beth!" he called ahead fifty-nine years.

But she didn't answer. All he heard were the insects out in the swamp and a dog barking on the camp perimeter. He was a little dizzy. Black motes swam in the black air. He had to pee, but he was afraid to. They had shoved a glass rod up the penis of one of the men and broken it, and whenever he peed, others had to hold him. There was a seam of light under the door. Martin stood in his shorts and his socks and shuffled toward it.

Out in the hall of New Eden he recognized the bathroom, but the screaming man with the broken glass up his penis would be in there. Martin turned toward the main part of the house. A chrome yellow moon staring through windows followed him from kitchen to dining room to parlor, past the painting of the Garden of Eden, and into another hallway. There were doors in the hallway, and he stopped before the first one. This was where Beth made him take baths, he thought. And when he pushed open the door, that was what he saw—the white bathtub in the middle of the room.

He grazed his hand up the wall but failed to find the light switch. It didn't matter. He could see a ghostly toilet next to a ghostly sink. Shuffling across the tile floor, he lifted the lid and the seat. He was going to go standing up, but the bowl presented a blurred target of concentric circles—rim, porcelain, water, drain—that seemed to agitate together and drift. Dropping the seat again and undoing his trousers, he sat down. It took a long time. His swollen prostate was like a drip-dry sponge. When he was done, he fumbled in the dark for the handle, and again the gradation of circles seemed to agitate together as if something moved there.

Back through the house he came, past the Garden of Eden, through the dining room and into the kitchen. He paused now, not certain where he was, where he was going. There were two doors and two arches, and when he had turned around once, he lost track of how he had come in. He tried one of the doors and found himself looking into a pantry. And then he tried the other, and it was a stairway leading down.

The steepness would have discouraged him, except that the dank earthiness wafting to his nostrils triggered remote associations from his past. And the past was all that mattered. It was more than the thinning connections of a failing brain that made time slip. If he came awake in the middle of the night looking back over his shoulder, it was a last search and rescue for all the failed rescues of Martin B. Bryce.

So down the worn cellar steps he went, finding the light switch but almost losing his balance as he fumbled for a handrail that wasn't there. At the bottom he turned and moved steadily through the storage room. He took small, even steps as though he were advancing on rails. He knew he had to keep going, that he was looking for something or someone—or something for someone. He did not specifically remember the starving men at Cabanatuan or his daughter Tiffany screaming for him from behind a wall of flesh-searing flame, but his heart was pounding with fear that he would fail again. The darkness in front of him was not a deterrent. The cellar could have been a lion's den and he would have pushed on. Sometimes there was nothing in the unknown that could be worse than what you knew.

But the darkness of the passageway beyond the storage room caused him to totter. He groped for the walls, pausing, pushing away. When the passage U-turned sharply, he bumped through the change and kept going. He kept feeling for a light switch, but there was only cold stone and silken spider trip lines. A few steps farther he reached out and the walls were gone.

Air was flowing against him from all sides now and it was very cool, so he must be outside. But where was the sky? Maybe he was in a cavern. His hearing wasn't particularly good, but there was a range in which he heard quite well. A shade going up, dead leaves underfoot, shingles flapping in the wind or the subtle spank of air above burning wood on a grate. He readily heard those things. And now it seemed that something was being dragged to his left in the darkness. It almost sounded like breathing—two-staged like that—except there was no pause. Bellows worked that way, or iron lungs for polio victims. And then the dragging changed directions, cutting in front of him, and he realized what it was.

Separate segments were slithering around him. Those nasty green snakes that waited by the wallows outside the camp. But it couldn't be avoided. You were glad to go to the dirty carabao wallows whenever they took you out on a work gang, because back inside the perimeter there was one spigot for twelve thousand men and the wait for a drink was twelve hours.

And then he heard the whirring wings, and they weren't trying to get out of his way; they were coming toward him. A dragonfly sound. A hunter sound. Straight at him, though for a few seconds he couldn't tell from which direction, just that the drone was getting louder. He raised his arms in the dark. Something brushed his scalp, and before it could come around again, there was another burst of wings, this one a flutter. It must have leaped from somewhere and intersected the whirring, because the dragonfly drone abruptly ceased.

Now the sounds were all of tearing and feasting. Martin Bryce had smelled the charnel horror before in the stench of a bullpen where diarrhetic men could not fall down to die, and again at the edge of a twilit grotto where other men hung, gutted and draining, upside-down over barbed wire. A universe without sanity was the most unsettling revelation possible. Once you had stared starkly over the edge of that immeasurable abyss, you could never forget it. Life thereafter had been hope but not trust in goodness or in order. And now, decades later, he was feeling it again: the rapacious and merciless appetite that drove the universe. One thing eating another until . . . *what?* What survived? What incarnation of life was the final cannibal?

He was listening to the blasphemies of creation sucking the marrow out of each other, and he didn't want to see them. But when the light burst around him, he did see. In the glare, one indelible glimpse at vespertine creatures on the floor of a tunnel. Two forms. Three, if you counted the bloody offal plucked up by the greedy thing that flopped quickly into the shadows. And the other one—that one was not involved in the grisly repast. That one was the slitherer. A red serpent. Bigger than the worm-size void in the Garden of Eden upstairs in the parlor from which it was growing, but not much bigger. About the size and length of a belt. Lashing its way out of sight and into the tunnel.

Amber thought she saw something beyond Mr. Bryce, though she couldn't be sure. He was across the laundry room and partially blocking her view of one of the tunnels. And the light was bright, even though she had only been in the dark for half a minute, feeling her way through the double-backed section to the wall switch. So she wasn't sure about the flash of red on the floor. It seemed longer than the spider, but then again, it was blurry.

"Mr. Bryce?"

He didn't turn, and she thought maybe he was embarrassed because he only had on underwear and socks. She went up and took him by the hand.

"This is the way out," she said.

He looked down, kind of breathless, and she knew by how hard he stared at her that he thought she was the other girl.

"What are you doing here?" he gruffed.

"I heard you use the bathroom outside my room, and then I heard you on the cellar stairs. Are you okay?"

"You should be inside."

"We are inside."

He looked around. "You shouldn't be here."

"Did you see something down here? Like maybe a spider?"

"It was a snake."

She hadn't painted a snake, but he got things mixed up sometimes. Telling her she should get rid of her Japanese money or her head would be cut off, and everything. "It's not safe down here," she said. "Why don't you come upstairs?"

"I don't care if I die."

"I didn't mean you were going to die. C'mon, let's go upstairs."

"You go. I've got to . . ." He looked around again.

"Got to what?"

"I don't know."

"Are you hungry? You should come to meals. You never come to the table for your meals."

"I ate."

"What did you eat?"

"Insects."

She laughed curtly. "You must be starving. I'll get you some yogurt."

"I don't care if I starve. I'm tired of living like this."

"Like what?"

She pulled him gently by the hand and he followed her. She thought she understood him. Lonely. Different. He needed her, and she needed a friend. He kept asking where they were going, and she kept telling him his room. But she knew it wasn't his room. Nothing in this house was ever going to be familiar to him. He had lived too long in other places and with other people, and he didn't want to change them. So she was Tiffany. She liked that. Whoever Tiffany was, maybe she was better to be than Amber.

"You're a good girl . . ." he said when she had tucked him into his bed.

"No, I'm not. You don't know me."

He grunted, and she could tell he was almost smiling.

"Little Miss Contrary. You're a good girl."

10

Rules of canasta in New Eden: bitch, subvert, manipulate.

The card playing went on at a snail's pace in little bursts of draws, discards and melds, while remarks and glances flowed within the matrix. Matronix. Four of them—Ruta Seppanen, Beverly Swanson, Marjorie Korpela, Helen Hoverstein—elbows on the card table, nose to nose to nose to nose, a canopy of gossip over the incidental game. Kraft Olson sat stone-faced in the morris chair, and now and then the Spy, Molly Armitage, passed through on one pretext or another.

Ruta was complaining sarcastically about their isolation, indulged to a point by the others, because, to a point, she was speaking for all of them:

". . . Yes, yes, thank you, Ariel, thank you for reconvening us in your little garden. Replanting us like cut flowers, rootless, to wither and die."

"Don't be melodramatic, Ruta. We aren't going to wither and die."

Three pair of eyebrows went up in response to Beverly.

"Well, Ruta makes us sound like those genocidal pygmies of Helen's. All we have to do is keep Ariel happy."

"Ariel is mad as a hatter—"

"Careful, Ruta."

"She *is*. Certifiable. It's wonderful that we're back, but for what? To be preserved in her little museum just the way she wants us? Unable to change a thing or pick up a phone or drive to Saint Paul?"

"Give yourself some peace," Helen weighed in. "Why do you want to make the same mistakes you made before? Stop logging the infractions. Time stopped for all of us once. Be grateful it started again."

"Mistakes? What mistakes did I make with Ariel?"

Marjorie played an ace on her meld of three and discarded. "Not just your mistakes, Ruta. Ours. We ought to recognize that."

"Well, aren't you the good trooper? I think you've finally gotten to the miserable point of our being here. Ariel will paint a gold star in the middle of your forehead."

"It's not about satisfying Ariel."

"No?"

"It's about where we were when she brought us back."

Their eyes came up and their postures changed. Composure was shattering like an icicle dropped from a roof.

"We ought to think about it. Where we were, and is that the only alternative there is?"

"I don't like to talk about this," Helen said.

"I'm just saying, we ought to think about it—"

"You think she's really God, don't you?" from Ruta.

"Of course not."

"You think giving Ariel what she wants will change where we go if we die again."

"Well, we've been giving her what she wants anyway, so that takes care of that," Helen sighed. "End of subject."

Ruta laughed harshly. "No, no, we can never give

Ariel what she wants, because she's just going to want more and more. I don't know why no one else can see that."

Marjorie tapped a card. "You're still missing the point. Ariel has her own motives, but now that we're here this is about us, our . . . attitudes. She may be right about one thing: we've all got a second chance."

"*I'm* not happy; *that's* the point," Ruta said.

Helen, who especially didn't like an argument being passed around like a baton, seized her chance to snuff out the metaphysical flicker. "At least your husband is here."

"Pardon me . . . pardon me, but you never married, so I don't see that your situation is any worse than mine."

"I'm not the one complaining."

"—and Beverly's husband died in the Vietnam war, didn't he? A hero too. So she's got closure."

Beverly—Our Lady of Perpetual Sarcasm—responded as if poked. "Maybe we should play Old Maid."

"And we have children—Paavo and I—don't forget that," Ruta said.

Beverly rolled her eyes.

Marjorie did not miss her own husband particularly and found Helen's spinsterhood admirable. Out of a sense of duty she worried sometimes that she should find out if her husband was still alive; but then what would she do about it? "Molly has children," she pointed out, "and a grandchild, I believe. And Dana's husband may be alive."

"Dana's husband is a brute. Cinderella is thrilled to be out of her marriage, dead or alive." Cinderella. Ruta's exclusive term for the wholesome-looking and now much younger Dana Novicki.

And then it happened—just like that. The thing that

hadn't happened for many months but which tethered
them to their creator and kept them in fear and trembling. Helen, who was facing the staircase, saw it first:
Ariel coming slowly down the staircase, no cane, one
hand on the banister, the other looped through the arm of
a companion. Ariel's face was incandescent, her brow
nearly geisha white, her eyes like ice at sunrise. A mad
artist's look, fresh from creation. But it was the companion who was the draw . . .

"Danielle . . ." Ruta whispered.

Marjorie and Beverly drew back with shock as they
turned.

Because it was not the beautiful Danielle Kramer, inamorata of Kraft Olson, whose death in middle age had
left them with the memory of a cowl of ebony hair, lan-
guid eyes, a serene mouth, a gypsy's flashing teeth and
nails, taut skin as luminous as moist marble and a
haughty confidence in all of the above. That was
Danielle Kramer when she had died. But what was coming down the staircase was a coffin-sprung travesty of
ragged flyaway hair the color of ashes, burning ferret
eyes and a slack jaw, yellowed teeth and a crone's nails.
The skin was stretched and sagging. Worst of all, in the
expression of this pitiful remnant there was a contradic-
tory mix of hideous joy and fear and shame at being
alive on any terms.

It was this trembling gratitude that struck the room
dumb. They could all be like this. The mocking husk of
what they remembered as Danielle Kramer was the object
lesson of a woman who could paint with the dust of creation. A few strokes of a brush here and there and another
decade would reside in their flesh. The paint would dry
and their bones would bend, their skin would loosen, their
heads would bow. And whatever was commensurate with

physical corruption would enfeeble their minds until they were like this ghastly drooling hag on the stairs.

So they froze around the card table, four vassals of their suzerain lady, unable to return Ariel Leppa's triumphant smile. And as the lone, last float of a grand mummers' parade that had started a year ago reached the bottom step and moved inexorably into line with where Kraft Olson sat, the women at the card table understood:

Ariel's revenge.

Ariel's test.

Ariel's vanity.

Here is your lover, Kraft. See how beautiful she is? Take her. Show me a sign that you haven't been deceiving me. Show me that you really have lost your memory. . . .

Ariel Leppa stared intently into Kraft Olson's face, searching for the slightest twinge of recognition from the man who still scorned her.

"See who I've brought you, Kraft? Don't you want to say hello?"

He may have guessed by Ariel's tone, then, who it was and even the unholy spectacle she had prepared for him, and maybe that was why he refused to lift his face from his chest. But when he heard *her* voice—a rag of the silken fabric that had been Danielle's soft voice, croaking his name—he slowly raised his eyes.

Five intuitive females, with their lifetimes of reading emotions, were riveted on him. They pulled in every nuance of color, avoidance, pace, breathing, posture. But Kraft Olson stared through the terrible corruption of his once and forever love as though waiting placidly for a distant star.

11

The jaw had been torn away, that was all. That explained why Denny Bryce hadn't been able to reconstruct the thing's mouth when he had stared down at the remains in the heart-shaped ivy alongside the road. Not because it hadn't had a mouth to begin with. That was clearly impossible. But he wouldn't mind having another look at it. Just to be sure. He hadn't actually picked it up and checked the first time. It was a bloody mess, after all, and the flies were swarming. And when it had loped across in front of his car, that was inconclusive too. How could you tell anything when you were fighting to avoid running down an animal with your car?

So now he was driving past the spot again on the way to New Eden, and he slowed and surveyed the ivy but couldn't pick out the place. Things didn't last long out here in nature's cemetery. No coffins, no embalming. Lots of undiscriminating appetites in the adjacent woods. So be it.

He feathered the accelerator faster. A minute later the driveway appeared, and he drove too fast up its shattered surface. The archipelago of asphalt hammered the suspension on his Tercel, making it hard to focus on the farmhouse. It looked so alien and impenetrable. Was his father really in there?

The link between them was forged of something he could follow to hell and back if need be, he thought, but he had an uneasy feeling that his old man was suffocating in that shadowy mausoleum of cellars and high-ceiling rooms. He still thought of him as sitting in the living room of their Cape Cod in Little Canada, his mother in the kitchen or putzing in the garden. In the evenings his parents had always been together, his father's head on his mother's lap on the couch, and she making her gentle outpouring of thoughts and feelings for the day while he listened. That was how they never lost track of each other. As simple and profound as that. How could one exist without the other? So it was natural that he, the son who had grown up witnessing that, had to adjust to a change of environment now, just like his father did.

But there *was* something different about the farmhouse today, some shade or texture. Denny swung around in a tight turn just short of the willow, whose nesting birds had taught him their range. As he got out of the car his gaze went to Paavo Seppanen. He had long since concluded that maintenance was one of Paavo's live-in duties, and the burly Finn was leaning wearily on the porch in long sleeves and bib overalls. The front door banged then and Beverly took two steps out, read in his expression that he had forgotten her cigarettes, turned back.

"Do you like filters?" he called lamely.

She put a hand to her hip and swung around not unlike Quasimodo. "They all have filters these days, unless you want to bring me a joint. Which is fine with me. I'm going to smoke my girdle if I don't find something illegal for my nerves."

"Sorry—"

"Oh, don't be sorry. I don't stand here at the door just waiting for you, you know. Standing there, listening to an old man spit"—she glanced at Paavo in disgust—"and Ruta prattling on about her nightmares. Why should I want to smoke? What I need is a drink. Bring me a five-gallon drum of schnapps and I'll give you a drum roll when you drive up."

"Sorry . . ." he repeated.

She saw that he was; waved her hand fussily. "Don't mind me. I'm a little nervous, that's all. I'll kill Ruta before nightfall, and then they'll put me in jail where you can buy anything you want."

Denny smiled to the side, and that was when he saw it: the chicken wire over the ground-floor windows. That was what had changed the light hitting the house as he came up the drive. And next to Paavo was a hammer and a coffee tin full of nails. He gave Paavo a flicker of a smile as he gestured toward the windows.

"Birds," Paavo explained, punctuating this with a throat-clearing cough and a glance at Beverly.

"Birds," Denny repeated and couldn't bring himself to break the poetry of that taciturn elucidation by asking him to elaborate.

He found his father curled up on the bed in his room, facing the window. Despite the heat, the old man was wearing a sweater. His left slipper was still on, the other floating in the folds of a thin green blanket.

"You awake, Dad?"

"Huh?" Martin rolled a quarter turn. "Oh." He rolled back, right hand pillowing his cheek. "Good to see you, son."

"Sleepy?"

"Just lazy."

"Not you, old guy. You've done enough in your life to qualify for the Goldbricking Anytime program."

"Hmm."

"Want your radio on?"

"No."

"I should bring your TV, but you never watched it at . . . you never watched it. Do you want me to bring it?"

"Want what?" He rolled onto his back, folded his hands on his chest.

"Your TV."

"No."

The commercials threw his concentration, Denny knew. He couldn't re-engage the story lines by the time they came back on. Maybe he had trouble seeing too.

"I don't see your glasses, Dad. Ah. Here they are. I'll put 'em right here on the nightstand."

"What is this place?"

"It's called Kenyon New Eden Assisted Living." He went through the litany again, explaining everything as he did at least once a visit, until his words stopped registering. "How's the food?"

"I don't remember."

"Well, I see a tray here. You must have room service whipped into shape, eh? Maybe you'd like to go eat with the others more. Get to know them."

"They're all women here."

"Mostly."

"Beth is dead, isn't she?"

"Yeah."

"That's where I should be."

"You've got a contract to live."

"A contract with who?"

"With God. With me."

"Hmm. Says you. I'm tired of waiting. It doesn't seem fair that everyone else is gone but me."

"Maybe there's a purpose for you being here."

"What purpose?"

"Maybe there's something you have to do. Maybe just be happy with life. Then God will take you home."

"I don't know if I believe in God. Bunch of ghosts floating around. Where would they all fit?"

"Mom believed in God."

"Hmm."

"What's that you've got in bed with you?"

The old man lifted his head, looked where Denny was fussing with the covers. Something bright red was nestled on either side of him. Bright red and shiny and—

"Fire extinguishers. Now where did you get those?"

They were the small household kind. Denny thought he had seen one of them in the kitchen. His father was genuinely bewildered.

"I don't know."

"You expecting a fire?"

"Yeah, I guess I am."

"Kidde. Good fire extinguishers, Pop. You steal the best."

"Hmm."

"You need a haircut, old guy. Can't let you go on growing hair faster than me."

"Hmm."

"I don't think they do that here, so I'll just have to bring some cigarettes—I mean, scissors. Now's my chance to turn you into a skinhead."

"Your mother's dead, isn't she?"

"Yeah. Yeah, she's dead. She was a great lady, and she lived her life, and you had all there was of it, and someday you'll be together again."

"I hope so." The poignancy of that wish squeezed his words as dry as a whispered prayer and seemed to penetrate the torpor. For a moment he was lucid again. "She was the best thing that ever happened to me. I loved her because her idea of romance was giving, not getting. You don't see that anymore. These women nowadays—their idea of romance is a man giving to them."

"Tell me about it."

"It's a two-way street."

"Yeah. When a woman gives to a man—afterward, that's called rape."

His father strained to bring him into focus. "Well . . . they're not all like that, Denny. There's some good ones out there."

"I keep looking."

"You aren't married, are you?" Starting to lose it again.

"No."

After a minute Denny reached out to lift the fire extinguishers. "I'd better put these back."

"Why?"

"They belong somewhere else, Dad."

"What about your sister? There might be a fire."

The forever fire, burning since 1956. Denny had been there. Whenever he smelled damp soot wafting out of a fireplace, smoke seared his six-year-old throat again. Why had his father looked for him first and carried him down the smoky staircase out of the house—because he was the youngest? Is that why Tiffany had to wait? His father had saved Tiffany too; saved her for operations and skin grafts and the disasters of her social life and ultimate damnation.

Denny let the old man hug his fire extinguishers. He sat by the bed until his father's eyes closed and the lids began to pulse and the bewhiskered jaw dropped slightly. Then he gently slid the red cylinders out from the thin green blanket and bore them back to their places. He found a bracket on the wall in the annex corridor, so he left one there, but when he took the other into the kitchen, there was Dana Novicki.

Waggling the extinguisher, he shook his head and gave her a crooked smile. "Besides having a killer right hook, Daddy's a kleptomaniac."

"That's better than a pyromaniac."

"Much better. I looked for you the other day. You were going to turn me down for lunch."

"Was I? It's just so . . . hard to get away. I don't like to leave here."

"Don't like to, or can't?"

The color in her cheeks flushed quarter-size and her slate blue eyes went flat.

"No one seems to go out around here," Denny said. "Beverly is getting ready to hijack passing cars for cigarettes. Is that a rule or something? Everyone has to stay down on the farm? Ariel told me no one ever took trips from here. She didn't say they couldn't."

"I wouldn't call it a rule. Ariel doesn't like to make things formal like that. But no one wants to disappoint her. She . . . created this place. She brought us together."

"Not to mention she's strong willed."

"Not to mention."

"So no one wants to cross her."

Dana averted her eyes. He saw that the redness where his old man had poked her was nearly gone.

"We're different here," she said. "Your father is the first one to come in the way he did."

"What way is that?"

"Not someone Ariel knew."

"So it's strictly by invitation only?"

"Yes. Invitation only. Everyone was surprised she let you in."

"I put a little pressure on her, and I met her price."

"Pressure?"

"You seem like such a closed shop, I'm sure she doesn't want anyone raising hell with the regulatory agencies. She must get tax considerations for being an assisted-living facility, and I don't know how much beyond that you've been scrutinized, so I fished in those waters a little. But going into town isn't big in my father's priorities, and I'm not going to rock the boat. The other places I saw were nightmares. This place is almost normal, in an abnormal sort of way."

"Good advice, Denny—about not rocking the boat. I hope for your father's sake you mean it."

"For my father's sake?"

"I shouldn't have said it that way. Now you think your father might be mistreated. I just mean there are circumstances that are unique to the people here. You don't have to know what I'm talking about. You just have to accept that your father won't ever fit them." She began shelving dishes from the rack in the sink.

"This just gets curioser and curioser. Which way to the Mad Hatter's tea party?"

"Well, Ariel may act like the Queen of Hearts sometimes, but that doesn't mean she should be taken lightly. Far from it. Like I said, we all knew one another before we . . . came here. We went through a lot together. The Great Depression, the wars—everything since. So we're like an extended family."

"Mother Leppa and her ancient children. Not you, of course. You can't be old enough to remember the Depression."

The laugh reached the surface this time, and the quarter-size splotches on her cheeks spread to a glow. "A woman doesn't tell her age, thank you."

"Well, whether or not you're too old for me or I'm too old for you, we still should do lunch."

    She tossed her hair coquettishly. "Why don't we make
it a picnic?"
    "Done! I've got a blanket in the car."
    "Whoa, whoa—not today."
    "When?"
    "In a week or two."
    "You expecting a long rain?"
    "It's buggy out."
    "Buggy? Does this have something to do with the
chicken wire on the windows? You must have some terribly big insects, if it does. Paavo said it was birds."
    She gave him a long patronizing look.
    "Okay," he surrendered. "Next week. Next month.
Anytime. Surprise me. Do you know where this fire extinguisher goes? And I'm glad your eye didn't swell up."

He went to speak to Ariel then, and he did it in the
wrong way, because he marched right up the staircase
where he had seen her go, calling as he went, thinking it
would be all right—that she had an office or something,
or at least that she would come out of one of the rooms
when she heard him. But when he reached the third
floor, the only thing that came out of a room was the
wheelchair that suddenly cut him off.
    The man who towered out of the chair looked like he
had been wedged into it. He had a massive mane of hair,
thick features and big, doughy white fingers that fumbled with the armrests. His lips were cracked and dried,
and flakes of skin clung to several days' growth of
beard. Only his huge eyes seemed to contain moisture,
and they were soulful lakes tinged red, as if something
molten churned in their depths. "Who are you?" he
wheezed leadenly from papery lungs.
    "Denny Bryce. My father lives here. Who are you?"
    "Oh. That one. You should get him out."

"Why?"

He tried to lean toward Denny as if to speak confidingly but only succeeded in tilting his shaggy head. "Get the hell out of here, if you want to stay healthy."

Denny pursed his lips. "Why is that? This place seems pretty healthy to me for an old-age home."

"It isn't an old-age home."

"No?"

"It's a nursery."

"A nursery?"

"These people were all dead. I was dead."

Third-floor dementia ward, Denny was thinking, despite what Ariel had led him to believe. He wondered if his father might eventually be brought up here. "Well, I'm glad to see you're alive now."

"You think I don't know how lunatic that sounds?" thudded back through the wheelchair man's crusted lips. "I'm telling you, we've all been brought back."

"From . . . the grave?"

He seemed to deflate a little then, breathing an affirmative with such sibilant horror that for a moment Denny Bryce wondered how real his nightmares were. This abject being believed what he was saying. Suddenly the man jerked a quarter turn in the chair and grew so rigid that he could have been having a seizure. Tortured cats, cornered dogs, looked like that. Breathing faucally, his eyes transfixed and slightly averted, it only gradually dawned on Denny that the pitiful wretch was reacting to something behind him.

"Well, I see you've met Thomas," Ariel Leppa said. "Isn't he interesting? I've been trying for almost a year now to get him to tell me what it was like to be dead. Sometimes he talks about burying himself. I think they call it delusional psychosis—or some term I can never get straight." Her mellifluous tone suddenly went flat as she warned: "He stays up here because he frightens everyone. And *they* stay downstairs."

Denny took a deep breath he didn't know he had been missing. "I didn't realize this is off-limits up here. I couldn't find Molly, and I wanted to talk to you."

She gazed at him coldly. "Will you excuse us, Thomas? I'll come see you later. Then maybe we'll re-bury you together. . . ."

Her words galvanized the helpless giant to desperation. "It's a nursery . . ." he shouted as Ariel led Denny down the hall. "A nursery!"

Ariel closed the door behind them in what was obviously a sewing room, complete with a disused spinning wheel and a slightly more recent Singer treadle machine. "This is why I told you that visitors to New Eden are unsettling, Mr. Bryce. If you insist on coming here to see your father, please keep to the lower level."

"Understood."

"Good. Now what did you want to talk to me about?"

"A phone. I'd like my father to have a phone in his room. I'll pay for the installation and the bills, of course."

The icy look of assessment was back, and he saw that this request too was an intrusion on her space.

"I don't think that will work out."

"Why not?"

"No one here has a phone in his room. I tried to explain to you when you insisted you wanted your father to live here that we were different. By any measure, we're isolated. But you said your father would fit in. 'A sanctuary,' I believe you said was what he needed. No stimulation, no interventions. He just needed to be left alone—isn't that right?"

"Right. But I'm not talking about stimulation. If he had a phone, he would only talk to me, and only when I call. I haven't seen him dial a phone for three years. He gets frustrated with the buttons."

"Then it's your need for a phone, not his, and you're not a resident here. I'm afraid I'm going to say no."

"It might mean I wouldn't have to come as often."

He had no intention of cutting back on his visits, and she wasn't fooled. "Nevertheless, no," she said. "It would make the others resentful. Really, Mr. Bryce, you must let me make the choices that will be in our best long-term interests, even if they seem unreasonable to you."

"I'm astonished . . ."

She stared down her hawk nose at him, refusing to be provoked.

Almost vindictively he switched gears. "Unreasonable seems too mild a word. Are you having a problem with birds and oversize insects?"

"Come again?"

"The chicken wire on the windows."

She paled a shade. "I believe you told me on your first visit: your father tends to wander."

"That's true, but I don't think he could work his way out a window. And I didn't notice any double-cylinder dead bolts on your doors."

"—then there's Thomas."

"In his wheelchair on the third floor?"

"You don't know all the residents here, Mr. Bryce. Your father isn't the only one who gets confused."

"But you told me you didn't accept dementia patients."

"I accepted your father." Her cold calculation ebbed a bit, as if she were making a decision. The supercilious tilt of her gaze suddenly lowered, and her clear eyes met his straight on. "Mr. Bryce, we do some miraculous things here—*miraculous*. I told you there haven't been any serious illnesses in New Eden—nothing that wasn't addressed—and we've never had a death."

"You're a small population. Naturally I hope that continues as long as humanly possible, but—"

"Oh, it will. Even longer than humanly possible."

He smiled thinly. "It's the water, I suppose. Look, I'm not unhappy with anything. I wouldn't have fought to get him in here if I didn't think it was better than his other options. I just want a phone for my dad. If that's a big problem, okay. It's not a hill I'm going to die on."

"Wouldn't you like your father to become healthier, younger even?"

"That's not going to happen."

"Oh, I don't know. A lot of aging is a state of mind, and that's what I control here."

He didn't try to answer that. She was more than an odd bird, and now she was showing her flightiness. People had a statistical success at something and right away it validated everything they ever did or thought. She thought she had all the answers, the magic beans, just because her little island was healthy. Wait till the first one fell facedown into the mushroom soup. It could set a trend. A couple cases of terminal flu in the same month and her salubrious outpost would be quarantined. Then see what a sage she was. But why burst her bubble?

"I couldn't help but notice that picture of your father when he was young," she was saying. "A Navy photograph, isn't it? My father was in the service, but I never had his photo. How I wish I did. Such a handsome man—your father—and his character is written all over his face. You must love that picture, or you wouldn't have carted it out here and hung it on his wall."

"As a matter of fact, I do."

"Well, then, wouldn't you like him to look like that picture again?"

He wanted to say "Sure," but she seemed more than just a basket case of excess optimism now. A little frightening, in fact, and he didn't want to explore how unbalanced she might be, didn't want to doubt her to the point where he had to rethink everything. She had made him promise that his father would stay here for life, if she let him in, and even though he had taken that with a large grain of salt, it was another hill he wasn't prepared to die on right now. So he didn't say, *Sure, I'd like my father to look just like that photo. Dose him with your magic well water and we'll watch the years peel away. And while you're at it, you could use a little de-aging yourself, if you don't mind my saying.* What he said was: "I just want him to stay the same."

"The same," she repeated, as though it were the saddest thing in the world. "'Same' makes death inevitable, doesn't it?"

"My father wants to die. I wish I could change that, but I can't. Everything around him has died or changed. Even if you could make him younger, you couldn't bring back that context. I just want him to be safe, comfortable and respected as a viable human being. He's not going to roll beach balls on the floor with a bunch of human artifacts sitting in a circle of chairs." He waved a retraction. "I didn't mean it that way."

"Oh, but you say it so well. The whole idea of New Eden is to get 'the context' back. Especially the context. We have no beach balls here, Mr. Bryce. You know that. We just . . . become as young as we like."

She seemed to be expecting him to say something, but he thanked her for her time. "Sorry for intruding up here in this part of the house," he added.

"That's your problem, you know," she called after him. "Making your father's death inevitable. You should stay away from him, if you feel that way. Let him go."

She was right, he thought when he was back on the solitary road, passing the long undulating waves of heart-shaped ivy. He was making his father's death inevitable because he was losing the battle to give him the will to live. It might have been different if they could have kept their lives together in the gingerbread cottage in Little Canada. If Denny could have continued like that. His mother had kept the old man going for years. The Freudian totality: mother-mistress. A lifetime of being the maternal consolation for the murder of his father's mother. And his father in turn had "kept her"— with apologies to Mary Chapin Carpenter. He had kept her the way she had wanted to be kept. If she had wanted it otherwise, he would not have opposed that. But however much they may have had to work at it, in the end they had just the right temperament for each other. He secured her. She created brightness just by being there. *I loved her because her idea of romance was giving, not getting.* How could you not keep living for that? And if she hadn't been killed in the car accident . . .

Well, we all die, thought Denny Bryce wearily. The gray regina of New Eden couldn't make death avoidable, despite what she believed. She could not be the sovereign of their souls, no matter how much she wished to be. And surely there were inner deaths that occurred while outward bodies yet survived.

12

"Haven't I made you the youngest?"

"Yes, but—"

"Why do you think I did that?"

"Because . . . because I was never cruel to you."

"And . . . ?"

"I don't know."

"And because I trust you, Dana. I *can* trust you, can't I?"

"Yes. Of course."

"Look at me, then. That's better. I know you've been talking to him. He has a certain boyish charm. I'm not asking you not to be friends with him. I'm just asking you to take his picture. Simple. Click . . . flash. That's all. It doesn't mean you're betraying his friendship. On the contrary, you're keeping faith with me."

"But . . . what will I tell him?"

"Tell him? Tell him I asked you to. Tell him you're my official photographer. That's true, isn't it? I want pictures of everything. He comes here every day. Surprise him."

Surprise me.

That's what Denny Bryce had said to her about pick-

ing a time for their picnic. But Dana Novicki felt hollow
and cold when she took the camera from Ariel and
started downstairs in the early hours of the night. Because she knew what Ariel used photos for. Knew any
photo she took would end up with the others. A surrogate
death row of images, waiting on appeal. Thumbs up;
thumbs down. Denny Bryce would be under that thumb,
then, like all the rest of them. No longer a threat to the
mistress of New Eden, but threatened by her.

But by the time Dana Claire Novicki reached the foot
of the long staircase it all became a moot point. Because
now she sensed something that eroded the thin plain of
existence she had returned to. Something that immediately froze her blood, suspended her rhythms, cleaved
emotions from her mind, flat-lining all the gentilities and
subordinate dramas of relationships on earth. The core
being within her contracted like a membrane—knotting
into a root essence as dense as a neutron star, excluding
light, shutting out any purpose but survival. It was as
though she had suddenly been returned to an obscene
flight of rodents, clawing over one another in the deepest
midnight rush up the walls of a flooding cellar to avoid
extinction. *And she was one of them. Fiery eyed, shrieking.* How could she have forgotten that? Only a year removed from the grave, and she had smothered the
memory.

But now the gulf was opening around her again, ex-
haling the dreaded stench of compounding decay while
receding into the horizonless vastness from which she
had been summoned by Ariel Leppa. She knew why it
was there. What it meant at this moment. It had opened,
like an overgrown gateway that is always present but
never quite discerned, to let something in. Something
new—or rather very ancient—had arrived from outer
realms. A corrupted thing. A wild malevolence escaped

from limbo. Here now. Physically *here* in this house, this night.

She turned slowly on the bottom step, breathing shallow breaths that sounded like katabatic booms across the Arctic, aware that her human essence was emanating like a feast to the other's numberless senses, and that it was homing in on every atom of her being in ways she could not prevent. But where was it exactly? Beyond the archway through the parlor, or lurking in the one leading to the old school wing? And what exactly was it like? Did it have leathery wings, stiletto claws?

"Amber . . ." she whispered involuntarily.

Because that must be how the vessel was created. The child painting things that didn't exist—had never existed—and therefore were just empty husks inhabitable by whatever desperate and raptorial anima broke in. A very deviant atman, this one. Something from the cosmic pit itself. A sediment, a residue of merciless passions that had swirled together like sewage, growing denser and more potent until the apprehension of its very vileness became toxic.

Dana Novicki edged off the step, feeling the late night air with raised hands as if it were palpable. To her right, she thought. And then again, maybe to her left. Could there be two? No. One powerful source. And it was on the left. Somewhere in the shadows that vaulted beyond the arch leading toward the added wing it was feeling her mortal warmth, just as she was feeling its alien chill.

Ariel had shepherded spirits to life as carefully as the unknown God of the universe itself. But Amber—what had she put together? The hints they had gotten the other night from the commotion on the roof and certain disturbing silhouettes in the fields had been all too familiar to the others, Dana was sure. Amalgams of the dead . . . composite corpses . . . banshee wails . . . nails scratching

on glass—fragments of a latent nightmare, the things
that had never been spoken of out of fear that they might
actually exist. But everyone who had come back knew;
everyone was one illusion away from the same sup-
pressed horrors.

She was one step into the dining room when she saw
it rise up. A baleful eye, crimson in the moonlight, and a
scar for a mouth, glistening wet with appetite. Its feet
moved—feet should not move like that. Half padding,
half clattering. Stentorian breaths heaving in cavities ter-
restrial morphologies did not possess. A satyr. A manti-
core. One part child-driven. The rest self-defined by the
intensity of its needs. Crashing into evolution. Gnashing
and shredding its way into the food chain. And the smell.
Worse than the suppurating rot that clung to Dana
Novicki's indelible nightmare, because it also bore the
pungency of its predator flesh. Rancid sweat, fetid
breath, carnal traces of its nesting among recent kills.
And if it had eaten, it knew how to hunt.

A great bowel-wrenching wave of fear swept over
Dana. The specter of returning to where she and this
feral entity had come from struck her with such violence
that she voided her bladder and began to regurgitate. Her
legs shook and started to fold like twists of paper; chill
sweat poured down her sides and sprang from her brow.
For a moment she wished for the shore beyond extinction. She did not want to hold on to her identity in the
face of such bone-pulverizing terror. Better to surrender.
Better to be torn asunder. To live with integrity of form
was to endure pain. To be cast upon the tsunami of un-
differentiated atoms that swept across the universe was
welcome.

But when the "it" uncoiled, raging from the darkness,
she instantly melded into a single force. Her calves
firmed, her ankles tensed as she launched herself into the

parlor, scrambling over the ottoman, around the morris chair, feeling her options narrow by slices as the thing cut off one direction, then another. Finally she shrank back and tried to look away as something loomed red in the moonlight through the window. She did not want to see it reared up at the penultimate moment before it struck. But its triumphant howl was inescapable: a maniacal, unbridled chord from multiple structures in its throat, splitting the air like some saurian bleat in a Mesozoic bog. And that bodeful sound seemed to acquaint her with every detail of its anatomy, as if it were already feeding voraciously on her flesh and a part of her, still conscious, was sinking through its maw.

In the wake of the howl, which must have shaken the house to its foundation, Dana Novicki grasped her bearings. The nearest door with a lock was the bathroom across from Amber's bedroom and behind her. A brass floor lamp with a marble base stood on her left, too heavy to heft as a weapon but a potential obstacle to use. Inching toward it, she placed one outstretched hand on its column just as the measured crepitations in the throat of her besieger turned into a hiss. As if the brass had turned blistering hot, she flung it down in a shower of sparks and jumped for the narrow darkness of the corridor.

The red stalker hurdled the lamp with ease but balked as she yanked the picture frame from the wall for a shield. It had the wariness of something that knew terrors greater than itself, and Dana took heart. Turning the painting of the Garden of Eden like a cigarette girl's tray in front of her, she fended it off as it dogged her step by step—a macabre samba of retreat and advance. Giving ground a foot at a time, she fell back into the corridor and abreast of the bathroom. *If only the door were open!*

But it wasn't.

It was closed, and God help anyone locked inside. She wanted to call out, but anything that broke the fragile equilibrium that was holding off the final lunge was going to be her last maneuver. So she swung the painting end to end like a great clumsy scythe and sprang for the door. The knob turned in her hand and then she was inside, slamming it shut, fumbling for the lock. It hit the panels with a roar of outrage, and the frame reverberated with a disquieting crack. She found the metal crescent that stuck out from the lock plate, twisting it against some impediment, unsure even if the bolt was still lined up with the recess. And then she sank down on the floor, surrendering in utter despair to whatever came next . . .

13

It was Paavo who incurred the wrath of the helldog. Paavo Seppanen, who had his own festering cesspit of obscene and blasphemous horrors. And it was he who inadvertently saved Dana Novicki, because he heard the bloodcurdling howl that resonated the very wallpaper of the room he shared with his wife, Ruta, and the Corybantic frenzy of flailing nails and thuds as the chase ensued, and almost against his will he swung his feet from the bed to the floor.

"Don't go out there!" Ruta warned him. She sat ramrod straight in bed, her hands pressed into the mattress, wearing a hairnet and looking oddly masculine without her makeup.

But of course Paavo did. There was no other male in the house capable of playing that role, and while his might be a mere intrepid gesture, peeking around the doorsill and then around the corner at the end of the hall, and from there to the dining room arch, and from there . . . well, by that time it was too late to outrun the thing. Never mind that his wife had leaped from their bed like a flea and locked the bedroom door behind him. There was no going back.

It smelled him before it turned. And Paavo knew, as

Dana had, that this was an anomaly from beyond known borders, a demiurge that had seized an empty form created in a Cartesian world. It had allegiances to neither laws nor species, and it would kill him. He wished he had not seen its eye. A flat disk with a misshapen red orb—red, like everything else about it. But he did see it, and he couldn't tear himself away from its cartoonlike simplicity. Its snout made vermicular contractions, pivoting like a perforated thumb in his direction, and after that something dropped open that must have been its jaws—slavering tissued things, badly formed and serrated. Even from that distance Paavo caught the rankness of half-digested prey from its gullet.

Its foreclaws, which were caught in the upper panel of the bathroom door, released then. It dropped into shadow, and that is when Paavo banged backward into the arch while turning to flee. By the time he stumbled into the resident corridor he was babbling, because the entire fugue of death was back, and he knew he was untethered, knew that like this chimera breathing down his neck he would seize any crag in the storm of life. That much he remembered on the border of chaos and disorder.

He banged on the door of his bedroom, but the only response was Ruta's sobbing. And he couldn't articulate the obvious, that she must open the door to save him, but instead went to the next door and the next. And the brute just played the same game it had played with Dana, advancing when he retreated, as if exploring the bloodlust of anticipation. And when Paavo reached the last door and his last bit of futile mewling, he turned to face it square on.

So it came at him, throat-straight, hitting him with gaping jaws and closing over him like a red canopy.

* * *

The screams etched every nerve from cellar to roof. Ariel heard them. Amber heard them. Molly and Dana and Helen and Marjorie and Martin and Beverly and Thomas and Kraft and Danielle and Ruta heard them. And except for Dana, who huddled on the bathroom floor, they remained on their beds as they had their cradles and their catafalques, mousy-eyed, understanding that one of the others was going down.

Only Ariel had the courage to rise up after a minute or so and go to her door and open it. She knew the carnage was related to whatever Amber had unleashed. It couldn't be ignored if they were to survive. So down she came, cautiously but imperiously too, because she really was the creator of New Eden. A year ago the farm had lain fallow, and now everything living owed its vitality to her. What breath there was under its roof she had quickened. This was a blasphemy against her creation, a transgression against her will.

It was eerily silent on the first floor. One by one she flicked on lights, revealing overturned furniture and the milk glass bowl of the brass floor lamp, broken in large pieces. The shade had torn so cleanly that it was unfolded like a scroll, and the painting of the Garden of Eden lay facedown on the parlor rug. With her cane she raised the frame to lean against the wall. She hesitated before Amber's closed door. Maybe it was good to leave her in there. It wasn't her daughter who had screamed, and a little prolonged anxiety over what was happening outside her door might make Amber more cooperative about returning the stolen paint. And then she heard faint weeping from across the hall.

"Dana?"

"Is it gone?"

Ariel tried the bathroom door. "Yes. Come out, Dana."

"I can't. Bring me some clothes—my bathrobe . . ."

But it was going to be a while before that detail was remembered, because when Ariel reached the residents' corridor, the blood trail began. A splash of it on the wall, a ghastly handprint on Beverly Swanson's door, and beyond that an unbroken chain of dribbles and smears on the floor tiles leading to the double windows at the end. Against the darkness she couldn't quite see that the glass was smashed, but the air flowing down the corridor was heavy with the smell of the fields and the woods. So the unholy thing had come in and probably gone out that way. Paavo's chicken wire had been a joke. Ariel rapped softly on the doors as she moved closer and closer to the shattered glass: *Come out, come out, little people, wherever you are. . . . It's all right . . . the Wicked Witch of the East is gone.* And so they crept out, bent and trembling, to take a census and determine who it was they had not tried to save. Only Ruta and Martin remained in their rooms, she refusing to unlock her door, he sitting in his undershorts on the edge of his bed, holding his shoe like a blackjack.

"It sounded like Paavo," white-faced Helen said.

That prompted Ariel to knock forcefully on Ruta's door. Hysteria erupted. She had told Paavo not to leave the room, Ruta wailed. It was impossible that her lament could have carried very far—certainly not past the corridor—but suddenly from the heart of darkness beyond the broken window Paavo's thin moan quavered. It went on for an intolerable time, and when it finally subsided, leaving a shocked silence, Helen said:

"It's playing with its food."

Ruta's door lock snapped open and she rushed forth, straight at Ariel, where she dropped like a stone to her knees.

"That's him, that's him! He's still alive. Make it stop!"

"Ruta—"

"Make it stop, *please*!"

"Ruta, I can't. If it overpowered Paavo, then how can I—"

"No, no. Not it. *Him*!"

A consensus of pleading looks came to rest on Ariel. Stop Paavo, Ruta meant. Make his suffering stop. A petition fit for a deity.

For just a moment Ariel Leppa looked like the inadequate rag of a woman they had taken her for throughout their mortal lives. Her lips pulsed, her eyes dulled, her fingertips slid nervously in the folds of her robe. But there were no dismissive looks from the major players of her life now, no sly confirmations of her inferior status. This was the moment she had fantasized, the one they had robbed her of by dying.

Another scream from the darkness, ending in a gurgle more pain than terror.

"It's eating him," Beverly whispered.

And then Martin Bryce appeared in his doorway, breathless and clutching his shoe. "They must have found Japanese money in his pockets," he said, shuffling toward the broken windows.

Gripping her cane like a baton, Ariel hastened to her studio while the others shrank back into their rooms like mollusks into their shells. Frantically she tossed Paavo's portrait flat on the workbench. With one pop she had the lid off a can of ordinary, nonmagic white paint and, without stirring, she poured directly onto the canvas. No need for this to dry. Underneath, the dust-impregnated vehicle for life was obliterated. Downstairs, Martin Bryce sidled gingerly among shards of broken glass, futilely attempting to climb out the broken window. Not many yards away in the darkness Paavo Seppanen's shrieks abruptly ceased.

*   *   *

At dawn, when nothing was sighted from the sewing room window save tattered clothing and dark stains in the dust of the yard, Molly and Dana went out with pitchforks. They went as far as the woods, probing along the brush and also the ditch by the road. And when they started back toward the house, they met something that churned the stark horror of the last ten hours all over again while resonating an uncertain joy. It was Paavo himself. On his feet and walking toward them.

"Paavo?" Molly called, raising the pitchfork a little.

He was unhurt, unmarked even. No blood whatsoever.

"She's painted him again," Dana warned.

And she had. Ariel had fretted only a minute or two after painting out the canvas the night before. Then she had pulled out a fresh frame and gotten the photo of Paavo and taped it to the top of her easel. For all she knew, there would be two of them on the farm when she finished—one dead, one living. And what if the first one somehow survived? That would be novel. Paavo Seppanens on either side of the dinner table. She would have to tell that fool of a son of Martin Bryce that Paavo had a twin.

But, of course, the first one was beyond reanimation. Whatever was left of him had ceased to exist when she slashed white paint across his portrait. She was all but sure of this. It wasn't like Amber, who had been born in the natural way. The inhabitants of New Eden were all extensions of what she had done with red dust and paint. Adams and Eves—if the dust was indeed something from God—or whatever else that powder represented in the way of cosmic events and interventions if it wasn't. That it was her father's ashes, she had come to doubt. She had once read of extraterrestrials returning to Earth like caretakers to a garden they had planted. Perhaps the red dust was their seedbed . . .

So the third Paavo came upon the earth, and he knew
nothing of the second, though he remembered the first
one, his natural life, which had come to a natural end.
The mechanics were such a muddle to Ariel. She didn't
want to understand them. She just wanted to move on.
And so she told Paavo the bare minimum again: that she
had brought him back after his death from a heart attack
at age seventy. She had brought him back younger, and
he was to be "the man about the place." And then she
sent him out to help the others look for his own remains.
Let the others help him sort it out if a body turned up,
she thought. It didn't.

Later in the day, when Dana and Molly and Paavo returned together and the tenantry of New Eden was gathered, nervous and stunned in the parlor, Ariel attempted
to clear the air and instill calm.

"I know you're all upset, but you see everything is
back to where it was. As long as I'm here, there's nothing we can't recover from."

"I don't like this. . . . I don't like this," Helen kept
saying.

Ruta, quiet for once, had already discovered differences in this new Paavo and sat a little apart from him.
Kraft Olson stared rigidly at the floor, and when he
raised his head he kept Danielle Kramer as far behind
his line of sight as possible.

"No one likes it," Ariel said, "but let's not overreact."

Beverly laughed sharply. "One of us was killed. How
are we supposed to react?"

"He was not killed"—a nod at Paavo, who sat numb
and disoriented, as they all had been on their return from
the Stygian darkness—"he's right here just like he was
yesterday, and the day before, and the way he'll be tomorrow."

"We don't want to die again," murmured Marjorie.

"Even if you bring us right back, we don't want to die. You don't know what that's like, Ariel."

Ariel softened as much from the use of her name as the sentiment. "That's true," she conceded, "I don't know. And none of you will tell me."

"There's no way to tell you," said Dana, hollow-eyed and listless. "Death is everything *wrong*. It's—"

"Don't!" Marjorie said curtly.

"You brought it up."

Beverly waved a hand at them. "Let's not lose track here. This is a crisis of survival."

"I've told you, survival isn't in question!" Ariel snapped. "You should all know that. You should be grateful—why aren't you grateful? Why don't you have faith in me?"

The silence crackled with nervous restraint, fear of imminent danger in Ariel Leppa's magic fiefdom. It was Molly who ventured the delicate reply. "I think they're worried about something happening to you," she said, as if she were not herself involved. And when the trial statement hung there and Ariel merely looked neutral, she added: "What if . . . what if that thing had attacked you last night? Who would paint you back?"

"Me? My, my. Someone is worried about me. Thank you. But nothing is going to happen to me."

"Something could, Ariel," Helen said. "You can't be foolish about that. None of us could paint you back, even if we knew where . . . where things were, or how to do it. If we tried, we'd end up with something like what attacked Paavo last night."

"Maybe I'll paint myself back when I'm on my deathbed. Maybe I'll leave you a number painting, and all you'll have to do is put the colors in." They were listening very hard, she noticed. "So you don't have to worry about me being around to keep you healthy."

"If you even *want* to keep us healthy," murmured Ruta.

A tactless thing to say, and they held their collective breath for Ariel's reply.

"That's so. 'If I want to.' That's the premise, isn't it? Even though I've given each of you the ultimate gift of life when you were dead, you still want more—a guarantee, a warranty on your bodies and your health. As if I owe you that. But I had nothing to do with your deaths, did I? You lived just fine without me in the only lives you thought you'd ever have. And now, instead of being sorry or grateful or trusting me, you want some kind of contract. Well, there isn't any. Just our feelings for each other. Our *sincere* feelings."

"You had something to do with my death," a small voice contradicted her. Amber, who had been sitting sullenly on the floor near the arch, looked surprised by her own outburst.

"You were paralyzed and living in misery. I made you better."

"You could make us all better," Ruta said.

"I could. I may. Or I may not. What would you do, Ruta, if you were a young woman again? Run off to the city like you did before? Whore it up for a few years? Yes, yes, I know, I'm just the dried-up old crone who never got her chance for a little fun, but some of us aren't equipped to get that chance. It's a superficial world, and we can't all be Danielles or Rutas, can we? Anyway, here we are in the encore, and all that matters is what we are inside. Make you *better*, Ruta? What could be better than this?"

The look of helpless agony became unanimous.

Off to one side Beverly stared poutily out the window. She rubbed the age spots on her hands. "What good is virtue untested?"

"No good at all." Ariel took a step toward her that seemed to re-center the room. "But it does keep the status quo for the time being. I'm not saying we'll stay like this forever. Forever is a long time. It's amazing how much paint I can manufacture, but it won't last forever. So virtue will get its acid test sooner or later. But for now we don't have a choice. We can't have our little situation here—our immortalities—if we're exposed before the rest of the world. We all know that. As soon as past paths cross or attention is focused on us, it will be just a matter of time before we're exploited by thieves or desperate people looking for the fountain of youth. Do you think I haven't thought about this? We might even be quarantined by the government in the name of science or national welfare or some damn thing yet to be invented. *But* . . . if we wait, maybe there will come a time when it can be different. When all the people who knew us have passed away. When we can move a little more freely. I haven't decided yet. It depends. But we've got all the time in the world."

". . . All the time in the world," Molly echoed vacantly. "Would you paint our children back, then?"

"I don't like this." Helen returned to her refrain. "Why are we talking about the future? We could all be dead in the next attack."

"I wish you wouldn't frighten everyone," Ariel said sternly. "Everyone is alive and healthy. That's all that matters. This little problem will get solved one way or another, and we'll still be alive and healthy."

"Little problem. You make it sound like all we have to do is call up Orkin. How is it going to get solved? Is your daughter going to get rid of them?"

Something in the light glazing across the painting of the Garden of Eden that still leaned against the wall troubled Ariel's eye. "Amber says she doesn't know where her paintings went."

"I told you, it was rainy and windy and I couldn't find anything," Amber said, scowling.

"Yes, you did." *What was wrong with that painting?*

Amber scrambled to her feet. "I don't care if you all hate me. I don't care. I didn't mean for anything to happen, and you just need someone to blame, so go ahead. That's all you do anyway—sit around and blame people."

"Amber—" Helen started to apologize, but a moment later the bedroom door slammed.

"At least she didn't call us 'beluga butts,'" Beverly said.

Ariel saw now what it was about the painting that bothered her. The paint had flecked off where the serpent was. How could that be? Either someone had scraped it off or the paint there had been different, drying and not bonding, or . . . or what? She wanted to drop down and scrutinize it, but she was talking about how everyone should just keep their cool here in New Eden and so she couldn't let them see her agitation, couldn't let them know her unreasoned fear—*because she hated snakes with a passion!* Ariel Leppa had an absolutely irrational terror of things that crawled or slithered. That, as much as anything else, was why she carried a cane: to fend off loathsome vermin that scurried from a baseboard crevice or dripped from a web in the high-ceiling old farmhouse, coming to horripilating life on the back of her neck. "Everyone is alive and healthy," she repeated for the third and final time, and when she had left for her lofty inner sanctum, Helen Hoverstein remained on the ottoman, murmuring, "But we aren't alive. . . . not really . . . not when we can be rescinded like this."

14

"Say cheese."

But the flash had already gone off before Dan
warned him. If Denny Bryce could have reacted in time
he would have shielded his face from the Polaroid camera. Instead he stood blinking across the parlor, having
just entered from the white blaze of an August afternoon
that rendered the flash anticlimactic.

"I wish you hadn't done that."

"You said I should surprise you."

"Surprise me about picking a time for a picnic." He
saw that his explanation was unnecessary. She knew she
had made a lame excuse. "Is my picture so important
around here?"

"Ariel thinks so. Visual things are important to a
painter."

"Are you telling me she wants to paint me?"

She gave him a look of raw intensity he couldn't read.

"I'll pose with a rose between my teeth, if you want to
cash in on the picnic," he said.

"Not a good idea."

"The posing or the picnic?"

"Maybe both."

"Bugs bad today? I don't see the chicken wire."

"Chickens took it back."

". . . And then they flew the coop. What are you doing living in a place like this, Dana Novicki? You're young enough to live out in the world."

He had followed her into the kitchen, where she began to fuss with dishes in the drain rack. "This *is* my world."

When she turned back from the cupboard, he moved in front of the drain rack. Color rose in her cheeks. Her expression held for a long moment, knowing that if she waited his mistake would become evident to him, and hoping he wouldn't press her.

He didn't press her.

"Your father has some cuts on his feet," she said. "He stepped in some broken glass. I think we got all the slivers out."

And while he was digesting that she made some further excuse and slipped out of the kitchen. Denny stood there, gazing at the heavily lacquered cabinets and white ceramic kitchen sink. Definitely colder, he thought. And he didn't know why, but he had the arrogance to think she was trying not to like him. Something had happened since his last visit. Was it the broken glass? His father had gotten broken glass in his feet how?

Molly was on her hands and knees scrubbing the tiles when he got to the residents' corridor, and she slackened her effort at the sight of him, as if to belie that she was removing something. He saw too that the wall in one spot and one of the doors had been scrubbed.

"An accident, Molly?"

She sat back on her haunches, plump arms going limp. "Your father stepped in some glass. We got it all out of his feet, I think."

"How did he do that?"

She gestured toward the end of the corridor where a Himalayan profile of jagged glass sat in the lower window frame. He didn't ask how it had been broken, and she didn't say, but he wondered if he had underestimated Ariel's caution about his father trying to get out a window

The old man was asleep when he entered the room He sat down to wait.

Denny Bryce was acting like she was eligible, Dana thought with mixed feelings. She felt like a decoy around which a live duck was hovering. A decoy because technically she might still be married and because she was drawing him to a woman who by natural age and state of mind could have been his mother, and a decoy because the muzzle flash of the camera she had used to take his picture hid the hunter Ariel Leppa.

The Dana Novicki who had died of a brain hemorrhage more than a decade ago would be seventy-four if she had lived, she reflected. Her husband would also be seventy-four, if he was still alive. For all she knew the great state of Texas had executed him at "the Walls" for murdering his ex-employer in 1986. Probably they hadn't, though. Probably he was still in Ellis outside Huntsville, ostensibly undergoing treatment. As if he could be rehabilitated. The murder had not been premeditated—hothead that he was—so he had that going for him. She had often wished him dead in the past, and felt guilty about it, and then she had wished him dead without feeling guilty about it. Now she didn't wish anyone dead. But she didn't consider herself married anymore. She had no desire whatsoever to go back to Detroit Lakes or to see the man who had turned her into a poster wife for abuse.

Nice men like Denny Bryce didn't know how to look for a woman. He had a certain awkwardness that made him read too much into contacts with the opposite sex. At his age he must have been hurt by that mistake before, and when he made it again he would be all the more vulnerable, because he would think this time he had gotten it right. She felt guilty because she didn't want to be the one to hurt him. He must be a very decent man to care for his father like he did. But she didn't dare feel anything for him.

Trying not to feel was how she had finally brought herself to take the photo Ariel was demanding. Probably nothing would happen to Denny Bryce, she told herself. Ariel would have the power to paint him from the photo, but she wasn't likely to use it. In any case, it wasn't her concern. How could she look out for a near stranger when her own preservation was at stake?

Let him hover. A decoy wasn't capable of responding.

She slipped past Martin Bryce's slightly open door with only a glance at Denny standing over the bed. She had to check on Kraft Olson and Danielle Kramer. Between she and Molly, they took care of Kraft and Danielle and Martin when he would let them, and sometimes, when Ariel permitted it, they went upstairs and helped Thomas Leppa.

The classrooms-turned-bedrooms in this corridor were so regular and barren that they seemed like oversize cells of an abandoned hive, and the inhabitants were like ancient larva deposited there by their gray queen. But of all the rooms, Kraft's seemed the most abandoned. He never put anything on top of the dresser or the table, and there was no whiff of aftershave or toiletries from the items Ariel had purchased and placed on his window ledge. The towels remained folded just as Dana left them, and the dust was always layered fine and undisturbed. Day after day she rapped lightly and entered to find him sitting riveted to his chair by the window, invariably wearing creaseless slacks and a seasonless plaid shirt. Except that today, instead of staring blankly, his eyes bore into her with a cognizance that was unmistakable.

"Kraft?" she said, pushing the door shut.

"What was it like for you, Dana?"

"Kraft." She came forward, not knowing whether to embrace him or address the urgency of his question. "What's happened?"

"What was it like before she brought you back?"

She sank down on the edge of the bed, facing him. Never mind that he had been faking dementia. The commonality of the dead was always front and center, and you didn't segue into it. It ran like a tape, reel to reel in the background of your consciousness, playing blackness and silence, and at any moment you could be seduced by its cabalistic lure, and then the images and the shrieks would glut your mind and you would wonder how you ever got away from it. That was reality. Life, it turned out, was the background hiss.

"Like a black carnival," she replied. "All motion and roar."

No one else had ever asked her about it. That was a futility. Only Ariel had wanted to know.

"Do you think we had the same experience?"

She closed her eyes and began to rock. "I don't know."

"Dana."

Eyes up.

"I brought it back. I let it in. I painted it with my finger on the painting downstairs. The one of the Garden of Eden, with the snake—you know?"

"What are you talking about?"

Her failure to grasp his meaning transformed his expression, and she saw how unbalanced he was. Could he have been in shock all this time, and now he was coming out of it? His mouth formed a kind of rictus, a Bell's palsy, as if he were trying to flicker back from rigor to spasm to life. The trouble was that she *did* understand him. If not the words then the trauma. Because it came from the same void the past thirty-six hours had opened for all of them again.

"It stopped," he tendered up defenselessly. "The voice stopped after I painted it. What does that mean?"

She wanted to scream. She wanted to tell him that it all meant the same thing. They were headed back. Candles out! Matter away! Cease. Desist. Dissolve. Lose your identity, join the howl. Become the zero wind blowing forever through empty space, nibbling at the mammoth columns, those pillars of the universe that tower above comprehension and disappear into the darkness beyond the stars. A black wind that carries the crippled scrape of purgatory's obscene army marching, marching, marching. Soldiers of saturnalia, lunatic, gaping wounds for medals, babbling from crusted orifices. Limbs do not come off like melted cheese, striding bodies do not truncate at the waist, eyes do not catch fire and roll out of—

"I must be all right, if the voice stopped," Kraft said with final hope. "Don't you think?"

She didn't think. Couldn't think. How many hours had passed since she had lain huddled at the foot of a bathroom door, trying to restore gravity, while an inch away something with earthly claws and earthly fangs raged for her flesh? Could Ariel's magic last forever? And if it couldn't, if somewhere there was an amorphous maggot in the food chain that would suck her soul out of the frail shell and spit it out, did it all end up the same?

"I could go back there now if I wouldn't be alone," Kraft said. "If I wouldn't be alone I think I could endure it."

Go back to it? How could he say that, if it had left him

so bereft? And then she began to truly understand. It wasn't shock from coming back. It was shock from something else. Something that had just happened. "How could you be alone?" she probed. "Everyone dies."

"I don't want to be with everyone. I want to be with her."

Her? There was only one "her" for Kraft Olson. Even if her outward form was a suppurating relic. "You *are* with her, Kraft. She's here in this house."

"No." Melancholy in his voice. A lilt of things lost beyond reclaim.

Dana digested the implacable syllable and grasped for the first time what this whole Grand Guignol conducted unexpectedly in his room was all about. A wave of fresh horror tingled at her hairline. Kraft was staring blankly again as she moved to the door.

Despite the clammy heat the corridor was cold as she walked to Danielle Kramer's room. This time she didn't knock, because she didn't want to have hope or expectation. She simply turned the doorknob and pushed.

Empty cell.

No larva here. The gray queen had visited. Had killed the competing queen with a few strokes of a brush. Just the bedcovers mussed, as if Danielle had wasted away to nothing. And Kraft had known. Had she caught them together?

Damn you, Ariel Leppa.

Trembling, Dana took the Polaroid shot of Denny Bryce out of her pocket. The resolution was sharp. Plenty of detail for a skilled painter to capture a soul. How could she let that happen? *Don't be stupid, Dana. . . . This will end up being about you instead of him.* Maybe she was the duck and he was the decoy. But with agonizing slowness she tore the photograph in half, again and again, until it was just macerated paper made moist by her sweating fingers.

15

Like old wolves the core group gathered, wanting the security of the pack but untrusting and staking out territories in the parlor. Helen, Paavo, Molly on the ottoman, Marjorie in the morris chair, Beverly leaning against the screen door as if to draw in the smoky, fermented ethers of an alluring but distant civilization. Dana in the dark of the dining room just beyond the arch. And Ruta moving, pacing, wringing her hands, changing chairs each time she sat back down. It was uncharacteristic of her not to settle in the center of things, where she could broadcast her daily tribulations. They took it as a sign of her fear. Fear and distress. There was no doubt about the distress.

"I didn't think Ariel would do that," she kept repeating in disbelief. "I didn't think she would actually get rid of one of us."

"Was Danielle ever one of us?" someone posed.

This was Danielle Kramer's wake, the postmortem, the inquiry. A head wind set the willow chattering across the yard, and a jay about to be dislodged from its crown hurled its single expletive. Storm coming. They sat listening for the first large drops to patter on the windowpane, waiting for Sturm und Drang nature to haul away a soul.

"She never could handle power." The words rattled up from Marjorie's private boil like steam from a covered pot.

"Who?"

"Who do you think?"

"Better watch what you say," Helen warned.

"Why? We're all in the same boat."

Helen leaned forward slightly to glance at Molly. "But some of us have life jackets."

The big woman sat with her elbows folded across her stomach, knuckles of one hand to her lips, liquid brown eyes red rimmed. "What's that supposed to mean?"

"Figure it out."

"Just because Ariel trusts me doesn't mean I can't be trusted by you."

"Doesn't it?"

"That's cruel, Helen."

"Oh, don't pretend, Molly. You've been snitching on us forever."

Paavo sat between them like a thin tenement wall hammered by fractious neighbors.

"And what did you do for Danielle, eh? Did you toilet her? Did you wipe the drool off her chin? No. You did as little as you could, because you're *old,* and that makes you privileged."

"Want to trade places?"

"Stop it," Dana said from the gloom of the arch. "Molly did more for Danielle than the rest of us put together."

"So now we hear from the other alter ego. Beautiful Dana. Just the right age. I'm not so sure about you either, my dear."

". . . Never could handle power," Marjorie repeated from the morris chair, deaf to the squabbling. "Once I made her shift manager for two weeks, and when I got back from a training seminar in Chicago two of the cashiers had quit and another had filed a grievance with personnel. We need to do something."

It was raining, but nobody had heard it begin. The trees were hissing and the windows drummed, and they listened like balcony figures in a cavernous theater cut off from main-floor applause rising to the mezzanine.

"Like what?" Beverly said, suddenly attentive at the screen door.

"It's clear enough."

"Not for me. What do you mean, 'we need to do something'?"

Everyone looked to Marjorie except Ruta, who had migrated to the raised hearth and sat rigidly on one edge of the worn brick, staring at a gilt mirror on the opposite wall.

"Ariel won't hesitate," Marjorie said. "Any time we don't make the grade, it's brush-brush—'off with their heads!' We used to call that murder."

"But she can bring us back indefinitely," Molly said. "She can keep us healthy."

"If living like this is healthy. Personally, I don't think it's going to get better. I think it's going to get worse."

"But at least we're alive!"

"Are we? I'm a copy of something that might still be out there in the darkness. Paavo is really the only one who has come back twice, and he hasn't said where he went the second time."

The subject of this speculation shrugged. "I don't remember. I don't remember being in this house before."

"That's what I mean. You aren't a copy of a copy. You're a second copy of the original. So maybe if we die again nothing will happen to us that isn't already happening anyway. We haven't escaped anything. The people we once were lived and died and are still wherever the dead go. The people we think we are now go nowhere."

"All I know is I'm here now, and I want to stay," Molly declared.

"What are you driving at?" Helen demanded. "What choice do we have?"

"We could stop her if we wanted. We could stop Ariel."

"But then . . ."

"Then we'd live out our lives and die. Again."

"Are you out of your mind?" Ruta laughed forcibly. "You're the one who said we should change our attitudes toward her, and now you want to eliminate her and let us all die, like . . . like those stupid pygmies Helen told us about. Paavo. Tell her she's crazy."

Paavo shifted his bony haunches uncomfortably on the ottoman. "She don't mean it, Ruta. Tell her, Marj. No reason to get everyone upset." But no one looked upset.

"We'd have the paint," Beverly said, refusing to give up hope of life everlasting. "We'd just need a painter."

And that seemed to provide a middle ground for action, whatever anyone believed.

Except for Ruta.

Ruta felt life coursing in her veins. Saw her image in the smoky glass flecked with gold. Still saw the once-and-forever woman she had decided she would become when she was in her twenties. Her eyes were *not* the bloodshot, filmy pools that gazed tragically at morning misrepresentations in the mirror. Her hair was *not* a thin, brittle remnant of what she had brushed a hundred strokes a night since her progressive if not impious mother had taken her to Loews Paradise Theatre in New York to be awestruck by Greta Garbo in *Flesh and the Devil* in the year 1927. All the decades of diets and supplements and exercise did *not* add up to this bony, long-neck hag rendered in mockery by Ariel Leppa.

They all thought she was so vain, but no one had laughed when she was named Miss Thief River Falls at Harvest Fest, or when she swam the Black Duck Lake freshwater swim in fifty-eight-degree water at the age of twenty-two and only thirteen others, including eleven men, finished the race. When had she ever promised to age gracefully? Let others surrender to the ravages of time; they had less to lose. The tucks and peels were her own damn business. Paavo had never complained. And none of them had the discipline to endure what she had endured. They thought she was weak, but she was a survivor—physically, emotionally. They could keep their little intellectual games. What was wrong with taking personal pride, of wanting to live?

Thunder rolled outside, making her jump. She didn't like storms. And going upstairs to see Ariel was like going out into a storm. But she had to do it. Even though she was appalled at the way things were turning out. How could she have known that telling Ariel what she had seen would seal Danielle's fate? Kraft had gone into her room—that's all she had said to Ariel. Not that they had deliberately met. Kraft could have been wandering. But Ariel must have caught them together. Ruta felt terrible about that. If she could undo it, she would. But she couldn't be held accountable for what Ariel did. And now she had to climb the stairs on this stormy night and address the source of all thunder and lightning herself, because the Creator of New Eden had as good as made a promise to her . . .

"I'll have to repaint you, you know," Ariel said when they had ghosted to chairs in the dimly lit sewing room.

"Yes, yes, of course." Ruta's plea came in a voice that crackled like the track of a 78-rpm record.

A small banker's lamp sat on a walnut ambo in one corner, its red glass cowl tilted toward the wall, leaving the chamber in gloom and grotesquely shadowed by the rebound of light. The spinning wheel's shadow in particular soared up the opposite wall, like some diabolical engine of medieval torture. Outside lightning flickered, dogged by a subsequent rumble that seemed to climb through the foundation to rattle the windows, rattle Ruta.

"Will I have to . . . ?"

"No, you won't die. I won't be making a new painting, just touching up the old."

Out of the corner of her eye, Ruta imagined the spinning wheel slowly turning. "Then I won't disappear like . . ."

"Danielle?"

"Paavo. I was thinking of Paavo."

"No, you won't disappear like Paavo."

"Will I just suddenly change?"

"Yes." Ariel, in a condescending fantasy voice. Magician to child. "I've done it before. Little things. In the middle of the night. No one seems to notice. But when did anyone ever notice anything I did?"

An invitation to suck up and Ruta seized it. "Oh, Ariel, nothing could be further from the truth. How can you say that?"

Ariel's artless laugh crushed her disavowal flat. "You were always such a liar, Ruta."

"Ariel! I mean now. No one ignores you now. We all treated you badly in the old days."

"And you treated me the worst of all."

"I wasn't your enemy."

"No. Enemies don't have the power to hurt that deep. For that you need friends." Crocodile smile—thin lipped and crooked. "Tell me, Ruta, who came up with the name Ariel the Leper? Was it you?"

"I never heard anyone call you that, Ariel. Maybe when you were in grade school, but I wasn't there then."

"No, you showed up for the morals-and-manners phase of our lives. You navigated us through an adolescence of winners and losers. You set the pecking order, and you promoted and demoted us more often than the schools. As long as I was around everybody else was at least one rung off the ground. If you missed a social cue you could always point to me, because I missed all of them. I was your comic relief. I boosted everyone's self-esteem just by being there to catch the bones and feel the claws."

"Ariel. I'm shocked." She *was* shocked. But it was because of the attack. "We had good times. You were always included—"

"Seldom."

"You went to the same parties and shows. You went to the rinks and beaches and . . . and you never liked to dance."

"Do you know that for a fact?"

"Well . . . did you? I don't remember you ever dancing."

Ariel threw her head back as if communing with the storm above the house, and when she looked at Ruta again her eyes were misted. "Did anyone ever show me the lindy or tell me what everyone was going to wear the next day? You were the oldest; you had the last word. If there wasn't room in the car or enough boys at the drive-in or theater tickets to go around, I was included out. You and I were before and after. Did you think I was a wooden post? Did you think I didn't hurt like you would have hurt?"

Ruta slumped. "I never knew you felt this way."

"What an act you put on. There was a time when I could have scratched your eyes out. But, you know, it got better, even though the inner circle never changed. All those years—you age and the past just gets silly. I ran out of revenge fantasies a long time ago."

The moment sizzled like a hot coal, and the shadow of the spinning wheel seemed to fly on the wall, and Ruta sat with her long neck oddly inclined, like an aging swan attempting graceful deference. For a long while neither of them could speak. Rain pattered, diluting and cooling, until just the red shade on the banker's lamp seemed to have any heat left. Then, granite hard, Ariel changed the subject: "I suppose they're all horrified about Danielle."

"A little."

"A little horrified. Did it occur to anyone that the only thing I really did was give her a little more life than God did? Should I be hated for that?"

"No one hates you, Ariel. They may be nervous—I'm not going to lie about that—but I don't think they actually hate you."

"I'm certainly glad you're not going to lie about that. So, who is the most nervous down in my parlor?"

"I don't know."

"Are you nervous?"

". . . Yes."

"Good. Because now I have the last word, and I'd like to know if anyone is saying things against me. Be very careful, Ruta. I'm not above testing you."

"They're upset." Ruta was flustered. "No one's thinking clearly."

"Who?"

"No one—"

"Beverly?"

"No—"

"Helen?"

"Helen wouldn't—"

"Paavo," she said, as if it was a conclusion.

"No, no, not Paavo. He told her . . . told everyone not to get upset."

"*Her?*"

No one could say Ruta hadn't tried. No one could say she hadn't lied to Ariel's face trying to protect them. But when the name "Marjorie!" came out with triumph and dismay, she couldn't deny it.

"Please, Ariel, it was just words. Don't do anything to her."

"I'll do what I have to do. You don't want to lose what you have, do you, Ruta? I've always protected you and the others. Which is why I won't make you younger just yet, Ruta. Because then everyone would understand how I knew about Kraft and Danielle. You see how I care? When everything is safe—when everyone understands that we need to pull together to make this work—then I can reward you. I can paint you as you really want to be."

She made the new painting first, and it was rending to her. Marjorie—of all people to betray her. If anyone among them had lived by principle, it was Marjorie Korpela. That she had always underestimated Ariel didn't alter that. A bit old-fashioned, fueled by misconceptions, as hard-nosed as a man sometimes, her good opinion was still worth cultivating and that was why Ariel had brought her back.

Practical, level-headed Marjorie should have seen what a thing it was that Ariel had created, should have appreciated it. In fact, Ariel would once have predicted that Marjorie would become her factotum instead of Molly. She had even seen a poetic balance in this, having been Marjorie's employee. But some ghost of their former relationship had held her back from painting patrician Marjorie younger and more able. And nothing in

the past year had stirred her to change that. There were
people who lived rigid lives according to the strictures
around them and never reached beyond that. Marjorie
seemed to be that way. She never talked about her husband or asked for anything, but just accepted a quiet,
dignified life as quite enough for the foreseeable eternity. And now to find that sensible woman speaking ill
of her behind her back was like discovering embezzle-
ment deep within her securest accounts.

So the new painting gave birth to Marjorie Kristen
Korpela, a living relic. Worse even than Danielle
Kramer. Her temples were translucent with blue veins
threading to the surface. Her limbs were draped in mot-
tled flesh, and her head—slightly askew where it came
to rest on her chest—was framed by the bony mantle of
a bowed and fusing spine. All that remained of her eyebrows were tufts at the bridge of her nose, and this thrust
the orbital ridge around her eye sockets into prominence.
Ulcerations crusted the few remaining lashes on her eyelids. Where flesh had not puddled like sediment it was
drawn taut, and the cartilage of her nose was receding
from yawning nostrils that pulled her mouth into a raw
wound fissured at the edges. She even pulled down a
tome of Ivan Albright's "magic realism" and borrowed a
morgue look from the galleries there. All was blue and
gray. All was pits and erosion. Only the eyes carried the
fading gleam of life, like flat pennies losing their luster.
Gravity and entropy were winning. Energy had lost. And
yet it was Marjorie Korpela—no question about that. The
genius of Ariel Leppa the uncelebrated painter was that it
could have been no one but Marjorie Korpela. And she
did it with the fast-drying *alla prima* technique—
the mark of her mastery.

When the painting had dried and the ossifying thing
actually lay bundled and wheezing against the wall,

Ariel studied it. She felt neither compunction nor compassion, only a vague sense of satisfaction that she had created precisely what she had intended. This was not the living being downstairs asleep in a room of her house. That version of Marjorie awaited a separate act of extinction. This was a separate entity, something that would never have existed except by Ariel's will. Marjorie then. Marjorie now. Same person. But they were not the same person.

And yet she herself would never see the two of them alive at the same time, so how could she be sure?

She flipped through the dozen frames stacked next to the workbench to pull out the first painting of Marjorie and set it upon the easel. Downstairs was a viable personality she had reanimated from her past, something lucid and capable of creative thought, of love and loyalty and appreciation. Only it hadn't felt any of those things. As if it didn't owe them to Ariel but had dredged itself up from its grave and endowed itself with breath, spirit and consciousness all of its own accord.

She glanced at the heap against the wall. It was watching her through its ruined eyes. What thoughts could it be thinking—born nearly dead?

She must see the other Marjorie, she decided on impulse. One last time. Must understand the distinction for herself. And so she left the dawn-streaked studio and made her way down the staircase to the new wing and entered Marjorie's room, which smelled of lilacs and liniment, and stood over the form on the bed. Wrapped in a cotton blanket like that, the sleeping woman could indeed be the swathed thing lying against the wall two floors above.

The light from the corridor streaming through the door got lost in the fold of the hood that peaked over the figure's head, leaving a deep emptiness into which Ariel leaned closer and closer. Why wasn't she breathing? Not even a dainty snore. Petite Marjie, ever the guarded aristocrat. Or perhaps she was sleeping more deeply and further into that shroud hollow than Ariel could imagine. Beyond apnea. Beyond mortal dreams.

Abruptly there was a sharp inhalation Ariel reared back just as an alabaster hand snaked out from the covers and threw off the hood.

"Ariel . . . ?" Marjorie squinted up from her bed against the light and came to one elbow, her pale blue nightgown falling from her corrugated throat. "What is it? What time is it?"

"It's *your* time, Marjorie."

"What are you talking about?"

"I've been painting, and I've made another portrait. It's upstairs in the studio. I put it next to yours just to see the likenesses and differences. There are lots of differences. But you can tell who it is. You might say you're beside yourself, Marjorie."

The woman on the bed shrank back as if to gain perspective, but it made her seem to stare down her nose. "You're losing it, Ariel."

"Wasn't I loyal enough when I worked for you? Did I ever talk behind your back?"

"You had no reason to. I never *demanded* loyalty from you. I was just your supervisor, Ariel, not your god."

"Oh, this is bad, very bad. I hope it's not too late to save the others by making an example of you."

"Yes, yes, love you or else. That's what all the worst religions do."

"That's a stretch and you know it."

". . . God on a rampage."

"How would you have done it?"

A rag of hope, an invitation to reason, but Marjorie

Korpela couldn't think of an answer. "I wouldn't manu-facture more suffering," she said.

"If giving you life is suffering, then I'm guilty of that."

"There are two Danielles dead now, two Paavos, and now you want to include me. You can't possibly imagine what that means."

"Are you begging me not to include you?"

"I will if that's what you want. Don't do this, Ariel."

Ariel leaned into the darkness, as if to distance her-self. "I wish I hadn't come down, but I had to know for sure. Go back to sleep, Marjorie. Let me remember you as someone whose opinion was worth cultivating."

The words evaporated, and suddenly Marjorie was kicking and thrusting against the entangling blankets. With her lame leg the issue was never in doubt, but Ariel retreated to the doorway in surprise at the raw physical desperation. Marjorie stumbled out of bed. And so began a snails' race through the house—dueling sloths—absurd but for the stakes.

Every coherent atom of Marjorie's being felt the peril. Survival versus extinction. But by the time she reached the staircase, Ariel was already on the first landing, her witch's fingers hissing along the wallpaper for guidance. In fear and dismay, Marjorie shouted at her. But she couldn't frame a genuine, groveling, have-mercy plea, despite what she had said. If she had, then she would al-ready have ceased to be Marjorie Korpela.

A lightning bolt carving through the upper stories of the century-and-a-half-old farmhouse and striking Ariel Leppa dead—that was the only hope. *In the name of God Almighty, strike this lesser god dead!* Marjorie prayed. But you didn't petition the whirlwind to save a mote of merely human flesh. Marjorie Korpela was on her way out again.

She stopped thinking about the present altogether then, because what was coming glutted her with its terrible roiling specter. And she tried to run. Blindly, instinctively, bare feet slapping the wooden floors and padding across throw rugs with the two-note beat of her infirmity, she blundered to the front door. There she had to grasp the dead bolt pommel with two fingers from either hand to stop shaking. Stiffening her arms and rolling her shoulders to control the violent trembling, she turned the old white enameled doorknob. Then, rushing the front steps, she pitched and sprawled along the path, her blue nightgown stretching and tearing. An explosion of sparks erupted through her sinuses when her nose struck the dirt. But up she came, without a pause, numbed to anything except flight.

The sparks somehow remained. Incoming now from the nether regions she had known before. Tardy emissaries of creation, lost from black space, from frozen time, like fireflies caught in a damp dawn. Gray all around her. The barn a great, looming mausoleum of agrarian death on a farm that was essentially fallow. And so she spun and stuttered past it into the cold mud of the fields that sucked at her feet, like the cosmos sucked at her soul. Fifteen rows in she mired and twisted back and thought she saw a lighted window in the upper story of the house and a figure there—Ariel in her studio—contemplating the whirling dervish flight below.

With animal grunts that defrocked her humanity, Marjorie lunged again, tearing free of the ooze. In a few furious steps she found the dead furrow of the field, which was carpeted with wet leaves and debris that supported her weight. The simple pain in her body was reassuring, because it meant she was still of the Earth. Bless the taste of blood seeping around her teeth from the fall off the steps, bless the cold stab of cavernous breaths, bless the downbeat sound of her good foot and the grace note of her trailing one.

But now she began to notice the things in the trees. Great, arcing silhouettes were advancing through the branches parallel to her path. They were not precisely flying but bouncing and flapping along like ungainly lovers of carrion who only had to arrive after the killing was done by others. But where were the killers? She wished she had her glasses. Was it better to be rent apart than to be exiled whole and aware by Ariel into the abyss again?

She didn't need her glasses to see the bloated thing that might have been red but looked dusky in the dawn. It stood against the largest tree at the edge of the field, and its great saucer eye stared out luminously as if straining to absorb movement or light. She wanted to cry out to it—*Here I am, come feast on me!*—but her throat was so parched that she only dredged up a faucal gasp that ended in weeping.

It was too late. Ariel was painting already, layering creation over creation, evicting her atom by atom from this beautiful Garden of New Eden. And she knew that it was being done with deliberate and excruciating slowness, whether out of hate by a sadistically demented Ariel Leppa or out of reluctance because the wretchedly lonely woman felt some loss of friendship after all. Either way, she was spared nothing of the journey.

Mist began to boil out of the earth, the miasma and effluvium of everything that had ever died here: corn and shrews and crows and foxes and people—settlers and gangsters. But she knew that the pumping, fulgent haze held much more than that and was far more ancient. It came from before the last century, before Indians or ice ages or reptilian denizens had slithered through time and slithered out again. Ephemeral billows disgorged herds

and flocks of things that had no name or niche in evolution. Vapors fastened onto her like clammy tentacles,
draining her, diluting her as surely as a whitewash over a
portrait in Ariel Leppa's studio. Liquid ashes of her flesh
twinkled into it, seeming to broaden her perspective until
it transcended the biases of vision. She "saw" beyond
and before the Earth to the seed itself of spinning nebu-
lae and accreting elements. A limberlost instant of time
fired by engines of motion and physics in concord with
unnumbered sister stars. Spinning down into ever
smaller universes of matter—clusters to galaxies to solar
systems to atoms and less—from what demiurge, what
state of being? This was important because she was
going back to it, whatever it was, and she must try to remember that she was an entity of light, that she had once
had form and substance. Let not the wildness pervade
that!

The fulminations of creation began to wink out then,
and a great shriek and moan rippled toward her. She felt
the mighty tsunami of space rushing in, unimaginably
vast and distant but closing like a fist around a palm
upon which she stood unclaimed by natural law. She felt
the crushing head winds and peered frantically into the
gulf to gather every last sensation. She saw a black
maelstrom seething with violence at the foot of sheer
palisades, each swell and ebb leaving hideous things on
the daggered rocks in the surf. Titan shapes flopped and
flailed for a handhold on the escarpment. Gnawed ap-
pendages were tossed up on the hiss and flume of chan-
neled waves in hidden grottos, having been wrenched
from voracious things with insatiable appetites that
dwelled in a murky domdaniel beneath the sea. And
from the ramparts she heard her name called with urgency and saw a tiny figure—Ariel—calling with remorse and pity (but not forgiveness), and she knew then

that she had already passed beyond the palpable world, and that these were the stored furnishings of her nightmares. From life. From deaths she had known before.

So she stopped in the field and took root, sinking into the primordial ooze while curtains of mosquitoes swept up, homing in on her signatures of heat and carbon dioxide, only to find her skin withering, her fluids gurgling inward toward some impossible source. And still she cried out—thought she cried out—grasping at the tether, trying to hang on to the silver cord, now hearing her phantom pulse, fading echo, fading memory . . . going, going, gone.

16

It was loathsome when they brought the new old Marjorie Korpela downstairs. The flesh slid like gelatin around the bones, and the skeleton was vividly palpable in Dana's hands as she and Molly lifted it. They had diapered her, but the odors went beyond bodily wastes, exuding in every breath and from every orifice. A metal tang hung above Marjorie's wispy hair and something like the pungency of rotting oranges wafted through her skin as though her bruised core had turned to mush. For the first time Dana felt repulsed by a member of the house.

Everyone else fixated in horror on the relic being borne down the wide staircase. But as soon as the bumbling cortege thumped through the archway, they spread away from each other and the shock of recognition like some immiscible substance. Beverly went to the porch, Paavo stood in the yard, the others disappeared into their rooms or wandered from one window to the next. Stalwart Molly kept at the necessary task of settling Marjorie in while Dana escaped the room, nauseated, a thin sheen of moisture on her brow and above her lip.

Dana didn't want to look at anyone else, didn't want to see what they were becoming. She ambled back into the parlor because that was now empty, her thoughts in full flight, her senses overloaded. Aimlessly her gaze skittered around the walls, noting eccentricities she had never noted before: the fireplace sealed with a rusted metal curtain that might once have been an awning; a blue wooden doll on the mantel with yellowed tatting for a dress; a metronome on a table, its pointer frozen out of plumb; and an empty oval among the family portraits clustered on that same table. From a rafter in one corner hung a Japanese gong, which she now realized was a propane cylinder cut in half and painted umber. How had this miscellany accumulated? Withered violets tied with brown twine, crossed swords, glass and wood barometers by the plethora, a pile of *Collier's* magazines, a tattered pincushion shaped like a porcupine with sailcloth needles impaling it, someone's leather driving gloves, and a cone of rusted iron oxide around something no longer definable on the hearth—the room was acrawl with truncated things and dislocations. Was it the mad consensus of disparate lives building over time, or the single derangement of a single addled mind?

And then her eye came to the large painting—the Garden of Eden—and she leaned toward it with sudden focus. A little helix of missing paint was torqued around the Tree of Knowledge. This is what Kraft had been talking about. *I painted it with my finger.* . . . The snake. He had painted the snake. And now the damn thing was gone, as if it had slithered right off the tree and out of the frame.

It sickened her to see that. Because even though she could construct rational explanations for it based on Kraft's irrational behavior, she feared it was exactly what he had said: *I brought it back. I let it in.* You had to have experienced death in order to connect the dots of insane things like that. You couldn't make quantum leaps unless you had visited a quantum universe. And she had.

So now she wanted to get out of this room and away from all of them. She wished Denny Bryce were here. Naïve, earthbound Denny Bryce would be a relief just now. She went to the kitchen, but Molly was leaning against the cast iron sink, staring out the window. The cellar door was right there, and it was so stultifying, hot and humid after the rain, that she just grasped the white knob and went down.

Beverly said you couldn't coax her to the cellars with Tom Cruise in a thong, but Dana didn't mind them at all. They were cool and quiet, and you had the sense that space ended when you stood within the earth-backed walls. The change in the sound of her steps going down was comforting too, an increasingly solid sound from the dry top stair to the damp-rot lowest one. She thought this might reflect a brief insensibility she had felt at death before being hurled into the phantasmal void. Terra firma. Subterranean closure. The sanctuary of a tomb before the blue marble fractured into something older than the universe, rank and festering with never-ending extinction. So. The cellars. She liked to feel underground.

The dampness was soothing, and for the first time since carrying Marjorie down from the studio she could think clearly. You were supposed to cross the river of forgetfulness when you died, but in reality it was the other way around. Birth was forgetfulness. Birth blotted out the origins of consciousness.

The dull thud of Amber's music from somewhere above intruded on her peace, and she moved through the passageway to the laundry room, where the lowered floor and doubled joists tamped all sound.

The washer, the dryer and the three slate set tubs seemed to confront her with geometrical smugness when she switched on the light. Out of habit she walked to the washer and thrummed her knuckles on the enameled corn-yellow surface. Hollow, empty. She lifted the lid with a click. *S'alright.* Dropped it. *S'alright.* Thank you, Señor Wences. Then to the dryer. Dust encrusted, be-linted. A faded laundry tag from someone's shirt collar lay in the grime on the floor, along with a blue button and a piece of straw that must have come in on her shoe and that was burnished to an almost incandescent hue. She thrummed the surface of that appliance as well. Dull this time. That was funny, because she was sure she hadn't left any clothes inside. But twenty years of lint baffles were probably built up inside the shell around the outside of the drum. It needed to be thoroughly cleaned before they wound up with a fire.

She popped the door, and it was the odor that hit her first because you couldn't see inside very well. She knew the gamey smell from her husband's duck-hunting days. It must have been jammed chock-full, because one of them rolled to the lip of the door seal and lay there, staring up at her with its filmy blue eyes, its jet-black wings shrugged up a little and folded tightly to its stiff-ened body, as if to say "Don't ask." She jumped away, because how could the dryer be loaded up with dead crows? And that was when a pair of large hands closed around her hips.

Denny Bryce had come up behind her unannounced just as she jumped back, but his apologies were sus-pended by what he saw in the dryer. "What the hell?" he said.

And likewise she could do no more than glance at him before her attention went back to the abhorrent mass of sodden plumage. "This is sick . . ." she murmured.

He sidled behind the machine and jiggled the corru-gated metal venting. "Where does this exit the house?"

"In back on the barn side. But you can't be thinking they flew into the dryer?"

"If the louvers, or the screen, or whatever seals it is broken—maybe. I don't know. In winter they might be looking for a warm spot, but not in this weather."

"I suppose they could have been looking to build a nest." The impossible heap of avian cadavers belied that, and she added that possibly an animal was stashing them there. "Storing them for winter, maybe."

"It must have been storing them for a long time."

"This dryer was empty two days ago."

"Then scratch that theory. Do you have a flashlight down here?"

"There are some candles and wooden matches back in the other room."

"Where do those tunnels go?"

"I don't know—storage mostly. No one goes back there. They were built by gangsters or something during Prohibition or something, but they leak, I think, and one of them may have collapsed."

"Then animals could get in."

"We would have seen them in the house, wouldn't we?"

"I'll go get the candles."

Like taproots to the living house, the crude tunnels had once nourished the farm with money and commerce from the external world, but isolation had ceded them to the past and to the rats or whatever else dwelled in their recesses.

"Igor returns," Denny said, returning in the cerise aura of two lit candles.

"I don't think we should do this."

"I've been sent to put a little excitement in your life. But if you want, wait here."

She regarded his little-boy smile and green eyes

gleaming in the candle's throw. "Men," she sighed. "Lead on."

At first she kept slightly behind him, cupping the candle he had given her. But each time he hesitated she came alongside and the twin nimbuses swept more darkness away. So she drew abreast and stayed there.

There were railroad lanterns on the shelves, rusted tins and empty Mason jars faintly luminescent through a coating of dust. Smashed empty wooden cases littered the floor and a roughly made cellarette, minus a door, stood shoulder high.

"We have some genuine rotgut in here," Denny said, withdrawing a green bottle from its cradle. "This could be very good. Here's to Al Capone." He started to work off the cork.

"What's that?"

"What's what?"

She moved the candle laterally. "That rustling."

The flame fled back toward her, a snapping pennant changing from chrome yellow to cerulean blue, and suddenly the darkness leaped in by half. Smoke threaded up from the exposed wick, but that too was lost as Denny's candle flame did its own swan dance and guttered out.

"Draft," he declared in the absolute blackness.

Of course it was a draft. She knew that, knew that, knew that. But the tunnel was a dead end; it should have been dead air. Something was there. Bigger than a rat. Something with a barrel chest and cavernous lungs— close, very close—but just out of range of the light and moving in as it huffed and puffed and blew their candles—

Scratch!

Denny had set down the bottle and struck a wooden match on the box he still carried, but his back was turned away from the draft and she didn't like that. The danger was in front of them. She took the box. But she had to keep scratching away, because the old sulfurous lucifer matches were getting no help from Old Scratch—ha-ha—until one of them finally popped and sizzled and flared. And she had a feeling that it was just in time. Because something that feared fire (or at least *obeyed* it) was shrinking back into the blackened crevices of the cellar.

"Let's get out of here," she said. "*Please.*"

Shadows were going up his face, making him look all wrong as he gestured toward the laundry room. She took the lead, shielding the flame with her body but feeling more heat from behind.

When the light of the single bulb surrounded them again, she saw that he had brought the green bottle with him.

"Know what I think?" he said. "I think our picnic is right here in this bottle. I think we've earned it. We could just slip into the cornfield and find out if this stuff is as good as it should be."

She looked at the dryer, its door still yawning open, vomiting out its virulent meal. Upstairs was more insanity, mirrored in the faces of her gray and tenuous companions. And here was this man who knew only oxygen and sky and firmness beneath his feet and laughing children and a world held together by cycles and seasons, like some great calendar clock with infallible gears, and he wanted her to taste some earthly pleasure on an afternoon in the summer of a year named 2001.

"Why not?" she said.

They made a furtive exit from the house, and he retrieved a fawn-colored comforter from his car and something called an MP3 player, which she had never heard of, and which he played over and over—a single song ti-

tled "Mambo No. 5"—and she could barely hear, because the MP3 player had little earpieces that he just left
lying on the spread comforter with the volume up fully.
Which was good, because it allowed them to talk. She
told him a lot about herself, even that she had a husband
somewhere in the Texas prison system, if he hadn't been
executed, and Denny Bryce didn't seem surprised that
she didn't want to know whether her husband was dead
or alive. She told him that New Eden was wonderful and
terrible, and that everyone here except his father had
known Ariel a long time. Why didn't anyone ever leave,
he asked her. She tried to *make* him understand without
telling him anything that would *let* him understand (how
could he accept the truth?), and they killed the bottle and
pretended it was better than it was.

"What if you came here one day and I didn't recognize you?" she asked him, and of course he thought she
meant what if she had Alzheimer's. "No, what if I
seemed to be someone else?"

He laughed at that and came off justifiably lost.
"Maybe I need your fingerprints."

She let him press his hand to hers, and they talked that
way—five fingertips pressed to five fingertips—until
their flesh seemed to weld together, and that made her
smile for the first time that day, because it felt distinctly
sexual and she had forgotten sexuality entirely. Life
could have been different for her, she realized. She could
have met someone like this man, and the sweet sting of
sex would not have been mixed with fear, as it had been
when she had married and lived unhappily ever after.

"Bottle's empty," she said with just a slight slur.
"Must get back to the scullery."

"Alas."

"You first," she said.

He left the comforter, and after a minute or so she

heard him start his car and drive off. She folded the
comforter and made her way through the rows of corn.
The rustling seemed to have an echo as she brushed
against the stalks, though of course that was because she
was half in the bag and her senses were definitely out of
sync. But a few rows from the edge she heard the ac-
cusative cawing of crows, and that brought back the
dryer and the rustling sound in the cellars and the piece
of rusty red straw on the floor. She stopped. How vehe-
ment they sounded. She had trouble picking them out,
but they were there in the willow—*were* there, because
when she saw them they stopped cawing and took flight.

Where had the day gone? It was late afternoon. Probably everyone would be sitting around drinking coffee or
ice tea. She couldn't stumble in like this, carrying a
comforter. Better to leave it in the barn and sober up for
a while.

She went around to the rolling door and tugged it
open just enough to squeeze past. The wheels in the
overhead track were all gummed up, and if someone
didn't clean it soon it was going to take a fire axe to get
into the barn. Not that the structure itself might not fall
down first. You could see daylight between the boards,
and you didn't need a ladder to get into the loft because
it had obligingly turned into a slide where the center
posts had rotted and collapsed. But it was a nice place to
go and get your head on straight—shady and aromatic
with a thousand residues that had once been pungent but
now lingered as a sachet of harvests and seasons. So she
dragged herself over to the lip of the loft where it dipped
to the floor, and fell back on the brittle hay while the
world spun round inside her head.

It was still spinning, but only at carousel speed, when
she heard the door wobble slightly on its track. *Shit,* she
thought, *who would come out here now?* Maybe they

wouldn't see her. It was gloomy and the garden tools
were close by the door, so maybe they would just grab
the hoe or whatever and saunter off to the garden. But
the door rolled open at least six or seven feet, judging by
the sound. So it must be Molly or Paavo—someone
strong. Still, she didn't sit up. She didn't sit up until
nothing happened for another minute, and the suspicion
grew that someone was just standing there, trying to find
her in the haze of shadows and sun-shot stripes that fell
on the floor.

So then she came up on her elbows and blinked at the
bright rectangle of the doorway. The silhouette there refused to make sense. Because the light from the opening
conspired to limn it with red in an irregular way, as if it
were jaunty and ragged, and no one in the house looked
like that. It responded to her movement too. She could
see that much. How it straightened suddenly and stiffened and . . . rustled? It was the same rustle she had
heard at least three times within the last several hours. In
fact, it seemed now that she had heard it a hundred
times, heard it all afternoon, in the cellars, in the tunnels,
in the field, unsure of what it wanted to do, or waiting
for her to be alone again. Only now it must be sure, because it had come into the barn looking for her.

What came next was so peculiar that she almost
thought it didn't happen. The figure moved, but it did so
in a strange hustly-bustly way, sashaying across the floor
toward her, twisting and thrusting as if it didn't have
enough joints, and stopping every few steps like a blind
animal trying to locate its prey. Sobriety began to kick
in.

The sun striping through the shrunken boards fell full
on it when it was twenty feet away, and despite her instinct to freeze, mouse quiet, she couldn't suppress a
gasp. Because it was a scarecrow, a red scarecrow—

pulsingly red—and she was transported instantly to the
outré regions from which she had never fully returned.
She knew, of course, that it was Amber's creation and
Ruta's nightmare—"Red straw . . . red straw!"—except
that no one had mentioned its rows of harrow teeth or
the nails tearing right through the gloves, stiletto length
and crimson. And the reason it moved in sudden bursts
was because it had no eyes—no eyes, but God knows
what other senses—and it had to stop and pick up . . .
what? Sound, scent, heat? It must have known that she
was alone, must have kept close all afternoon, sensing
her somehow. Maybe it had even stalked them from the
cellars. And now it had her in the barn.

She thought of the dryer full of dead crows, and she
had no doubt whatsoever that this was the predator that
had amassed them. It was a killing thing, after all, and it
must be a very effective killing thing to have captured
the wary crow in such numbers without benefit of sight.
The way it twisted and leaned sharply forward made her
think it was hypersensitive—as if it were exposing some
sensory organ to minute vibrations. She tried to hold her
breath and stay calm, but it knew. With that horrible
rustling it was zigzagging toward her.

The alcohol still buzzed in her brain. But then she
wasn't going to have to outthink it. She was going to
have to outrun it, and she thought she could do that.
Inching upward, she rose to a crouch, and when it
fronted her with a terrifying burst to within six feet, she
made her dash.

She sprang off the loft. But before she could take a
second step it was in front of her again, and she had to
sidestep back onto the hay just as its arm rived the air
with a sweep of nails. Sliding, backpedaling she went,
gaining maybe two seconds while it struck one of its odd
tilting postures as if to determine the nature of the loft

from sounds or smell or the way the air moved—or, more probably, all three. By the time it had placed one red boot on the fallen fascia board, she was scrambling for the pitchfork that hung on the wall.

"Back off!" she quavered, brandishing tines.

A mistake, of course. As if she had issued an invitation to embrace her, it leaped, Ray Bolger–style, head askew, limbs bent, harrow teeth unmistakably grinning. But it landed stiffly, bristling with power, and so close. It had called her bluff. *Here I am! Surrender, Dorothy!* And she could do nothing more than thrust the pitchfork into its chest—through its chest—with the tempered steel finding no resistance at all in the red straw.

Worse, with the precision of a catch in a ballet, its right glove clamped instantly onto the haft and with a twist of its torso yanked the weapon from her. Then it yanked the tines out of itself and snapped the pitchfork in two. Then it tossed both, clattering and clanging, to the floor.

So she was going to have to outthink it after all.

It seemed momentarily confused by all the rustle and vibration as she rolled sideways and scrambled higher into the loft. But it was relentless, and it was sorting out her heat from the sound or whatever it was picking up. Heat. Faint flicker of hope, flicker of an idea, flicker of a match. She had the wooden matches she had taken from Denny in the tunnel. If she could get one lit, if she could set the obscene thing on fire. . . .

She fumbled with the box, hands shaking, spilling matches in her lap. But then she had one, and without sliding the cover shut, she tried to scratch it on the friction strip on the side. But there wasn't enough support with just the cover, so she tried to slide the box back into it, but it was hanging right on the end and her trembling fingers jammed it a little sideways. It dropped out of the sleeve and fell in the hay. *Take your time, girl!* But when she reached for the box, it disappeared into the hay like a drowning hand slipping under a wave.

The red scarecrow twisted, harrow teeth working, nails fanning like hackles.

She still had the matchbox cover and one wooden match. Bracing two fingers of her left hand on the inside of the sleeve, she pressed her right index finger against the head of the match and snicked it on the friction strip. This time it started to hiss. But her hands were sweating and the dampness of her forefinger must have soaked into the match head, because it fizzled and died in a copious puff of yellow smoke.

She knew without lifting her eyes when it had found her. She was ground zero and the countdown was at one. But all the same she was groping through the hay for another match. And when she actually came up with one, the scarecrow still hadn't hurled itself on her. She thought fleetingly that the smell of sulfur had arrested it. It wasn't sure. It was hesitating. If she could just . . .

This time she pressed her index finger a half inch higher up the match, and the grit of the friction paper resonated grain by grain into her sense of touch. She felt each nuance, each subatomic transfer, as if the reaction were aggrandized to a cosmic scale for the entertainment and edification of every consciousness in the universe. *Dana Novicki has struck a match. Will the antimony sulphide and potassium chlorate melt and ignite the little stick? Will she combust the red straw of Amber Leppa's diabolical horror before it leaps in rage upon her?*

She looked into the scarecrow's blind face and serrated maw and jerked the match forward. Touched the red straw, in fact. But the match was already falling from her violently shaking hand as she reached out. And the flame that had burst so promisingly a moment ago vanished in another gush of smoke. She could smell the cloyingly sweet red straw. She could hear it rustling. The sibilant sounds took her back so close to where she had lain after death that all the old nightmares came rushing over the rim.

Once again she stood before ramparts and ageless pylons rooted in space. Pitted faces loomed near, shunned things sucked her breath, fused entities warred for her soul, and from all sides susurrant legions rustled and giggled, devoid of pity, incapable of empathy or unity or anything but the solitary and savage predation of the disconnected. But from three feet away, the empty vessel of red straw seemed suddenly unable to sense her presence. It contorted into a hyperextended Saint Andrew's cross, impossibly tall, a bristling thing of receptors, seething, smoking, and suddenly bursting into flames—purely red flames—that singed her face as she shrank away.

She crabbed backward in the loft—a loft filled with flammable hay—rejoicing that she had lit her attacker on fire after all, because even though she knew that she had absolutely not done it, she told herself that there must have been an ember or a spark that had taken a few seconds to catch hold. So now the combustion had her in its thrall. Even after the thing was thoroughly immolated and tongues of flame were gesturing like melodramatic arms in a silent film, she kept sliding sideways, back and forth, as bereft as a spider in a bottle. The fascination was utterly irresistible because she could see that the malign creature was starting to break up into discrete particles. And that was a glimpse over the wall that all who live must take. This was not just another earthly death, or even the hastened transformation of matter to energy. It was annihilation—the reverse of creation. How could she have caused such a thing? In the midst of her calamity, she wanted to understand that.

Now the red scarecrow was fire within fire, as if each wisp was being torn loose to be seared into oblivion as it rose toward the rafters. Up went the embers, a diaspora of red straw, everywhere and nowhere. *Red straw, red straw . . .* Absurd and innocent, but now a cry of tramontane exile, a catch phrase of warning, given reinforcement by the others of the household as the barn went up and they came first to the windows of the house and then to the porch and the basswood. *Red straw . . . red straw.* The ululation of an exanimate population, wailing with horror as they rose like bits of straw into galactic winds that blasted them back to the far side of infinity.

Dana didn't remember letting herself slide off the gradient loft, or passing slowly through the firestorm of cinders raining down from the roof, or coming out into the sunlight from that orange hell and seeing her companions. She said nothing, remembered nothing. No one called the fire department. Ariel watched stonily from not more than thirty feet away, leaning on her cane, ash pelting her like condemning angels.

When the pillar of fire had undulated to the ground and a huge pyre of shingles and beams flickered and smoked, Molly put her arm around Dana, grounding her from across the universe, reeling her in, restoring a human circuit that instantly lit up with what seemed an impossible denial: "I didn't do it. . . . I didn't do it," Dana said, laboring, birthing the words like a half-drowned person glutted with water, the phrases beginning with forced exhalations and ending in whispers. "I tried to do it, but the match was already out. I didn't do it."

17

It was pretty amazing how you couldn't really feel the heat inside the cupola. You could smell the smoke some, but even that didn't seem to stop the sauerkraut smell that had been coming up through the house since early afternoon. Molly always made sauerkraut when she was sad or mad, and Amber thought she was both today. Even before the fire she had been sad or mad about Mrs. Korpela. Everyone was. Except her mother.

And that made Amber sad and mad, because there wasn't anyone else to talk to. No stories of the Taron pygmies who were dying off one by one in far-off Myanmar because the world shouldn't have them anymore. No Sir Aarfie. No friends her own age. Just herself to talk to and whatever friends she made up. She still had the red paint, though, and she was going to get good enough so she could paint friends and pets and stuff, the way her mother did, and then she would never be lonely again.

That was why she had come up here on the roof to the cupola early this morning. And why she had taken the almost washed-out picture of her scarecrow and touched it up a little. She didn't think that would hurt, and it was good practice. But when she had come back this after-

noon, she saw Mrs. Novicki and Mr. Bryce in the cornfield, and she had watched, hoping they would do kissing and stuff, but they never did, and when he finally
left, she saw Mrs. Novicki go into the barn. And then she
saw the scarecrow—*her* really, honest-to-God red scarecrow, just like she had painted him—go into the barn,
and she knew she had made a mistake. She shouldn't
have touched it up at all.

Her heart was doing flip-flops because you could tell
by the way the scarecrow was following Mrs. Novicki
that it didn't want to be seen, but then when it went in
the barn, it must have known it would be seen. So that
was bad. And when Mrs. Novicki didn't come out afterward Amber felt sick. She had seen the blood in the hallway the night of the break-in, and heard Mr. Seppanen
screaming, and now she was going to hear Mrs. Novicki
screaming. She should have painted the scarecrow out
with white as soon as she had found the rain-streaked
picture that day. But she hadn't had any white then, and
she didn't have any white now. She only had the magic
paint in the cupola. So she did the next best thing. She
painted him out with red. Red fire. Fire was easy. She
had always been good with fire. And she prayed.

Dear God, make my fire real.

She thought there must be a God, because who had
painted things before her mother came along? So then
she saw the smoke, and then the roof started to glow and
the shingles began to curl, and she knew it had worked.
But Mrs. Novicki still wasn't coming out. She shouted to
her, and then the people in the house started to come outside, and she didn't want them to see where her hiding
place was up on the roof, so she didn't shout again. But
no one looked *inside* the barn. They could see it was on
fire, but they just stood there. So she was going to have
to yell again and tell them that Mrs. Novicki would burn

up if they didn't go inside and get her. But then she
thought, her prayer had worked once, so she tried it
again—*Dear God, make Mrs. Novicki come out okay*—
and sure enough, out she came.

So everything was okay now. Except that she couldn't
come down until everyone left. She had to stay up there
and smell the smoke and the sauerkraut and watch
through the slits in the louvers. Her mother was standing
right there too, and if she found out that her daughter
had caused the barn to burn down, Amber didn't know
what she would do. Kill her, probably. Take away TV
and make her live in her room on sauerkraut and water.
She wished her dad was better, and that he'd tell her
mother to "lighten up," like he used to.

And then she saw Mr. Bryce—old Mr. Bryce, not the
young one who had almost been kissing Mrs. Novicki in
the cornfield. He came out all upset and shuffling as fast
as he could. But when he got to where the others were
standing, he went right on by. He was trying to run, but
he couldn't lift his feet that good, so he just shuffled
straight toward the fire. Then Mr. Seppanen and the others grabbed him and wouldn't let go. He tried to slug Mr.
Seppanen the way he had Mrs. Novicki (that was funny,
when you thought about it: old Mr. Bryce slugging her,
and young Mr. Bryce taking her to the cornfield). But it
wasn't funny the way old Mr. Bryce yanked and pushed,
trying to get free so he could run into the barn. And then
she heard him shout.

"Tiffany!"

And that just made her feel sick again, because of
course he was trying to save her.

"Tiffany!" he bellowed.

And when the barn finally collapsed, old Mr. Bryce
collapsed too. Sitting down there in the dirt, like he was

a little kid or something. Everyone moved away from him in a circle and just let him get it out of his system.

A couple of times she almost shouted down to him, because that's all it would've taken to make him feel okay. But she didn't. Even though she felt ashamed, she couldn't give herself away. Finally old Mr. Bryce just sprawled out in the dust and looked exhausted. Some of the others helped him into the house then, and pretty soon everyone was gone. Miss Hoverstein was the last to go in.

So it was over. And Amber was tired and had to pee, and she didn't know what she was going to eat if all they had was sauerkraut and sausage. It was going to be one of those sit-there-until-you-eat-it-young-lady meals that would end when she gave up dessert or went to bed early. But all in all, she was relieved. Things had started out really badly, and now they were okay, if you didn't count the barn or how badly old Mr. Bryce felt. She would take whatever medicine went with the meal and just say another little prayer tonight, thanking God that her mother wasn't any the wiser about things, and if she didn't see Mr. Bryce before everyone went to bed, she would go to his room tonight.

So she scuffed down the roof to the chimney and made her leap to the pipe and then down to the lightning rod and the window to the sewing room, and it was all pretty quiet in the house. Scrambling inside, she quietly lowered the sash. *No problemo,* she thought. And there wasn't. Except that when she turned, her mother was sitting there in the dark in the high Queen Anne chair.

"Is that where the paintings are?" she said. "Up on the roof? Very clever."

Amber was too shocked to answer. She was trying to figure it out—how her mother knew—and of course it must have been when she shouted down to Mrs. Novicki in the barn. Her mother had probably been upstairs and could tell where the shout had come from. She had responded to the fire and never once looked up at the roof, Amber was sure of that. That's how subtle her mother could be. You might fool her for awhile, but never forever. And when she stopped being fooled, you wouldn't know it. Worst of all, you couldn't tell what she would do about it.

"I can't go up there, of course," her mother said. "None of us can. Except for you," she added with a hush of magic in her voice. "It's too bad you don't remember your previous life past the age you are now. Then you might have learned your lesson about climbing dangerous things. It's not fun being in a wheelchair, Amber."

"It's not fun being killed, either."

"What are you talking about?"

"You killed me," she asserted breathily. "You killed your own daughter."

She could make out her mother's face in the gloom now. The "dead-on look" her father used to call it. No one could look straight at you like her mother. Eagles looked like that. Burning eyes and everything just sort of aimed at you so you knew you couldn't escape.

"I made you better."

"You made me dead. You showed me my grave in the cemetery."

"I should have known you would eventually accuse me of this."

"It's true!"

"What's true is that you're alive—young, healthy, and impertinent. I didn't know what was going to happen when I gave you life again. In fact, I didn't know I was giving you life. I just painted you as my last act."

"What do you mean?"

"Never mind. You've succeeded in putting me on the

defensive, because I'm a caring mother and I dwell on
my mistakes. But a caring mother tries to keep her
daughter from making the same mistakes. I want the pictures you have, Amber."

Dead-on. All silhouette except for her eyes and a little
bluish gray on the left side of her nose, cheek and brow.
Demanding in that way she had that made you feel that
all the right was on her side. All the right and all the
might. She had made the people in this house—*made
them!*—so she was like God. Only she had done some
awful things too. Making people go away and come
back, and maybe, like with Mrs. Korpela, she shouldn't
have made them come back at all—

"Right now, Amber!"

"I don't have any paintings. Honest, I don't. They all
blew away when we had the storm, except for two that I
found in the fields, and one of them was no good and the
other was almost no good, but I tried to fix that and . . .
and that's how the barn got burned down. It was me! See
how honest I'm being? The red scarecrow went in there
and he had Mrs. Novicki, and I saved her—I did, Mom. I
painted fire and that made the scarecrow burn up, only
the barn got burned up too."

She was crying now, the final punctuation of a child's
confession, because while the appeal was exhausted, the
fear of punishment remained. But Amber's fear was
partly because the lie was still coming out, and she didn't
know if her mother was going to see through it—her all-
powerful mother who was never fooled forever.

"So you still have paint," Ariel said quietly.

"What?"

"You heard me. If you painted fire, then you must still
have my paint."

"I—I think I used it all up."

"Bring me the empty jar."

"You said not to climb on the roof."

"I'll make an exception. After all, if something happens to you, I can always bring you back. Can't I?"

Terrifying words. Especially the "*can't I?*" A question that implied *If I want to.* Ariel Leppa nonchalantly twirled an umbilical cord that now stretched over two births, assessing whether it could possibly extend to three. And her reigning daughter was feeling the centrifugal pull of this. So it was really, really dangerous, what Amber did next. But she had to do it. Because she feared what her mother would do once she had the paint back. Then Amber would have nothing to bargain with. And no one could imagine the things her mother could imagine, being a painter and all.

"I threw the jar away," she said. "I threw it at the barn when it was burning."

"I see. Well. That takes care of that. You can go now."

Danger, danger. Why was she talking that way? What was she going to do? Amber couldn't let it go. Couldn't walk out of that room not knowing if her mother really was satisfied with the way things were, or whether she had just given up persuasion in favor of something more drastic.

"Aren't you going to punish me?"

"Do you think you need it?"

"No."

"Good."

Amber took a couple of quick steps toward the door, slowed, pivoted on one foot. Her mother's face caught a little more light from this angle, and she was no longer looking dead-on.

". . . Maybe just a little," Amber amended about the punishment.

"What do you suggest?"

"I shouldn't get any dinner."

"Done. No sauerkraut and sausage for you."

"No dessert either."

"Good. I don't think Molly had time to make any anyway."

"No dessert all week."

"My, my."

"And I shouldn't listen to music or watch TV."

Silence from the Queen Anne chair. She was overdoing it, and her mother was no longer amused. Nothing had changed. The danger was still there. Amber didn't know what might happen to her, wouldn't know. Better to shut up and just go to her room.

"We won't be using this window anymore," her mother said when she got to the doorway. "I'll have Paavo nail the sashes together. You'll want to make sure he doesn't do it while you're up on the roof."

Amber lay awake in the massive bed frame her grandfather had supposedly hewn together for her mother before he went off to fight in WW II. White oak corner posts as big around as water heaters and sideboards thick as curbs. You lay in it and you felt like you were anchored to the center of the earth. In her imagination Amber had survived storms and stampedes in its embrace, earthquakes and a direct meteor hit from outer space. But tonight it felt like a coffin. Tonight it paralyzed her with dread. Physical movement seemed impossible. When the sheets got hot and her legs itched, she didn't roll to a cool spot, she *thought* about rolling to a cool spot and then she just lay there. She didn't even get up when she heard old Mr. Bryce passing in the hall, his hand hissing along the wallpaper the way it did whenever he was unsteady. But later, hearing shuffling outside her window, she dragged herself up on one elbow and saw him standing in the moonlight in front of the still-smoldering barn.

His arms hung limply at his sides, and he seemed to lean a little, as if he were listening to something. What could he hear from ashes? Maybe he was hungry, she thought. Maybe she should take him some nice lemony yogurt. But if she got caught, her mother would think she was getting it for herself, despite her declaration that she should go to bed without eating. So she flopped back on the pillow.

She heard Mr. Bryce come back in and then go out again. She lost count of the number of times he went out to stand looking at the ashes of the barn. But at some point she began to cry for him—or maybe it was for herself—because he was looking for her, wasn't he? His Tiffany. And in a way she was just as doomed as if she really had been in that burning barn. Because when she went to sleep, she might wake up ancient. In fact, she might not wake up at all. So maybe it was better to just let him think she was dead.

At last it occurred to her that what her mother had said about having Paavo nail the window shut was good, because it meant that she expected Amber to be around. If she didn't, then it wouldn't matter about the window. And if she really needed to get up to the roof, she could probably still do it. Because her mother didn't know exactly how she got up there—that she used the lightning rod and the side of the house—and if she had to, she could do that right from the ground, she thought. She could climb up using the brackets probably, even though she wouldn't have the gutter to relieve some of the weight until she got to the sewing room window ledge. Like her father said, the trick was to pretend you were on the ground. You could dance and jump on a two-by-four on the ground and never fall, so climbing with hands and feet should be no problem. If the lightning rod held.

But her mother had also said that about Paavo nailing the window shut while she was up there, which meant that she expected her to try, and also that she didn't believe Amber had used up the paint and thrown away the jar. Not that it had been a very good lie. But any lie—even a transparent one—was better than just defying her mother to her face. Whatever happened, she had to hang on to the paint in the jar, Amber decided. Her father couldn't protect her anymore, couldn't tell her mother to lighten up, couldn't coax his little girl through her darkest feelings in that fade-away voice of his:

I hate Mommy.

No, you don't.

I do. I wish she was dead.

No, you don't. Your mother loves you.

Hah.

And you love her.

Double hah.

Someday you're going to have to work this out—you two. Someday you're going to have to find a way to communicate. Your mother doesn't know how to tell you she loves you. She thinks so much of you that she wants you to be perfect. But you just want her to love you.

Triple hah. Like I could care.

You want that more than anything else in the world.

He was good about that. Understanding her and her mother. Her parents had fought a lot, and you could think they hated each other, but if anyone knew her mother and could make her change her mind about anything, it was her dad. That's what Amber wanted to believe. But now her mother had done all these cruel things, brought her dad back in a wheelchair even—why? And she was checking people in and out like they were clothes in her closet. Trying to get them to fit perfectly too. So maybe her father had been right, and maybe now her mother had gone over the edge.

And he was wrong about her wanting her mother to love her.

She didn't care anymore. Not at all.

At last, reluctantly, she drifted off to sleep while Mr. Bryce stood watch outside the ashes of the barn, unaware and unable to save her from extinction.

And that was how she died.

Only it wasn't as bad as she expected. Because, in the first place, nothing much really changed when she opened her eyes again. In fact, she didn't know she was dead until she heard the barking. No dog barked like Sir Aarfie, and no dog came skidding down the hall on the wood floor and then windmilled his nails on the seam of her door like that, as fast as a gerbil's paws on an exercise wheel. So she must be where Aarfie had gone when he died. But then she heard Molly hollering "Where did that dog come from?"—and what was Molly doing here where Aarfie had gone? So then she knew she wasn't dead but that somehow, some way, Sir Aarfie had come back to life. And by the time she was sprawled on her bedroom floor, laughing and trying to keep him from licking her lips, she was already thinking that it had to be her mother. Her mother had painted Sir Aarfie back. She had found a photo somewhere and made the painting last night after their big confrontation in the sewing room.

And Amber didn't know why, but that made her start to cry again.

How could she have thought her mother would really hurt her? Hadn't she given her life twice? And even though she had caused her first death, it was because she wanted to bring her back, wanted her to be okay again and not in a wheelchair. Her mother had stayed up all night probably, looking for a photo of Aarfie and doing the painting, and now he was back! *(Your mother doesn't know how to tell you she loves you.)*

So what could she do to show her mother how thankful she was? Because neither one of them was any good at saying how they felt. *(Someday you're going to have to find a way to communicate.)* And she guessed she knew what she had to do, even though now that the first wave of relief had passed she felt just a tingle of doubt, as if maybe her mother had known all along how it was going to turn out.

But she got dressed anyway, putting on her Skechers and giving Aarfie one of her ragged felt-top boots from last winter. Then, while he was chewing industriously on the sole, she closed her bedroom door behind her, so that he couldn't follow and betray her intentions by barking. But the old floorboards snapped like a whole pack of barking dogs as she darted quickly through the house. And Molly and Beverly were in the parlor, though they only nodded as she raced past, thinking she was going upstairs to thank her mother. Which she was, of course. But she was going to do it not with words but with the thing her mother wanted, even though it meant she would have to trust her now, because she would have no more leverage. The jar of red paint was up in the cupola, and she would get it and bring it to the studio, and her mother would understand and they wouldn't have to say a thing.

That was what she intended to do.

And she would have done it too, except that when she got to the sewing room and tried to raise the window sash, two slotted screws stared out of the wood at her like silver dragon's eyes.

18

Get Amber!

When had she last said those words? 1968? '69? Before Woodstock but after Kennedy and King were assassinated, Ariel thought. The year of the three deaths. Like the rest of the nation, they had been traumatized by all the madness, and then—that summer—Sir Aarfie ran out in front of the pickup on the curve, and that third death was childhood's end as far as Amber was concerned. But until then Ariel could say *Get Amber!* with an intonation of excitement to the eager toy collie, and he would look up at her, half understanding, and she would slap her hands on her thighs, making him flinch and scamper off without so much as a sniff,. as if he knew by telepathy where his young mistress was. He always found Amber, always barked when he did.

So now he was recalled for duty as a sleeper saboteur, a mole, a plant who would perform his Judas act at the proper time, *because Ariel absolutely could not risk everything on a child's perspective!* If her daughter managed to retrieve the paint from the roof, or if she had more hidden elsewhere, or if she was holding back some monster painting like this scarecrow of hers, then she must find it. She would watch for Amber's furtive exit, leaving Aarfie behind, and then when Amber had time to reach whatever hideaway she was visiting, Ariel would free the dog.

Get Amber!

The thirty-six-year-old painting of Aarfie she had used as a model stood side by side with the new one, virtually identical except for the brightness and the subtle densities in color that she achieved now with brush strokes rather than pigments. She had found the canvas flat in a drawer, where she had left it after reclaiming the mount board for another project. It wasn't until she finished the new painting and noticed the shaky crayoned inscription MY DOG on the back of the old canvas that she remembered the circumstances of that year: explaining assassination and war to Amber, the accident with Aarfie in August, "Hey Jude" for a dirge that fall because its lyrics and slow recession at the end seemed to sustain them, and then "Oliver" at Christmastime for consolation and new beginnings.

They had taken their chances in a world that was falling apart back then and had survived. Why was everything going wrong for her now when she had control? Should she risk everything, put Amber in school, send everyone back to the families who had buried or cremated them? The world would overrun her if it knew what she could do. She could paint back saints and prophets, presidents and Elvis Presley. It would be chaos if she did, of course. And yet, her little circle might be grateful to her then.

Another possibility was that she could destroy the paint and free them, trusting that she would not be forgotten again. But they would still be discovered for what they were and surrounded with sensationalism. She would be derided by the world for throwing it all away—the Elvises and Gandhis. Her "friends" would feel pressure to ridicule her too.

She stood at the window while the *alla prima* was drying sufficiently. She didn't watch—not watching had become a superstition with her—but just stared out as the night thinned away, shuddering a little at the sounds behind her. She cried for the living Ambers she had lost, but the tears formed so slowly that there was no relief, and when at last dawn came and she heard the spasm of paws on the studio floor, her brittle mood annealed into something less vulnerable.

"And where have *you* been?" she asked Aarfie when he stretched his paws up to the windowsill.

She waited until the room filled halfway with light, like a bathtub full of sunrise, and then she led Sir Aarfie across the studio and opened the door.

"Get Amber," she said.

Later, she asked Dana to bring some coffee up to the sewing room for both of them. Of all the household, Dana was still the least likely to lie or talk behind her back, she thought, and if she did either of those things, they would show on her face like a slap. One on one, Dana read like a diary.

"You have a little sunburn," Ariel said when the coffee was poured. "Or is that from the barn fire yesterday?"

"Sunburn. And how are you today, Ariel?"

"Lovely, thank you. You should put something on that sunburn."

Dana nodded once. "I see you've gotten Amber a dog. You had one in the sixties, didn't you? Is that . . . ?"

"Sir Aarfie."

"Funny name."

"Amber says she saved you yesterday."

"Amber?"

"She started the fire."

"Amber did it?"

"She was watching you in the barn." The slapped look was evident, even with the sunburn, and the longer Ariel stared, the brighter it became. "Nasty habit of hers. Spying on people."

"I wasn't hiding anything, so she wasn't spying."

"No, of course not."

"If she didn't tell you, Denny Bryce and I were having a picnic, and I went to sit in the barn afterward."

"It's none of her business. No one's business but yours."

"I guess you're wondering about me taking his picture." Tremor in the voice. "It's really awkward. I don't know if I can do it."

"Yes, everything is awkward. This whole arrangement . . . being alive when you shouldn't be . . . awkward."

"Ariel—"

"Much easier to just follow conventions, niceties . . . natural laws."

"Ariel, I'm not complaining."

"Yes, you are. Why is everybody making this so *awkward* for me? Can you tell me that, Dana? Why don't I have"—she gestured—"cooperation or . . . gratitude or . . . sympathy?"

"You've got all of those things, Ariel."

"Really? You've been dead, Dana. What was it like? Tell me that and I'll believe in your cooperation." She waited a full ten seconds, even though her companion adopted a pose of settled long suffering. "Well, so much for enlightenment. I feel better now that you've . . . co-operated. Take Mr. Bryce's photograph, Dana. You can do that, and I expect you to."

Neither of them touched their coffee.

The brittleness Ariel had felt last night was diamond hard now. Like it or not, she was at her best as judge and executioner. She saw this as a role that had been forced upon her by a lifetime of alienation, but her great fear was that it was her native element. Perhaps these second comings were about punishment and revenge after all. She didn't know how to be loved. Would she even recognize it if it came? Or would it be lost in her own resistance and suspicion? Even Amber's gushing gratitude for Aarfie's return seemed pasted on. *Thanks, Mommy, thank you SO much!* rendered in a remembered voice from a still younger child. Not her. Not really Amber. But what was Amber? A hybrid of two little girls thirty-five years apart. "Beluga butt" and "freaky scene" with Dylanesque overtones all in the same sentence. "Groovy" and "cool" were her bridge over decades.

And then at lunch Dear Dana, sitting across from Denny Bryce, who had come for his afternoon visit to his father, lifted the Polaroid camera from below the line of the table. And when Denny pulled back from looking over his father's shoulder, she said: "Oh, come on now. Your dad's all spruced up. Pose with him."

Ariel's appraising scrutiny sharpened. Martin Bryce, shaved and freshly barbered, was wearing a new long-sleeve shirt his son had brought him, but that wasn't the incentive for Denny's cooperation. It was the relationship that was unmistakably deepening between him and Dana, Ariel decided. She could see it in his eyes, wide and boring into Dana's. The premise there was a mix of doubt and tentative trust, and she could tell which one was winning by the fact that he leaned forward with a reluctant smile. The electronic flash left his expression floating in the air, and Ariel memorized it, certain that the image would be all she needed to combine with her artistic eye on canvas.

Denny Bryce was the one exposed element in New Eden. He had insinuated himself through implied threats and an open wallet in order to get what he wanted. And now Ariel could recognize the daily surge of his little foreign car up the driveway. It seemed likely that sooner or later he would know too much So she needed some insurance, a little implied threat of her own. She could paint him to life in the house now, handicapped in some way, and that would end the natural-born Denny Bryce in the natural world, just as it had the natural-born Amber. But that wouldn't end the danger he posed. He was active in society, and there would be an investigation if he broke his connections. So, unfortunately, she would have to deal with him terminally. Once he was created here at New Eden, she would immediately paint him out again. Presto. No corpus delicti. Ariel the judge and executioner would have to protect New Eden. The world had no jurisdiction here.

With a nascent whir, the Polaroid snapshot slid out of the camera and everyone craned to see. An image emerged from the chemical wash. One more toss in the wishing well of immortality for those who stood in line.

Ariel loomed in like a towering adult casting a shadow over her children's discovery. "Let me see," she said, reaching across Dana for the prize.

And Dana, smelling lavender water and talc and something horribly eager, was suddenly repelled. Just before the bony wrist passed her cheek, she dropped the photo—some thought flicked it—into her soup. It was tomato soup. Dana's white cotton blouse looked like it was spattered with gore.

Ariel's gasp was palpable. "Well, I'll just take another," she said, reaching for the camera, which Dana—now standing as she dabbed at her blouse with a napkin—held in one hand.

The grandstand understood all of it, of course: Ariel's motive, Dana's taking of the photograph, the change of heart. They cheered inwardly when the photo went in the soup. But it was too much to expect Dana to refuse to give up the camera. So when that object seemed suddenly to slip from her grasp, fracturing its plastic shell and cracking the lens on the hardwood floor, mitral valves hung up and lungs quit respiring. For a long moment no one dared a living breath.

But Ariel was set this time. "Poor Dana," she said very evenly, "your arthritis must be killing you." And then she looked at them in a slow pan, smiling benignly.

Hearts jump-started, lungs filled to capacity, and in the wake of Ariel's gray retreat victorious smiles broke forth. But Dana was not smiling. She sat back down in a cold sweat, eyes averted, oblivious to the goodwill burbling around her. She didn't have arthritis.

Yet.

19

Ariel slept three times that day—two and a half hours, forty minutes, twenty-five—but despite being up the night before, she wasn't tired. Old people who slept were either ill or bored, she told herself. In reality her body was shedding its long-term needs like a dead skin. Beneath the surface she was beginning to consume her final resources, like a fiery star-bound meteor.

So the naps were only to preserve her strength, because there was no doubt at all now what she must do tonight. Tonight she would be altering six portraits— Helen's, Beverly's, Paavo's, Ruta's, Molly's and Dana's—the able-bodied of her disobedient second comings.

She didn't dare think about it during the day. If she thought about it while she was still smarting from the nearly open rebellion, she would very likely succumb to her basest instincts. A lifetime of eating crow, playing second fiddle, bringing up the rear, and now that she had a taste of control, a rebuff. That made it doubly tart. But even with the delay and the naps, dark images were simmering inside her. Artistic blasphemies she couldn't suppress. Ruta with no mouth. None at all. And Molly with a thunderous butt—a beluga butt!—so big that she couldn't climb the stairs. Dana turned into a cinder of Cinderella, left scarred, as if her sunburn were indeed the searing, weeping wounds left by the barn fire. Paavo with his sleeves pinned up because he no longer had arms. Or maybe she should take his legs, leaving him in Amber's old American Flyer coaster wagon to get around. Horrors all, tinged with gallows irony.

But she put off the conscious decisions of what to paint, because in the end it had to be more measured than that. Otherwise how would it be explained to Denny Bryce? Yet she wanted them to know without ambiguity. She couldn't take Ruta's mouth away, but she could make it smaller. Just enough to make her want to scream through it (ha-ha). Paavo's strong hands could become gnarled and stiffened, like Dana's were going to be, and "Helen the Hunchback" was an appellation waiting to happen. Beverly would be runtier still, thinned and weakened. Accelerated aging, that was all. Weaker, stiffer—Molly staring at her enlarged and infantilized thighs in the mirror, noting the flaccid flesh of her arms. Enough change so that Ariel's Edenites would see it in each other's eyes—the common terror, the realization of what they were and that Ariel could run the clock in either direction.

Denny Bryce might notice, but he wouldn't recognize the suddenness of the process. All in one night. Passover. Her first-born smitten to a soul. The tenth plague. Unannounced. No Paschal Lamb's blood on their lintels to save them.

20

Maybe it was the silver dragon's eyes staring out at her from the sewing room window sash, or maybe it was the fear she sensed everyone had for her mother, or maybe it was just her own streak of wildness, but Amber knew that she wasn't going to give back the paint. She would have after Aarfie came back—she had tried to—but now it was too late. She didn't care if that meant she was ungrateful and disobedient. She already believed she was a bad person, because she had no friends, no real father anymore, and because her mother didn't love her even though she tried. You couldn't fake that.

The magic paint almost made up for it. The paint was power and control over her own life, if she could just get good at using it. Sure, she had made mistakes, but she wouldn't make any more. She would just hang on to the paint until she figured out how to use it to make things better, and also because as long as she was the only one who knew where it was, she was protected. But if she wasn't going to give it back, she *was* going to have to move it. Sooner or later her mother would figure a way to get it off the roof, so it had to be moved.

Night was the best time. Night was the only time, now that the third-story window was sealed. Amber went to bed at ten o'clock without being told, and at twelve thirty, while the house exhaled the heat trapped in its walls, she rose up again and pulled on her jeans, her Mudd T-shirt and Skechers, and stroked Sir Aarfie, whispering: "You stay here, Aarfie. . . . And don't bark, okay? No bark."

He barked once as soon as she closed the door on him, a throaty "woof" that registered his indignation, but she moved away quickly, because if she lingered he would think it was a game.

In the parlor, luminous with moonlight, she stopped and listened. She had a funny feeling, like everything around her—the wooden blue doll on the mantel, the pincushion porcupine on the corner shelf, the metronome that seemed to be clicking its tongue with disapproval, the oval picture frames gaping like open mouths hanging on the wall—was alive and warning her not to go. Her mother said she had fallen while climbing in her other life and that was how she had ended up paralyzed, and now she had to climb from the ground to the roof, so maybe that was why she was anxious. But she had to go. Because if she didn't, she wouldn't have that much of a life anyway.

The moonlight was so bright that she could see mosquitoes rising off the screen as she pushed onto the porch. The air was very still and muggy under the overhang, but as soon as she passed the corner by the willow she felt the uneven current, as if the wind were circling the house in waves. And by the time she got around to the back it was flooding against her like water crashing along an invisible moat. The old TV antenna wires slapped rhythmically against the clapboards, reminding her of Colonel Klink slapping his riding crop on his thigh in *Hogan's Heroes (. . . Don't even think about trying to climb that wall, Hogan)*. But the thing that both-

ered her the most now that she stood behind the towering farmhouse was the light on the third floor. Her
mother's studio. That meant she was painting.

And even though she could be painting anything, the
fear that she was altering her horrid little daughter right
this instant grew to a conviction. The picture could already be done and just drying. And when it dried what
would she be? Too old to climb up on a roof and get the
magic antidote? Too old to climb down if the change
came when she was up there?

Seizing on her own fear, Amber went straight to the
lightning rod and clamped her hands as high as
she could. Then she drew her hips up parallel with the
ground and planted both feet against the side of the
house. The rust on the rod gave her a grip, but it tore her
skin too. Hand over hand, foot over foot she climbed, a
right angle of pulling and pushing. Now and then she
rested her hip against the rod to take a little weight off
her arms and legs. Only, each time she did that, she
heard a wrenching sound from the brackets. There were
three of them, so rusted that you couldn't see the screws.
And there was no window on the second floor within
reach of the pole.

The wind was tossing her hair in her mouth and her
arms were burning and her legs felt like sand was draining out of them, so she had to stop every few feet and
just hang there. But she still thought she could do it. She
thought she could do it right up until she got halfway,
when without any warning at all the rod began to pull
away from the house.

Her feet left the clapboards and her body swayed out
past the vertical. She almost let go—she would have, instinctively, if the pole had kept on going—but miracu-
lously it stayed vertical and her legs swung back,
banging against the side of the house. And now as she

twisted and scrabbled to get her feet back in place, she saw that it was the middle bracket. When she had come even with it, it had popped out of the rotting board. One of the screws was missing and the other was rusted into the hole, its point inches away from the side of the house. The lower and upper brackets were still holding though, and lightning rods went down into the ground, so maybe the brackets didn't matter.

She could feel her movements thrumming through the metal as she went higher, making her think that the upper bracket must not be very tight either. But the sewing room window ledge was there just below it, and she got a foot on that. Numbed and exhausted, she clung there. One more hard pull and she could reach the galvanized gutter. Drawing close against the clapboards, she gathered her right foot under her and pushed . . . and pulled . . . and now she had her right elbow above the gutter. The thrumming stopped as she climbed past the upper bracket, thrusting herself onto the roof with her left hand. And there she lay, flat to the pitch, letting the blood flow back into her limbs and the pain subside where the skin at the base of her fingers had been pinched against the metal pole.

Below her the TV antenna wires still slapped the side of the house, and to either side loose shingles flapped with the gusts. Nevertheless, she felt safer now than she did in the house. This was her realm. This was where no one else could reach her. Even the wind seemed to be different now, soothing on her forehead instead of pushing at her back. It wasn't until she made her zigzag to a higher point and then to the pipe and then to the chimney that the feeling of being out of reach from things that could hurt her underwent revision.

Because now she could hear something inside the cupola. But she had already thrown herself up the pitch, and if she stopped, she would slide down. So she kept going until she got one hand over the saddle shingles at the ridge. And before she could pull herself up, it came at her with a rush of wings and golden eyes. She never saw the claws. They scraped her ear and cheek as she turned away, and then the thing was gone. By the time she got one leg over the ridge, all she saw was an edge-on silhouette gliding into a line of trees against the blue green glow to the west. An owl, probably. That's what happened when you burned down a barn. Owls went looking for new homes.

She touched her cheek. There was blood, for sure—black and slippery. Her mother used to warn her about cuts and rusty nails and stuff, so she knew you could get lockjaw from that, and now she had gotten rust from her fingers in the scratches on her face. She'd better hurry up and get done so she could wash out the cuts, she thought. Straddling the ridge she edged cautiously to-ward the cupola. Half standing, she wormed her way through the broken slats.

It still smelled funny inside, like the mud that stayed icky in the canals along the road, but she thought she could smell the owl too. A kind of warm, gray odor, like a dog that had been out in the rain. Everyone laughed when she said she could tell colors with her nose, which she could. Gray. Definitely gray. She waited for her eyes to adjust, but the stripes of moonlight stayed silvery blue and the black was just black. So she felt around very slowly where she had snugged the paint jar down next to the platform, until her fingers touched the glass shoulder just below the screw cap. There wasn't any point in sav-ing the paintbrush or the poster paper, so she just tucked the jar against her side with one hand and started back down.

It was easier than going up, even with the paint. But

then she came to the lightning rod. She was going to
have to put the brakes on gravity, and for that she was
going to need both arms. Encircling her Mudd T-shirt
over the jar, she tucked the hem deep into her jeans. The
glass was cool against her skin right where her heart
thumped, and she could actually feel the red liquid
sloshing around like it was blood or something. She kept
her legs bent to stop the T-shirt from pulling up as she
worked her way off the edge of the roof onto the lightning rod. Then she began walking down the side of the
house, controlling the descent with her arms and the
pressure of her hip against the pole. Her father had read
some of *Adventures of Huckleberry Finn* to her—the
part where Tom and Huck climb up and down a lightning rod in order to help Jim—and Amber grew a little
heady remembering that, thinking she could do the same
even though she was younger and a girl. No one could
climb like she could. But her hands slipped just above
the second floor, along with some of her confidence, and
she had to press her forearms against the rusty metal to
stop a slide. Chastened and scraped, she came down the
rest of the way fighting for breath.

For a few seconds after she stood at the bottom her
legs seemed to be sinking into the ground. She squatted
down, curling her body around the cool glass in her shirt
and resting her head against her arms. She felt nauseous
and her gashed cheek was starting to sting. The wind
washed over her face, reviving her gradually and carrying the smell of damp ashes to her from the charred heap
that had been the barn. If it wasn't so messy and so close
to the house, she could hide the jar there, she thought.
But then again, it could still be hot underneath the ashes,
and maybe the paint would dry up or the jar crack. No,
she would stick to her plan. She had a hiding place she
had discovered a long time ago. It wasn't high up like

she wanted, but it was all overgrown, and it had a
wooden cover.

Rising shakily to her feet, she started off for the fields.

Her dad had told her about the cistern—how the gangsters used it to dump bodies—but when she had actually
stumbled on it one day, she was surprised and maybe a
little disappointed that there were no skeletons at the
bottom. She knew this because she had climbed down
the rickety ladder that stood inside. On a bright day, with
the cover off, you could see all the way down. And when
you stood on the bottom you could look up against the
light and see pretty much everything about the cistern. It
was lined with old, crumbling bricks with roots sticking
through in a couple of spots, and some of the bricks
were lying in the dirt. She thought the ladder was probably there because someone had used it to move the dead
bodies.

So now it was going to be her new hiding place. Her
studio. She would keep the magic paint there, and she
would get another brush and poster paper and regular
paint so she could practice. The field on whose edge the
cistern lay was shielded from the house by a long strip of
trees. She wouldn't be seen if she circled around and
came up that side. It took a while to get there, but that
was good, because no one else would go walking this
far.

She had to kick around some to find the cistern now,
because even though she knew exactly where it was, all
the weeds and briers looked the same in the moonlight.
But then she stepped on the wooden cover and it made a
clunking sound on the rim. She bent and clawed aside
some dog fennel and spurge, exposing the weathered
edge. With her legs braced, she got her fingers under the
seam and slid aside the heavy cover.

What Amber Leppa smelled evanescing up from that

storied hole in the field evoked the color green in her
portfolio of visual scents. The green didn't go with its
history, she thought, though it could have been the green
of snakes or frogs of the kind that showed up with spring
rains. It was not the green of anything that survived in
sunlight. Once, she had turned over a piece of slate in a
ditch and been surprised by a ripple of emerald as vivid
as sequins from the City of Oz. But the exposed glitter
had faded to a dull brown residue so quickly that she
doubted what she had seen. That was what she thought
of when she smelled the hole, as if the sunless emerald
fungus, or whatever she had unearthed beneath the slate,
grew there between the bricks. She descended the rickety ladder and the green smell sharpened like a whiff of
cinnamon when you got it up your nose.

An irrepressible voyeur moon followed her, peeping
straight down into the bore of the cistern. By its light she
could see many more broken bricks than there had been
on her last visit. It occurred to her that another might fall
out of the walls and break her bottle of paint, so she set
up a small enclosure of bricks behind the base of the ladder and placed her precious jar within that. She was just
finishing when a moment of darkness swept past, as if
the light above her had blinked. Her gaze shot upward,
but the moon stared down innocently.

Brushing her cheek above the scratches, she stood and
climbed the shaky ladder. Funny how she felt safer
climbing a tree than a ladder. Ladders always bothered
her. And just as she reached the top it happened again. A
flicker of shadow. Only this time she saw a silhouette
rocket across the field, something massive wheeling behind the tops of the trees.

A jumble of branches filtered it there, but she had the
impression that the arcing thing continued to move, gliding like the owl she had flushed from the cupola. Only

this could not have been the owl. It had to be ten times bigger than that. In fact . . . maybe the owl had hidden itself in the cupola to get away from it. Maybe it had come at her because it was terrified.

So now she squinted, trying to make sense of the moonlight coming through the branches. Only, it didn't really make sense. Like looking at one of those color blindness tests where everything blurs together if you can't pick out the color that makes the numbers. Down lower, where the shadows filled in, she could see a bunch of fireflies. But now she was starting to see the numbers, too—the pattern that was way too big for the treetops—and it just couldn't be what it looked like.

It couldn't be a spiderweb.

One big spiderweb raying out like floating stairways all leading away from a center. And when the breeze lifted it, just the silhouettes that made up a web moved, and that was why she saw it—thought she saw it—in the first place. But if it was that, then where was the spider that should have been waiting in the middle?

Silly.

A spider couldn't get that big. What would it eat?

And then she thought about the red spider in the bathtub, and what if that was just a baby of the ones she had created? Maybe it had crawled through the drain because it was so small, and this was where it had come from. She had painted lots of spiders, and they had all been big compared to the other things she had painted. As big as the picture she had made of Aarfie. As big as the scarecrow.

And that was when her stomach dropped out and she felt hollow and cold. Because the fireflies she saw arranged against the blackness at the base of the trees were still clustered the same way—like pairs of headlights, some big, some small—and they weren't blinking.

21

Passover.

While the six slept, Ariel set their portraits in a row on the workbench: Helen, Beverly, Paavo, Ruta, Molly, Dana. She couldn't suppress a small spark of self-righteousness about their fate as she mixed her colors. She had begun New Eden without a scintilla of revenge in her heart, but they had forced her to this. Not her doing but theirs. And she was sick to death of their willfulness.

She couldn't just throw them away and start over, because they would be the same aloof, unappreciative, backstabbing, disloyal covey who had determined the course of her life for all those years. They had to change from within. Recognize the error of their ways and how badly they had underestimated her abilities and her worth. And the only way she could hasten that was to discipline them, force them to rethink who they were and the consequences of their choices.

The pointel's worth of red ashes she transferred to each jar as she mixed her paints was negligible compared to what remained in the flask. She could not conceive of ever running out. And yet she would. In time. Finite ashes; infinite time. What would happen when the last reanimation from the last drop of the last mix was lived and they all inevitably died? What kind of reckoning would the final death provide?

Such a wind outside! The gusts slapped the antennae wires against the side of the house—*and what was that?* She put down her brush, went to the window. She flicked the latch and tried to raise the sash, but it was swollen shut and she managed only an inch or two. The humidity touched her fingers like webs and she pushed the window shut again and drew the shade. Another thrum came through the walls as she returned to her brush. Oh, bother, the damned house had stood for a century and a half, it would stand another night. So she tried to ignore the elements outside, though twice there were distinct thuds above the ceiling that made her lift her eyebrows. Something in the rafters? Not the first time, particularly with a storm in the neighborhood.

And then she became wholly absorbed in the metaphysical oneness of creating. Even without miracle paint she knew the ecstasy of invention. Before she began encroaching on God's seminal act with the red dust, creating on canvas had been as close as she could get to worship. Legends of what if, histories of what was, myths of what wasn't. Art: worshipping the ideal and dreaming aloud.

She worked rapidly, and as always the intensity of concentration sustained her. Like a medium channeling energy, she took on the identities she was trying to create. She even felt a kind of self-pity, if not compassion, as if the frailties and deformities she was painting were actually hers. And she awoke to the moment of completion feeling that the universe had gathered at her shoulder, that she could throw the shade up and close by the window there would be stars, benign furnaces sighing with approbation. But even after she cast off this disorientation, a feeling persisted that she had assembled a

whole new order. She gazed critically at the afflictions
of her Passover and thought *These are not the people
who held power over me.* She saw the stiffness and in-
fantilization, the humpback and the shrunken mouth, the
atrophy and kraurosis, and they inspired an odd mater-
nalism in her. She was pondering this mystery when she
became aware of distant barking. It was something she
hadn't heard for more than thirty years. Aarfie, of
course. In exactly the same volume and muffled timbre
she had heard hundreds of times, acting like coordinates
that placed him in Amber's room.

How late was it?

Question: Why was Aarfie locked in there, and why
wasn't Amber quieting him?

Answer: Because Amber wasn't there, of course.

And then it all fell into place like shuffled playing
cards. The thrum of the lightning rod . . . the flutter of
something against the clapboards . . . the thumps on the
roof . . . Aarfie barking. Amber was relocating the stolen
paint. Ariel hadn't expected it to happen so quickly, and
certainly not in the middle of the night, but there it was,
not a moment wasted. Like mother, like daughter.

Well, she was ready too. She took her cane (because
there might be snakes or even spiders—and how she de-
tested vermin!). Downstairs she went, first to the kitchen
to get some twine for a leash, then to Amber's room
where she still remembered how to use her knee to keep
the frenzied toy collie from wriggling past before she got
the tether on. He was hyper tonight, and that was good
because he wouldn't need coaxing. By the time she
moved out of his way, *Get Amber* was redundant.

She had forgotten a flashlight, she realized as they
crossed the yard, and almost reined Aarfie in. But the
twine might not withstand dragging him back, and anyway, Amber must be well into her business by now.

Never mind the flashlight. She would trust the silver complicity of the moon with Aarfie's noisy rush and the parry of her cane, hovering back and forth along the ground, to keep her safe from crawling things. And besides, she didn't expect they would have to go far.

She was depending on the dog not to bark too soon. He had enough hunter in his blood to go with the herder until the moment of confrontation. And then he would create a triumphant racket, having come to the end of his instincts. But that would mean they were in sight of Amber.

When they entered the fields Ariel began to have second thoughts about the flashlight. She had expected the hiding place to be close by in the old pump housing or the machine shed or perhaps the rubble of the barn. Her own childhood caches had all been near the house: an old rubber tire, an upturned crate, the abandoned 1926 Minerva Landaulet that had sat on its rear axel near the light pole and later was used for a chicken coop. But, of course, Amber the undaunted would not shrink from crossing all borders as her shrinking-violet mother had.

So Ariel found herself knifing between stalks and plunging through sinks. There were no obvious signs beyond Aarfie's surges that a human had come this way. "Get Amber," she reminded him in case he had gotten sidetracked by the scent of a rabbit or a raccoon. And then, two fields removed from the house, the dog suddenly stiffened. "Bingo, Aarfie," she said. But his ears and tail went down and he began to slink forward, whining a little, nosing from side to side. Ahead of them was a thick swathe of trees.

She quickened a little at recognition of the tract. It was a parcel where she had picked wild blackberries as a child, a refuge for does with yearlings. And now it was her daughter's secret hideaway. But Aarfie's ears went up and he woofed truculently, then immediately whined a contradiction. Ariel could feel his tremor right through the twine. A few seconds later she heard faint crashing in the undergrowth. There were moving silhouettes, an insoluble mix. And finally a scream.

Amber's scream.

The caterpillar of abject fur Aarfie had become answered with sudden urgency. Ariel took a single step and that launched him. But if it was the right course for a canine, it was the wrong one for the tandem human. The disturbing tumult was coming toward them so rapidly that it was obviously not a timid nocturnal chase. Ariel stabbed her cane out front, trying desperately to slow down without letting go of the twine.

A silken something filled the air, distinct from the humidity that bathed her skin. The swaying trees and staccato thumpings planted an idea in her head of what it was. She had to tell herself, *These are not filaments floating over me; it's only mist.*

Aarfie's ears were on swivels: up for Amber's screams, down when they stopped. He must have smelled or heard or sensed the enormity of the horror even before Ariel discerned it in the shifting blackness. On the next piercing scream Ariel let go of the twine, knowing that, brave little shepherd that he was, Aarfie would keep going straight into the valley of the shadow of death.

Afterward she would pretend that the twine broke— this is what she would tell Amber. But the shrill accusations against her then would not be stilled. And she did let it go. She had to let it go, because it bought them a little time. Even though the mismatch between the dog and the emerging obscenity wasn't going to last long.

There were thick silhouettes that were too high in the trees to be growing there, too disjointed in their sudden swaying to be rooted, as if whole groups of trunks and limbs were suddenly transplanting themselves. And there were the fireflies, pinpoints of demon light flickering through shadowy lace. Something so huge that it couldn't squeeze through the branches darted there, searching for a way down. And unseen but heard, a little girl was struggling in the underbrush.

Despite the fact that its silk was extruded all over the tract of trees, the horror could not move freely. But Sir Aarfie could. He barked and worried the thing, forced it to recoil and dodged when it suddenly solved the inter-vening foliage with a rush of legs. But in the end, the toy collie's blood went coursing through the obscene fangs of a behemoth that had been created by the very child he was protecting.

They would think of that afterward, but no one was thinking of it while they fled: mother and daughter pounding across the field hand in hand. Ariel huffed dazedly as she tried to keep up, and for once in her life she was using her cane for its intended purpose.

When they were back in the house they lay in a cold embrace, too numb to cry for Aarfie or themselves.

"I painted it, Mommy," Amber confessed in a drained voice about the spider just before dawn.

"I know."

"I did it because you hate spiders."

"I know."

Later that day Amber had the temerity to go back and look. The spider was a nocturnal thing, her mother had said, and that meant it wouldn't bother anyone until nightfall. As if she knew. So Amber went looking for Aarfie, but mercifully never found the drained wad of fur in its silk coffin.

She found his paw prints mixed in with her mother's shoe tracks, however, and that was when she understood. Her mother could not have heard the screams when she was in the house. She had been waiting for her to move the paint. That was why she had painted Aarfie back to life. So that he could betray her when she hid the paint. And he would have too, but what happened in the woods kept them from finding the cistern.

If her mother had accidentally saved her from the spider, the spider had accidentally saved her from her mother.

22

Denny was thinking of the dead crows in the clothes dryer as he drove up. Dana hadn't mentioned them again, and he hadn't thought to ask. All that business at the table with having his picture taken, and then the photo dropping in the soup and then the camera getting smashed—what was that all about? A token event of some deeper schism going on? Beverly Swanson had warned him that letting his picture be taken was a bad idea, but Dana had already taken one the day after his father stepped barefoot in the broken glass, so what was the big deal? Maybe they were just upset about the barn burning down. Lightning strike, Molly had told him. But it didn't look like there had been a storm.

Shit, he had forgotten Beverly's cigarettes again.

At age fifty-one Denny Bryce knew this much about himself: that he had become a high school counselor because he didn't like being on the defensive, and almost everything in life made him feel defensive. He wished he could blame it on childhood deprivations or abuse, but it was simply his nature. His mother's nature before him. Yes, his father could have been more demonstrative— hugged him, given his unqualified thumbs-up without holding back the last carrot of motivation, witnessed his few triumphs on ball fields and in concerts—but Denny would have been full of self-doubt and yearning anyway. Maybe that was why he was still here every day, seeking his father's approval, seeking his own approval of who he was, who he should be. Being a school counselor put him behind the bench in the courtroom of human jurisprudence, when all he really wanted was just not to be in the dock. Nevertheless, he was a profoundly sympathetic judge. Everyone who stood before him left acquitted, absolved, exonerated. But New Eden was not one of the safe houses of his life. Coming here put him on the defensive in the extreme.

He had expected a comfort zone to eventually set in as he became familiar with the place, but when he pulled open the screen door and stepped across the threshold, he still felt the formality of borrowed space. There were protocols of age and perspective here he could never meet. The dusty bric-a-brac and worn fabrics were helplessly mute with history, the high ceilings swam with ghostly echoes, and the totem objects enshrined in cabinets or frames remained arcane mysteries to him. Worst of all, the eyes of the elders who lived here grew more distant instead of closer with each visit he paid. They were *not* sympathetic judges. They were an increasingly disinterested panel of jurors consigning him vote by vote to the irrelevant world of external things.

Except for today.

Today the gazes bore into him like bloodied iron pikes, stabbing again and again but failing to hold. Red-rimmed eyes, great gluey eyes, muzzy orbs wide with fear or desperation—not just on one person but on all of them. So he understood that whatever had agitated the table at yesterday's meal had progressed to this. Or deteriorated. And in part, because of the eyes, he glimpsed the vague travesties of Ariel's Passover without really seeing them, recognizing that something had changed but blind to the details. He saw that everyone looked older, more defeated by life than he had seen them before, but that was just a thing you noticed suddenly. And they kept moving, like so many ravaged salmon dying in the shallows of their final migration; this too confused the impression.

It was almost comical, their restless stirring in slow motion from room to room. He lingered longer than he normally would have in order to observe it, trying to start a conversation but getting only barely civil responses. How odd. It aroused all those counseling instincts that made him comfortable with distraught students sitting across a desk from him. Only, no one wanted to sit near him now. From parlor to dining room to kitchen they turned aside, slowly dying salmon casting raw-eyed pleas before wriggling away.

"What's going on?" he plied Dana when she came up from the cellars with a clothes basket only half full.

"Laundry," she said.

She looked haggard and pained, he thought. He followed her outside where she had strung a plastic clothesline from the stanchion at one end of the porch to a sugar maple thirty feet away.

"That's going to sag," he said about the clothesline.

"I couldn't fling the rope up through the first branch."

"Sounds like a job for Paavo."

She made a neutral sound, rubbed her fingers. He was startled by the knobbiness of her knuckles. This wasn't temporary swelling; it was the chronic deformity of arthritic hands. How had he not noticed before? That business with pressing his fingertips to hers the other day in the field—her hands had been smooth then. But, of course, he must be mistaken about that.

"Want me to clean out the dryer?" he said.

She looked at him with a glint of gratitude. "I couldn't ask you to do that."

"You aren't asking. I'm offering. Dana . . . *what's going on?*"

"You can't see?"

"See? Why don't you just say it? Then I'll know if it's what I see."

Her slate blue eyes were already receding, like the others. Doomed people looked that way. People on an ice floe drifting away from the mainland looked that way.

"There's nothing you can do for us," she said. "And your father . . . will be all right, I think."

"You *think?*"

She shook her head. "He'll be all right. I shouldn't have said it that way. I meant that you shouldn't interfere. There isn't any problem for you if you don't interfere."

"Listen, if I thought there was any danger to my father here, I'd be on it like—you'll pardon the expression—a fly on horseshit. So what exactly are you talking about? Why is everyone dragging around like mourners? Did someone die in that barn fire and Ariel is trying to hide it?"

But she wouldn't confirm, wouldn't deny. He played *Twenty Questions.* Got no satisfaction. It wasn't about the two of them or the photo or the camera, she maintained.

"You did drop that picture in the soup though?" he pressed her. "I mean, that wasn't an accident?"

She fussed wearily with the wet clothes going over the plastic clothesline, as if he had made a statement. Maybe it had been an accident, he thought, staring at her deformed hands. She could be embarrassed about her arthritis.

He went straight to his father's room then and recited the litany of contact, looking for clues to the subtext of his old man's life: "How are you, guy?" *"Lonely."* "That's because you sit in here all day." *"Says you."* "Well, don't you?" *"I don't remember."* Sometimes it was *"I don't care."* But Martin Bryce never spoke of events or the people around him. When he was stimulated enough, he would launch his own mantra:

"What is this place?"

"What time is it?"

"Beth is dead, isn't she?"

When she was alive, his father had always referred to her as "your mother." But increasingly now, as if it hurt to remove her even that far, it was just "Beth."

"You need a shave, old man," Denny said.

"No."

"I promise I won't cut you this time." His father remembered. Good sign.

"Use the electric shaver."

"Can't get any whiskers that way. You're a lumpy old man. Getting rid of your whiskers is like trying to shave parsley off mashed potatoes."

"Says you."

Did it matter if he shaved? Did it matter if he wore a cheap flannel shirt buttoned to the neck on a muggy day? He wasn't breaking a sweat. Denny's mother had sent away for that shirt—some catalogue filled with deception and offering hope to a woman still vital but without the energy to argue her husband into going shopping.

Denny asked half a dozen questions, knowing his father would tolerate no more than that. He tried to sculpt them so that they could not be responded to with clichés, hoping that something of the undercurrent in New Eden would emerge from the answers. His father would begin inventing things if the demand on his memory grew too great. He would simply snip out years of intervening reality to find some parallel that pleased him, something that fit comfortably with the continuum of the life he had known when his wife was alive. Thus the food was fine at New Eden, though he could do with another helping of Beth's apple brown Betty; and the people were fine, though he wished they wouldn't honk their car horns at all hours of the night; and he was getting along with everyone just fine—no arguments—except that he wanted to be left alone. Alone. He had complained about being alone when Denny had entered. Meaning that no matter who else was around, without Denny he would always be alone. His boy, the only living being who was still admitted to the estates of shared time and memory. When had his father ever trusted anyone this much? It hurt Denny to the core to be trusted like that. He wasn't worthy of it.

And that was funny, because he had spent most of his life trying to secure just that demonstration of paternal love and endorsement. And now it was his by default, by derangement. No, not derangement. His father would simply die if Denny let him. He was alive because Denny demanded it. Because Denny couldn't let him go. Didn't want to ever, ever, ever have to look back and know that he had just let him go.

So why wasn't he doing something about all this weird stuff going on here? He should at least be looking for the right questions, if not the answers. Dana Novicki's reticence was proof positive that there was something going on. Could he trust her when she said his father would be all right if he didn't interfere?

"I'm not trying to interfere," he said, face-to-face with Ariel later on. He had asked for a few minutes with her through Molly (pallid, flabby Molly who seemed to have succumbed to gravity overnight) and was struck at how composed Ariel was and how nervous Molly became before she left them alone in the sewing room. "Believe me, the last thing I want to do is to interfere with something that attracted me in the first place because . . . because it seemed to be working." He lost track of where he was going. He was a lousy performer, and he should not have rehearsed that little preamble about not interfering.

"And now it isn't?" Ariel helped him crisply.

"Isn't . . . ?"

"Working."

"I don't know if it is. I mean, if I said that, I meant I'm just a little worried about my father."

"Then it's your father who isn't working?"

"No. No, I don't mean my old man. Something is going on here, and I don't know what it is. I think it's personal between you and . . . and your circle, so I really don't want to know. But if it's threatening to my father—and frankly, if everyone is at each other's throats, then it's bound to affect him sooner or later—then I'm worried. You can understand that."

"How is it threatening to your father, Mr. Bryce?"

"Well, for one thing, I can't get hold of him, and he can't get hold of me."

"Ah, the phone. What else?"

"I don't know what else. It's just the atmosphere. My first impression of this place was that it was so informal that I thought it was just what my father needed. A real home—natural. I guess this is the downside of that. But there are limits—" She looked at him so steadily that he forbore raising the possibility of taking his father out of New Eden.

"I'll remind you of all my reservations, Mr. Bryce. You wouldn't listen. Even after I made it clear to you how unorthodox we were, you wanted your father to come here. You implied that if I didn't let you in, you might raise questions with the authorities. Specifically, I believe you mentioned taxes and state subsidies and certification. I compromised rather than deal with that, because no one wants to do back flips for nearsighted inspectors. As you say, we're informal here—"

"I pay you more than the going rate."

"Yes, you do. Your choice again. All your choices. And when I told you I wouldn't accept anyone who didn't agree to stay here for life, you accepted that too."

There it was. So, what if he took his father out? The two of them would be right back where they had started. No place to go that wasn't a warehouse for the dying, and maybe a waiting list besides. The papers were full of horror stories of neglect, abuse and incompetence at one facility after another. At least his father wasn't getting worse here. In fact, what had he personally suffered? "I'm not trying to interfere . . ." Denny murmured, lifting his eyes above her, absorbing the countdown of her stare.

"I'll tell you what, Mr. Bryce. I can't ask Paavo to do it, but if you want to manage the work yourself, you may put a phone in your father's room. The phone jacks are quite old, so you'll have to fuss with whatever they do to make them fit the new phones."

"I can put in new jacks."

"Good. Then you'll be able to check on your father whenever you're worried."

He nodded. "That would help," he said. "I'll pay part of your phone bill."

She waved it off. "If it gets to be an expense, I'll let you know."

He went looking for a hardware store and found a Menards twelve miles away, sharing a dying strip mall with lilliputian boutiques and a Kentucky Fried Chicken. Back with a crimp tool, hardware and a new phone, he kneeled at the baseboard of his father's room.

"You don't have to do this, son," the old man said, and Denny knew he was pleased. Even though his father would probably never use it, maybe not even pick it up if it rang, he was registering the attention, the fuss over him by the flesh of his flesh.

And Denny in turn prolonged the dependency of father on son. "It's a button phone, Dad. Big oversize buttons, and they light up as soon as you lift the receiver. Just push the numbers you want. Okay? It's easier than a rotary dial. And I'm writing my phone number right here at the base in big numbers. See?"

He could have set the speed dial so his father only had to push one button, but he couldn't count on him remembering that or even following instructions if they were written down. So he was betting on habit. His father would understand that it was a phone number written at the base, and might even recognize whose it was or at least figure that it had to be his son's. It was better than nothing, because this was his dad, and yeah, it mattered whether he was shaved or had the right shirt on. Because if he stopped preparing for life each day, then he was that much closer to becoming part of the rapacious mystery that had devoured all but the final two of the Bryce dynasty, and Denny wasn't ready to let him go, or to go it alone to extinction. Not by a long shot. So he shaved him and clipped his nails, which were so brittle that they puffed powder into the air, and helped him into a nice cream-colored pastel long-sleeve of light cotton that Beth Bryce had bought at Target. "Didn't cut you, did I, old man?" he said, even though he had nicked a tiny wen in the crease around his mouth. And then he let the old man lie down, all spruced up with nowhere to go, and kissed him on the forehead and said good-by.

He hadn't forgotten the crows though. So he spent the next half hour cleaning out the dryer drum with a pair of gloves on and putting the rank, feathered travesties with their blue-lidded eyes into a plastic garbage bag. The two dark passages on the far end of the laundry room yawned like railroad tunnels, and he had the feeling that something kinetic was building there, as if a huge engine were gathering power in the blackness. A long, mournful whistle from the right-of-way across the road cued into his thoughts, and he wondered just what way station this farmhouse was in the destiny of its earthly inhabitants.

23

Amber sat in the middle of her bed, rocking. The huge oak corner posts were rooted to the floor, but the side-boards creaked: her nocturnal lullaby, sung to herself whenever she felt insecure. Her thoughts were flying and her heart was pounding from bad dreams, but gradually both slowed to match the rhythm and the sound she was making. As anxiety subsided, she stopped rocking, slumped, slept. Three times during the night she sat up and resumed her catharsis, and three times it worked its magic and she went back to sleep. The midmorning sun found her kneeling in the middle of the mattress, bowed over the pillow in her lap.

Why hadn't anyone called her?

She should have known then that something was wrong. Sometimes if her mother thought she had been restless, she let her sleep. Though even then she would hear the house murmuring drowsily and the smell of bacon and toast might drift under her door. Other doors would click shut, and Ruta's shrill complaints would start. Someone might laugh, toilets would flush, faucets would run, or the Philco radio in the parlor would drone with news. But today, with the sun through the slats already striping the far wall, there was dead silence.

And no Aarfie.

The only time that the house stayed quiet like this was when her mother wanted to surprise her, like on Christmas or her birthday. So now she tasted a vague excitement, because the only thing she could think of was that her mother had painted Aarfie back. That's why everyone was being so quiet. Not because they were scared and hunkered down in their rooms, like she had thought at first, but because they were all waiting for her to be surprised when she saw Aarfie again.

Only, why didn't he bark?

So then she thought it probably wasn't Aarfie, and her spirits fell a little. Still, you couldn't be sure he wasn't coming back. The painting had to dry. So she stayed kneeling in the middle of the mattress, not wanting to end hope. But the house was so quiet.

Exhaustion, in fact, had stolen a scene from Amber just after dawn when the household had begun to stir. The earliest murmurs—Paavo's, Helen's, and Beverly's self-conscious voices—hadn't penetrated her sleep. The three of them had been sitting in the parlor, not wanting to awaken anyone else, when suddenly a fourth person had appeared and demanded: "Who are you?"

"Who are we?" Helen had said. "Are you walking in your sleep?"

And then there had been a long pause. And then Beverly, trembling and with awe, had said: "It's not her. *It's not her.*"

And that left the hush Amber awakened to later—the hush of retreat and stifled whispers and abject fear. For two hours no one had stirred except that fourth person, who wandered the house and yard that were so changed from the mid '60s, when she had last seen them. It was her tread that awakened the sleeper, as she came down

the familiar hall to the familiar room and without knocking opened the bedroom door.

You couldn't tell which one of them screamed first.
Twin screams. Twin faces. Twin Ambers.

Amber One stood on the mattress; Amber Two took a
step backward but clung to the door handle as if welded
there by an electric current. In the far reaches of the
house everyone else knew what they were discovering.
*Welcome to your new pet, Amber One. Ditto, Amber
Two. Much better than a toy collie, eh? Your own Barbie
doll come to life. But there are going to be some problems. Who gets to wear what, sleep where? And who gets
Ken? You get the picture, don't you, girls? You* are *sisters, but you've still only got one life—*

Ariel could have told them of each other's existence,
of course. Told one or both of them. But it was an experiment, after all, and the politics of the thing were yet to
be determined. A little leverage for the creator, let's say.
No telling exactly how it was going to go. Let them sort
it out, discover enmity, fear. Because they didn't know
yet if they could coexist. And Ariel was betting they
could not.

She had gotten the idea with Marjorie's doppelganger.
A copy of a copy. Not like painting a natural-born person, who, if they were still naturally alive, would then
cease to exist. No, she could make them proliferate like
rabbits, all alive at the same time. What fun! Of course,
there was a certain moral inertia that had to be dealt
with. The mere sanctity of life for one; divine provi-
dence for another. But why should she be bound by
purely mortal concepts? Creation was the very antithesis
of rules. She would not be bound by the tiny voice of a
fleeting moment of time out of eternity. That first morning after her intended suicide, lying on the Chesterfield,
hearing Amber's little-girl voice call out "Mother?" after

so many decades—that was one such tiny voice. You couldn't get too sentimental about life when your power effectively meant the end of death. No one could understand this who had not performed the magic by his own hand. Holy or hell-spawned magic, it didn't matter. The power was the same.

> *"We must all invent God for ourselves."*
> —Ariel Leppa, New Eden, 2001

Not that she believed a scintilla less than what she had always believed about God. But she had finally separated it from man's inhumanity to man. Need a war? God will provide. Need genocide? God will provide. Hate, intolerance, dominance, insecurity, greed, fear, ego—all sanctified through the next prophet. Or the last, if you were too lazy to start your own reformation. God on the dashboard. God in plastic icons. God made real by accumulated dust. (We are proud of our humility, and absolutely obstinate about our open-mindedness.)

The only way you could really know anything about God was to be ostracized from the marketplace of divinity. Blessed are the alienated. Blessed are those upon whom derision and cruelty are heaped by their so-called friends for the first seven decades of their lives. That was how you came to know God. And if you happened upon the dust of creation, well, my, my, but it could be fun! So Ariel was over the sentimentality. One Amber. Ten Ambers. Count them on Sesame Street. No matter. A commodity now. All the same. So let the two downstairs sort it out for a while. No chance they would get along with each other. And the dynamics of not getting along would be instructive to Ariel.

But she was dead wrong about that. Two little girls, each inhabiting the other's life, not quite united, not quite independent, were like hostages to each other. Hostages and captors. So don't forget the old Stockholm syndrome. Make your captor into your friend. And that is why, as soon as the dual screams were uttered, the two Ambers immediately registered the fact that the other one was afraid.

It was reassuring, if only marginally. It meant that some robotic assault by a mindless impostor of themselves was not under way. Each was tensed for whatever came next, but when nothing came, the edge of alarm dulled. The insatiable stares softened. Anxiety ebbed.

An imagined dialogue went through each of their minds, questions that seemed to be answered before they were asked. *Who are you? Where did you come from? What are you doing here?* The answers would obviously be the same for both of them. So when the first words were actually spoken, the question was not about themselves. It was about the person who had created them.

"Why did she do this?" Amber One murmured breathlessly, sinking back to her knees on the bed.

Amber Two let go of the doorknob and for the first time dared glance around the room. It was no longer yesterday's room, but a new one. Different paint, different pictures on the wall, everything out of place except the bed and the dresser. Her glance darted back. "How long have you been here?"

"A year."

"A year? Then it must be true. She said I was gone for a long time."

"Did she tell you about before? About the climbing accident and being crippled and everything?"

"She said I died. She said I was forty-four when I died. It was scary. I thought she was crazy or kidding me, but she looked so old, and . . . and everything really is different." She edged into the room, puzzling at the CDs piled on the floor. "But I can't believe this."

"Believe it. It threw me for a long time too, because you feel the same way you always did. You keep thinking it's going to go back the way it was. But you can't go to school or anywhere now. Mom's afraid of what will happen if people come here, so you can't make friends. I've only been shopping twice, and both times she drove me straight there and straight back and wouldn't let me talk to anyone when we went in the stores."

"Freaky."

"Freaky is uncool."

Amber Two looked stricken. And the look only deepened over the next half hour as too much of thirty-six missing years replaced too much of yesterday too fast. The cassette player was a boom box, John Lennon was dead, beads and bell-bottoms were ancient history, tattoos and body piercing were in, shoes looked funny, hats were plain, cars looked like trucks, cells were phones, songs were videos, and TV shows had funny names like *Malcolm in the Middle*—all this coming from her mirror image in a blur of words and magazine pages.

Amber One was getting frustrated too, because how could you explain karaoke and a dubber to someone who only knew vinyl records? But she couldn't restrain herself, and she scrambled on and off the mattress, retrieving Harry Potter and Lemony Snicket books and makeup with glitter until she saw her twin's face flag hot with tears, and then she stopped.

"You can't go back, you know," she said.

"Yeah." Big sniff, pressing the back of her hand to her nose.

"Just about everyone here was dead, and now at least they're alive. We're alive. So we must be better off."

"Yeah."

"Except . . ."

"What?"

"Nothing. You didn't see a painting of me up in the studio, did you—I mean, like a second one of you?"

"Uh-uh." She shook her head. "Just the one. And a bunch of Mom's friends. I guess I met some of them down here. Weird."

"They're old, but they're not that bad. Except for Ruta—she needs to take a chill pill. Sometimes they're grouchy, but they give you stuff."

"What's a chill pill?"

"I mean she's all hyper and everything."

"Oh." She touched the dresser. "Are there any other kids here?"

"No. Just us."

A speculative look passed between them, the thinnest bridge, swaying with uncertainty.

"I guess . . . in a way . . . we're sisters," said the Amber on the bed.

"Yeah."

"Maybe that's why she made you."

"I don't know. It's hard to know what she thinks. She's so old now, so different. It's spooky to see her like that."

"Did she tell you what she can do with the pictures?"

"What d'you mean?"

"She can paint them out. She can make us disappear. She can make anyone disappear. In fact, she already has."

Renewed fear flashed green in her counterpart's eyes.

"She's done it to people in the house. And Dad is in a wheelchair—did she tell you that?"

"No."

"And Aarfie's dead."

"She said he ran out in front of a pickup truck."

"That was a long time ago. She brought him back, and then he was killed again."

"How?"

"By . . . by something else that got painted."

The newly incarnated version of herself looked sicker and sicker as these revelations unfolded, but Amber One continued on. She had a full year of her own disorientation to unload, a year of loneliness, a year of gossip, a year of pent-up freakish isolation from any kind of peer. And that single year had thirty-six more years of lost time in it. Zipped up like a compressed computer file ("Oh yeah—I haven't told you about computers. We don't have one, but everything is computers now.") And almost in the same breath she was telling her about the red spider in the bathtub and the thing that killed Paavo the first time. Amber in Horrorland. Incomprehensible stuff. And it wasn't just family history. By definition the dawn of the twenty-first century carried its own estrangement. So to the newly arrived child the fantastic aberrations brought about by their mother were hardly distinguishable from the realities of cargo pants and spiked hair, and naked people right on television, and herky-jerky music shared through ear buds by the two Ambers—"That's Britney Spears, only you gotta see the video." And the reeducation went on until the ancient munchkins beyond the bedroom walls crept out of their rooms again and the household began to rustle and sigh with movement, with cautious conversations, with water running and the smell of tomato soup and tuna fish from the kitchen. The two girls ended up side by side, looking at their twin reflections in the dresser mirror: Amber One with slightly darker skin from the summer's sun and faint scratches on her cheek; Amber Two with slightly darker hair for lack of a summer's sun.

"So if we're sisters, then it's share and share alike,

okay?" said Amber One. "It'll be spifferific, you'll see. You'll get used to everything, and I'll help you. Okay?"

"Okay."

And they played and shared for six days, and God looked down from Her studio at Her handiwork and saw that it was good. . . . *And She was furious!* So on the seventh day She called Amber One up to her studio and said, "You've certainly taken to your little soul mate, haven't you? I'll bet you've shared *all* your secrets by now. But it's so confusing. I thought I'd be able to tell you apart, and here you are, so alike that you might as well be the same person—which, come to think of it, you are." And then She rummaged through the stack of canvases leaning against the wall and pulled up two, and Amber began to tremble because they looked exactly alike. "Just like these paintings of you, my dear. Can you tell which is which? I can. I suppose I'll have to paint one of you out, if it gets too confusing. But which one? What a dilemma. Let's see, what kind of test could I use? I know. The paint. Whichever one of you brings back my paint, that's the one who stays."

24

Martin Bryce saw flames before he woke up. Saw flames and smelled smoke and heard Tiffany screaming for him. So when he opened his eyes, he was already agitated, already trying to swing his shoulder across his body to sit up.

He blinked at the room, yellow in the glow from the night-light. Beth was dead, and this was the place where his son had brought him. There were old people here, mostly women. He knew these things, but that didn't quiet the other impression. The fire. Tiffany. He could no longer trust the evidence of his senses.

On his second try he rolled to a sitting position and sat breathing hard, waiting for the dizziness to subside. He coughed once, and when his heart had been given ample notice of what was to come, he felt around with his bare feet for his slippers and stood up. A smaller wave of dizziness was accommodated by another rise in blood pressure, and then his heart was thudding strongly and steadily. He reached out for his robe on the chair, fell a few inches short, took a step, reached again. His arms felt like plumb bobs, but the act of swathing himself invigorated the muscles somewhat. Fitting on his glasses with both hands, he wandered into the corridor.

Without pondering why, he took the small fire extinguisher off the wall and lugged it with him through the
house to the parlor. There he turned around twice in the
gloom before locating the shadowy front door. When
he stood in the front yard a few feet from the porch, he
looked around again and took stock. He didn't specifically remember his previous midnight forays, but he
felt a familiar imperative. This was right: coming outside . . . the path around the side of the farmhouse . . .
the big pile of rubble that smelled of smoke out back.
The barn fire had affected him profoundly. Like a long-
awaited beacon on a dark journey, it linked where he
had been with where he must go. Shuffling through the
dust in his slippers, he passed around the side of the
house.

Something wide-winged and jagged, like an ani-
mated kite, glided to the top of the basswood, but he
didn't see it, didn't feel it when it swooped down from
behind and passed within six feet of him. He was too
absorbed with the charred remains of the barn, and he
just kept padding through the soft perimeter of ashes,
searching for a way in. The smell of smoke was damp
and acrid; there must be flames in there. And he didn't
know, but maybe this was where Tiffany's screams
came from at night. Lifting the extinguisher and aiming
it at the debris, he tried to squeeze the handles together,
but nothing happened.

The kitelike silhouette lifted off the roof of the machine shed for a second ponderous attack, beating its
ragged asymmetry, lifting its talons, arrowing straight
for the upright human being.

Martin fumbled with the extinguisher mechanism,
twisting, pushing and finally catching his finger in a
plastic loop. He pulled out the pin and squeezed the handles again. This time the extinguisher gushed foam, and

the prolonged hiss drove the swooping silhouette away. When the extinguisher sputtered its last, Martin dropped it and listened hard for a cry.

"Tiffany?" he called.

Then he shuffled back to the house, head down—a line of steps, a pause, a quarter or a half turn to reorient himself. Inside he passed through the parlor, but the inky darkness threw off his balance and he grasped a wooden post that suddenly appeared on his left. For a few seconds his chest lifted effortfully. Why couldn't he find Tiffany? He glanced to the side, saw that he was leaning on a newel, looked up a staircase that led to darkness.

He didn't remember the staircase, didn't think he had ever climbed it. That must be where she was. Where the fire was. He hoped he wouldn't be too late this time. She would be horribly scarred if he was late. He started up, pushing on one knee, sliding his elbow along the banister and winching himself to each successive step. But he made only a few before he had to sit down. There were days (or nights) when he could climb this staircase, but this night wasn't one of them. He felt lousy. And he couldn't remember why he had started up now. He was tired, and he knew he had a bed here somewhere. Downstairs. Wearily, he stood.

"You there," came a whisper.

He looked to where the whisper had come from; saw nothing.

"Mr. Bryce? Come up here."

Martin peered wide-eyed in the gloom. "Who are you?"

"I can't come down. I'm in a wheelchair. I've got something for you."

"What is it?"

"Something that belongs to . . . Tiffany."

And that galvanized him a little. His focus came back, and he climbed one slow step at a time, hesitating to strain up at the darkness until he could see the face peering through the balusters on the landing. He reached the second floor, and there was the man, a shaggy man with a huge head. But he wasn't in a wheelchair. He was sitting on the carpet.

"I've been waiting for you, Mr. Bryce. My daughter told me you walk around at night, so I knew if I could just get to the landing, sooner or later I'd catch you."

"Where's Tiffany?"

"She hasn't been up in a while. I think her mother is keeping her away. But I've got something for her. It's a secret, and there isn't anyone else in this house I trust. Can I trust you?"

"I don't know what you're talking about."

"Come and I'll show you." He began to drag himself up the next flight. "Come on, Mr. Bryce."

They weren't that different when it came to climbing stairs—octogenarian Martin Bryce, legless Thomas Leppa, sighing like steam locomotive pistons working in tandem up a steep grade. At the very top the wheelchair was outlined in dim light cast from an open doorway. With his farmer's biceps and a little dexterity not unlike a gymnast's on a pommel horse, Thomas Leppa stiff-armed himself onto the foot stops and hauled himself onto the seat. Releasing the brakes on the wheels, he spun silently through the open door.

"Under the cedar chest," he said when Martin caught up.

Maneuvering slowly, he brought the chair alongside a brass-bound chest and adjusted the green shade of the lamp that sat on its lid. With the light spilling squarely on the floor, he reached down again and slid out two objects.

"You see?" he said. And Martin Bryce saw. "I want you to take them to Amber—to Tiffany. Hide them until you get a chance to show her in private. Will you do that?"

25

So now Amber knew. It was in her mother's icy eyes, wide and staring like a cat's. She had even sounded like a cat, purring when she offered a test to see which of her daughters would survive.

And that was why she had to get the paint out of the cistern *now*, no matter what the risk from the thing that lived in the woods. She had to move it far, far away this time, so that her mother wouldn't follow her. The creek that wound through the property and came out at Crookshank Road had a culvert there with cattails and mud on either side, and that's where she thought she would go. Aarfie had gotten into that mud once, and it had taken them a couple of hours to reach him. Her father used to joke that he was going to leave the family jewels there, because no one would touch them in all that muck. So she would take a spade with her and dig a hole near the culvert and bury the paint jar there.

But it had to be now. Only, she was afraid to go at night because of the spider. And anyway, the other Amber would know because they slept together in the big bed.

The other Amber. She didn't know what else to call her. That was the one big awkwardness between them.

They talked so intimately and shared everything else, but they couldn't decide about the name. Did that mean they were competing? She had been thinking about it and she was going to suggest that they pick different names. She would be Christina, or maybe Buffy the Vampire Slayer.

The other subject that they had never talked about in the week before her mother made her veiled threats in the studio was the stolen paint. She hadn't been able to bring that up either. A couple of times she had been on the verge of telling her, and something had interrupted— Alicia Keys singing "Fallin'" on the radio, and another time Ruta glaring cow-eyed at them from the porch. But now that her mother had threatened to make it a test between them, how lucky was that? She would have revealed the hiding place today or tomorrow. Lucky but sad. Because when her mother told her twin it was going to change everything.

When she came back from the studio that night and got into bed, she started to cry.

"What is it?" came at her shoulder. "Was she mean?"

"Sort of."

"What did she say?"

"She wants to split us up."

"How can she?"

Hesitation. "She can't."

But she could. She would. One way or another. Amber wasn't crying because her mother didn't love her. She was crying because yet another dream of having a companion had been shot through the heart.

Which may have had something to do with why she procrastinated going for the paint the next day. It was like admitting that she couldn't trust her only friend, ending their friendship, in fact. So she didn't move the stolen paint right away. After all, as long as they were together, she would know if their mother called her twin aside to tell her about the test.

There were other excuses to delay her trip back to the cistern. Everyone in the house was watching them out of the corners of their eyes, as if something was going to happen, so it would be hard to slip away. And late in the afternoon they got into some boxes in the cellar filled with stuff from their childhood, and that was really strange—

"Oh, remember this?" (Of course she remembered the coloring book. They couldn't contradict each other's memories because they were exactly the same.) "Look at the green hair." "I know." "I was heavy into green then." "I know." "This was my best one—Cinderella at the ball." And then with sudden social deference—"What was your favorite?" "Duh?" "Oh. Yeah, it would be the same. What does 'duh' mean?"

They found the witch costume from Halloween and the azure love beads and the first five Nancy Drews. An Argus 75 camera that had been old even in the '60s was still in its brown case, and there were the contraband lapel buttons (GIVE A DAMN, GOD IS DEAD, BAN THE BRA, STONED) hidden from their parents, which apparently their mother had known about all along and preserved. And Snoopy, chewed and hugged to piebald alopecia, unexplainably wrapped in a Jimi Hendrix psychedelic poster.

They sensed the anticlimax of these discoveries, but didn't understand where the drain was coming from; felt the echo, but couldn't identify it; saw their common source, yet lost the thread of sameness in the fact of being two people on either side of an old trunk. The only difference was mathematical and inscrutable: three-and-a-half intervening decades had shrunk to one year for Amber One, one week for Amber Two.

And by the time they climbed the stairs from the cellar dinner was ready, and then it was getting dark again, and so there was no trip to the cistern that day.

Amber the stealer of paint understood that her mother was giving her time. It was the simplest solution. Scare her, then reward her when she gave up the paint. But Amber couldn't trust in that. Even if she gave up the paint, she wouldn't be able to trust it. Safer for both she and her twin if she called her mother's bluff by just holding out. And she wanted to tell her companion that. Wanted desperately to share *every*thing and make a pact never to give their mother what she wanted. But, of course, if they both knew where the stolen paint was hidden, then their mother could paint out either one of them. And Amber wasn't ready to sacrifice her only chance for survival. Her mother was giving her time to figure all this out, because once her twin knew what the stakes were and how expendable she was, it was going to get very, very bad.

And then the next day, at exactly five o'clock, Molly came in and said that the newest resident of New Eden was wanted upstairs. She looked soberly at Amber Two, but clearly she wasn't sure which of them was which.

"Let me go," Amber the thief whispered to her twin when Molly was out of earshot.

"Why?"

"Because I know her better than you, and she wants to split us up. *Please* . . ."

"It won't work. You're more tanned than me, and you've still got that mark on your cheek. She'll know if we switch. Don't worry. I can handle her."

Amber wasn't worried. She was panicked. Watching her twin go off, she realized it was over. The clock that had been running had stopped. Or was this another scare? Her mother might not really be telling her twin

that only one of them was going to survive. Because
what if her twin freaked out? What if they got in a fight
and she was killed? Then her mother wouldn't get the
paint back and wouldn't know if it was someplace where
someone else might find it.

So Amber waited downstairs, drifting back and forth
between the porch and her room and the parlor. She
wanted to be ready to dive out the window of her room
but at the same time keep in range of the staircase, so
she could see her companion the second she appeared.
She would read her face, her eyes, and she would know.
Either there would be the connection they had made or
there would be something different, like her mother's cat
stare. What would be her twin's look if she was suddenly
surprised by Amber looking steadily up at her? She
would turn her eyes away, that's what she would do. So
Amber had to be right there to look up when her twin
wasn't expecting it. When you looked down a staircase it
was hard to pretend you didn't see what was at the bottom.

And if she did look away, Amber would just turn and
run. She knew the fields, the woods, the places you
could hide and where to jump to avoid the mud, so probably her twin wouldn't be able to catch her, even though
they were physically the same. And if she did catch her,
what then? Probably nothing, unless she went totally
ballistic. She had to get the paint first. And their mother
wouldn't tell her everything without giving her time to
do that. It could turn into a long game. So she probably
wouldn't go ballistic until their mother ran out of pa-
tience.

It was a sketchy strategy, full of uncertainties, and
Amber changed her mind a half dozen times. She went
to her room and put on her Skechers; she got the spade
she thought she would need to dig a hole at the culvert

and set it by the porch; she even opened the window in the bedroom in case she had to get out that way. But she kept listening for the closing of a door upstairs, for quick steps on the staircase. And she always came back to the same hope that it wasn't over, that the friend she had so desperately wished for in this everlasting childhood was still her friend and not her enemy.

Dinner was a minor production. Molly and Dana exaggerating the motions. Plates set down on the table with slow deliberation. The kitchen faucet on and off at low force, as if they knew there was trouble. No one asked Amber to sit down. When it was over and people straggled out, Mrs. Novicki left a plate of gingersnaps on the table and gave her a glance. But she couldn't eat.

What was taking so long upstairs?

It would be dark soon. In her mind she saw her mother glaring steadily at her twin, her voice like a melody but the words chilling: *I suppose I'll have to paint one of you out, if it gets too confusing. . . . Whichever one of you brings back my paint, that's the one who stays.* Only, it must be a lot more than that. Explanations, plans, plots. Maybe tears and doubts. But it was taking a long time, so someone was listening. And finally, with dusk falling, she had had enough.

Backing slowly away from the staircase, her eyes directed upward until the last second and counting down— *three, two . . . one*—she retreated to her room and closed the door. Then she wedged a slipper under the seam, hoping they would waste time thinking she was in there pouting. Maybe, if she was lucky, she could even do what she had to do and get back here before anyone was the wiser. She pulled the shade so they couldn't look in. Then she wiggled behind it and climbed out the window, drawing the sash down behind her.

Stooping below the parlor window, she retrieved the

spade she had left by the porch and scooted to the basswood side of the house. From there she followed the line of trees along the drive, circled back behind the charred remnants of the barn and dashed out into the fields.

There was a mahogany cribbage board on the credenza in the dining room. The pegs had long since been replaced by small finishing nails, but she liked to push and pull them in and out in sequence, dreaming that each hole was another step in a journey. The journey led to a treasure, and sometimes she had to dodge other pegs, or cross rows to escape imaginary pursuit. And that was what she felt like now, crossing the furrowed fields and darting among the broken stalks. Each step followed a row until she crossed to the next.

She thought of the spider and the other things she had painted: red eyes in red bodies with red fangs and red claws. The sun was half under the horizon, so they would be coming to life soon—nocturnal, like her mother said. But she had been out at night before, and so far so good. If she could just get in and out of the cistern before the spider started to hunt.

She ran a little harder, her heart flip-flopping like a fish on a dock, perspiration on her brow (*That kid never sweats,* her father used to say, and she had tried not to, wiping her lip or her brow before she came into the parlor on hot days). When she saw the stand of trees, the warmth in her chest went out like a snuffed candle. Ice churned in her belly. She had to pee. How could she have thought she could do this? The spider was probably watching her with all its pairs of firefly eyes, as unblinking as her mother. She had hoped the light would be bright enough in the tops of the trees so that she could see if it was up there. But maybe it was sitting on the ground in its hole or something—there were spiders that did that. She would go around the woods as far as she could, she decided. She would try to come up on the cistern from the other side.

And then she stumbled, and it made her remember another thing her father had told her. That some spiders used trip lines. They ran them along walls or out on the ground, and when passing prey touched them the spider knew. It felt the vibration and it could tell everything, like how big you were. And then it came, and if you were what it wanted it attacked and bit you and wrapped you up with silk as strong as steel cables, and it would stick something in you like a needle full of poison. Then you were paralyzed. Sometimes the poison dissolved your guts. Sometimes the spider just laid eggs in you and the eggs hatched and ate you while you were still alive, and—

She caught her balance again, but instead of slowing, she ran harder, faster. Going for the far side of the field. Fighting off the shucks in her face and staggering. Dodging nimbly, like a peg on a cribbage board.

When she got to the edge of the field she calmed a little. The sun fire on the horizon was just cold orange now. Nothing much lit the earth. She stared intently along the rows, trying to detect any motion, but it was very still. Unnaturally still. It was the moment right at sunset before the hunters came out. Which was why she had to hurry. No time for caution. As soon as it was dark, she was doomed.

Moving up the edge of the field to the end, she went straight to the cistern. She had pushed the dog fennel and spurge back in place the last time, but she could see one of her footprints in the mud. Reaching down she found the edge of the wooden cover and dragged it off.

The green smell was overpowering this time, and there was no sun or moon to dispel the darkness of the hole. She could just see the weathered ladder ends like two paws reaching for the rim. Tucking the spade in her waistband, she buried her fingers in the spurge and dangled one foot in search of a rung.

She had a sudden premonition then that there was already something down there, maybe on the ladder, and that it was going to grab her by the ankle, but her toe found support and she let her weight sink after it. Down she went, one hand letting go of the spurge, then the other. Coolness came, then the pungency of the emerald fungus she sensed, and even the wisp of cinnamon sharpness she had smelled before. The ladder shivered less and less as she descended. Her left foot encountered the floor and she stepped off.

The spade was cutting into her hip. She rotated it slightly. Then she felt around for the brick enclosure she had built around the precious jar and, to her relief, she found it smooth and whole to her touch. She sidled around so as to be able to pull out her treasure without knocking the glass on anything hard. But as she squatted she sensed something whiz past her cheek, followed by scraping like a violin bow across flaccid strings. She looked up just as the geometry of the ladder was disappearing over the edge of the cistern. Against the dusk a small face peered over, green eyes lucid with remorse.

"You should've told me," echoed down. "I would've trusted you, if you'd told me."

26

They had been watching her all along. Watching when she left the house, probably from the second floor. The long delay had been to make her run for the paint so that her twin could follow.

The little girl at the bottom of the cistern heard the voice and saw the face slide back and knew that the only possible escape was walking away. "She lied!" she screamed at the empty rim.

Slowly the face came back.

But what could she say? She couldn't really blame her twin for knuckling under to their mother's threats. What did she have to save herself with except cooperation? A torrent of desperate persuasion poured out of the cistern: "She won't let you live for long. . . . You won't be able to please her. . . . She's crazy, and the first time you do something wrong, she'll repaint you. . . . You can't live like that. . . . Let me up and we'll do something . . . see, I've got the paint. . . . We can stop her! . . . C'mon, *Amber*"—there, she used the name—"let me out. It's not too late. We can gang up on her, if you put the ladder back and let me out."

The answer that came down was much softer but almost as mournful. "She's got the paintings."

So now the prisoner switched to raw pleading. "Don't do this. Please don't. It's almost dark, and the spider will come if you leave me here. Please, please, please, *don't do this!*"

And then it was just a circle of graying light above her, the last daylight she would know before the night and the spider came. But she yelled and yelled— "Amber! *Amber!*"—until the shaft in the earth rang with her voice and her head was exploding with the sound. The pressure of the voice in her skull was red. Red needles jumped into line like a stockade fence and sank back into the green stench of the hole. And then it struck her that if the spider hadn't known she was here before, it would know now because of her shouts. Even if it was deaf, it would feel vibrations. She stopped yelling.

Think. Think! What was going to happen? Her twin would tell her mother where she was and that the paint was here. Then her mother would take out the portrait of her and paint it over. No. She would want to see that the paint was here first. She would come see for herself. Then she would paint her out. But what about the spider? Her mother knew about that, so she probably wouldn't come at night. So Amber had until morning. If she survived that long.

The spider knew where she was and it would come, and of course it could crawl down the wall. The specter of that huge hairy creature filling the circle above her and creeping down, demon eyes never blinking, until it had her with its legs and its fangs made her clammy and faint. It would eat her right here. Or maybe it would paralyze her and drag her back to its web to feed its young. And even if it couldn't crawl down one side, it was big enough to brace its legs across the circle and come down that way.

If only she could reach all the way across the cistern

herself. But she couldn't. Not by a mile. And then it occurred to her to use the length of her body instead of just the spread of her arms. So she pressed her palms into the bricks on one side and lifted one foot against the opposite side, then the other. She had to spread her arms a little on the curve to shorten the distance, but she got everything up in the air.

Except the paint . . .

Forget the paint. The ladder must still be up there, and once she got out, she could lower it in and come back for the paint. Her arms were already starting to get heavy from pushing so hard, and her spine was killing her, so she had to keep going while she still had the strength. She felt like an elephant trying to back out of a bucket— right foot, left foot, lifting butt first, but only a couple of inches at a time, because otherwise she couldn't reach all the way across, and—*crap, she couldn't do this!* Her arms felt like goalposts and her backbone was splintering. She let one leg drop and that pulled her down like a bobber on a short fishing line. With a whimper she collapsed to the bottom.

There were things she couldn't quite frame but that sat in the anteroom of her child's logic like numbered puzzle tiles waiting to be set in order, as in: Amber One, who was really Amber the Second if you counted a forty-four-year-old woman who lay moldering in her grave, could not coexist with Amber Two, who was really Amber the Third. And there were things she couldn't know or grasp for their horror. Such as the fact that her mother could birth her in legions! *I am Amber.* Numberless. No bond-engendering gestations, no womb-ripping travails—the industrious strokes of a brush laden with red dust from an ancient site on the other side of the world would create dispensable armies of Ambers marching off canvases. What she did grasp, lying there, was that she was no longer special.

She cried soft, aching tears that made her throat hurt. It wasn't fair. She wanted to be nine again in 1965. She wanted to go to school and listen to the Beatles and see back on her wall her poster of Twiggy in mod stockings and a miniskirt and talk to her dad out in the yard while he tinkered with the old Ford Fairlane, and no one said "far out" anymore or wore mood rings. But she felt too gritty and thirsty to mount a good cry. Bone dry. Funny. Here she was at the bottom of a cistern and she was dying for a drink.

Dying.

And that was the lightning that set the dry tinder of rebellion inside her on fire again. Because now she was thinking of another way she might get out. The cistern was falling apart, and there were bricks all over the bottom. Ignoring the burning where she had scraped her palms and the bruises on her knees, she stood up.

This time she put the precious glass jar of paint in her shirt, and with the spade she had brought for the mud at the culvert, she began to dig at the loose bricks in front of her. To her intense relief the first one came out like a cookie on a spatula. And the next. She could almost build her own staircase out of bricks, she thought in a burst of jubilation. But she wouldn't have to try that. Using the cavities that were already in the wall, digging out others, stabbing the spade into the crumbling joints, she began to climb. She had to lean close like a rock climber to keep from falling, but that was the kind of thing she did instinctively. Never mind that the natural-born Amber had become paralyzed in a rock-climbing accident at age thirty-three, this was her prototype, the nimble child who danced in the bonnets of trees and sprinted on fence rails. The Skechers slid into the open slots that her fingers abandoned as if they were stirrups, and in less than five minutes she was clawing at the fennel and the spurge at the top.

She kept to the field because it was already too late to avoid the spider. If it was there, she would have to outrun it. Too late too for the culvert. Too late and too dark. She had a stitch in her side, and the paint sloshing against her chest like blood from her heart made her feel queasy. Hunger pains alternated with faintness. She wished she had eaten the gingersnaps Mrs. Novicki had left out for her. When she crossed the dead furrow, she slowed. And when she got to the field nearest the house she began to walk.

In the charred debris where the barn had stood she dug into the ashes with the spade and buried the jar. She buried it deep enough where she didn't think it could be broken or accidentally uncovered. She would have to clean the ashes off the spade before she put it back, she thought dully. And she couldn't go inside the house until she figured out what to do. But she was too tired to think. Or maybe it was just that, even after tonight, she didn't want to accept the truth: that she couldn't share her life with a twin after all. They were like the newborn queen bees her father liked to talk about. First one out of a cell must kill the others.

She slipped toward the machine shed where her mother parked the old Plymouth Fury that she still drove to the strip malls. She could sleep in the car for a while because no one would dare go look at the cistern until daylight. But the shadows and the smell of things around her—violet smells, deep black violet—made her uneasy.

She didn't feel like she was really inside the shed when she passed under the sagging header and stood in the gloom. It was not like a room of the house where you could see everything and you knew what each object was. The oily smell and the uniform color hid things. Her child's mind grasped only that everything was blending together, that it was rotting or rusted or somehow changing into something that she would become too if she stayed long enough. She curled up and hugged herself on the car seat, and she thought that maybe blending wasn't so bad after all, and that if she sat really, really still she could become part of the shed. Then she would be hidden too.

From the rearview mirror her white face ghosted back at her, whereas nothing else in the car was reflected. There could be things on the backseat watching her and she wouldn't know. Things in the shed too. Guarding her, she told herself. And that self-deception allowed her to close her eyes.

She didn't mean to fall asleep, but exhaustion and the hour of the night dictated otherwise, and it wasn't until she heard a series of short, even scrapes that she opened her eyes again. The nightmare stalkers in her imagination tried the sounds on for size—snakes that moved like inchworms and jackbooted centipedes and trudging spiders—but there was something helpless and lost about this sound that correctly informed her at last. Opening the car door, she scrambled to the entrance of the shed.

"Mr. Bryce," she called.

He paused his shuffling gait.

"Mr. Bryce . . . over here."

"Tiffany? You'd better come out of there."

"Why?"

He concentrated hard for a moment, but his thoughts, like his slippered steps, came in disconnected segments. "Do you want me to come in and get you?"

And that little paternalism was all it took to drive her crying into his embrace, her arms around his waist, her face buried in his concave chest. She blurted out her own disjointed segments then—all the way back to Aarfie and the scarecrow and the spiders, and he just kept patting her on the back of the head and crooning that it was okay now.

". . . You're the only one I can trust, because you're the only one she hasn't painted," she babbled. "I don't wanta disappear like the others, and I'm scared. She makes people disappear who go against her, but I stole her paint, so now she won't do anything to me until she gets it back. But she's already made another person like me, and she's got a painting of me. That's the big thing. The painting. I've got the paint, but she's got my picture."

"It's okay . . . it's okay," he said.

"It's not okay." She pushed herself away. "She's got pictures in her studio, and she's got mine. I've tried to get in, but the door is always locked. So nobody can get their picture."

He looked at her, thinking hard. "I'll get it," he said and turned toward the house.

"Where are you going?"

"Inside."

"I'm not safe in there."

He looked around, looked at the house. "You'll be safe in my room."

She couldn't stay outside forever, and if she ran away her mother might paint her out anyway, she thought. Even though the jar of stolen paint would not be accounted for, her mother might take the chance. She had thought a lot about running away, but it always came down to the fact that her mother would paint her, or maybe everyone, out, if attention were drawn to the farmhouse. The stolen paint might not even matter anymore if the risk to her mother got big enough. So she couldn't leave. Maybe she could hide in Mr. Bryce's

room for a few hours until she figured things out. It had
windows she could escape through, if she had to, and her
mother and her twin wouldn't know she was gone until
they went back to the cistern in daylight.

So she took Mr. Bryce's hand and they went to his
room. One long segment of shuffling to the porch, then
another segment from the top of the steps to the new corridor where the seam of light from under his door made
her hesitate. But he had left a lamp on himself. When the
door was closed behind them, he went directly to the
brown wardrobe that stood next to the windows. The
flimsy metal tinned as he rummaged behind his clothes,
and then he had the edge of something that had a white
corner on it, and as he hauled it out she froze in disbelief.

It was her portrait.

For just an instant she had the ridiculous thought that
it was something he had done, but of course it was her
mother's work. No question about that. Her. Amber
Leppa. Exactly the portrait she had seen more than a
year ago. No question at all, as exultation rose in her
breast. *This was it!* Somehow. She couldn't believe it.
Old Mr. Bryce had walked out of her mother's studio
with the painting that kept her a prisoner!

"Take it," he said as offhandedly, as if he were offering her a peppermint.

"But how did you get it?"

"A man gave it to me."

She studied his face, but there was no way to tell the
truth. He made up things when he couldn't remember.

"You can have it," he repeated.

It didn't matter how it had come to him. She had it.
She had it. She had it. She took the frame, then leaned it
on the bed and hugged him. She hugged him twice.

The problem was going to be where to hide something

that big, she decided about the painting. She could take the canvas off the frame like she had seen her mother do, and . . . and suddenly her world came crashing down. Because it had taken her a minute but now it occurred to her that this might not be *her* picture. It could be her twin. Squatting down on her haunches, she breathed painfully as she scrutinized the image. It looked the same as she remembered, but her mother had probably made the second one from the first. She hugged her knees and rocked and thought. And then she knew what she had to do.

"Thank you," she said, mouse quiet. "You don't know what you've done." And giving him another hug, and carting the frame along, she hurried from the room.

Martin Bryce stood staring after her for a moment, wondering if there was something wrong. Then he turned stiffly to regard the wardrobe. Shuffling to its open doors, he pulled back the clothes and made his slight genuflexion. It was still there. The second of the two paintings the man in the wheelchair had given him at the top of the stairs. One for Tiffany, one for him.

There were a half dozen bottles of liquid shoe polish down in the cellars. All but two—one black, one white— were dried out. There was more of the white, but Amber chose the black. Black felt right.

You could get along with just three fingers and a thumb on one of your hands, she thought. The Simpsons had only three fingers and a thumb on each of their hands. So she would probably never miss her little finger if she guessed wrong. She chose the left hand, even though it would be harder to separate the little finger from the finger next to it in the painting. The shoe polish applicator was just a blob of fuzz too thick to use for a brush. She tried a pipe stem cleaner from a yellow sleeve on the shelves but that was still too thick, and then she tried a broomcorn stem from the whisk hanging from the end of a shelf but that was too unsteady, so she ended up using a small finishing nail. She wiped the nail as clean as she could—and she remembered then to wipe the ashes off the spade, which she still had in her waistband—and then she dipped the nail in the black polish and practiced making a straight line on the side of the shoe box that held the shoe polish bottles.

Upstairs her twin was probably asleep in their bedroom. She wondered if it would cause pain to lose a finger this way—if, in fact, her twin would wake up screaming. If it did, she would paint out her head next, because that would end the pain.

And what if it was her own finger that went away? She didn't dare scream, because if everyone woke up, she would have to leave the house in the middle of the night carrying the painting, and what if the pain was so horrible that she couldn't run?

Don't think, don't think . . .

She tried to catch just the tip of the finger first, but there was barely any paint on the point of the finishing nail at all. Not even a drop. And her hand was trembling. So she dipped the nail deeper in the shoe polish this time and came back to the canvas, kind of resting the side of her right hand against her left. But her left little finger was right there, practically over the one in the painting, and that made her want to wince when the drop of shoe polish squiggled on.

. . . Do it!

And it was more than she wanted to get on the painting, so it kind of smeared around, and then her left hand began to tingle and then burn. At least she thought it did, but after she jerked it away and held it up in front of her face, already whimpering and gasping against the tightness in her throat, it was still there. Chewed fingernails and all.

So she listened.

But there wasn't any scream. None. Zip. Nada. Zilch.

Feverish, excited, fearful, she dipped the nail back into the polish, and this time the black flowed where she wanted it to, and she was sure she got all of the finger blotted out—all of two of them, in fact. And she was about to take the fuzzy applicator and just go at it, but then she thought: *Maybe it has to dry first before anything happens.*

She read the label, which said that Kiwi shoe polish was nontoxic and had extra scuff protection, but it didn't say anything about fast drying. She knew from her mother that paintings sometimes went on drying for weeks, even months, so you couldn't always tell. Still, the polish looked dry already. Upstairs, her twin might be missing part of her hand. She could wake up any second and start screaming. And if the rest of her wasn't painted out right away, then however much longer she waited to do it, that's how much longer it would take before the screaming would stop. She was almost sure now the polish was dry. But what if it *wasn't*? If it wasn't, she could be committing suicide. She wouldn't know it was really her own picture until it was too late.

Do it!

Dropping the finishing nail, she dipped the fuzz-ball applicator back in the bottle and brushed out the left hand, then the arm, then the face. She thought of the monsters she had done in the cupola—how, no matter how badly she painted them, they came to life exactly like that—and now, in a way, she was making another monster: one-armed, headless Amber flopping around on a bed upstairs.

Choking with passion and fear, she poured the shoe polish over the canvas and began spreading it with her hands. It seemed to gush from her fingers and palms now. But to her horror, she could still see the feet. Frantically she pawed over the saw-toothed canvas until the stain transferred to the lower part, and when she was satisfied that every discernible part of the image was obliterated, she jerked her hands up reflexively, allowing the last of the liquid to trickle down her arms like black blood.

27

The clothes dryer still reeked of dead crows. The drum
had been scoured with bleach, but you couldn't turn the
thing on without being bathed in a warm acridity that
quickly led to nausea. It was up into the duct and inside
the frame, the crow stench, bonded to every mote of dust
and felt snubber on the old Maytag, and it "fuzzed" into
the air through the lint filter and the seams around the
venting. Clothes came out smelling putrid. Even Paavo,
whose nose had no more functionality than a nose on
Mount Rushmore, wouldn't wear his shirts unless they
had been line dried.

Twice Denny had tried to rake out the batts of lint that
curled around the drum and inside the shell, but the odor
persisted everywhere in crevices and in foil corrugations
and in syrupy patches of congealed grease. That was
why he was outside looking up at the sugar maple. He
had fifty feet of new plastic clothesline still in its sleeve,
a cordless Black & Decker drill and a pair of twenty-
gauge screw eyes. But he saw now that he was going to
have to get up in the damn tree to remove the old line,
which hung at an absurd slant. Paavo or someone had
managed to loop it into the first crotch. The person had
cinched it tight, like a lariat, and if he cut it off from

below it was going to leave the knotted part hanging up there.

He could swear a kind of stasis was setting in down on the farm. Everyone frozen by pain or favoring the muscles of the day, palsied extensions where yesterday steady hands had prevailed, and still no one making much eye contact. Maybe he was just now getting it. Maybe he had rationalized a more Pollyanna-like atmosphere because he wanted his father to fit in. Maybe it was time to get his old man the hell out of here.

He went inside and found a six-foot stepladder in the pantry and carried it back out, but he couldn't stop the polemics in his head. It was nice and simple to think *Get the hell out of here*, but then what? Truth be told, it was still a better deal than the depressing diaper decrepitude of the institutions. Hired compassion in eight-hour shifts, where you were buying a benevolent prison and the guards came and went and the one-size-fits-all rules were administered from afar. Flowers and carpet couldn't hide sanctioned family abandonment. Guilt. You could smell dead crows everywhere.

The ladder got him halfway to nowhere, because unless he wanted to stand on the very tippy top, he still couldn't work handily with the knot. He should have brought a kitchen knife; then he could have severed the lasso. Easier to pull himself up on the branch now. Easier if you were sixteen and you didn't have hemorrhoids or bruise easily. But he managed it, sliding along like chiffon over a pineapple, catching his pants, abusing his privates. He hoped it wasn't going to be a Gordian knot.

And then he got distracted by a nest in the crotch of the sugar maple, and that was fairly odd for midsummer, because even if you couldn't see that it was freshly built you couldn't mistake the single egg therein. Fairly odd too that the egg was just sitting there yet he had neither

seen nor heard any squawking from momma bird. Most
of all, it was a fairly odd egg. Big, for one thing. And for
another, it was bright, bright red. Not just some off-hue
brown, but Fabergé crimson.

Ha-ha. Someone playing a joke. The old folks at
KNEAL, who could barely get off their whoopee cush-
ions, had planted this thing up here, anticipating that he
would drive up today with plastic clothesline and two
twenty-gauge screw eyes and climb this tree and hump
along this branch to discover a Jurassic Park egg. It wasn't
Easter, it was summer, he repeated to himself. What was
a leftover Easter egg doing up here? And then he remembered the mouthless creature he had struck with his
car that day, and this egg was exactly that shade of ver-
million.

Someone was jerking him around and he didn't know
why, but he felt very, very threatened by it. Red fur, red
carrion, red straw, red egg. Not funny at all. What was
causing mutations around here—a rogue pigment in the
food chain?

Like his mother—like the sympathetic school counselor he was—he could rationalize anything. But now
the evidence was done tapping him on the shoulder; it
was staring him in the face. The shaggy eccentric in the
wheelchair upstairs telling him the place was a "nursery," the barn burning down, and then there was Paavo's
chicken wire all around the windows. Denny scrutinized
the egg. Definitely not poultry. Ostrich maybe, except it
wasn't buried in the sand. Maybe he'd been burying his
head in the sand. . . .

He resisted the impulse to confront Ariel. One of the
underlying premises he was good at was manipulating
other people's credibility, usually by inflating it. He had
done so to navigate young people through the shoals and
reefs of maturation, done it to keep his parents afloat, re-

versing it a bit to get his father installed at New Eden, and now he was at the far negative limit with Ariel. People could be dangerous when you bankrupted their credibility.

He untied the old rope, drilled one hole in the tree and another in the porch stanchion, twisted in the screw eyes, strung up the new line, and took the ladder back. Then he went to see his father.

"How are you, old man?" he said.

"I've been better."

"Yeah? You need a shave, but I guess that doesn't bother you."

"Not a bit."

A Kleenex lay on the floor, one slipper was under the bed, the eyeglasses were on the window ledge. The newspaper Denny had brought last Sunday lay undisturbed on the dresser. Even if he could read well enough with the magnifier, his father couldn't concentrate through a whole story.

"Looks like the Twins are starting to fold in the pennant stretch," Denny said with the brass brightness of small talk.

"Do you have enough money?"

"I'm fine, Dad."

"Take all you want."

Anachronistic philanthropy. The money had dried up years ago. "Thanks, Pop. You always took care of everyone. Good planning. Everything runs well because of you."

"Not everything. Your mother is dead."

"You can't blame God for wanting her in His garden."

"I wish it was time for me." He was lying on the bed, staring up at the ceiling, and he drummed his fingers on his chest. "I guess they don't take weeds."

"You're not a weed, Dad."

"Hmm. At least Tiffany is okay now."

"What do you mean?"

"She finally came out of the house. She wanted her picture."

"Yeah?" (*Attention, please: today's lucidity is now ended.*)

"I kept one, gave her the other."

"A picture?"

"Yeah. I'm keeping it in the wardrobe."

It bothered Denny to play along with these mirages of memory, as if he were disrespecting his father. And that was why, a little later when he walked to the window, he opened the wardrobe. He had hauled it here from the basement in Little Canada—his sister's old clothes closet from the tiny front bedroom she had chosen over the larger one at the rear because she wanted to look out at the park instead of the alley. He remembered thinking, as he had trundled it step by step into his father's room, that the hollow boom of the metal was like the empty descent of Tiffany's life. So now he stared at it again, the dull sculpted coating like metallic surf, scratched at the corners, the even duller patch where a sticker (RAINBOW GIRLS) had once adhered.

"How are you doing for clean shirts, Dad?" he said.

But his father had closed his eyes, so Denny didn't need a pretext to check and make sure there really wasn't a picture.

Only there was, of course.

He pushed the hem of the champagne-colored bathrobe aside and lifted out the frame. Amber. The little girl he seldom saw, who bore more than a passing resemblance to his sister, Tiffany, at age nine. Tiffany had looked almost exactly like this: blond hair, green eyes, rosebud mouth, a certain serenity that said she was in control. But after the fire that had scarred her face and

scarred her soul, she hadn't been in control. Not for almost four decades. Dead seven years now, she would be
fifty-four if she hadn't overdosed. But she would always
be nine years of age and unscarred in their father's resur-
rections.

So his old man had somehow swiped the portrait, and
Denny supposed he ought to bring it to Ariel's attention.
He could take it with him and do a quick check for missing pictures on the first floor, even though he was pretty
sure he would have noticed if he had seen it before. So it
must be from the second or third floor.

Despite the clanging of the wardrobe, his father's
breathing was deeper, his thin eyelids closed and trembling with rapid eye movements underneath. What right
did he have to mess with the old guy's dreams, Denny
thought. Let him have the picture until someone hollered
about it. Waggling it back behind the champagne-
colored bathrobe and a line of shiny trousers hanging by
their unstylish cuffs, he gently closed the wardrobe
doors.

He went looking for Dana then, and found her behind
the house, puttering listlessly in the small garden on the
side opposite the rubble of the barn. She probably knew
he had parked out front; probably she was avoiding him.
But given that she felt hopeless about having a relationship beyond the confines of New Eden, he would regard
this as not entirely a rejection. In fact, you could almost
read something flattering in the fact that she felt she had
to avoid him.

"How are all the little cabbages and tomatoes today?"
he said, barely glancing at the seared rows.

She straightened, fired a slate blue glance at him.
"The rabbits and the caterpillars like them."

"Safe to say you won't be becoming a vegetarian any
time soon?"

"Safe to say . . ."

"Ah, well, there's always green eggs and ham."

"Not on this farm."

He surveyed the fields and the yard. What she said was true. Other than the mangled remains of a small chicken coop, the farm had clearly kept its commitment to cash crops. "You can see why I'm a city slicker. I still think the cow's in the meadow and the sheep's in the corn." His eye paused on the sugar maple. "Then again, red eggs are not out of the question."

She offered him mild perplexity.

"You practically lassoed a redbird with your clothesline," he said.

"What are you talking about?"

"There's a nest in the maple right where you looped the rope. And it has an egg in it as big as a Ruby Red grapefruit and twice as bright."

She wasn't very good at hiding shock, this Scandinavian woman with fair skin and high color. And he almost joked, "That's the shade," but the way her glance skittered from roof to tree to sky brought him back to his own misgivings and the question he kept putting to her.

"Dana, what's going on here?"

"I don't know," she said, and she murmured a couple of half phrases, half aloud, half focused, that came together with startling vehemence. "Let's kill it!"

"What?" "The red egg. I think we should destroy it."

"Why?"

"It's red. It's unnatural. Just show me where it is." And she started off walking toward the maple.

He picked up at her shoulder, "Okay, but I'd still like to know why. So what if it's unnatural? Better red than dead."

She wasn't going to laugh today, and she just kept marching along until she was at the base of the sugar

maple, where she began to circle, craning upward at the
first branch.

"I'll get the ladder," he said.

By the time he returned, lugging the stepladder, she
was farther out but still circling, and he had more questions, all of them off the mark.

"Does this have something to do with the crows in the
dryer? . . . Is there something about birds around here?
. . . Is that why Paavo had the chicken wire around the
windows?" This last even though he knew the chicken
wire had only been around the lower level. And then he
said: "What's with the color red?"

"Ask Amber."

"Amber?"

Dana was three steps up the ladder before he put his
hand on the back of her knee. "I'll get it."

"Just steady me."

"You can't reach far enough. You have to climb out
onto the branch."

She hesitated. "How will you kill it?"

"How?"

"Bring it down. I'll take care of it."

She backed off the ladder and up he went.

The branch felt solid, but the leaves were shaking and
he searched the upper foliage for another source of dis-
turbance. It was a mature tree at the zenith of the season
and there were many dense clusters of leaves. Whatever
laid the egg could still be up there, as aberrant as the
thing itself, a Mayzie bird gone missing or mad after its
involuntary act of motherhood. But nothing came at him.
And the egg was still there, garish and mysterious, dis-
played on a nest that was more like a pile than a weave.
He looked for a feather or any other sign, but no, nothing. Just the egg.

He lifted it and, like a drop of mercury, it seemed to

dance in his hand. All the way down the ladder he never took his eyes from it, and he imagined Dana watching him as carefully as he was watching the egg. At the bottom he discovered she had the shovel, so she must have gone back to the garden while he was up there concentrating on the prize.

Still moving slowly, he extended his hand to show her, but before he could react, she knocked it to the ground. It hit with a muted crunch, defying gravity as it rolled upright. Something quite red shot out to hold it in that position. The thing was alive at that instant—he was sure of that—incubated without heat beyond the ambient temperature, and already consciously performing its single trick of balance in a desperate bid for survival. With unbelievably gratuitous venom, Dana slammed the shovel down and crushed it flat.

She smashed it twice more, pained with the effort but swinging her forearms and hunching her body weight into each blow. The almost hatchling was mangled into a literal blood pudding of red feathers, red fluids, red membranous skin and red scaly legs, with only the sclera around its flattened remnant of an eye showing white.

Denny could not abide cruelty—could not clean a fish or kill a mouse—and though he was trying to understand the threat that this deviant embryo posed, he could not. He looked at Dana, and the repulsion in his eyes must have penetrated her manic act, because she suddenly burst into tears and covered her face. He caught her as the shovel clanged to the ground.

He had wanted to hug Dana Novicki for a long time, he realized, but there was nothing romantic in it now. It felt paternal. If he could have somehow known that she was twenty-three years of age the day he was born, it still would have felt paternal. He held her buried against his chest, her arms crossed between them, and her remorseful shudders contradicting the ghastly act she had just committed. Things were very wrong throughout New Eden, but all he had to substantiate this was the eccentric and circumstantial evidence of a bizarre summer.

In a moment she regained her composure and, with her arms still hugged against her breasts and her eyes downcast, she stepped away.

"Tell me what it is, Dana. What's all this about pictures and red things?"

She looked dazed and weary, not even a distant relative of the woman who had swung a shovel three times against the defenseless thing at their feet.

He caught her wrist to stop her retreat.

"All right, I won't ask you anymore. But listen, I've decided to take my father out of New Eden. Things are too shaky around here. And since I don't know what's going on, I've got to take him out—even though I can't take care of him myself. In fact . . . in fact, I'm asking you to go on taking care of him. If you'll come with us back to where I live in Little Canada, I'll pay you everything I'm paying Ariel—"

She shook her head vigorously.

"You can live there the same as you do here, Dana— independent, no strings attached—except that I can help when I'm home from work. You can drive a car, go shopping, have a life. Don't tell me you don't want that. I know you do."

"You don't know what you're asking."

"The hell I don't."

"It would be over as soon as she knew."

"You mean Ariel? Why?"

Each flurry of head shaking gained celerity, as if she were trying to convince herself. He took her by the shoulders, but she wouldn't look at him.

"No strings, Dana. I swear."

"You can't take your father out of here."

"Watch me."

"Don't do it, Denny." And now she looked him dead in the eye, repeating: "You don't know what you're asking."

"I don't think you know what you're turning down."

"Yes, I do. Is that what you want to hear? I can give you that. I'd love to leave here. I'd *love* to go live with you and your father. But trust me, I can't leave. And neither can your father."

It was absurd. It roused what small capacity he preserved of the warrior man. *Do not tell me what I cannot do.* An old woman like Ariel Leppa couldn't hold anything over him the way she seemed to with everyone else in this odd household. More than that, he was uplifted by Dana's bold assertion that she would love to accept his offer. That alone was reason enough not to argue, not to risk poisoning the sentiment. It wasn't the thought of a relationship with him that was holding Dana in check. She had opened up to him that much in order to stress some other imperative. But what?

"Trust me," she said again. "Leave your father here. He'll be all right, if you leave him here."

28

Painters preferred the north light. Ariel had read that somewhere. Painters and surgeons from the days when operations were performed by candlelight favored the "cool, clear light of the north." Sixteenth-century studios and operating theaters had skylights oriented to the north. Ariel's studio window was pointed north, and she stood there in the weathered frame high up on the third story, where a year ago she had contemplated suicide, feeling cosmic and apocalyptic.

But there was no cool and clear light out there now. Out there in the darkness was the cistern, and in it her child—a copy of her child. If Amber lived till dawn, then she could surrender the paint as her petition to go on living. And if she didn't make it—if, for instance, that ghastly spidery spawn of her own artistic endeavors caught her at the bottom of the hole—well, what was a mother to do?

A mother.

Not the right term. At risk of profaning the sacred, Ariel had to be honest about her role. She was Amber's creator in every sense of the term. The implication beyond biology was intriguing. Could a mortal act of genuine creation compare with a divine act? She would have to think about this, come to a conclusion once and for-ever. Up until this point she had been timid about using her powers, and that was natural because she was a good person, one who had no intention of usurping higher pre-rogative. But, in fact, what was the difference between the mortal and the divine? She painted, and it was her design, her rendering, her will that controlled the out-come. Of course, the paint was procreative in some or-ganic and palpable way, but it was still just paint. An inert thing by itself. The way it was used, on the other hand, could be . . . well, godlike.

She had to be ruthlessly honest about this because it would be just as bad to be too humble as too vain. It wasn't a sin to maximize what you had, as in the parable of the talents. You could make the argument that some-thing had created the red dust that went into the paint, and you could reason that the creator of the red dust was therefore the ultimate god, but Ariel had mixed the paint and shaped the images, and how could that not be the heart of it? Was it a universe of overt creative acts that included her in its pantheon of creators, or was the uni-verse just a single creative act from which all else de-scended?

Downstairs in a bedroom a perfect facsimile of Amber slept. So far she had obeyed to the letter, following her predecessor twin to find where the stolen paint was and even taking the initiative of trapping the disobedient Amber before coming back to report to her mother-creator that the missing paint was in the cistern. A little better than Eve had done, wouldn't you say?

When dawn raked its fingernails through the canopy of night to the east Ariel got her cane, and it was only fear that she might encroach on the hours of the hunter spider that made her wait a little longer. Light spread like surf up a Plutonian shore, and when it touched the

far horizon she glided through the house where her creations slept, dreaming dreams of the immortality that
was hers to bestow. She was the cynosure of all hope, all
morality, all judgment for those things she had made.
Within that sphere, she need answer no one.

She opened the door to Amber's room without knocking and found her sitting upright in the middle of the big
bed, rocking. In the diluted light of dawn, the dresser
and the oak bedposts were black, the walls and the
sheets white. And something of this contrast extended to
Amber in a way that was faintly shocking to Ariel. Her
daughter's face and cotton nightshirt were white, but her
hands were black. Jet-black trailed up her wrists as
though she were wearing ragged velvet gloves.

It looked like blood, except for the fact that nothing
transferred to the white sheets, and mud wouldn't have
dried in such thin rivulets on her forearms. But as she
opened her mouth to speak, Ariel grasped something
else: the rocking, the lack of focus, the steady gaze at the
wall opposite the bed—a few hours ago she had spoken
to her anointed one, and there had been none of this obvious trauma. This was not the Amber she had recently
created.

"Thank God you got out of that old cistern," she said
smoothly. The fact that her clever little girl had escaped
should have infuriated Ariel, but instead she smiled
calmly. "Amber? I couldn't come for you in the dark—
you know that. I can't imagine how you made it back
here, but it would have been suicidal for me to go out
there in the dark. Of course, I want the paint returned—
that's a matter of survival for all of us—but I've been
fretting over you all night."

No reaction, no expression, just a little girl in ebony
gloves, rocking, staring. What *was* the black stain on her
skin?

"Amber? Where is she?"

"In the cellar," came back abruptly.

"The cellar?"

Suddenly the child's face turned, and her eyes lit up with awareness, and she looked squarely at her mother and spoke with just a hint of tremor. "Here's the way it is. If you paint me again, then I'll paint too. I'll paint spiders and snakes, and I'll let them loose in the house. If you do anything else to me, you won't ever get your paint back. It will just be there where someone else will find it. And I wrote a note, so whoever finds it will know where it came from and what it can do."

As abruptly as she had turned, Amber faced back to the wall and resumed rocking.

Outrage sizzled like a lit fuse in the high-ceiling room, but it was a long fuse. Time was on her side, Ariel decided. She stood up, walked slowly to the door. "How dangerous," she said. "How very, very dangerous."

But the rocking continued.

Ariel went straight to the cellars, where she found the blackened canvas, and that snuffed out her rage with cold fear. She scratched at the black coating, searching for confirmation that this was indeed one of her paintings. But of course it had to be. There were the familiar corrugated fasteners and copper staples she used on frames.

She thundered up the steps, breathing hard but driven to assess the damage to her security. She reached the studio electrified, fumbling with her key. Wheezing, shaking, she unlocked and threw open the door.

Everything had looked in order a few minutes ago, and it still looked in order, but that must be a lie, because she had just held one of her sacred paintings in her own two hands down in the cellar, so someone had been in here. Someone had access. She rifled through the stacks

of frames, one after another, against the wall: *Ruta* . . .
Paavo . . . *Molly* . . . *Dana* . . . *Helen* . . . *Marjorie* . . .
Beverly . . . *Thomas* . . . *Kraft*—even the younger sketch
of herself waiting to be painted in. But NOT *Amber*! Not
Amber One. Not Amber Two. *Both* missing.

She sat down hard on the floor. It was over. The little
menace had her, could expose her at will. She felt like an
old hag again. White-faced, bloodless, suddenly facing
the merciless fate of all fallen deities. But why hadn't
Amber said something about possessing her own portrait? Why threaten with just the paint and not mention
that her mother could no longer change the painting?
And why was she worried about another Amber being
created—why hadn't she just taken her portrait and the
paint and run away?

Of course, this was a little girl reborn into a world she
had not seen for more than thirty years. Running away
would be daunting. But then again, this was tempestuous
Amber, indomitable flesh of her indomitable flesh,
climber of roofs, painter of monsters, who ventured out
at night with stolen goods—very little truly daunted her.
Then what could one conclude except that Amber didn't
know her portrait was missing?

My, my.

Another thief in the house. Who? They had gotten into
the studio without breaking in. A key? Ariel didn't think
this was possible. She must have left the door unlocked
briefly. So it had to be someone relatively mobile
(Molly? Dana?). Or someone opportunistically close at
hand (Thomas?). Or with a reckless hate for her (Kraft?).
She would search each room. Put the fear of God in
them. Find the answers to all the questions. But first she
would do another contingency portrait, like the one she
had done of herself.

This one from a newer photo—Amber at eleven. Unfinished for the moment, because it was done only with pigments that were not mixed with the dust of creation. This one her warrior. This one her gladiator who would defeat the younger, smaller Amber anytime in order to live. Anytime Ariel wanted.

Behold, Amber Three.

29

A warm, breathing twin of herself had lain on the bed a few hours before, and Amber had painted her out, made her disappear, sent her . . . where? What was death like? Everyone in the house knew except her and her mother. And Mr. Bryce.

So why did she feel like the other Amber was still here? It was incredibly real and spooky, almost like they were together on the mattress, touching knee to knee, face to face, eyeball to eyeball, her twin staring goggle-eyed into her brain and her soul. The only thing missing was breath in her face. But even that was sort of there, because she felt air moving against her skin, only it was ice-cold.

When her mother came in, something prickled at the base of her neck and squeezed her throat slightly all the way up behind her ears, as if her insubstantial twin were suddenly trying to smother her. It made her keep her eyes open, watchful that her mother wasn't orchestrating something she had created with her magic paints.

Amber was figuring things out. She had gotten rid of her competition, but it wasn't going to end there. Her mother was saying nice things, fake things about how she had wanted to save her from the cistern, and Amber had to let her know that she couldn't be fooled anymore. She hadn't planned to say those things about painting spiders and snakes if another Amber came along; they just came out. Then her mother went away.

And now she couldn't stop rocking.

Rocking kept the world in balance, like a swing, like a teeter-totter. Stop rocking and you fell or slid or tipped over. When the door opened again she stopped rocking.

Mrs. Armitage came in first and then Mrs. Novicki. The rest of them, Mr. Seppanen and his wife, Miss Hoverstein and Mrs. Swanson, stayed outside the doorway. Her mother had made them older and they were slower now, but she didn't like the way they stood there holding their arms out a little like a game of Red Rover, where kids tried to block you from running past. She had felt bad for them—Mrs. Seppanen with her mouth shrunk up like that, and Miss Hoverstein all hunched over, and Mrs. Swanson so tiny that she could have been one of the twelve Taron pygmies waiting to die that Miss Hoverstein talked about—but now they looked threatening.

"We want you to come with us, Amber," Mrs. Armitage said, moving to one side of the bed. *(Red Rover, Red Rover, let AMBER come over!)*

Mrs. Novicki moved to the other side, mumbling an apology, and Amber jumped off the foot of the mattress, almost into Mr. Seppanen's arms as he blocked the doorway. She dodged back, squealing with fear. Mrs. Armitage's plump fingers flexed, catching the sleeve of her nightshirt for a moment. The room was too small. She couldn't get away, so with both hands she grabbed one of the bedposts and squeezed until her fingers were white. But then as they closed in from three sides, she jumped back onto the mattress and jounced to the other end.

The window there was closed but not locked, and she

took hold of the handles and yanked as hard as she could because it was always swollen shut this time of year. She only had a couple of seconds, and if she didn't get it up the first time, there wouldn't be a second. So she put everything into it, shrugging as she lifted and pushing with her legs, but her feet sank down into the mattress and the frame barely slid up on the gray metal tracks. Then dry fingers closed around her ankles and a heavy hand clamped over her shoulder.

"We're sorry, Amber"—Miss Hoverstein's swollen shoulder blades forced her head into her neck and made her voice strained—"but we've got to make sure you don't interfere."

"Interfere with what?" she whimpered.

"With what we've got to do. You know we can't go on like this."

Amber had no idea what they were talking about. "I promise I won't interfere! I'll just stay in my room."

"She's your mother. We can't take that chance, child."

"When we're done, we'll let you out of the cellar," Mrs. Novicki assured her.

They were all in the room now, and a half dozen hands were pulling her off the bed. The air had that mad quality of a humming beehive. They were going to attack her mother, she realized. They were going to try and take over New Eden.

"She's got your pictures," Amber said between ragged breaths. "She'll kill you!"

The momentary hush told her this was very much on their minds, but it was only a second before Miss Hoverstein conceded with resignation, "That would be acceptable. It's living like this"—she waved her hand at the stooped and hoary company—"that we have to stop. Your mother can make us suffer anything and anytime she wants."

Amber's feet barely touched the floor as they lifted her toward the door.

"I won't interfere, honest, I won't!" she begged, but into the corridor went the eerily infirm cortege, bumbling along through the house to the top of the cellar stairs. "I could help. You need me. Mom's just gonna lock herself in her studio and do whatever she wants to your pictures!"

They were like some slow machine that couldn't stop running, a sump pump with a stuck switch gurgling dry air or a car dieseling on with a dead ignition. The reason they wouldn't listen to her wasn't just because she was a kid and they were old, Amber thought, it was because they were practically zombies while she had been alive when she was painted for the first time.

Someone threw the light switch and the vague glow from the storage room rose halfway up the stairs. Amber was edged onto the dark top step. Dry fingers slid off her arms like limp fronds a moment before the door firmly closed. She saw the ghostly white ceramic handle twist, heard the lock snap.

Tears burned hotly in her eyes as her captors shuffled away, but she fought them down. It wouldn't be so bad, she thought. Being locked down here while a battle raged wouldn't be so bad. Then she thought, what if her mother painted her out along with the rest of them? Her mother didn't know she was locked in the cellars. She might assume she was part of the rebellion. The others might be willing to die, but she wasn't! She had to get out of here, had to tell her mother she wasn't part of it. Or else she had to become part of it and make sure they won. Because if they didn't win, she would lose with them.

She jiggled the white handle. Banged on the door. It would take an axe to get through the oak. She had once

seen her father tear down a shed with a wrecking bar and
a sledgehammer, but if those tools existed anymore they
were probably in the machine shed. Skating her hand
along the wall, she descended through the storage room
looking for anything she could use to beat down the
door.

When she snapped on the light in the laundry the two
tunnels at the far end seemed to leap toward her. The old
stories of passageways and collapsed sections were
vague in her memory. Somewhere within that clutter the
secrets lay buried. Maybe she could find a path this time,
she thought. But she wouldn't go in without a light. If a
spider could come up through the plumbing into the
bathtub, then there could be lots of them down here, so
she wouldn't go feeling in the dark.

Back for the candles and matches in the cupboards she
went. She tried not to look at the dried black shoe polish
all over the floor as she lit a pair of sputtering wicks. Returning through the double-back passageway, she went
straight to the tunnel on the right. But she got only as far
as the furnace when she saw all the debris: shelves and
crates and barrel staves and broken, gluey, green glass
mixed with a slope of dirt and stones and . . . red straw.

It could have just looked red because of the light.
Holding both candles in her left hand, she picked up a
piece and held it close to the flames. The vividness of
the color brought back the vividness of the scarecrow
lurching into the barn that day and the fire that she had
made happen. The red straw could have been here since
before the fire in the barn, of course, but she had an eerie
feeling that something was watching from just beyond
the collapse. There could be undamaged tunnels on the
other side of the debris. No telling how big they were or
what might be in there.

She started to back away, moving the wicks side to

side, trying to keep them from making blind spots in her field of vision. But a couple of steps brought her up hard against the furnace. She raised the candles to reassure herself that she had caused the metallic thrum, and the light revealed the ghostly robot limbs of the old duct-work that wound round each other, heading off to every room in the house. She and her friends—back when she had friends—had hollered through them sometimes, room to room, pretending they were telephones or microphones or that they themselves were gods making booming pronouncements from on high.

The house was big and old and the ducts were big and old, and it suddenly occurred to her that she could crawl through them—crawl and climb—if she could just get inside. And she could. Because one of them, right where the Lutheran school had installed square ducts to go to the new wing, had rusted through on the bottom, and her father had cut the rusty part out and laid another panel in its place inside the duct. She had watched him do it. "Guess that's not going anywhere," he had said, and she thought that was funny at the time—the idea that it could go somewhere. Only, now it did. Because she dragged boxes in place and climbed up and pushed the panel until it slid back enough for her to lift one of the lights and poke her head in.

It looked like oatmeal inside, a gray blanket of dust all wavy and pilled, but there were squiggly lines along the bottom too, like rivers that had dried up, so it must have leaked, and that was why her father had replaced the rusty part. She could see the bare metal in the riverbeds. And every few feet there was a rib where one section joined the next. A ways down she could see a dark opening where the oversize duct turned up. *I can do it,* she thought.

Daddy's little monkey . . .

She was barefoot and in a cotton nightshirt, but whatever was happening upstairs left her no choice except to try to defeat her mother before she herself was destroyed. So she wormed her way in and slowly crept forward, mindful of the hot wax dribbling onto her hand as she maneuvered a few inches at a time. Dust clung to all four inner surfaces and stirred into the stifling air as she planted her elbows commando style. The fine tickle in her throat thickened until it felt like she had swallowed a washcloth, and then she coughed and that made her bump her head, knocking wads of the stuff loose. Like cotton candy, it vaporized. She barely had time to realize it had caught on fire. Embers, smoke, ash—all in a burst.

So now she knew the gray lining could all go up at once, and her grip began to sweat, making the candles slippery. One touch to the blanket of dust and—poof!— cremated Amber. Old Mr. Bryce would blame himself.

She would have turned back at that point, except that she was near a vertical shaft. Squiggling her bare toes forward in the soft blanket, trying not to create a tear that would bring down curtains of flammable dust, she twisted her neck and peered up the intersecting riser.

It wasn't as dusty up there, and she could stand up. In fact, it wasn't a duct at all. Vaguely she remembered her father joking about how the furnace must have been built by the same people who had done the Tower of Babel, because it had round ducts and square commercial ducts and sometimes no ducts at all but something he just called chases. She must be standing in a chase, she thought, because most of it didn't have any metal. It was a wood-frame shaft with metal sections here and there that she thought maybe the church people had put in as part of the agreement for their school. The ribs every couple of feet would make it easy to brace her feet, she thought, and unlike the cistern, it was just narrow enough for her to use the sides. The problem was the candles. She didn't think she could climb and hang on to the candles, pushing with just her elbows and wrists instead of her fingers.

There were voices—shouts—coming from high up in the house, and that spurred her on. Pawing away the coating of dust on the horizontal shaft right below the chase, she dribbled a little wax on the bare metal and stuck both candles straight upright. Even if her body kept the light from shining past, at least she would be able to look down and see what progress she had made.

Cautiously she tried the first handhold, simultaneously feeling with her toes for the first ridge. It took a little adjustment to her balance, pushing just right against the sides as well as down, but it wasn't all that hard for Amber the Human Fly. Up she went, faster than she had been able to crawl in the horizontal duct. She kept looking down to make sure she wasn't dislodging dust onto the candles. And each time she looked up again, she had to give it a couple of seconds for her eyes to get used to the darkness. Enough light made it past her so that she could pick out the dark openings that came into the chase, and when she reached the second of these a fall of light was tantalizing close.

It took only a few seconds to slide on her butt through the horizontal shaft and discover that she was looking up through the floor register of the downstairs bathroom by her bedroom. And that made her wonder if the red spider she had drowned that day had gotten into the bathroom through this very shaft and afterward gone down the tub drain. She pushed as hard as she could on the grid, hammered with her palm. Then got her feet against the lattice with her knees up against her chin. Nothing budged. She cried out in frustration, but the tinny echo just blended with the general tumult from upstairs.

And now there was another thing. Was it her imagination or was it growing hotter in the duct? She couldn't get a full breath. Too late she realized that she was dragging a carpet of dust with her as she wriggled back to the vertical shaft. And as she shoved her feet over the edge into the chase, it went raining down on the candles below. She peered past her toes at the feathery clusters as they hit the flames and set them winking. For just a second she thought they would go out. And when the wavering stopped and the light steadied again, she almost wished they had. Because now she could see every detail of the crimson eyes in the crimson head and the crimson serpent's tongue flicking up at her.

She screamed and screamed.

Screamed until she was deafened and the metal that surrounded her hummed. But the vibrations only seemed to excite the thing below, and its split tongue flicked up at her like a fork probing for tender morsels.

For a few dizzying moments her arms and legs wouldn't move. It was clear to her that if they did, she was going to pass out from sheer fright and fall down the chase, and then the snake was going to unhinge its jaw and work its mouth over her head. It was probably starving, probably able to swallow her bit by bit by unhinging its jaws the way she had once seen in science lab when she had been in school. And this snake looked terrifyingly real, not at all like the ones she had painted, but more like the one in the painting in the parlor. It was still writhing into view out of the horizontal shaft, and it was incredibly long. Anaconda long. And it was red. She understood what the wriggly lines in the dust of the bottom shaft were now. They were not leaks that had rusted out the panel. They were tracks where the thing had come and gone. It must have crawled in and grown and grown until it couldn't get out.

But suddenly her heart surged, flushing the cobwebs out of her mind and allowing her to reason that the snake wasn't all that fast, not going up anyway. So that's what she had to do. Go up.

She began to scramble for footing in the ductwork, but she must have dragged more dust out of the horizontal chase she had just left, because the light around her began to pulse like a strobe, and when she looked down the last thing she saw before first one and then the other of the candles winked out was the flattened viper head much, much closer.

30

Ariel walked right into them on the stairs. She came out of the studio, intending to search the cellar for the other missing portrait of Amber, and there they were, a guilty little huddle of rebellion halfway to the second floor. She looked down with scorn but they glared back, and she saw that they didn't look guilty after all. Their haggard, burning eyes were anything but conflicted.

Then she noticed that Paavo had a hammer and a chisel and Molly carried the jack handle from the car. The others—Dana, Helen, Beverly, Ruta—seemed to be holding things at their sides. But the really shocking sight was the seventh figure, the one bringing up the rear. Kraft Olson looked disturbingly sentient for a man clutching a serrated carving knife with homicidal intent.

And yet the vivid reality of what they were attempting seemed absurd to her. A more desperate act by so inadequate a group was hard to imagine. Her first reaction was to confront them, and she actually took five or six steps down the staircase as if she were not afraid. But they kept on coming, a ridiculous slow-motion coup straight out of a B horror film: arthritic knees lifting, flaccid arms pulling on the banister, fingers catching on steps. Ruta's obscenely small mouth strained for air, and runty Beverly struggled to get both feet on each step behind Helen the Hunchback.

Ariel balked. Farce or not, she did not like their intensity or the very fact that they were unafraid. Better to retreat to the studio. Put a heavy oak door between her and them. But as she turned, her eyes came up sharply to the wheelchair that sat poised at the top of the stairs. Massive and shaggy, her invalid husband leered down at her.

"Wait for me, dear," Thomas Leppa rumbled, and yanking as hard as he could he launched the big silver wheels over the edge.

The heavy chair plunged straight at Ariel, thrusting her husband upright, his arms outflung to prevent any possibility of her escape. But the right footrest caught the second step, pivoting the wheelchair on its side and altering its trajectory. Ariel was already losing her balance when a flailing hand clutched the throat of her blouse. It was an irresistible force, and she spun after her husband while the misdirected chair tumbled to the landing. She fell elbow first against the small of his back, and she actually heard the snapping of the vertebrae, though she couldn't tell whose. But they rode only a couple of steps before he slid out from under, leaving her gently sprawled halfway down the flight.

She had hit her lip and now she tasted blood, tasted reality. The blur of open rebellion rising from the lower level was palpably threatening. By the time Molly and Paavo were past the upended wheelchair and Thomas' grotesquely twisted body, Ariel had crawled ponderously to the top step on the third floor.

She threw one white-eyed glance over her shoulder as she gained her feet, then hobbled toward the studio, fumbling for the key in the pocket of her slacks as she went. A chill went through her out of fear that the object was lying on the staircase. But it hadn't fallen out, she discovered with relief, and that little triumph infected her with insane glee.

"Do you know what you've just thrown away?" she shouted to the climbers on the stairs, then slammed the door thunderously and turned the key.

She staggered to her workbench and collapsed beside it, allowing herself the luxury of several racking shudders and a single dry sob. Why had everything gone so wrong for her? She had been at the bottom of the food chain and at the top, and each time she had been devoured by the ravenous pack. There was no reason for it except the capriciousness of human preference and resistance to change. They hadn't liked her looks. It was as simple as that. Children on a playground nearly three-quarters of a century removed had decided at a glance that she lacked the symmetry and grace of the rest of them. So they had practiced their own "natural selection" ever since. And nothing was going to change that.

Her wallow in self-pity was suddenly interrupted by a scream. The fact that it was a distant scream from deep within the walls of the house failed to register. More screams. She thought they were coming from the horror-struck and damned collection at her closed door. Like a raft of doomed sinners they had arrived on Charon's ferry to the far shore of the river Styx, and their screaming drove the self-pity out of her mind, because it was their turn to suffer the full consequences now . . . really suffer.

"You've lost!" she shrieked, half rising, half scrabbling to the door. "You threw it all away!"

She landed on the inner panel as if she had been hurled, and she spoke hoarsely into the wood, letting it resonate her condemnation and her laments to the faithless inhabitants of New Eden on the other side.

"I gave you a chance to redeem yourselves, and you

were too selfish, too proud, too WEAK to take it. Do you think I'm made of stone? I cared . . . I cared enough to let you back, and all you could do was look down on me. Ariel the Leper. Ariel the Doormat. How could *she* be in charge?"

The first blow jarred her from the door. It was Paavo hitting the middle with the hammer. A mediocre thud. The door was heavy; Paavo was weak. They could pound until they dropped, and the door would hold.

"Do you know what I'm going to do now?" Ariel amplified. "I'm going to make you so hideous that you'll wish for hell again. Did you hear that, Ruta? You think Marjorie is a festering ruin? Wait till you're too weak to brush the worms out of your sores. Wait until your bowels leak and your skin is so thin that it bursts when you move. You'll wish for hell to save you from me!"

More blows from metal objects—and fists—as she set about getting the portraits ready. She would paint them as she had said: a rogue's gallery of living agony that would put the ugliness of their souls on their outward bodies. Fit company for Dorian Gray. And if, by some chance, they were able to penetrate the door before the changes could dry, she would have open containers of paint ready to spill onto their images, obliterating them forever.

But the hammering on the door suddenly stopped of its own accord. Too suddenly to be exhaustion.

Ariel heard movement as if they were stepping aside. And now there was a thin, gritty thud in the center of the panel so impotent that she almost laughed. But why had the others stopped? And then she knew what it was, and it did indeed have its effect. Kraft Olson had cast his hand in her symbolic assassination. He didn't need to get any closer in order to wound her. The knife came out and went in again and again, so vindictively, and she wanted to tell him how Danielle had suffered, how ugly she was before annihilation, but she couldn't. Because she felt uglier than any of the travesties she had described. Ugly and hated. A tremendous pain filled her mind and body, so paramount that she feared she could not exist another instant if she examined it. Everyone and everything had betrayed her. Even the pain threatened to betray her by yielding reasons she didn't want to hear. So she let the outrage that lay at the bottom of her heart scream it down—that ravenous outrage that had lain mute all her life while it grew bloated with hurts. Such a scream it had pent up. So deafening that now it blinded her. And she was glad because she could no longer hear the knife in the door. And she was glad she couldn't see Kraft's face. And most of all, she was glad he couldn't see hers. . . .

31

The soles of Amber's bare feet tingled and the cotton nightshirt, ending at her calves, felt like a wind tunnel exposing her to every breath of heat rising in the duct. That she could actually feel heat from the nightmarish reptile, that its scorching breath would touch her naked heels first when it caught her, seemed rational. A red serpent, a flickering flame for a tongue—its whole aspect was heat. Burning fangs would close around the tendon at the back of her foot, and she would be dragged down, down, feverish from the poison that was paralyzing her as it began to swallow and digest her in the hot acids of its stomach.

She caught the vanilla smell of the gutted candles then, and it was funny, but that sane association with unbaked cherry pies and cookie dough rekindled her with hope as strong as fear. She began to climb furiously in the dark. Hand following hand, foot following foot, grasping, pressing, clinging to successive ridges where sections of the old chases and newer ductwork met. She thrummed her way upward, listening beneath the reverberations for pursuit, and the unfairness of the fact that the snake didn't make any sound at all made her want to cry.

Her response to the next hint of light in a connecting shaft was just as desperate. She scrambled into the horizontal duct and banged her way to the grillwork. There would be no time to go back now. And then she saw that it was a second-floor bedroom that was used to store books and boxes. One of the boxes sat on half the floor grid, and from the way it bulged, she knew it was heavy. She got her foot up on the lattice but gave up after one push.

So now the panic hit her like ice dripping from the top of her spine to the pit of her stomach. Which way to go? The red snake might be up to the connecting shaft by now. She tried to remember where the registers were in the second-floor rooms, tried to figure where the duct might go. It would be a dead end, she thought, and before she could reason that *any* direction was going to be a dead end, she had started back to the vertical chase. But moving toward darkness was disorienting, and in her haste she miscalculated. Reaching out, she brought her right hand down into nothingness. Like a slow surface dive, she pitched headlong into the shaft.

The fact that she stiffened her legs, which were still in the horizontal duct, was what saved her. She was rigid when her shoulder jarred against the opposite side. Pain radiated from her waist to her neck as her right hand clawed for a seam and her left grasped the horizontal lip of the crossing. She pushed, wriggling backward one awkward inch at a time until her hips were supported and she could rest both elbows on the opposite edge.

But now her body was bridging the intersection, with her stomach bowed downward as if to invite the scaly red serpent to strike. She thought about all the high places she had climbed, roofs and trees and a lightning rod, and here she was inside a simple long box that had edges like a ladder on all four sides. All she had to do was get her feet under her. Her arms felt like rags and her spine like straw as with one last trembling effort she pushed herself upright.

Bruised and scraped, she positioned herself across the emptiness again and started to climb. But the surge of adrenaline passed after a few feet, and another wave of nausea made her want to just let go. Maybe she would be unconscious before she was eaten. Maybe she would crush the snake. She thought she heard her heart thudding. But no, it was pounding overhead. Her mother was yelling something. Not a cry for help. Something drawn out and angry.

Too exhausted and sick with terror to figure it out, feeling less and less through her fingers, she climbed mechanically until at last she came to the third-floor crossing and saw another pocket of light like the others. This was it. Endgame.

The meager light patterned across her face as she dragged herself a few feet into the shaft behind a wall register. But this grid wouldn't budge either. And then she saw the room beyond, and it was the studio, and there was her mother.

32

The banging resumed with such fury that it alarmed Ariel. She twisted to see before realizing that it wasn't coming from the door but from the inner wall near the baseboard. How the hell had they gotten in there? She went to the radiator grid and stooped far enough to make out a tear-stained face and battered fingers.

"Amber! What are you doing?"

"Let me out."

Let her out? That would be letting her in. Then what?

"Let me out!" Bare feet tattooed against the grid, sending flakes of loose paint from the plaster around the frame. "Let me out, let me out, let me out!"

"Stop it!"

But it didn't stop. Her brash young daughter had never been this frantic before. It half persuaded her that they had done something to her. Maybe Amber wasn't on their side after all. Why wait until the grid broke out of the plaster?

"All right, all right, I'll get you out. But then you have to leave the studio. Do you understand?

"Yes, yes, hurry!"

Ariel had a small metal spatula for working paint, and she applied its edge to the slotted screws one by one. But the fourth screw was still partially threaded into the plaster when Amber added a final kick to the effort and the grid shot off. The child tumbled out then, and Ariel was struck by the spectacle. Two small patches of her nightshirt were blood soaked, and her hair was matted and powdered like a nineteenth-century periwig. More crimson trickled through the caked dust between her bare toes, as if it flowed up from wounds on the soles of her feet, and dust obliterated the pattern of her nightshirt where it covered Amber's knees. Her arms hung limp and her shoulders sagged as she stumbled toward the door.

"Not that way. Out the window."

A look of agony. "I can't."

"What do you mean, you can't? You've been up and down on that lightning rod, and you can reach it from this window as easily as from the sewing room."

"I can't!" She flexed her knees slightly for emphasis, and before Ariel could stop her, she pattered to the door and turned the key.

Had the seven who stood in the corridor known what to expect they might have forced their way in, but the rattling in the lock was taken as a sign that Ariel was coming out. Whether in resignation or with a weapon, it would be Ariel, and they backed away. So when Amber emerged they were distracted just long enough for Ariel to slam the door and twist the key again. Dismay changing to anger, they turned on the child.

"Now look what you've done!" Ruta blistered.

"I didn't do anything. I opened the door for you."

"You're just like your mother. . . . "

"No—"

"You painted those creatures," Molly said. "You made the thing that got Paavo the first time."

"You made the scarecrow," Dana added.

"Yes, but I didn't know they were going to hurt any-one."

They had her hemmed in. Paavo took her by the arm. "How did she get out of the cellar?" he posed.

"We're sorry, child," Helen said. "But we can't let you go. You've got the paint."

"I don't want it anymore. I'll tell you where it is!"

And as if that offer devastated Ariel behind the locked door, the studio suddenly erupted in shrieks. Something overturned, something else clattered as if hurled, glass shattered. Only Amber understood. Her mother was throwing things, breaking the windows to see if there was a way to escape. And it wasn't to get away from the other members of the household. Her mother would go down kicking and clawing, if it was just human beings she was up against. The reason she was trying so franti-cally to get away was because *it* was coming through the open wall register now—*it*—and she really *hated* snakes. . . .

When the key rattled in the lock this time, they were ready. They took hold of Ariel the instant she stumbled out, and it seemed unreal that they actually had their hands on the cause of their damnation and that her power over them could be at an end. Paavo let go of Amber, and for the moment she was forgotten. What did the offspring matter when you had the queen bee sur-rounded? Nothing, unless you believed in royal succes-sion. Because the daughter of the queen suddenly jumped back into the studio that held the magic paint and all their portraits and locked the door behind her.

The red serpent was gone. In the turmoil, Amber stole a look in the studio to see how imminent the threat was and caught a last glimpse of it rippling back *into* the duct. For a moment she was uncertain. Why hadn't it at-

tacked everyone? Then again, it lived in the cellar; it
could have attacked before and didn't. It was almost like
it had been after her mother and now her mother was
caught. So Amber took her chance—hadn't Ruta said
she was just like her mother?—darting back into the studio and locking the door.

Once before she had been in the studio alone with
the paints. She had thought then that she could get
good enough like her mother and that she would paint
her father healthy again and then he would be able to
get out of his wheelchair. But she hadn't gotten good
enough. Instead she had unleashed a bunch of hideous
things, things that didn't fit in, things that had no way
to survive without killing. They were like Miss Hoverstein's pygmies, who married each other and whose babies were all deformed or had sick brains, and so the
world shouldn't have them anymore. Only, her monsters weren't going to let themselves die out. They had
to be killed.

But now that she was actually in the studio, she realized the choices. *You're just like your mother. . . .* Yes,
she was, in some ways. She had the artistic ability that
ran in the family. And she could learn the rest. And she
had all of the paints now. She could do it. Here were the
pictures. She could paint them all out. Then she could
practice, practice, practice with just regular paint—all
day long, if she wanted—until she got good enough to
use the magic paints. She could start again with a different world. She could paint Aarfie back, and her dad, and
any friends she wanted. Maybe even a sister. That's what
she could do.

That's what her mother did. Because her mother
couldn't trust anyone, couldn't share with them, and so
she could only be below or above them. And she had
been both. She had made everyone come back, but not

equal with her. So that was kinda her own choice too, Amber thought. And she was like her mother, sure, but not *just* like her mother.

They were pleading with her when she went to the door, begging her to give them their portraits.

33

Denny punched the speaker button on the ringing phone because he was putting on his sunscreen, in order to go out and mow the lawn, and his hands were greasy. "Hello?"

"You'd better get out here."

"Dad?" He grabbed the phone out of the cradle.

"You'd better get out here, son."

His father actually calling him on the phone, getting the number right to boot—the first call he'd received from him in, what, a dozen years? "What's the matter, Pop?"

"I dunno. I hear things."

"Like what?"

"Screams and guns."

"In the house?"

Hesitation. "Yes, in the house."

"Is anyone else right there? Dana, maybe. You know, the one you bipped on the beak, old man."

"Everyone's gone."

"Gone?"

"They're screaming."

"Okay. Okay." Screaming. Guns. His father still had nightmares now and then. The Bataan thing his mother had told him about had never healed—never would heal. "You're sure you hear screaming?"

"Yeah." Straining with impatience. "And guns." A raspy remnant of a voice. "Turret guns."

This is what Denny had gotten the phone for. To reassure his father when he couldn't be there. Cauterize the hemorrhaging of events that flowed without sequence. Chase away the nightmares 24/7. Tell him where he was and what year it was. But all at once Denny heard the "guns" for himself. Right over the phone. Distant and tinny, like backstage thunder, but it must have sounded like Tin Pan Alley if you were right there in the house. It could have been the metal wardrobe. It could have been someone banging on the furnace. But his father said turret guns. And screams. "I'm coming, Dad. Stay right where you are, okay?"

He left the mower out in the drive, and he kept wiping his hands on his yellowed sweatshirt as he drove. How could he have been so stupid, so reckless with his father's well-being? Something was very wrong with that farmhouse in the middle of nowhere. Unless there was a totally innocent explanation for all this, he would bring the old man home with him tonight.

On the seat beside him was the pack of cigarettes he had finally remembered to buy for Beverly the night before.

34

Amber could hear them dragging her mother downstairs, but she knew that others were still in the hallway. They had quit begging for their paintings, but they were still there.

In point of fact, it was Paavo and Kraft and Molly who were taking their captive to the cellar while the rest passively stood by, riveted by Ariel's baleful warnings as she was pulled down—kicking and screaming—into her own apocalypse. Behind the door Amber listened, and a whole range of feelings beset her. The leaden pall over her life was literally sinking down the staircase like a counterweight, lifting a curtain of anger, mistrust and doubt and revealing a thinner fabric of pity for her mother that must have always been there. It would always be there, visible but not impeding anything. And a lot of fear remained too. There was fear on both sides of the door. But when the others returned and her mother's dire sputterings were just a smothered murmur in the distant cellar, Amber decided to take a chance her mother never would have taken.

Turning the key, she opened the door on seven startled faces.

"God bless you, dear," Miss Hoverstein said, reaching

out a waxy hand that looked shrink-wrapped over blue
veins.

They doddered into Ariel's inner sanctum like
awestruck children, and for a few moments the studio re-
sembled a life-size music box whose figurines turn
slowly with the last dirge-soft notes. Here was the castle
tower, empty of its lightning-hurling sorceress, and it
was just as warped and faded as the rest of the house.
How strange that the gateway between the two contrast-
ing dimensions they had known should be so mundane.
Dust crawled for the corners and plaster sagged along
the exterior edge of the ceiling. But the miserable creature in the castle keep was not finished with them yet.

"Look," Dana warned, drawing their gazes as she
glided toward the appalling portraits lined across the
workbench. "She had already started on Paavo."

They saw; they slumped. Eyes refused eyes. The air
seemed to go out of the room.

"But it hasn't dried yet," Beverly noted.

Paavo came slowly toward the image of himself with
the left arm torn out of its glistening socket and braced
his hands on the edge of the workbench. His eye fell on
the open jars of paint that Ariel had been using. "Doesn't
matter," he said. He pushed himself erect and hefted a
can of commercial alkyd from the shelf. "I don't have to
be here when it's dried."

Molly raised her head as if in affirmation. "No, it really doesn't matter, does it? None of us have to be here
anymore."

Amber sensed the drama of a decision circling round
the room.

Dana walked to the window. Ruta looked at each of
them in turn, as if to borrow a resistance she wanted but
could no longer feel, then wrapped her arms around her-

self. Kraft was stone solid. It got very still then, very posed. Even the dust stopped crawling for the corner.

"It's what we talked about before, child," Helen said to Amber, because she was the only person in the room who didn't understand.

But they hadn't talked about it. Not in specific terms. Just a few remarks posed by Marjorie Korpela when they were playing canasta. And now it was Helen's role to make it concrete.

"We didn't want our portraits just so that we could stay alive, Amber. We wanted your mother to stop changing them."

"What are you saying?"

"I'm saying that maybe your mother was right about what we were. You never knew us when we were younger. Maybe we needed a second chance to come to terms with that. But now we have seen it, and we're as ready as we'll ever be."

"Ready to what?"

"Ready to die."

"You're going to make yourself extinct like the pygmies."

"The Tarons . . . very apt. Yes, the Tarons. This is all wrong. The world shouldn't have us anymore."

The elder faces were concentrating on Helen now, thinking profoundly what they hadn't wanted to think since returning from the nonplace, the infinite paradox where existence meant you couldn't corroborate that you existed. Limbo, purgatory, hell, Sheol, Tophet, Gehenna, Hades, perdition, the abyss, the pit—it mattered not what infernal region it was. It was not paradise. Or even serene oblivion. And death was coming again, no matter what. If they lived another day, it subtracted a mere twenty-four hours from their final and eternal disposition. Forever minus twenty-four in their present condition. Twenty-four followed by twenty-four followed by . . .

". . . Better to go now," Helen was saying, "while we've got the perspective and the will. It's as close as we're going to come to a state of grace."

"State of grace?" Kraft Olson growled in a voice none of them had heard for years. "There's nothing graceful about life. I've never seen anything that makes me believe in a God of grace."

"God made Danielle," Dana said.

"Whatever made her let her die."

"Get over it, Kraft."

"I think I'll paint my portrait pink," Ruta mused, surveying the paints as if they were cosmetics. "If Ariel's got any pink."

Beverly caught the spirit of bravado. "Wish I had one last cigarette."

And Molly: "I don't know if there's a heaven, but there has to be something better than where we were. If there's a dark place, then there must be a light one. A white universe all crystal and warm. If I can't be me, then I want to dissolve in a white universe."

"So who's going first?" Ruta asked nervously. "I don't want to go first, but if we stall around any longer, I'm going to change my mind."

"What about Ariel?" Molly said. "We can't just leave her locked in the cellar."

"Leave that to me," Kraft said. "No one is going to be painting over my picture. I'll let Ariel out when you're gone."

Helen glanced at the shelves. "Her paints have to be destroyed." And looking pointedly at Amber, she added, "I hope there aren't any more around the house."

They all looked at Ariel's heir then, who like them

was a painting come to life, but unlike them had never been dead.

Amber stared at a point more or less in the middle of the room. "I'm going to burn down the house like I burned down the barn," she recited with perfect composure.

Helen dropped down on the ratty Chesterfield. "Are you sure you can do that?"

"Yes. I can. If you want, I'll paint you all out. I did it to my twin, so I know how it works—it won't have to dry if it's not the magic paint. And then I'll paint fire all over the studio. I'm really good at painting fire. But you have to help me get my father and Mrs. Korpela out of the house first. I can get Mr. Bryce out by myself later."

Trembling, Helen reached out to her hand. "Amber, your father is dead. His chair went down the staircase."

The all-seeing lambent eyes of the shriveled figure on the sofa swallowed the child whole, while Amber's eyes welled and shimmered emerald but held fast. He had never really come back—her father, bound in that wheelchair—so he was no worse off than before. But what if he was where the rest of them had been? A dark place, Molly had said. She really didn't get it all, but she understood that they were going to go back because they thought they were ready now and because they were suffering. So it was probably all right for her dad, too.

But not her mother.

In a little while the house would be on fire, and she would be standing outside with her and Mr. Olson and Mr. Bryce and Mrs. Korpela. But she wasn't afraid of her mother anymore. Without the paint her mother would just be an old woman.

Amber tugged her hand free of Miss Hoverstein's frail fingers and went to the few canvases left against the wall. The one she wanted was in front: a picture of herself. She was surprised that up close it looked different from the one she had destroyed in the cellar. It looked older, in fact.

Beverly nodded. "You'll have to keep it with you. Guard it all the time."

"I know."

"Are you ready?"

Amber sat her portrait by the sofa and nodded. At the workbench Paavo had the lid off the can of paint, but Molly had another frame that she had found in the stack.

"Marjorie is suffering," she said. "If she could say so, she would want this. Start with her, Amber."

There was a certain poetic balance in an act of annihilation by the daughter of the woman who had created them. If the line between deity and mortal had been crossed, it was made inviolate again by what went on over the next quarter hour.

Amber painted quickly with the largest brush she could find. She painted facing away from them, afraid to look, afraid to falter, afraid even to listen. The silence at her back was solemn and profound. The alkyd was white—alas, no pink for Ruta—and that was good too, Amber thought, because Mrs. Armitage had said that about finding a "white universe," a place of light instead of darkness. She did Mrs. Seppanen second and Miss Hoverstein last, thinking about the Taron pygmies of Myanmar and wondering if, in whatever was to follow, Miss Hoverstein would meet them.

It must have been terrifying behind her. No matter what they hoped or how much they were suffering in their present conditions, it had to be terrifying. She wondered if they were watching each other, or if they closed their eyes. She wondered if it was even working, because there were no gasps or whimpers or clues. And when she was done and she turned around, it was just Mr. Olson staring at her with dull, flat eyes.

"Are you going to start the fire?" he asked in a voice that rattled like an old car engine shaken by winter.

"Yes," she answered.

"Good. Fire is cleansing. I'll go tend to your mother now."

"Don't you want your picture?"

She took his portrait off the workbench and brought it to him, and he rolled himself up off the Chesterfield almost jauntily, an elbow leading from his side, and steps that were almost nimble. Amber was surprised at his energy. For the first time she could imagine what she had heard whispered in the parlor, that this man had been the object of her mother's desire before she married.

As soon as he was gone she turned her attention to finding a smaller brush that would fit through the mouth of the open glass jar of red paint on the workbench. It was important not to think too much about what she had just done to all the old people or that her father was dead or about the horrors in the house, but she couldn't suppress a little rush of power that came with standing in her mother's studio with all her magic paints. It was scary and exciting. And it almost seemed like her painting was made better by the power too, because she had never done fire so well. Getting the curves just right with yellow mixed in, and the flames at different heights all around the walls. The way the fire might spread or the house might collapse were not things she considered. There were chemicals that would explode in the studio, she knew, like the thinner, like the stuff that was used to seal finished paintings, but by then she would be outside with Mr. Bryce.

When she got to the workbench, she hesitated. Her mother's magic paints were right there in the glass jars.

There were a dozen of them, all different colors, but the three largest jars must be the ones she mixed the others from, Amber knew. She knew this because they were red, blue and yellow, and back when she was alive the first time, she had seen her mother use primary colors many times to mix regular paint. So there they were. Red, blue, yellow. The source for everything that had come alive in the house.

(Did she dare . . . ?)

She had promised to burn down the house, and she would. But she already had more than half a jar of the red paint buried out by the ashes of the barn, and what if her mother was sorry—truly sorry—for what she had done? What if—not now, of course, but someday—she wanted to bring everyone back and let them be free and healthy again? It could be done if—

Red, blue, yellow . . .

There wouldn't be any danger if she herself kept the paints under control, Amber thought. She had kept the red hidden, hadn't she? And she wouldn't be stupid about it. She wouldn't even tell her mother about them unless things really, really changed in the future.

There was a large portfolio bag her mother used to haul things when she painted outside, and impulsively Amber snatched it up. She would use it to protect her portrait, she told herself. And she did. She stuffed the frame into the widest pocket. But there were other pockets. Each padded to protect the contents. She had carried this bag for her mother decades ago.

(Red, blue, yellow . . . and she already had lots of red.)

It couldn't hurt to keep her choices open until she saw how things went. She would have to destroy the red anyway if things didn't change. What was the difference if she had three bottles to get rid of?

The pockets were too small, as it turned out. But she placed one jar on either side of the portrait frame. Blue and yellow. There was plenty of room.

She finished her task of painting the fire by the door, and by that time the flames she had painted first were almost dry. She could feel the heat as a sketch her mother had hung of a sunset began to smolder and turn brown. Lifting the canvas portfolio bag by its shoulder strap, she left the studio for the last time.

35

His soul was ruined already, so what did it matter? He could never be sorry, never forgive. Danielle's roots ran deep inside him, synergistically intertwined with his own, and so to kill one was to kill the other.

He was dead, you see. Still dead. Ever dead. His feet on the stairs echoed the dead steps of dead legions. He had heard them in the cosmos, scrabbling talons and mammoth four-toed pads, scraping up red dust and hurling it across collapsing galaxies. Energy sucked dry. Replaced by sheer will. The animus of nether regions croaking to him as Ariel drew him out of his grave: *March . . . march . . . march with us. Open the gate.* And he had. And he would again. Because it was all in the cellar now. The charnel cellar filled with the echoes of old violence and new blasphemies. Silhouettes slipping through, gathering there like desiccated cadavers awaiting the drench of blood to reconstitute them to grayness for their horrific hour. *His* kind of phantoms now.

Such a dark act of love he was going to perform.

He listened at the cellar door to make sure Ariel wasn't on the top step. But no, he could hear her sobbing somewhere down below. Foolish Ariel, still thrashing in self-

pity. If she could stop, she might hear the ululant sighs
coming from the damp walls or the slither and rasp of
papery things unfolding like yellowed parchment. He
turned the key, paused to listen again, jerked the door
open.

She was sitting sideways on the bottom step in the
dim illumination of the storage room's single bulb, and
her great gluey eyes followed him as he clumped down
one slow step at a time.

"You spoiled it," she said when he stood next to her.
"You spoiled what could have been paradise, Kraft."

He put his hand on her gray head as she cried, and it
was only a shudder or two before she blinked uncer-
tainly at him. And then he said: "I'm sorry, Ariel."

She blanched, sat straighter. "You are?"

"Very sorry."

"You mean . . . because I'm down here?"

He let his hand slide off her hair. "Are you all right?"

She inclined her head with just a twitch of disbelief.

He moved beneath the light with his back to her, anticipating that she would follow.

"Kraft?" She came up behind him. "What did you
mean? You're sorry for what?"

When he turned they were as close as they had ever
been face-to-face, and he tried to keep his eyes trained
on hers while he reached up to the searingly hot bulb
with his left thumb and forefinger. "Not just because
you're down here," he said. With a twist they were in
darkness. "I'm sorry for *everything*."

Her faint exhalation of joy was blasphemous to him.

The staircase high above them gave off its tattoo beneath Amber's descending feet. It was irreversible now.

Ariel said: "What are they doing up there?"

"Dying."

"Dying?"

"Amber has painted over their pictures."

"Oh. How stupid. I can just paint them back again." A door slammed in the distance. "At least you didn't go with them, Kraft."

"I couldn't."

"Couldn't?"

"I stayed because of you."

"Me?" She made a girlish sound—half laugh, half disbelief. "Then you're over being angry with me? You know, I didn't really make things worse for you, Kraft. What I did to Danielle was stupid and desperate, but I wanted you to see—you most of all—I wanted you to appreciate what I gave you back."

"I know."

"I can't believe this, especially now. You talking with me like this. What a difference it makes. You have no idea—do you hear that sound? What *is* going on up there?"

"It's just Amber."

"It sounds like she's running water or something. Oh, Kraft, I can start over. I can make New Eden again. We can all start over. Get it right this time. Would you mind turning on the light?"

". . . Yes."

"Yes?"

"I'd mind."

"Why?"

"Because I want to kiss you."

Stung silence. A terrible joy. Her arms groped as his circled smoothly around her withered body and drew her onto his withered lips. Soft at first, then firm, then hard. Hard. HARD!

She snapped her head back. "Kraft!"

There was a distant sound of something collapsing.

Air sieved out of the cellar, leaving parched, vapid breaths.

"Do you hear it coming?" he whispered excitedly.

"I smell smoke. . . . Let me go!"

"Not the fire. Listen."

She listened. Heard the scrapings and draggings coming from beyond the laundry room. Not a singular thing, but a procession—twin processions—coming toward them. And for just an instant she had a connection with the insanity, the outer chaos from which she had summoned back the gallery of her life. It was the answer to the question she had incessantly asked: What is death like? And now she could feel it—*feel* it, because she couldn't *know* it. How could you know total aberrance? How could you order disorder? No rules, no form, no stability—a total shattering of bonds. Except for the hell of consciousness. That was the one glimpse she got, the one foretaste of her imminent fate. But she was still a part of the rational world and she couldn't let go of that, even for the handful of remaining seconds. Not here in this century-and-a-half-old farmhouse that remained on its foundation. So she told herself that her little family had found another way into the cellar. They hadn't painted themselves into extinction at all, but were coming in some ridiculous mummers' parade to frighten her, punish her, show her that they had her precious paints (which they would never be able to use) and—

Something even more insidious reached her now. Something similar but distinct from the spank and hiss of flames overhead. A sinuous rush like the undulation of a wave along a breakwater. And then a long, subtle sigh, as of an ancient ache about to be satisfied. *Something just around the corner.*

"You didn't think it would stay up in the studio, did you?" Kraft whispered, cinching her to him, heart pounding against heart, triumphant with betrayal. "It's down here. This is where it lives. Shall I turn on the light now?"

36

Amber didn't count on seeing her father's body on the stairs. When they said he had died there it didn't occur to her to white out his picture, and here he was, twisted and slumped over one wheel of his chair. His shaggy head felt like a cold marble bust beneath her fingers. But he had died before, she assured herself, so this didn't really count. It was like Miss Hoverstein had said. Being alive for the second time in her mother's world was all wrong for them.

Chest heaving, Amber stood. "Good-by, Daddy," she mouthed in the searing air, and with the old dried frame of the farmhouse sending out tentacles of fire along its interior seams, she resumed her awkward descent, clinging to the shoulder strap of the portfolio bag.

The first floor had an eerie stillness to it, as if the air in the middle of the rooms couldn't figure out where to go. She passed through the dining room, and there, leaning against the jamb to the kitchen, was Mr. Olson's portrait. He must have left it there to go to the cellar, she thought. And if she took it outside with her, he might go looking for it when he came up with her mother. So she left it and hurried on to the residents' corridor, where the old school had been, and where all the doors now stood ajar the way they once had at the end of each class day. All the doors ajar, that is, except one. Without pausing to knock, she grabbed the handle and flung it open.

She could see right away that Mr. Bryce didn't know there was a fire. He was sitting in his chair by the windows with his flannel shirt buttoned up to the neck, even though his forehead was starting to glisten and even though two floors up there was an inferno eating its way to the ground. The heat was building and smoke crawled out of the radiator grid in little puffs that backed into one another.

"Mr. Bryce, we've got to get out of the house right away," she said, plucking urgently at his sleeve.

He turned so slowly that she realized he had been nodding off. "Tiffany . . ."

"We've got to get out of here, Mr. Bryce. It's a matter of life or death."

He looked around. "I don't care about dying. You go."

"Stop talking like that, you've got to come *now*!"

She let go of the portfolio bag strap and tugged his wrist, but he simply let the arm extend until the dead weight of his body anchored her.

"What is this place?"

"Your room, and you've got to leave it. Please, Mr. Bryce." And then she remembered how he had warned her—warned Tiffany—on so many nights in his wanderings that she had to get out of the house because there was a fire. She thought of how she had burned down the barn, and of how he had been out there calling her name and trying to go into the flames while the others held him back. And when the barn had collapsed, he had collapsed in the dirt like a little kid not caring anymore what happened to him. So now she played on that, telling him she was Tiffany and that there was a fire, and he had to save her.

Tiffany. What made no sense at all to Amber Leppa living in the present made perfect sense to Martin Bryce living in the past. Color sprang into his cheeks and he tried twice unsuccessfully to push himself out of the chair, coming up unsteadily on the third try. And then he got his "land legs" and took her hand while she lugged the portfolio bag, slung by its strap over her shoulder. She had to cue him in which direction to go in the corridor, but by the time they reached the end of it, he was actually leading her instead of the other way around. Decades after the fact, Martin Bryce was saving Tiffany at last.

Out of the house and off the porch they went, the old man's grip on her fingers hurting in its ferocity. Thirty feet from the steps he came around in a wide circle, still holding her hand as if leading a grand cotillion. His gaze came down slowly from the blazing upper story of the farmhouse.

"What's that?" he asked.

"What?"

With his free hand he gestured to the picture frame sticking out of the portfolio bag. "That."

She unlimbered the bag and pulled the portrait up so he could see it. "That's me."

"Like the one I've got in my wardrobe."

"You mean like the one you used to have. You gave me that one already."

"I did? Yeah, that's right. I gave you one of them. There were two."

She heard this without impact, his little confusion, the nonhappenings that popped up as facts in old Mr. Bryce's failing memory. But the insidious truth began to drip like ice into her consciousness. Because even though Mr. Bryce could get lost easy as pie, he was very good with numbers. He might not remember his age, but whenever Mrs. Armitage told him what year it was and what year he was born, he would tell her how old he was without missing a beat. And now he was sure he had had two portraits, and he had given her one—the one she had destroyed to annihilate her twin.

Amber looked hard at the painting she had been carrying precisely as if her life depended on it. The reason it looked different was because it *was* different. She was older in this picture. Her mother must have painted a *third* picture of her, only this one hadn't been finished with the magic paints yet, and that was why there wasn't another Amber around. And the real portrait of her—the one Mr. Bryce was talking about—that one was still in his room about to burst into flames.

She squealed with fear, tried to pull away. "Let me go, let me go! My picture is in your closet and it's gonna burn up!"

He peered hard at her, and he had her hand in a literal death grip, trying to fathom, trying to understand why she wasn't saved now that he had led her out of the burning house.

"I'll die if I don't get that picture. I'll die!"

And then she yanked away and ran for the porch and danced up the steps and down again, because the heat was blasting out the door and the parlor was already an unearthly orange. Mr. Bryce was coming after her and she thought: *his bedroom windows in back!* So she ran around the house, which was billowing smoke and popping with small explosions of glass, and she couldn't tell which windows were his. So she broke two of them with bricks from the edging Dana had put around her garden, but all that happened was that yellow smoke came pouring out. With a cry she ran back around the basswood to the front, and there was Mr. Bryce. Only it wasn't old Mr. Bryce. It was young Mr. Bryce.

"Is everyone safe?" he hollered at her. But she was too terrified to make sense of anything, and he had to grab her by the shoulders and brace her. "Is everyone safe?"

She cried and shook her head and tried to lunge for the porch.

"Where's my father? Listen to me. Where's—"

"He must have gone inside. He was here, but he went back for something."

The words were barely out of her mouth before he was vaulting up the steps.

She tried to follow. Making it as far as the parlor, in fact, where the wallpaper high in the corners was starting to curl and turn brown while fire raced down the seams. The last thing she saw was the yellowed sweatshirt the younger Mr. Bryce was wearing, throbbing white against the archway as it collapsed on top of him.

37

She didn't remember coming back outside, but she knew she was waiting to die. Only it was taking forever for the flames to reach the painting in Mr. Bryce's wardrobe.

He must be dead now, old Mr. Bryce. His son too. And where was her mother and Mr. Olson? Half in shock, her emotions hardening into the armor of aftermath, she walked slowly to Mr. Bryce's car and got in the passenger's side.

A pack of cigarettes sat unopened next to her and she focused on it as if it had profound implications. Did Mr. Bryce smoke? The question hung sealed up in her wounded mind like the cigarettes sealed in the pack and the people sealed in the house and her portrait sealed in the wardrobe, and it suddenly slipped into her mind without a breath of emotion that the metal wardrobe might somehow be protecting her picture, even though the house must be hot enough to melt it.

Casually she got out of the car and casually she walked toward the back of the house again, pausing for a moment in the cool refuge that the basswood provided when it eclipsed the conflagration of the house. But the top of the tree was already on fire, and burnt leaves and flaming twigs were drifting down. She moved away. She continued toward the back of the house, and when she reached the windows she had broken, she saw it.

At first she thought it was a piece of uncharred debris from the roof, but no, it was a picture frame. And as she sprang forward, she knew already that it was hers—her image, her salvation, her life—lying facedown where old Mr. Bryce must have thrown it out the broken window. He had saved her, saved her for real this time. But why hadn't he saved himself? The house was collapsing in showers of cinders that drove her back, and there was no way he could be alive. Why hadn't he just fallen out the window or something? He had wanted to die, but to just give up like that, like he was too tired to care . . .

She was standing far enough away from the house so that the heat no longer blistered against her skin, and she turned the picture frame over and gazed at the likeness her mother had painted. She didn't understand how people could not want to live. The Taron pygmies or the other residents or Mr. Bryce. She was going to live, and not just an ordinary life either. Because she was the daughter of a painter, and she was going to become a painter. Then she would paint a world around her to her liking. Maybe she would bring back Sir Aarfie, and maybe the Taron pygmies, and certainly she would bring back her mother. Give her another chance. But she would have to do it in a way that her mother couldn't be in control. Amber Leppa was going to be in control.

The firemen found her like that, standing in a rain of white ashes drifting down like lost souls or feathers from the moon. A portfolio bag hung from her shoulder, which she would not relinquish to anyone. The only other thing standing was a blackened lightning rod sprouting from the earth, as if it were trying to reach into the cosmos.

Thomas Sullivan has been a gambler, a Rube Goldberg–style innovator, a coach, a teacher, a city commissioner, and a born-again athlete. His short stories have been published in every magazine from *Omni* to *Espionage*. He lives in Minnesota.

Your worst fears are born...

Born Burning

by
Thomas Sullivan

It's a chair that has been passed down from generation to generation. But ten-year-old Joey doesn't dare go near it—even though it seems *terribly* important to Joey's father and uncle. Because the chair is part of a family tradition. A tradition in which Joey must take his place—now matter how terrifying.

0-451-20754-8

A Signet Paperback

S756

Bestselling author

Michael Slade

is the "GENUINE RIVAL TO STEPHEN KING."*

Bed of Nails

Isolated in the Riverside Insane Asylum is the
Ripper. He believes he's the notorious butcher
who terrorized Whitechapel more than a
century ago. In the black hole of his
imagination, he reenacts the crimes. In the
darkness of his heart he still craves the thrill of
the kill. Thank God he can't escape.

Unfortunately, in Riverside, there is no God.

"WHO KNOWS WHAT EVIL LURKS IN THE HEARTS
OF MEN AND WOMEN?
MICHAEL SLADE KNOWS."
—*NORTH SHORE NEWS* (BRITISH COLUMBIA)

0-451-41115-3

*Book Magazine

0769